WINGS *of* PROMISE

Books by Bonnie Leon

Sydney Cove series
To Love Anew

Longings of the Heart

Enduring Love

The Queensland Chronicles
The Heart of Thornton Creek

For the Love of the Land

When the Storm Breaks

Alaskan Skies
Touching the Clouds

Wings of Promise

WINGS *of* PROMISE

A NOVEL

BONNIE LEON

a division of Baker Publishing Group
Grand Rapids, Michigan

© 2011 by Bonnie Leon

Published by Revell
a division of Baker Publishing Group
P.O. Box 6287, Grand Rapids, MI 49516-6287
www.revellbooks.com

Printed in the United States of America

Library of Congress Cataloging-in-Publication Data
Leon, Bonnie.
    Wings of promise : a novel / Bonnie Leon.
       p.   cm. — (Alaskan skies ; bk. 2)
    Includes bibliographical references.
    ISBN 978-0-8007-3360-5 (pbk.)
    1. Women air pilots—Fiction. 2. Bush pilots—Fiction. 3. Alaska—Fiction.
I. Title.
PS3562.E533W56 2011
813′.54—dc22
                                                      2011010718

Published in association with the Books & Such Literary Agency, 52 Mission Circle, Suite 122, PMB 170, Santa Rosa, CA 95409-5370, www.booksandsuch.biz.

11   12   13   14   15   16   17   7   6   5   4   3   2   1

Dedicated to
Gayle Ranney—
a woman who followed her dream.

— 1 —

Kate pulled her Plymouth coupe to the side of the road in front of the Townses' place. They were good friends, and she was thankful for their invitation to share Christmas with them. Still, she was unable to hold back a sigh as she turned off the ignition. Bear Creek, with Paul, would have been more fun, but frigid temperatures had cornered her in Anchorage. She knew better than to count on anything when it came to the weather in Alaska.

She sat in the car a few minutes to rein in her thoughts. The calendar said December 25, but without Paul, it didn't feel like Christmas. It was to be their first Christmas together as a couple. They'd planned a celebration with a tree, gifts, and dinner. And maybe even a trip up Bear Creek on the sled with the dogs. Kate had imagined a romantic evening huddled together, sipping hot chocolate and gazing at a glittering Alaskan sky. They'd talk about their future and with any luck share the beauty of northern lights dancing across the sky.

Maybe she could get Sidney's permission to use the shop's radio to call Patrick out on the creek. Paul would most likely be there. Would calling him be too forward?

Maybe we can celebrate the New Year together. It was almost as good as spending Christmas with each other. According to predictions, there was reason to rejoice—1937

7

might be the year the country actually crawled out of the ruinous depression.

Her thoughts turned to family in Washington. They'd be celebrating with friends in Yakima. She could still hear the veiled melancholy in her mother's cheery voice when they'd talked that morning. She missed them.

Kate reached out and patted her dog, Angel. "You ready for a party?"

The husky/malamute mix answered with a wag of her tail and a small bark.

"Okay, then." Kate stepped out of the car and Angel followed. Clutching a bag of gifts, she carefully made her way up the frozen path leading to the front door. She knocked and waited. Helen had said Mike Conlin would be here. Just the thought of spending time with him made Kate ill at ease. She and Mike had been good friends from the first day they'd met back in the summer of 1935 when she'd first arrived in Anchorage. He'd been the one who had introduced her to Alaska and piloting in the territory. But since she'd refused his marriage proposal two months ago he'd been distant and reserved. She missed the camaraderie between them and knew spending the day with him would be awkward. If only she were with Paul.

The door swung open and Albert Towns greeted Kate with a broad smile. "We were beginning to think you weren't going to make it." He swept a hand over thinning hair where he was nearly bald in front. He pulled her into his arms.

Albert's happiness was contagious, and Kate felt the joy of the season envelop her. He was more father than landlord. "Sorry I'm late."

"Angel. Good to see you, girl." Albert buried a hand in the dog's thick coat.

"I hope you don't mind my bringing her. I just couldn't bear to leave her home alone on Christmas."

"She's always welcome here."

Helen joined Albert, her pale blue eyes sparkling with Christmas delight. "Kate, dear. Come in. It's freezing out there." She ushered Kate inside. "Did you hear President Roosevelt's address on the radio this morning?"

"No. I didn't get a chance. My parents called."

"How are they?"

"They're well."

Truly they were fine, but Kate also knew that Christmas without her had created a hollow place for them. Holidays had always been a special time for family. If only there was a way to spend the holiday together. Maybe one day she'd convince her parents that Alaska was a fine place for them to live.

"Next time you speak with them say hello for me." Helen rested a hand on Kate's back. "I do wish you'd heard the president's speech. I just love his fireside chats. And this morning's was especially inspirational—so encouraging during these hard times. And it was very kind of him to speak to the country on Christmas morning."

"I think I heard that one before," Albert said, his voice laced with sarcasm. He closed the door. "Figure it was a recording. Kate, let me hang up your coat for you."

Kate set down her bag, pulled off her gloves and stuffed them into the pockets of her parka, and then handed the coat to Albert. Combing her fingers through her short auburn bob to fluff flattened hair, she stepped into a cozy living room. Warmth and the mingled aroma of sweet rolls and roasting meat greeted her. "Whatever's cooking smells fabulous."

"That's my Helen," Albert said, draping an arm around his wife.

Mike, who had been sitting on the sofa, stood. Surprisingly, he wore a smile and his casual stance had returned. "Afternoon, Kate. Good to see you."

"Hi." She put on her friendliest face.

Angel padded across the floor to greet Mike.

"Hello, girl." He gave her a good rubdown, and then walked toward Kate.

She stiffened, not certain what to expect.

Mike stopped just out of arm's reach. "We were thinking

we'd have to eat without you." He gave her a quick hug. "It's good to see you."

"I'm glad to be here. This should be fun." She dropped her tight shoulders and let out a relieved breath, puzzled over Mike's change but thankful for it. "It'd be a tragedy to miss one of Helen's meals." Kate realized she was happy to be there. These people were more than friends—they were family. She'd only been in Alaska for a year and a half, but they already shared a history together.

"I had a few things to take care of." Wearing a wry grin, she held up the bag of gifts. "Left my Christmas wrapping to the last minute." She glanced at a small fir standing in a corner of the room, then asked Helen, "Do you want these under the tree?"

Mike reached for the bag. "I'll do that for you."

Kate held it out of his reach. "Oh, no you don't."

"You get me something?" He cocked an eyebrow and grinned.

"You'll have to wait and see." Her step light, Kate headed for the tree. She wondered what Paul was doing. Did he have a tree? She doubted it. Maybe next year they'd have one together . . . if they were married. The thought set off a thrill inside Kate and she couldn't suppress a smile.

The little fir was festooned with shiny glass balls and homemade ornaments. Kate gazed at it, envisioning the tree she knew stood in her parents' living room. They always put up a large, stately pine. She fingered a smiling snowman. "Helen, did you make the decorations?"

"Some of them. Muriel did quite a few." She glanced about. "She must be in the kitchen."

Kate removed packages from the bag and added them to those already stashed beneath the boughs. She straightened and looked out the window. "The snow has started again."

"It wouldn't be Christmas without snow." Helen stood at the front window, her hands stuffed into the pockets of her apron. "It makes everything look brand new."

The Townses' daughter, Muriel, and her husband, Terrence, stepped into the front room. "Hi, Kate." Muriel blew damp, blonde hair off her forehead and wiped her hands on an apron. "So glad you made it. Mom's whipped up a great meal."

Helen smiled at her daughter, her eyes brighter than usual. "You've done as much of the cooking as I have."

Kate thought Helen looked especially happy, even for Christmas. "From what I hear, Muriel, you're as good a cook as your mother."

Helen moved to her daughter's side and circled an arm around her, pulling her close. "She's better." Beaming, Helen continued, "I know I'm supposed to wait until after dinner, but I just can't." She glanced at her daughter. "We have news."

Muriel slid a sideways look at her mother and smiled, a dimple appearing on her right cheek. "Go ahead."

Helen didn't speak up immediately, and then she blurted, "I'm going to be a grandmother!"

"A baby? How wonderful!" Kate said. "I'm so happy for you." She couldn't help but think about her and Paul. He'd make a good father.

Muriel rested a hand on her abdomen. "I'm not very far along." She glanced at her husband. "I'm thankful we moved back to Alaska. Now I'll be close to Mom and Dad when the baby gets here."

Helen gave her another squeeze.

"Congratulations," Mike said, his voice sounding less than celebratory. He glanced at Kate.

What was he thinking, that they should be married and beginning a family? Kate turned her gaze back to Muriel. Being a mother and wife was what Muriel had always wanted. Kate was happy for her.

Terrence smiled and pushed wire-rimmed glasses farther up on the bridge of his nose. "It's a lot of responsibility, having a family. But we always hoped to have children."

Muriel moved to her husband and snuggled against him as he draped an arm around her slender shoulders. Her blue eyes, so like her mother's, shone with delight.

What if it were her and Paul making such an announcement? Kate allowed her thoughts to stray, wondering what that would be like. She'd never given it much consideration. Her career had always been foremost on her mind. Kate forced herself to rein in her thoughts. Paul hadn't even asked her to marry him, not yet anyway. And they hadn't seen each other since they'd proclaimed their love for one another weeks ago.

She looked up to find Mike staring at her. Even though he'd put on a friendly façade, Kate could see his sadness. He'd hoped to share his life with her. He loved her, but she could only see him as a good friend.

A spark of fear ignited in Kate. Could that happen between her and Paul? His wife had been gone for almost six years. And there was something about his past she knew gnawed at him. He hadn't told her what it was. Could it affect their relationship? Kate was the first woman he'd allowed himself to care for since Susan's death. Was it possible he regretted his declaration of love? *No,* Kate told herself. The last time they'd spoken on the radio he'd been just as excited about their Christmas celebration as she was.

But things could change. She knew that. She'd walked out on an engagement with Richard, her lifelong friend in Yakima. They'd been buddies and then somewhere along the way, they'd fallen in love. But he wanted an ordinary life with an ordinary wife. She wanted more.

When she'd canceled their wedding only one week before the ceremony and then flown off to Alaska, she feared he'd never forgive her. But time had healed the wound. He'd sent a Christmas card with a chatty letter. To have his friendship now was comforting. She'd write to him first chance.

Everything was as it should be. She had Paul now. They were a good match, and one day they'd get married. She was certain of it.

"I hope everyone's hungry," Helen said. She walked to the door between the front room and the kitchen. "Dinner's ready." She stood there while everyone filed past, opening

12

her arms as if guiding a flock of sheep into the large dining area off the kitchen.

Albert placed a platter laden with a golden brown turkey on the table. Helen and Muriel set out the rest of the feast. Kate settled onto a chair at the table and Mike took one beside her. Angel investigated the delicious smells emanating from the table.

"This isn't for you, girl," Kate said, her voice uncompromising. "Go lay down." The dog ambled to a corner between the kitchen and back door and settled on a colorful braided rug.

Mike elbowed Kate. "You should get some of Helen and Muriel's recipes. You can try them out on me."

Mike seemed overly friendly. Was he just trying to recapture the closeness they'd had before? "You know I'm not a cook," Kate said, thinking she ought to learn. One day she might need to know how to prepare a meal like this. "There's not much room for cooking in my tiny apartment anyway." She glanced at Albert and Helen, who leased the room to her. "I love it, though. It's cozy."

"It's small," Albert said. "We'd sure understand if you wanted to move."

"I enjoy living there." She rested her arms on the table. "I do hope to get a place of my own one day. But since my plane is sitting at the bottom of a lake—"

"I can still barely believe that you crashed into that lake," Muriel said. "And then survived out in that wilderness all those days."

Kate's mind flitted back to the accident that had nearly taken her and Nena's lives. They never would have made it if not for Mike and Paul's persistence. Kate would never forget the flood of relief and joy she'd felt when she saw them emerge from the forest.

"It was awful, but we made it." Kate smiled. "But my savings will have to go to replacing the plane. After I'm back in the air, I'll rebuild my bank account."

"The room is yours as long as you need," Helen said.

13

"Thanks. I'll be there awhile. But I do have a line on a plane—a Bellanca Pacemaker just like the one I cracked up, only two years newer."

"No need to worry about flying today," Mike said. "Even Sidney took time off."

"Oh?" Helen set a Jell-O salad on the table. "Where is he?"

"Out at Kenai. Couldn't wait to see his parents and that passel of nieces and nephews of his." Mike leaned back in his chair. "He's a family man at heart. Should have had one of his own." He eyed Kate. "Never did understand why he stayed single."

"He loves flying and managing the airport." Kate picked up her fork. "He works harder than we do, and our kind of work takes everything we've got. There's not much time for family." She glanced at Muriel. When she'd first set out to be a pilot, any sacrifice seemed worth it. Now she wasn't so sure. If she became Mrs. Paul Anderson, she'd have to reconsider some of her convictions about flying.

Helen placed her napkin on her lap. "I think a person can have a career and a family." She sat beside Albert. "We've worked the store for years and managed quite well." She smiled at her daughter.

Muriel flipped blonde hair off her shoulder. "I remember hanging out at the store after school. I loved helping."

"You and your friends were more interested in raiding the candy jar than you were in working," Albert said with a grin.

"That's not true." Muriel smirked. "Well, not completely. I must confess to eating more than my share of buttercreams."

"It's been a struggle—both of us working." Albert took Helen's hand and kissed it. "But we did it together and we've had a good life."

"And we've been blessed," Helen said. "Just keeping the business afloat through this horrible depression is a gift from God. So much of the country is suffering, so many out of work and losing their homes." She shook her head. "It's terrible."

Albert looked around the table. "Let's thank the Lord for the food and all his blessings."

14

Everyone at the table clasped hands. Muriel's felt small in Kate's. Mike's was warm and callused. He gave hers a squeeze. His sudden affection made Kate uncomfortable.

"Our heavenly Father," Albert said. "Thank you for friends and family. And thank you for your abundant blessings. We have more than we deserve. We ask that you will provide for those who have so little. And on this special day, when we remember the birth of your Son, we think about the price paid on our behalf and we are grateful. Please bless our time together and continue to build the bonds of friendship between us. Amen."

Mike gave Kate's hand another squeeze. She quickly let go.

When everyone had finished eating, the men retired to the front room while the women cleaned up the kitchen. Muriel cleared the table, Helen washed dishes, and Kate dried.

"I'm so full I can barely breathe," Kate said. She glanced out the window. Winter's early nightfall had descended. "I need to walk. I wish we had longer days."

"I love being outdoors after dark," Muriel said. "Especially when the northern lights put on a show. Sometimes when I stand under the sky with the lights dancing, I feel as if I'm getting a glimpse of heaven."

Helen studied her daughter. "You need to keep your heaven-gazing to the church sanctuary. You're in a delicate condition and shouldn't be out when the temperatures are extreme."

"I'm fine. Don't fuss."

"I'm not fussing." Helen turned back to the dishes. "You've got to think about the baby."

Muriel set an empty casserole dish on the counter. "You worry too much." She leaned over and kissed her mother's cheek. "But I love you for it."

"When is the baby due?" Kate asked, adding a plate to a stack.

"The doctor thinks mid-July," Muriel said, glancing at her stomach.

"It's the perfect time for a baby." Helen handed Kate another dish. "The days are warm."

"Don't let Terrence drag you off on a trip into the bush this summer. I'd hate to have to fly Paul in to some remote spot to deliver your baby." Kate laughed.

"Terrence loves to get out of town, but I doubt he'll be leaving in July."

Helen chuckled. "When your time gets near, he'll be like all expectant fathers—nervous as a rooster locked up in a chicken house with a hungry fox."

"I can't imagine Dad being like that."

"Oh, but he was." Helen smiled as she scrubbed gravy off a plate. "The day you were born I thought he would walk a path right into the floor." She chuckled. "But he's been a good father."

"It'll be nice to have a doctor tending to people who live out of town." Muriel dipped a washcloth in the sink water and wrung it out. "I think what Paul's doing is very kind."

Helen immersed the plate in rinse water, and then handed it to Kate. "It's such a shame he couldn't join us today." She turned to Kate. "How does he feel about being a bush doctor?"

"He's excited. But it's been awhile since he did any doctoring, so he's kind of nervous."

"Why did he give up his practice in San Francisco?" Muriel asked.

The muscles in Kate's stomach tightened at the question. She'd wondered the same thing, but the topic was off limits. "I don't know," she said as nonchalantly as she could manage. "He doesn't talk about it. And I don't want to pry."

"I'm so happy for you two. I think it's wonderful that you've found each other," Muriel said. "When I met Terrence, I knew right away that he was the one for me."

Kate smiled. "I'm sure he's the one for me. He hasn't proposed yet, but I hope he will. When we were making plans to get together for Christmas, he mentioned talking about our future."

"I'll bet it won't take him long to ask you," Helen said.

Kate ran a towel over the plate. "I hope you're right."

"How do you feel about being a flying hospital?" Muriel asked, gathering up the napkins.

"I'm thrilled. I'll love working with Paul. And there's such a need for a doctor. I think it will be wonderful."

Helen dunked a cup into soapy water, and then glanced toward the front room. "I'm so glad Mike came tonight. He's not been himself since . . . well, since you two—"

"I know. But he seems fine now. Maybe we can still be friends."

"I'm sure he hopes so too. He seems pretty comfortable tonight."

Mike stepped through the kitchen door. "Almost done in here?"

Helen untied her apron. "We're nearly finished."

"Good. It's time to open gifts. I think I have one under the tree." He winked at Kate.

What had come over him? He'd been morose since her refusal, and now all of a sudden he was his old charming self? Maybe he'd accepted things as they were and was ready to move on. The thought made her feel relieved. He could have stayed mad, but that wasn't like Mike. He was a good man, and hopefully they'd resume their friendship.

With the kitchen sparkling clean, the women joined the men in the front room.

"I was thinking it would be nice to sing some carols," Helen said. She settled on the divan beside Albert and patted his thigh.

"How about 'Jingle Bells'?" Albert said.

Remembering her own rendition of the song, when she'd flown packages into the villages the previous year, Kate nodded and wondered if she ought to teach the group. They'd get a kick out of it. Before she could say anything, Albert began, "Dashing o'er the snow in a one horse open sleigh . . ."

When the song came to an end, Mike said, "How about the new one that's out, 'Winter Wonderland'?"

"They've been playing it over and over on the radio," Muriel said. "I love it."

Soon everyone was singing the new melody. After that, Helen insisted on a religious carol, and then it was time to open gifts.

Albert handed out two packages to each person, explaining they were from him and Helen. One was a canister of assorted homemade candies and the other a knitted muffler.

Kate wrapped her deep green scarf around her neck and then took a bite of fudge. "Thank you so much. You know how much I love candy, and the muffler's beautiful."

"I wish we could have done more, but with things slow at the store . . . Well, you know how it is."

"Thought we were coming out of the depression," Terrence said. "But it looks like we've plunged right back into it."

"Everything will work out." Helen leaned against Albert and smiled at him, her love for her husband, even after all their years together, evident.

Kate's gifts were next. She'd managed to purchase several hand-carved pieces of ivory from Joe Turchik. He'd offered to give them to her but at her insistence had finally accepted a token payment. She handed them out and watched while everyone unwrapped their gift.

Helen held up a delicate mother seal with a baby at its side. "Oh, this is lovely. Where did you get it?"

"You remember the Turchiks—Nena was with me when my plane went down."

"Yes, of course. Such nice people." Helen ran a fingertip across the seal.

"Joe Turchik made these."

"Is he a native?" Terrence asked, studying his plump walrus.

"Yes. Eskimo," Mike said, as he unwrapped a native man holding a spear.

"Whenever I'm in Kotzebue, I stay with them. They're good friends. Although I doubt Nena will ever fly with me again after what happened."

"It's a miracle—the both of you surviving that terrible crash," Muriel said.

"Please tell Joe how much we love his work and thank him for us." Helen studied her ivory seals. "I'll write a letter so you can take it to him on your next run north."

The rest of the gifts were opened, all except one. It was from Mike, for Kate. The package was small. Kate couldn't imagine what it could be.

Everyone watched as she carefully removed the Christmas paper. "I know you didn't wrap this yourself. It's much too nice," she teased.

"I did." He gave her a tender look. "Only the best for the best."

With the paper removed, Kate held a small box in her hands. She was suddenly afraid. What if Mike had decided to do something foolish? Her hands trembled slightly as she lifted the lid.

When she looked inside surprise radiated through her. "Oh, Mike!" She lifted out a tiny gold airplane attached to a gold chain. The words *Fearless Kate* were inscribed in red on the plane's side. "It's beautiful!" She held it up in the light and tears sprang to her eyes. "It's my plane."

He smiled broadly. "Thought you'd like something to remember it by."

"I love it. Where did you get it?"

"You're not the only one who knows an artist." Mike winked. "I'll help you put it on."

Kate draped the chain around her neck and let Mike hook the clasp. His hand rested on her neck for a moment.

Choosing to ignore the gesture, Kate studied her tiny plane, and then let it drop against her chest. "Thank you. It's a wonderful gift." She wanted to hug him but didn't dare. Instead, she looked into his quiet blue eyes and said, "I'll cherish it always."

— 2 —

The sound of a plane set Paul's pulse racing. He stepped onto the porch and searched the skies, hoping it was Kate. He'd missed her, couldn't stop thinking about her. Then he spotted it, a new red Pacemaker. "Kate," he whispered.

He ran down the trail, but when he caught sight of Kate as she stepped out of the plane, he was suddenly unsure of himself. He hadn't seen her since that day in Anchorage when he'd told her of his feelings. How should he greet her? What did she expect? Should he kiss her or just give her a respectful hug? What if she'd changed her mind about him?

Kate waved, and he returned the gesture. Angel galloped toward him. Thankful for the distraction, Paul knelt in the snow and caught the dog in his arms as she slammed into him. With a laugh he avoided her wet kisses and gave her a rubdown. "You're in a fine mood," he said with a final hug.

Paul pushed to his feet and headed toward Kate. She stood tall and trim like one of the reeds that grew along the creek bank in summer. His heart thumped and his body shivered with anticipation. She brushed short hair off her face and smiled at him, her amber-colored eyes warm and expectant. Love swamped Paul, and he knew exactly how to greet her.

He hurried his steps and when he reached Kate, he pulled

her into his arms. "I've missed you." He pressed his face against her hair and breathed in the lingering fragrance of Breck shampoo.

Kate wrapped her arms around him and held on as if she'd never let go. "It seems like forever since I've seen you."

They stayed like that for a long moment. Kate looked up at Paul. "I've dreamed about this reunion. It's been too long."

He kissed her, a long lingering kiss. When they parted, Kate smiled and hugged him again. "I was afraid I'd imagined it all, and that I'd get a howdy and shoptalk. I'm so glad I was wrong." She hugged him again.

"No shoptalk from me, at least not today." Paul held her against his chest and rested his chin on her head. "When I got up this morning and saw that the sun was out, I hoped I'd see you."

"I left at first light. All I've thought about is you. I missed you so badly at Christmas."

"Well, we've got New Year's." Paul grinned. "We'll bring in the New Year together."

Paul turned his attention to Kate's Bellanca and studied it. "So, this is your new bird. Pretty sharp. Red just like your last one."

"It's my favorite color." Kate gazed at the Pacemaker. "I was lucky to get her. She's a couple years newer than my last plane. And she has a radio."

"I'm glad to hear that." Paul continued to look at the plane. "No 'Fearless Kate' this time?" He grinned, remembering how Kate had painted the name in florid script across the fuselage of her last Bellanca.

"No. I figured once was enough." Kate touched the tiny gold plane hanging around her neck.

"What's that?"

"This?" She lifted the ornament. "It's a replica of my Bellanca, the one I cracked up. Mike gave it to me for Christmas."

Paul felt a stab of jealousy. "That was nice of him. Didn't know you saw him during the holidays."

"He was at Albert and Helen's for Christmas dinner."

Kate looped an arm through Paul's and leaned against him. "I was thinking of you."

"Good thing." Paul dropped a kiss on her forehead.

After a dinner of roast chicken, Paul and Kate moved to the porch and huddled together to stare at the night sky. A wolf howled in the distance, but tonight it didn't make Paul feel lonely. He wasn't alone anymore.

Kate took a sip of her hot chocolate. "This is just how I imagined it would be. The two of us, a clear night sky, and hot chocolate." She smiled at him and he kissed her. "I don't think my life could be better than it is at this moment. Except, I wish we had more time together like this. But it's back to work tomorrow."

"Yeah." Alarm, like a barb, jabbed Paul's insides. What if he wasn't good enough? What if someone died . . . because of him?

Get hold of yourself. You're ready. But the words didn't convince him he was either competent or ready to be a bush doctor.

"I'm so excited. I love to fly and I love you. We'll make a good team." She squeezed his arm.

"I love you too." The venture he and Kate were about to set out on was suddenly real. And the dangers it involved were real too. He loved Kate. He hadn't loved anyone since Susan. A picture of his wife flashed through his mind. She'd been tiny with blonde hair and blue eyes—nothing like Kate. Fear raised up its ugly head like a cobra, threatening to strike. What if he lost Kate too? Flying with him would only increase her hours in the air. He tightened his embrace.

"Oh, I almost forgot." Kate stood and darted inside the house. A few moments later, she reappeared with a small package in her hand. "I got something for you."

"For me?"

Kate grinned and held out a small box. "It's not much, but I thought you might like it."

Paul unwrapped the box and lifted the lid. "What in the world?" He studied an ivory carving of a dog that looked like Buck, pulling a sled. "Where did you get this?"

"Joe Turchik made it. I would have had him include all the dogs but there wasn't time. So I thought if you had to pick just one it would be Buck."

"It's beautiful." Paul ran a finger over the polished figurine. "Thank you." He hugged her, and then with a slight grin, he said, "I got something for you too." Kate followed him inside. He retrieved a small box from the bookcase. It was festooned with bright red Christmas wrap with a red bow on top. He handed it to her.

Kate carefully removed the bow and gift wrapping to reveal a gift box. She glanced at him, her eyes alight with anticipation. Her hands trembled. She lifted the lid and inside a pearl necklace nestled in tissue paper.

Kate stared at it, not saying a word. Maybe she didn't like it? Was it too feminine? "I took a chance," Paul said with a shrug. "I can take it back and get something else if you want."

"Oh no. I love it!" Kate lifted it out of the box. "It's beautiful."

"The last time I was in Anchorage, I spotted it in a store window on my way out of town. I thought you might like it."

"I do. I love it." Kate studied the perfect ivory string of pearls. "Can you help me put it on?"

"It won't look good with the one you're wearing." Paul wondered which one Kate liked best—Mike's gift held special meaning.

Kate quickly reached up and unhooked the necklace Mike had given her and then turned her back to Paul so he could fasten the clasp of the pearl necklace. "I'm sure you spent too much money on this."

"Never too much for you." He dropped a kiss on her neck.

Kate turned and faced him, her hand resting on the pearls. "It's a wonderful gift."

"I'm glad you like it." He kissed her. The love he felt for her swelled and his heart seemed as if it would burst. He tried to quiet the emotion. He adored Kate, but loving her also reminded him that he could lose her. And he couldn't bear that.

"We better get some sleep," Kate said. "We have a long day tomorrow."

"Let me get the lantern. I'll walk you over to the Warrens'. Sassa has a bed ready for you."

The following morning they headed for the frozen creek. Paul shaded his eyes and gazed at the azure sky and tried to quiet his nerves by taking a couple of slow, deep breaths. He was capable and ready, but what if he loused things up? He turned to Kate and said as confidently as he could manage, "Good day to fly."

"It's perfect."

Paul turned his attention to his cabin, where smoke trailed into the unspoiled air. "Would you mind if I bring along some pelts? I was hoping to sell them at the winter carnival."

"Sure. I have room."

Paul placed his bag and pack in the plane. "I'll be right back." He headed toward the trail.

"I'll give you a hand," Kate said, falling into step beside him.

Their arms loaded with furs, Paul and Kate walked back to the plane. "Not much in the way of pelts this year," he said.

"Seems like a lot."

"Not really. Last year, I had four times this many." He shrugged. "Doesn't matter. From now on there won't be much time for trapping anyway."

"Is that going to be a problem . . . financially, I mean?"

"No. I'll be fine." Paul hoped she didn't ask more. Between his inheritance and the money he'd put away while working in San Francisco, he had more than most. But he wasn't comfortable talking about finances yet. That would lead to other questions he wasn't ready for.

He stowed the furs while Kate cranked the flywheel, then climbed into the cockpit and started the engine. Angel took her place up front.

"Sorry, girl, not today." Kate hauled the dog off the seat.

Angel padded to the back of the plane where she settled on a stack of blankets. Looking dejected, she rested her head on large feet.

Paul folded his tall frame into the passenger seat and glanced back at the dog. "She's not happy with me."

"Don't worry about her. She's fine. When I have passengers, that's her spot. She's just pouting." Kate gazed out at the brilliantly white landscape. "It's a great day for new beginnings."

"Sure is." Paul felt tight. Was he ready?

"You all right?" Kate asked.

Paul nodded, but his insides churned. When he agreed to work as a doctor for people living in the bush, he'd been caught up in the moment. Had he accepted Kate's offer recklessly?

"Nervous?" Kate throttled up.

"Yeah, a little."

"You'll be fine," she said and leaned over and kissed him. "In fact, you'll be great. Remember, I've seen you work."

Paul felt a spark of elation. "Thanks. It'll just take awhile for me to get into the swing of things."

Kate turned her attention back to flying. "Who cleared the landing site?"

"Patrick and me. We figured since you'd be making extra stops here, we ought to make sure you had a safe place to set down."

"You did a good job. Thanks."

Paul and Kate fell silent, the drone of the engine the only sound.

They lifted off and the white world fell away below.

"You sure it's not too much trouble, your coming all the way out here to get me?" Paul asked.

"Can't lie—it'd be easier if you lived in Anchorage. But I'm just grateful that you're willing to do this and it gives me a reason to come out to get you. I love it here."

"I said I'd give it a try. We'll see how it goes."

"Oh . . . right." Kate's voice trailed off as if she wanted to say more.

"That was our agreement, remember."

"Yep. That's what we said—just a trial." Kate stared straight ahead and chewed on her bottom lip.

Paul knew she wanted more from him, but he wasn't ready. He hadn't practiced medicine since his wife had died and that had been nearly six years ago. If Susan's death hadn't been his fault, he might feel differently, but it was clear to him she'd still be alive if he'd taken her condition more seriously.

"We'll be gone about a week. Who's looking after your dogs?"

"Patrick's boys. Since Douglas is the oldest and most responsible, he's in charge."

"They're good kids." She glanced at him. "Has there been any word from Lily? I know Sassa misses her. It must be especially hard since she's Patrick and Sassa's only daughter."

"Yeah. It's hard on them, especially Sassa. Patrick said she writes pretty regularly, though. She found a job and an apartment in Seattle and decided to stay. I think she might have found a man too."

"How does Sassa feel about that?"

"She knew it was bound to happen. Lily's easy on the eyes and she's sweet. My guess is Sassa's fine with it, although I'm sure she'd have preferred Lily had fallen for an Alaskan. That way she'd be closer to home."

"Lily has a whole new life. Seattle's a big city—a far cry from Bear Creek. Kind of like when you moved out here from San Francisco." Kate gave him a sidelong glance.

Paul clenched his teeth. He knew she was fishing for information. He couldn't tell her everything about his past, not yet. "Yeah. S'pose it is."

"Do you think Lily will ever move back?"

"Hard to say." Paul folded his arms over his chest. "'Course from what I've seen, once an Alaskan, always Alaskan. It's hard to get it out of your blood."

"I already feel that. When I left Yakima, it was hard on my

mother. My dad understood, though. In fact, he encouraged me to go after my dream. Mom wanted me to stay put, but I think she's better now. Especially after their trip up during the summer."

"It's been nearly two years since you moved, right?"

"In July."

"Well then, I'd wager you won't return to the States. The territory either runs you out the first year or it snags you for good."

Below, Susitna Station looked serene, resting along the river with a forest of bare-limbed trees hedging it in from behind. Smoke drifted from cabins, and Paul thought he spotted Charlie Agnak, out on the dock in front of the mercantile. He glanced up and waved as they flew past and headed north.

"This is my home now," Kate said. "But I miss my family."

Paul felt the familiar tightening around his heart. He kept his eyes on the scenery. "Don't suppose a person ever completely gets over missing loved ones." He rolled his shoulders back, trying to relax his muscles. "So, what's on the agenda?"

"Our first stop is a homesteader's place not far from here."

"What's the problem?"

"It's the Kennedys. One of their boys is sick. Sidney didn't say with what."

Kate landed on a well-packed airstrip in the midst of a broad white field. A small cabin huddled amidst piled snow, stunted spruce trees, and naked birch.

Before Kate brought the plane to a stop, the door of the cabin opened and a black dog barreled toward them, lunging through chest-deep snow. Kate moved to the door and opened it.

"Hey, Max," she called.

Angel leaped out and sprinted toward the other dog. They nearly collided, then gave each other a good sniff before bounding off, nipping at one another and taking an occasional tumble as they frolicked in the white meadow.

"Angel has friends everywhere," Paul said.

"Good thing she gets along with other dogs. Otherwise

I'd have to leave her in the plane most of the time. Out here, everyone has dogs." Kate took Paul's hand. "Thank you for giving her to me."

Paul gave her hand a squeeze. "Nita had a fine litter, but when I picked up Angel I knew she was the perfect pup for you."

"You were right." She flashed him a smile, then trudged toward the cabin.

Paul followed. Cold air stung his cheeks and seared his lungs. He wanted to put an arm around Kate but refrained. He didn't know how she felt about showing affection in front of people.

Kate glanced at him. "Jack's not as friendly as Max, but he'll be all right."

"Jack?"

"The Kennedys' other dog. He's an old man, but isn't about to give up his post as guardian."

"Hope he won't mind my visiting."

"He will." Kate grinned, giving Paul's arm an affectionate squeeze.

As they approached the cabin, a man with thick curly red hair and a beard to match stood at the top of the porch steps, his hands shoved into the pockets of his overalls. "Howdy."

"Hello," Kate called.

Jack pushed his aged hulk up off the porch, and with his hackles up, he woofed as he charged to the top of the steps.

"It's all right, boy," the man said, resting a hand on the dog's head.

Kate approached the house. "I've brought the doctor."

The man moved down the steps. Jack stayed at his side, bristling and warily eyeing the newcomer.

"I'd like you to meet Paul Anderson, our new bush doctor."

The man extended a hand. "Good to meet you. I'm Bill Kennedy. Grateful you could check on my boy."

Paul grasped the man's big hand. "My pleasure."

"Come on in," Bill said. "Too cold out here for dallying."

Paul stepped forward, but Jack growled and blocked his way.

28

"That's enough, Jack," Bill commanded.

"He's just protecting his family." Paul figured the dog was more bluster than bite and knelt, tugging off a glove. He extended a bare hand to Jack, palm down. The dog sniffed it. Cautiously, Paul placed his hand on Jack's head and stroked his thick fur. The animal relaxed and moved forward, running his head under Paul's palm and rubbing his heavy, tufted coat against his leg.

"Guess you've passed the test," Bill said with a laugh. "He won't forget you. Come on in."

After introductions, the Kennedy boys hung back, obviously lacking enthusiasm over a call from the doctor. "Come on, now. Nothing to be afraid of." Bill turned to Paul. "Carl's the one who's having trouble. His ear's been hurting him for more than a week."

Paul listened to the boy's heart and lungs. He placed a thermometer in his mouth and then examined his ears. "That left ear's infected, all right." He glanced at the boy's mother, Iris. "Has he had this before?"

"Yes. Pretty regular in fact. Probably four or five times a year."

Paul took out the thermometer and checked the reading. "A hundred and one—not too bad." He returned the thermometer to its case. "You might want to think about having his tonsils and adenoids removed. That usually takes care of the problem."

Iris paled. "That seems kind of extreme for a sore ear."

"It's done all the time. Repeated infections can damage hearing. And . . . I don't want to alarm you, but sometimes infections can settle in the mastoid bone, here." He touched Carl's head behind his ear. "If that happens, it's a serious problem."

"Really?" Iris's fingers played over the collar of her dress. She glanced at her husband. "I suppose we'll have to talk about it."

Paul smiled and reached into his bag. "In the meantime, I'd like you to put two drops of this oil in his ear three times a day." He handed the medicine to Iris. "And a hot water bottle placed on the ear will help with the pain. Do you have aspirin?"

"Yes. I always keep some on hand."

"Good." He closed his medical bag. "Give him one tablet every four to six hours. It'll keep the fever down and decrease pain." He rubbed the top of Carl's head with his knuckles. "He'll be fine in a few days."

"Thanks so much for your help, Doc," Bill said. "We don't have much money, but I was hoping you'd take a couple of pelts. Been a good year for marten."

"My traps have been mostly empty this season. I'd appreciate the pelts."

Kate and Paul left the Kennedy homestead behind and moved on to a mining camp. Several men who needed to be seen were packed into a small room in the back of a general store. It stank of sweat and stale bodies.

Paul introduced himself and dove into work, diagnosing and treating the men's ailments. Time slipped away from him, until he looked up to see Kate watching from the doorway.

"Where you been?" Paul asked.

"I took care of the mail and dropped off supplies."

"Can you give me a hand here?"

"Uh . . . sure," Kate said.

"One of the men had sliced his hand pretty badly while cleaning a fish. As soon as I took off the wrappings, it started bleeding," Paul said. "Can you keep the blood clear while I stitch it up?" He handed her several pieces of gauze.

"Okay," Kate said, glancing at the wound, then turning away from the man's splayed skin.

"I'm going to need you to watch what you're doing," Paul said.

"I'm a pilot, not a nurse."

Paul let out an amused grunt as he began to clean the wound thoroughly, then went to work sewing up the injury. Kate managed to keep it clear of blood, even though she looked away a lot of the time.

30

Once back in the air, Paul blew out a breath and leaned back in his seat. "I'm beat."

"I didn't know doctoring was so much work," Kate said.

"It can be." He opened one eye and looked at her. "You did a good job. If you ever decide to give up flying . . ."

"Sorry—not my cup of tea. I hope you won't need me to help very often. I almost gagged a couple of times. Especially with that man who had the infected toe. Didn't know a toe could get so ugly."

Paul chuckled. "It was pretty bad."

Kate took Paul's hand and gave it a squeeze. "You're a good doctor. If I'm ever in need, I know who to call."

Paul winked at her. "Thanks." He looked at the frozen tundra below. "It's kind of nice to be back at work." All Paul had remembered about being a doctor was feeling like a failure, a murderer. He hadn't expected the satisfaction he'd felt today. He was glad he'd come.

"Did you get paid at the camp?"

"A couple of fellows paid me. Don't figure miners have much. Money's not what I'm after anyway." Paul looked at her. "How you getting paid for your flying time?"

"While you've been doctoring, I've made some deliveries and there were goods to pick up. I don't have any extra passengers this trip, but there'll be more than enough in the weeks to come."

That night Paul and Kate stayed at a roadhouse in Mc-Grath. After a supper of caribou stew and fresh-baked bread, Paul walked Kate to her room.

"Well, I'll see you in the morning." Paul wasn't sure just how to say good night. He didn't want to tarnish Kate's reputation, but he also didn't want to leave without a kiss.

"I had fun today, stinky feet and all." She leaned in to Paul. "I'm proud of you."

"It was pretty simple stuff," Paul said, but her respect made him feel good.

Kate gently kissed his cheek, then circled her arm around

his neck and pulled him closer. "I'm so glad we're working together." She pressed her lips to his.

Passion flared and Paul pulled her to him, answering her kiss. He longed for more, but forced himself to step back. "We better say good night."

"Okay," Kate said, her voice breathless. "I'll see you in the morning." A soft smile touched her lips.

"Tomorrow, then," Paul barely managed to say.

———————

The next few days Kate and Paul hopped from village to village. At the end of the fourth day, they moved up the coast of the Bering Sea. Paul was eager to get to Kotzebue. He hadn't seen Joe or Nena since Kate's accident. He wanted to see how Nena was getting on.

He gazed out at the endless bitter landscape. "I've never seen anything like this—miles of . . . nothing."

"A lot of ice and wind. Once in a while you'll see a pack of wolves or a bear. The villages are spread out. Nome's the main hub. They have a doctor there, but we'll stop anyway from time to time to drop off and pick up supplies and passengers."

Paul's eyes turned to the ice-covered ocean. "Hard to imagine that much water being frozen."

Kate glanced out at the ice. "This area always makes me feel small."

"More like microscopic."

"I never really feel alone, though. It's such an amazing place—huge and endless—and I'm reminded that God created it. I feel his presence here. And I know he sees me flying along." Kate smiled.

"You think so? I'd like to have your faith. Some things in life make it hard to believe."

Kate gave him a questioning look, but didn't say anything. Instead she glanced at her watch. "We're nearly to Kotzebue. Good thing. By three thirty it'll be dark."

Paul didn't want to think about how God had let him

down. He willed away thoughts of Susan and all that had happened in San Francisco and let his gaze roam over a ridge that flowed across the frozen arctic. "The mountains and the land blend together," he said, studying the white wasteland. "It's incredible." He turned to Kate. "Thanks for introducing me to Alaska. I've been holed up all this time and didn't realize there's so much to see."

"By this time next year you'll be well acquainted with the territory . . . and its people." Kate's lips curved up into a soft smile as she surveyed the expanse sprawling north. "I love Alaska."

She turned her gaze toward the sea. "I can't imagine what Amelia Earhart is experiencing right now. It must be amazing. She's flying over places people have never even seen. I'd love to do something like that."

"You'd like to fly around the world?" Paul shook his head.

"Yes. Can't you imagine it?"

"It would be an adventure." Paul chuckled. "But she's got to be a little crazy, don't you think? A woman and a navigator, on their own, flying across thousands of miles of unknown territory and up against all kinds of weather conditions. Not to mention how undependable planes can be."

"She has the best equipment and she's in touch with people on the ground." Her eyes alight, Kate didn't seem to be concerned with the dangers. "Just imagine seeing India and Australia and—"

"Don't you get any crazy ideas." Paul's stomach tightened. Sometimes Kate seemed to lack all reason. And yet, her adventurous spirit and her courage were part of what he loved about her.

"I won't. I couldn't afford it anyway. But I'd love to meet her someday."

By the time they approached Kotzebue, the sun, looking as if it had been drained of color, rested on the horizon. Firepots were lit and set out along the airfield.

As soon as the plane was down, Joe Turchik headed onto the airstrip. Paul opened the door and Angel bounded out with Kate following. Joe smiled, his almond-shaped eyes nearly disappearing in his round, tanned face. "Glad to see you."

"It's good to be back," Kate said. She turned to Paul. "You remember Paul. He was at the hospital when Nena was hurt."

"I remember. You helped save my Nena. Thank you." Joe grasped Paul's hand. "Welcome to Kotzebue."

"Glad to be here." Paul turned to look at a small village that huddled against the frigid Arctic. Icy wind tugged at the ruff of his hood and burned his cheeks. He pulled his hood closed around his face. "It's freezing out here."

"Outsiders," Joe said with a laugh.

The three worked together to secure the Bellanca. The oil was drained, the engine covered, and the craft securely tied down before they headed toward the village. Wind swirled particles of ice off the frozen ground, creating a sparkling mist in the fading light.

As they'd traveled, Paul's respect for Kate had grown. She was an incredible woman. He grabbed hold of her arm and stopped her. Joe kept moving.

"Kate." How did he say what he felt?

"What is it?" She stared at him with a puzzled expression.

"I just want you to know . . . I didn't understand." He blew out a breath. "All this time . . . I didn't get it—the risks you take, the kind of life you lead, the lives you touch. I'm so proud of you." He glanced at Joe's back, then gave Kate a quick kiss. "You're amazing."

"No, I'm not." Tears washed into her eyes and she shook her head. "I'm not even close to anything like that."

"You are," Paul said. "Don't let your past hold you back."

"I'm not. Why are you?"

— 3 —

Wind and cold chased Paul into the Turchiks' home, a combination mercantile and living quarters. It was small, overly warm, packed with provisions and furniture, and smelled of cooking meat.

Three youngsters barreled into Kate and hugged her. The littlest one, a girl, clung to Kate's legs. Paul wasn't sure he'd ever seen more beautiful children. Straight black hair framed tanned round faces.

Kate hugged the youngsters all at once. "Oh, how I've missed you."

Angel pushed her way in. The children buried their hands in her fur, and the smaller of the two boys wrapped his arms around the dog's neck. "Hi, Angel. You're the best dog ever."

The taller boy smiled up at Kate. "We're happy you came."

"Me too." Kate gave him an extra hug.

The youngster hanging on to Angel said, "I have something for you." He hurried to a table, picked up a piece of paper, and ran back to Kate. "It's a picture of the flowers and mountains—the way they look in summer." He held out his artwork and pointed at the drawing. "And that is the sun."

"What fine work, Nick." Kate took the gift. "It's nice to be reminded how beautiful it is here when the sun is warm."

35

He smiled broadly. "We have a lot of sunshine in the summer."

The little girl lifted her arms, demanding to be picked up. Kate hefted her and rested the child on one hip. "Mary, I swear you've put on ten pounds since I last saw you."

"The way she eats, she'll soon outgrow her brothers," said Nena, who looked like an older version of the little girl.

"She has a way to go to do that." Kate rested a hand on the older boy's head. "Peter, you're getting tall." He straightened, as if trying to add more height to his stocky frame.

Kate looked around the room. Even though it was packed with store goods, Nena had managed to give it a homey feel. "It's good to be here."

Nena wrapped Kate and Mary in a hug. "We are thankful for you." She turned to Paul with a smile. "And it's good to see you again."

"You're looking well." Paul gazed at her healthy brown face as he tugged off his gloves. "How are you feeling?"

"Good."

"No headaches, dizziness?"

"No. None. My balance isn't always just right, but it's getting better." She smiled, showing off-white teeth. "Thank you for coming. There are many villagers who wish to see you."

"Good. And I'm glad you're feeling fit. For a while there, the doctors weren't sure you'd pull through." Paul felt a knot in his gut at the memory of Joe's vigil at Nena's bedside. Not so different from the one he'd once held, only Joe and Nena had been given a happy ending.

"I have God and good doctors to thank." Nena glanced upward. "He was with me and so was Kate. I'd never have made it if she hadn't dragged me out of that plane and then watched over me." She gave Kate an extra hug.

"I could never desert you," Kate said. "We had quite an adventure." She gave Nena a one-armed hug.

"We are grateful," Joe said, then turning to Paul added, "and the people of Kotzebue are very happy to have a doctor here."

"I hope I can be of help." Fear niggled at Paul. What if he let them down?

"These are my children." Joe nodded at one of the boys. "Nick is five." He smiled at Paul. The tallest of the three stood beside his father. Joe rested a hand on his shoulder. "Peter is seven." He turned to Kate and the little girl in her arms. "And Mary is two."

Nena moved to a small kitchen range. "I made caribou stew. I hope you like it." She lifted a lid from a pan on the stove and steam billowed into the air. Using a wooden spoon, she stirred the meal.

Joe moved to the front room and dropped into a chair. "Paul, sit." He picked up a pipe and tobacco from a table made out of an empty barrel. He offered them to Paul.

"Thanks." Paul took the pipe and dumped tobacco into its bowl, pressing it down with his thumb. Joe lit it and Paul drew on the pipe until smoke drifted into the air. He took several puffs, and then held up the pipe. "Good," he said, although it tasted of cheap tobacco.

"Not so good," Joe said. "But it will do." He filled another pipe, clamped his teeth on the bit, and sucked air through the stem. "You been to Kotzebue before?" He settled back in his chair.

"No. It's a lot different from where I live on Bear Creek. But it looks like a nice little town." That wasn't exactly true. There didn't seem to be much commerce, and the homes and businesses were tiny and in need of repair, but Paul wasn't about to hold back a compliment. He understood how important a person's community could be to them.

"Most people never been here." Joe crossed one leg over the other. "You like it on Bear Creek?"

"Yes. There's lots of timber, and I've got a snug cabin and fine neighbors. The fishing and hunting are good too."

Joe nodded and then concentrated on smoking.

Paul rummaged around his mind for something more to say. "You do much hunting?"

"Sure. Seals and bear. Sometimes caribou or moose. And fish

fill the rivers in the summer." He drew deeply on his pipe and, without looking at Paul, asked, "You want to catch some cod?"

"This time of year? Up here?"

"They're under the ice. Just cut a hole in it and you can get 'em." He smiled. "I'll teach you if you want."

"I'd like that."

The sound of giggles carried out from the kitchen where Kate and Nena stood side by side finishing preparations for the evening meal. A memory of Susan and his sister ambushed Paul. They'd been standing just like that, cooking together and chatting. An ache rose from his chest and into his throat. Would he ever stop missing her?

"I think there will be many people here to see you tomorrow." Joe's words cut into Paul's thoughts.

"Oh? How many do you expect?"

Joe shrugged. "Most of the town. Even if they're not sick, they will come to meet you and to see if you are a good doctor." His eyes smiled.

"I look forward to meeting them."

"Some don't trust people from the outside." Joe removed the pipe from his mouth. "They're used to Alex Toognak, our medicine man. He's wise and able."

"Maybe you can introduce us." Paul respected traditional practices, believing there was room for both modern medicine and the old ways. He knew if his views got out to other physicians he'd be ridiculed, but he couldn't deny the power of natural healing. "Joe, it might help if you let people know I'm not from the outside. I've been living in Alaska nearly five years now."

Joe grinned. "Anyone who does not live in the Arctic is from the outside."

Paul chuckled. *It does feel like the end of the world.*

After dinner, the family gathered in the front room. Joe had promised to tell the children a story.

Kate sat on the floor beside Paul's chair. He noticed a

glance between the women, and Nena held back a giggle. Kate must have told her about them. Contentment warmed his insides and he gave her shoulder a gentle squeeze. She leaned against his leg. He liked that.

Lanterns and candles flickered, creating wavering shadows on the walls. The children waited, their eyes alight.

"Tell us the one about the great whale," Peter said.

"No. I want to hear about the bear that hides in the snow," said Nick.

Joe sat on the floor with the boys. He was quiet for a few moments, and then he said, "Tonight I will tell you a new story. It is about birds that saved a man's life."

"Birds saved a man?" Peter asked. "How can that be?"

"With God all things are possible." Joe smiled.

"Tell us," Nick nearly shouted.

"The Bible says that long ago there was a man named Elijah. He was a prophet of the one true God."

The boys' eyes didn't move from their father. Resting in her mother's arms, Mary looked sleepy.

Paul had been enchanted by the idea of storytelling, but he wasn't interested in a Bible story. He wished there were a polite way to excuse himself.

"In the land where Elijah lived, there was no rain for a very long time. Elijah had told the people that would happen."

"Why would he stop the rain?" Peter asked.

"He didn't stop it, God did. But Elijah told the king that a drought was coming."

Peter nodded but looked perplexed.

"We don't always understand why God does a thing, only that he is always right."

When Joe finished the story, Peter asked, "Why would a bird feed a man?"

"It was the power of God, who can do all things." He smiled at his son, his eyes crinkling at the corners.

Paul forced himself not to grimace at his answer. *What was right about taking my wife and son? Why would you do such a thing?*

Nena stood. "It is time for sleeping."

The children gave hugs all around, and then Nena bundled them off to their room in the back of the house. She returned a few minutes later, her arms full of blankets. "Kate, we have a bed for you with the children. I hope you don't mind sharing with them."

"Not at all."

"We have a tick mattress you can use," she told Paul. "Joe will bring it out."

"That suits me fine." Paul stood. "I'd better get some sleep. Tomorrow will be a busy day."

Accompanied by the children's quiet snores, Kate snuggled beneath her blankets. Her mind wandered back over the last several days. Working with Paul had been gratifying. The more she watched him, the more her admiration grew. He was highly skilled. And she didn't mind assisting, at least most of the time.

The bond between them had grown stronger. Yet she felt as if Paul were holding back part of himself. He didn't speak about his life before Alaska, and each time it came up he'd deflect the conversation. What was he hiding? It must be something really bad, because it seemed to have stolen his faith. He was angry at God.

She rolled onto her side. Whatever it was, Kate couldn't pry it from him. He would have to tell her in his own time. She whispered a prayer for Paul as she fell asleep.

Kate opened her eyes and looked around the dimly lit room. With a yawn, she stretched her arms over her head and looked about. The children were gone. Then she remembered that soon people would be arriving to see Paul. They might already be here. She flung back her blankets and sat up. She'd be needed.

By the time she made her way to the kitchen, Nena had a meal of flapjacks and eggs prepared. Paul was already eating. Someone had placed a cabinet between the kitchen area and the front room. Kate guessed it was there to serve as a privacy wall.

"You like some coffee?" Nena asked.

"Thank you." Kate sat across from Paul. "So, you ready?"

"Absolutely," Paul said, a little too emphatically.

Kate wondered if he was nervous. She was sure it had been awhile since he'd seen patients regularly.

Nena set a cup of coffee in front of her. "No milk. Sorry."

"This is fine." Kate took a sip. "Where's Joe?"

"He's helping a friend fix a sled. You hungry?"

"Starved. Breakfast smells delicious." Kate looked up and found Paul watching her. Feeling as if she ought to say something, she asked, "Did you sleep well?"

"I did." He leaned back in his chair. "You?"

"Like a log." Paul continued to gaze at her, his expression a mix of humor and adoration. A shiver of pleasure moved through Kate.

Nena set a plate of flapjacks and eggs in front of her.

"Thanks, Nena. You didn't have to go to so much trouble."

"Yes I do. You will work hard today. You need good food."

"It smells good." Kate spread butter on the pancakes. "Since I didn't help with breakfast, I'll do the dishes."

"No. You are a guest, and you and Paul will need your strength. He said that you help him."

Kate looked across the table at him. "So, I'm to be a nurse again?"

He speared the last bite of pancake, dipped it in a puddle of syrup, and forked it into his mouth. "Hope you don't mind. You're good at it."

A knock sounded at the door. "People are already here." Nena hurried to open it.

A woman and two children stood on the stoop, huddling against the cold. "We heard the doctor is here?"

"Yes. Come in." Nena opened the door wide and stepped back. She had the look of a child on Christmas morning. "Paul, your first patient."

Paul stood. "Give me one minute. I'll get my bag." He

carried his plate into the kitchen and set it in the sink, then hurried into the front room and grabbed his medical bag.

Nena cleared the table. "Sorry, Kate, you'll have to finish your meal standing."

"I don't mind." Kate picked up her plate and cup and stood at the sink, where she ate the last of her eggs, took a final drink of coffee, and set the mug on the counter, then looked around, wondering what to do.

Paul placed his bag on the table, opened it, and then turned his attention to the woman and children. "Good morning. Have a seat," he said, nodding at the chair.

There was another knock at the door. Nena rushed to answer it, her mukluks scuffing across the floor. Kate hovered near Paul, just in case he needed her for something.

It wasn't long before the entire front room was crowded with patients. Some looked well and others seemed quite ill. Kate wondered if they'd manage to see everyone in a single day. She kept herself busy writing down people's names and recording their reason for seeing the doctor. Those who were especially ill were moved to the front of the line. Occasionally Paul needed her help to calm a child, or to hold a compress, or to assist while he sutured a wound.

As a teenage boy moved out of the examining chair, Paul turned to a white-haired man shuffling across the room toward him. "Good morning," Paul said. "What can I do for you?"

His eyes suspicious, the man studied Paul. "I always go to Alex Toognak. He knows the old ways."

"I'm sure he's very good," Paul said. "You may go to him if you like."

The man glanced at his hands. "I did. He said I should come here." He lowered himself onto the chair.

Paul pulled up another chair and sat across from the elderly man. "I'm Paul Anderson. It's a pleasure to meet you . . ."

"George Chilligan."

"What can I do for you, George?"

"Well, I got a lot of . . ." He glanced toward the front room.

Lowering his voice, George said, "My nose runs all the time. I go through two or three snot rags a day. Can't stop it."

Paul reached into his bag and took out a flashlight. "Guess I better have a look." He tilted the man's head back and, using the light, he checked the inside of his nose, and then using a tongue depressor, he examined his mouth and throat, and finally palpated his neck. "No sign of infection." He thought a moment. "What do you use to light your house?"

"Oil lamp."

"Whale oil?"

George nodded.

"Does it smoke a lot?"

"Sometimes. They all do."

"That might be what's causing your trouble. If you keep plenty of oil in it and cut the wick short, there should be less smoke. Also, I'd like you to try using a saltwater rinse. That should help."

George stared at him for a long moment, and then asked, "How do I do that?"

After Paul explained the procedure, George went on his way, without a thank you.

"Don't worry about him," Nena said. "He's always cranky."

"I'm not worried," Paul said with a grin. "Actually I like people who are a little rough around the edges. They make life interesting."

All day people kept coming. Paul treated bronchial infections, stomach ailments, sore throats, and skin infections, and he pulled bad teeth, something Kate remembered all too well. Although the villagers usually went to Alex Toognak, they seemed glad to have a real doctor. Most thanked Paul before leaving. He was paid with coins, furs, and tobacco, and one woman gave him a jar of crowberry jam.

As Kate witnessed Paul's generosity and genuine concern for his patients, her love grew. Why had God given her such a fine man, and why did Paul love her? She didn't know the answer, but she was grateful.

The last patient left just as Nena finished preparing

dinner. Paul and Kate hadn't eaten since breakfast. There hadn't been time. Kate suddenly realized she was ravenously hungry.

"You like some soup and biscuits?" Nena asked.

"I'd love some," Kate and Paul said at the same time. They looked at each other and laughed.

Everyone except Peter sat down at the table.

"Where's Peter?" Kate asked.

"He said he's not hungry, that his belly hurts." Nena looked at Paul. "I didn't want to bother you over a stomachache."

"No trouble. I'll take a look at him." Paul stood. "Where is he?"

"In his bed." Nena led the way to the children's room.

The boy lay on his side, pale and fevered. Alarm thumped through Kate. He'd seemed fine earlier.

Paul kneeled beside the bed. "So, you're not feeling so good, huh?"

Holding his stomach, Peter shook his head.

"Can you tell me where it hurts?"

The boy touched his upper abdomen.

Paul nodded and rested a hand on Peter's forehead. He glanced over his shoulder at Nena. "He's running a fever. Probably just a bug of some kind. I doubt it's anything to worry about."

Nena's brow furrowed with worry. "After lunch, he said he wasn't feeling good. And he seems worse now."

Paul turned back to his young patient. "Peter, can you roll onto your back?"

With a quiet groan Peter managed to do as he was asked. He looked at his mother, eyes fearful.

Paul gently probed his stomach. "Does this hurt?" Peter shook his head no. "How about this?" Paul pressed two fingers gently into the right side of the boy's abdomen.

Peter winced. "Ouch!"

"And here?" Paul moved his hand to the other side of his stomach and applied pressure. Peter shook his head no.

"Hmm. The pain's sharpest in the area of his appendix.

No way to tell for certain if that's it." He straightened. "We'll keep an eye on him and see how he does."

Nena stayed with Peter while the rest of the family returned to finish their meal.

With her hunger satisfied, exhaustion swamped Kate. She struggled to keep her eyes open. Even so, Nick talked her into a game of Go Fish. With Paul and Joe chatting, she tackled the tenacity of the five-year-old, who had obviously played a lot of card games.

After Nick beat her three times, she headed to her make-shift bedroom. Joe had made up a place for her in what looked like a storage room. He'd apologized but didn't want Peter's illness to disturb her sleep. Finally comfortable and warm beneath the covers, she drifted toward slumber, her mind on the people of Kotzebue. It had been a good day.

One of the highlights had been a woman who was advanced in her pregnancy. Paul had let her use the stethoscope to listen to her baby's heartbeat. When she first heard the muffled thumping of the child's heart, her eyes lit up and she'd exclaimed her joy. To her, it was a miracle. Kate's eyes closed and she wondered if she'd ever hear the sound of her own child's heartbeat.

Kate didn't know how long she'd been asleep when Nena roused her.

"Kate," she said, her voice tense. "Wake up."

Her mind still feeling muzzy, Kate pushed up on one elbow. "What is it?"

"Paul needs you."

"Me? Why? Is something wrong?"

"It's Peter. He's very sick."

Now fully awake, Kate hurriedly dressed and followed Nena to the kitchen.

Peter lay on the table, looking terrified and quite ill. Joe stuffed wood into the stove even though the room was already unbearably hot.

"What's wrong with him?" Kate asked.

Paul had set out instruments on the table. "I'm pretty sure

it's an inflamed appendix." He took Kate aside, out of reach of Peter's hearing. His voice soft, he said, "If it ruptures, he could die. I've got to get it out."

Kate's stomach plummeted. She glanced at Peter, unable to imagine the rambunctious little boy dying. "Do you know how to do that?"

"Yes." His expression was grim. "But I've never done a surgery under such primitive conditions."

"I have confidence in you," Kate said, resting her hand on his arm.

Paul's gaze moved to Nena, then back to Kate. "I need someone to assist me. Nena's going to take care of the anesthetic."

Kate's heart sped up. "I can barely tolerate a man's stinking feet. How do you expect me to do surgery?" She glanced at Peter. "I can't do it."

"You'll just be helping." Paul's dark brown eyes bore into Kate's. "I need you." He glanced at Joe. "Better you than Joe."

Kate took a quaking breath. She had no choice. "What do you want me to do?"

— 4 —

Paul washed his hands and dried them, then moved to the table where Peter lay beneath a sheet. He leaned over the boy and smiled down at him. In a soothing voice he said, "We'll have you good as new in no time."

Kate blew out a shaky breath and tried to relax tight muscles. Could she do this? She glanced at Joe. The worry in his heart lined his face and darkened his eyes, and then she looked at young Peter. Yes, she'd do whatever was needed.

"What you going to do?" Peter's voice trembled.

Paul rested a hand on the child's shoulder. "I'm going to take out your sick appendix." He squeezed gently. "Your mama and daddy are here. And Kate too."

"How you gonna get it out?"

Paul didn't answer right away. "Well . . . I have some medicine." He removed a container of ether he'd been heating over a burning candle. "It'll make you sleep, and when you wake up, your appendix will be out. You'll feel much better."

Wide-eyed, Peter looked at his mother, then his father, who stood at her side.

Nena gently stroked his hair. "Your daddy and I are right here. Dr. Anderson is a good doctor." She pressed a kiss to his brow.

Paul covered a small handheld mask with gauze. "I'm going

to put this over your nose. Just breathe like you always do and soon you'll be asleep." He placed it over the boy's nose and mouth, then dispensed two drops of ether onto the gauze. Peter's eyes closed.

Paul watched him for a moment, then said, "Nena, keep the mask over his nose, and if he stirs or acts like he's waking up, place one drop of ether on the gauze. No more than that." He raised his eyebrows. "Let me know if his lips look the least bit blue or if his skin becomes abnormally pale. Also keep an eye on his breathing to make sure it doesn't slow down too much."

"I'll keep watch," Joe said.

"This is a dangerous medicine?" Nena asked.

"It's good medicine, but we need to be cautious." He offered her an encouraging smile. "I know what I'm doing. He'll come through just fine."

Fear glinted in Nena's eyes as she took hold of the mask and accepted the ether. And yet, her hand was steady.

Paul turned to Kate. "I'll need you to stanch any excess bleeding. And it's hot in here, so if you can keep the sweat off my forehead and out of my eyes, that'll help."

Kate realized she was clenching her teeth. She couldn't remember being more terrified. "How do I stanch the—"

"Use this clamp." Paul held up what looked like long-handled tongs. He placed a piece of heavy gauze in the instrument and handed it to Kate. "Get more dressing as you need it."

Kate took the clamp. She tried to keep her hand from shaking, but couldn't quite manage.

Paul placed a hand over hers. "You're a natural for this." He smiled encouragement, but Kate could see trepidation in his eyes. Was he afraid too?

Paul examined Peter, opening each eyelid and looking closely at his pupils. Using a stethoscope, he listened to the boy's heart, and then folded back the sheet and watched the rise and fall of his chest. Next, he doused a cloth with liquid from a bottle and wiped it on the child's stomach, leaving a reddish-brown smear. With a glance at Nena and then Kate, he asked, "All set?"

Both women nodded. Kate didn't feel ready. She was a pilot, not a nurse. The last place she wanted to be was in this room.

With meticulous care, Paul picked up a small-handled knife. Every nerve in her body taut, Kate forced herself to watch. He palpated the boy's stomach, and then pressed the blade to his skin. As he cut, flesh fell away and blood oozed.

Kate felt woozy. *I'm not going to faint. I'm not.* She swabbed blood as Paul opened the incision farther and probed for Peter's infected appendix.

"Here it is," he said. "And definitely toxic. Good thing we didn't wait."

While Paul worked, Kate forgot that she didn't know what to do. Paul was patient and precise in his instructions, and her insecurity and queasiness was replaced by interest. She'd never seen the inside of a person's body.

Paul glanced at Nena. "He still in a deep sleep?"

"Yes. How much longer?"

"Nearly finished." He snipped off the inflamed appendix, lifted it out, and dropped it into a bowl. "Got it. Before you know it, he'll be out pretending to be a mighty hunter and chasing after his brother." He went to work suturing the inner incision and, when that was done, moved to closing the wound he'd made in Peter's abdomen.

Finally, he tied off the last stitch. "That's it." He smiled at Nena and Kate. "Good job, ladies." He wiped blood from his hands, then checked Peter's pulse and respiration. "Keep him warm and quiet. He'll sleep for a while." Paul turned to Kate. "How you holding up?"

She lowered herself into a chair. "I'm fine." She closed her eyes for a moment, and then looked at Paul. "I'm glad it's over, though."

Paul smiled. "Like I said, you're a natural. You ought to think about becoming a nurse."

"I'll stick to flying, thanks." Kate's tone was dry, but she felt elated. She'd done something she'd never thought herself capable of, and Peter was going to be all right.

Paul and Kate remained at the Turchiks' another full day until Paul was certain Peter would recover well. He left thorough instructions for his care, and then he and Kate set off. They had additional stops to make, but thankfully encountered no further emergencies.

When Kate set down in Anchorage, she was glad to be home.

"The Winter Festival ought to be in full swing by now." Paul squeezed Kate's knee. "We could use a little fun."

Kate nodded, but she was worn out, and even the festival felt like too much. Working with Paul had turned out to be more than she'd counted on. It consumed a great deal of her energy and time. Plus she flew fewer hours and made less money. Exhausted, she longed for her bed, but she needed to get back into the air and hoped Sidney had work lined up. She glanced at Paul. He was counting on spending the time with her, and the idea of sharing the merriment of the festival with him made it hard to think about work. Maybe she ought to take a couple of days off.

Wearing his usual relaxed smile, Mike Conlin met them at the plane. "'Bout time you two got back."

He gave Kate a one-armed hug and shook Paul's hand. "How'd it go?"

"Good," Kate said, glad to see Mike was his usual friendly self.

"You guys look beat. How about a cup of coffee?" Mike grinned. "Helen dropped off some fresh-baked cookies this morning."

Kate was so tired even Helen's cookies didn't sound enticing. "Thanks, but I've got to take care of the plane and then I'm going to hit the sack."

"What, you too tired for some of Sidney's sinkers? They're only a couple days old." Mike grinned.

Kate loved doughnuts, but not the kind that had been sitting around the shop. "Not interested."

Mike chuckled. "I'll help you guys with the plane. Oh yeah, we have a new pilot. I'll introduce you."

"Sidney found someone, huh?"

"Yeah. A fella down from Fairbanks."

"Good, now maybe Kate won't have to work so hard." Paul draped an arm over her shoulders. "It'll give us a little more time together."

Kate leaned against Paul. "I love being with you, but I need all the work I can get. I've got a house to save for."

"We'll have to do more *work* together." He grinned.

"That sounds good to me."

After the plane was secured and the oil drained, the three walked toward the shop. The mingled odor of overcooked coffee and diesel assaulted Kate's nose when she stepped inside the building. She glanced around.

Sidney, who'd been studying a map, looked up. "Howdy."

"Hi."

Kenny crammed parcels into a pack. He glanced over his shoulder at her and Paul. "Hey there. Was beginning to think you two had taken off for good." He grinned and whiffed at a strand of curly hair that had fallen across his eyes.

"It was a good trip. But I'm glad to be back." Kate's gaze landed on a tall, sturdily built man wearing a red flannel shirt. He was clean shaven except for a heavy mustache. Stepping toward Kate, he extended a hand. "You must be Kate."

His grip was strong. "I am. And you are . . ."

"Alan Weber, pilot."

His tone was friendly, but by his demeanor, Kate guessed he was shy. "Glad you're here. We really needed another pilot."

"I'm thankful for the job." He turned to Paul and shook his hand. "I take it you're the doctor."

"Paul Anderson—glad to meet you."

Sidney leaned back in his chair. "He showed up just in the nick of time. With you gone, Kate, I needed a pilot."

"Glad to be part of the crew," Alan said. "And it's good to be based further south. Too cold and too dark in Fairbanks."

Mike slapped him on the back. "Glad to have you. Sidney's been working us to death."

Kate massaged sore muscles in her neck and turned to Sidney. "Speaking of which, I'm wondering if you'd mind my taking a day off."

"A day off? I've got flights stacked up."

"I was just thinking—"

Sidney laughed. "You bet you're taking a couple of days off, young lady. Go home and get some rest—enjoy the festival."

"Thanks." Kate could have hugged him, but decided not to embarrass him.

Paul scratched several days' growth of beard. "I could do with a bath and a shave." He turned to Kate. "Can I catch a ride with you?"

She looped an arm through his. "I was counting on it." They headed toward the door and stepped out.

"Hey, Kate," Mike called.

She stopped and, looking back at him, saw hurt and longing in his eyes. She let go of Paul's arm.

"When you planning to go to the winter carnival?" he asked.

"Maybe tomorrow." She looked at Paul for confirmation.

"Sounds good to me," Paul said. "I brought along some pelts to sell and tomorrow seems as good a day as any to put them on the market. Thought we'd go together."

"Well, I guess I'll see you there, then." Mike's voice had lost its enthusiasm.

Kate cringed inwardly at the wounded look she saw in his eyes. She nearly invited him to join her and Paul, but held back. She wanted time alone with Paul. And this was the first day since they'd headed into the bush that they'd have time just for fun. "Okay. See you tomorrow sometime."

Paul took Kate's hand and they walked toward the car. She couldn't wait for the next day.

After dropping Paul off at his hotel, Kate gratefully walked into her apartment. She dropped onto the sofa, unlaced her boots, and pulled them off. She wiggled her toes and considered going straight to bed. Instead, she ran a bath, stripped out of her clothes, and sank into steaming water.

Resting her head against the back of the tub, she closed her eyes, savoring the warmth. Thoughts of the last two weeks drifted through her mind. Working with Paul hadn't been what she'd expected. They'd spent a good deal of time together, but she still felt as if she knew very little about him.

He was a kind and a highly skilled doctor, but why he'd left San Francisco remained a mystery. She wished he'd tell her about his life there and wondered why he kept so much of his past a secret. She closed her eyes. What if he'd done something so horrible he couldn't speak about it?

No. Not possible. Not Paul.

After a good soak, Kate put on pajamas, added wood to the fire, and climbed into bed. She shivered between chilly sheets. Pulling wool blankets up under her chin, weariness engulfed her, and she fell asleep.

Muted morning light greeted Kate as she forced her eyelids open. She gazed at the window. It was late. She rolled onto her side and looked at the clock on the bureau—ten o'clock. Reaching her arms over her head, she yawned and stretched, enjoying the luxury of not having to get up.

She remembered the carnival and wondered when Paul wanted to go. They hadn't decided on a time. The aroma of baking pastries made her mouth water, and hunger convinced her to get up.

With a fire crackling in the woodstove, Kate stood at the window and marveled at fragments of light that were dispersed through an icy prism on the glass. She hummed "I'm in the Mood for Love." Just the thought of Paul made her smile. Today would be fun.

She splashed her face with water, brushed her teeth and hair, and stepped into clean clothes. Taking only a few moments for makeup, she headed for the store at the front of the building.

Helen stood at the large window facing the street. She turned when Kate walked in. "Good morning. I thought you were going to sleep the day away." She opened her arms and pulled Kate into a hug. "Nice to have you back. How was your trip?"

"Good. No real problems. Paul's a wonderful doctor."

"I'm not surprised." Helen moved to a table set with breakfast goodies. "Would you like some coffee?"

"Love some." Kate gazed out onto the street congested with people. "I never expected such crowds for the winter carnival."

"Folks from all over the territory have been flooding in." She handed Kate a cup of coffee along with a sweet roll. "Baked these just this morning."

"I could smell them from my room." Kate took a bite, her tongue appreciating the mingled flavors of apples and cinnamon. She sipped her coffee. "I didn't realize how hungry I am." She took another bite of the roll. "Delicious," she said around a mouthful.

Helen filled another cup with coffee for herself. "Do you plan to join in the festivities?"

"I'm supposed to pick Paul up at the hotel this morning, but we didn't set a time. I'll have to call him." Kate watched a group of children dart back and forth across the street, tossing snowballs at one another.

"Mike called this morning," Helen said.

"Mike? For me?"

"Well, not exactly. He wondered if you'd already left for the carnival."

"Hmm. That's strange." Kate finished off her roll and sipped her coffee. "He said something about seeing us there, but I'm sure he doesn't plan to join us."

"Sometimes it's hard to shut off feelings . . . like love." Helen joined Kate at the window. "Mike's human, like the rest of us, and I suppose he hopes to see you around."

"He knows how things are between me and Paul."

Helen gazed out the window. "He'll adjust. Give him time." She took a drink of her coffee. "How did things go between you and Paul on your trip?"

"Good. We work well together. I even assisted in a surgery."

"Really?"

"Yes. Paul removed Nena's boy, Peter's, appendix."

"My goodness. Is Peter all right?"

"Yes. Or he was when we left." Kate took a sip of coffee. "It was amazing to help in a real surgery. At first I was so scared I couldn't keep my hands from shaking, but Paul was very competent and calm, and he told me exactly what to do. Before I knew it, I wasn't scared anymore." She let out a sigh. "He's a wonderful man. We're crazier for each other than before we left, except . . . I still don't know much about him, his past anyway. He's kind of private."

"Some men are like that. He'll open up eventually."

"You think so?"

"Absolutely."

Fear made Kate's insides feel tight. What if he never trusted her enough to share his past? Could she love a man who couldn't trust her with his past? And worse yet, could she trust a man who would hide it from her?

Helen draped an arm over Kate's shoulders and gave her a little squeeze. "Try not to worry."

Hanging on to Paul's arm, Kate cautiously walked along the icy sidewalk. She hoped they didn't run into Mike. She still wondered why he'd called. He knew that she and Paul were a couple. It didn't make sense for him to inquire about what time she was going to the festival. It felt like he was trying to horn in on her time with Paul, and that was out of character for him. He was better than that.

"Don't think I've ever seen crowds like this in town," Paul said.

Anchorage teemed with people, and the air buzzed with excitement. Fur sellers talked up the quality of their pelts while buyers talked them down. Deals were made. Children created snowmen and built forts where they bombarded one another with snowballs from behind frozen fortresses. Some raced sleds, their dogs yapping and sometimes stopping in the middle of a race to fight one another.

A huge bonfire warmed a crowd at one end of the street. Not far from there, a group stood shoulder to shoulder around a blanket made from hides. They tossed a young boy into the air. When he flew up, he'd wave his arms and kick his feet before falling back to the blanket.

"That looks like fun. Let's join in," Paul said, heading toward the circle of people crowded around the blanket.

Too late, Kate saw Mike. He was part of the group holding the blanket.

He looked over his shoulder, and when his eyes found Kate, he hollered, "Come on. Over here."

"Looks like fun," Kate said, making sure Paul stood between her and Mike. She grabbed hold of the hide as the young native boy flew into the air. Everyone cheered. When he dropped to the blanket, he was immediately tossed back up. Leaning against Paul, Kate laughed as she watched the boy fly.

"You want to try it?" Mike asked Kate.

She shook her head no.

"How about a little mushing, then?"

"That sounds like fun," she said, turning to Paul. "But I thought you were going to sell furs."

"I decided tomorrow would be better. Today should be all about having a good time—no work."

"I've got some friends with sleds and dogs," Mike said. "You ever do any mushing, Kate?"

"No." Kate felt a weight in her stomach. She didn't want Mike butting into her time with Paul. "Paul's going to teach me."

"Oh. Sure," Mike said, his tone glum. "That makes sense."

Paul took Kate's hand. "You hungry? I saw a fella down the street roasting meat."

"Sounds good," Kate said. "See you," she tossed at Mike as Paul led her away.

After finishing off a baked potato and a chunk of roasted

moose meat, Kate and Paul watched a game of ice hockey and competition between dogs pulling weighted sleds, then they headed toward the end of the street where there were sled dog races. Kate couldn't remember having so much fun. She wasn't sure if it was the events or that she was with Paul.

"Hey, Paul, how you doing?" asked a tall, friendly looking man. He separated himself from a group of men and walked toward them. "Haven't seen you for a while."

"Jake. Good to see you. I'm well, just not in town much—either working on my place or out and about with Kate here." He put an arm around her and pulled her close as if to make sure Jake knew they were together. Kate liked the feeling of belonging to him.

Jake turned friendly hazel eyes on Kate. "So, what is it that you do that keeps Paul out of town?"

"I'm a pilot, and since Paul's working as a bush doctor, I'm usually the one flying him from place to place."

Jake's eyebrows lifted slightly. "I'm impressed. Never met a woman pilot before, and I didn't know you were a doctor, Paul. You're one for keeping secrets."

He is at that, Kate thought.

"I used to work as a doctor when I lived in California. Gave it up when I moved north, but with a little encouragement from Kate I decided to go back to work." He grinned. "I like it."

"I'll look you up if I need a doctor." Jake turned to Kate. "So, you ever drive a dog sled?"

"No. Never."

"You want to take a ride?"

"Sure. Sounds like fun."

"Well, I've got a team that's raring to go. I'll give you a ride." He headed toward his team of dogs.

Paul led Kate to the sled. "Climb on."

Kate sat on the sled. "What should I do?" She pulled her hood closed around her face.

"Just sit. I'll do the rest." Jake chuckled and then asked Paul, "You want to drive?"

"You bet. I'd love to take my girl for a ride." He stepped onto the boards.

Kate's heart warmed—*my girl*. She looked at him and smiled.

"How about a race?" another man, Billy Johnson, called.

"Nah, this is just for fun," Paul said.

"What, you afraid I'll beat you?"

Paul's eyes narrowed and he looked down at Kate. She gave him a nod. With a smile, Paul turned to Jake. "So, your dogs worth betting on?"

"Not a problem. They're a good team. In fact, I've got a five spot says you win." He pulled a wallet out of his back pocket and fished out a five-dollar bill.

"That's pretty steep," Billy said.

"Well . . . if you're afraid—" Jake acted as if he were going to put away his money.

"I ain't afraid." Billy pulled out a five-dollar bill and waved it in the air. Several others joined in on the bet.

"If this is going to be fair, Billy, you've got to add some weight to your sled," Jake said.

Billy looked around. His gaze landed on a woman who was much smaller than Kate. "Hey, Sooz, you wanna ride with me?"

The tiny blonde smiled. "Sure." She pranced over and settled herself on the sled.

"You ready?" Paul asked Kate.

"I guess so."

"Hold on. Don't want to lose ya." He looked at Billy. "Anytime."

Jake held up one arm, then as he dropped it, he yelled, "Go!"

Paul lifted the lines and hollered, "Hike up." The dogs lunged forward, and he and Kate charged into the lead. Billy soon caught up and moved ahead. Win or lose, Kate didn't care. She loved the feel of the snow flying beneath the sled blades and the cold air splashing her face.

In the end, Paul and Kate came up short, but they made a good showing. Paul and Billy shook hands. "Good race."

Kate climbed off the sled. "That was fun."

"Want to learn how to drive one of these?" Jake asked. "It's okay with me if Paul gives you a lesson."

"Really?" Kate's blood pumped with excitement. She looked at Paul. "Would you mind?"

"This is as good a time as any, if you're game." He stepped up to her and pulled her close. "You sure you want to do this?"

At the moment, Kate would have preferred to remain in Paul's arms, but she wasn't about to say that, not in front of everyone. "Yeah. I'm sure. It can't be as hard as flying."

Kate stepped behind the sled. She caught sight of Mike. He huddled inside his parka and was heading back up the street. By the set of his shoulders, it looked like he was not happy. Kate felt a flash of sadness.

"You can ride on the boards or run behind if you want." Paul handed her the traces. "These control the dogs. If you want them to go, you just tell them to 'hike up,' and if you want them to turn right, say 'gee' or to go left is 'haw.' When you need them to slow down, all you have to say is 'easy' and to stop them it's 'whoa.'" He rested a hand on her arm. "Got it?"

"I think so." Kate stepped onto the boards, took the towline in one hand, and held on to the sled bar with the other.

Paul stepped up behind her and showed her how to hold the lines. He stood so close Kate could feel his breath. She turned and looked at him and her eyes locked with his. She wanted to kiss him, but didn't dare, not in front of everyone. The two lingered for a moment and finally decided they didn't care who was watching. Their lips met. Hoots and hollers of approval arose from onlookers. Paul stepped back. Feeling heat in her face, Kate glanced at the faces of friends and strangers.

She smiled at Paul, then turned and faced the front of the sled. "Okay, I'm ready. Hike up!" she hollered.

The dogs lunged forward so abruptly that Kate lost her balance and fell on her backside. "Whoa!" she called, thankful the dogs listened and stopped instead of heading off down the street without her.

Laughing, Paul helped her to her feet. "Don't worry. Almost everyone has a rough beginning."

Kate brushed snow and ice off her pants. "It's not funny."

"It's not?" He grinned, and then his expression turned more serious. "You're not hurt, are you?"

"No." She looked at the band of men still snickering.

"Maybe today's not the best time for a lesson," Paul said. "I'll teach you with my dogs out on the creek." He kissed her cheek.

"That sounds like a good idea," she said, casting a caustic look at the spectators. "I'd rather it was just you and me anyway."

— 5 —

Trudging through freshly fallen snow, Kate headed toward the shop. She looked up through a flurry of white flakes. "May in Alaska," she muttered, pulling her hood closer around her face. It was spring—didn't it know better than to snow? She was ready for summer.

Why had she even bothered coming to work? She had more chance of joining Amelia Earhart on her round-the-world flight than she did of getting a run on a day like this. She imagined herself copiloting with Amelia—what an incredible adventure that would be. Miss Earhart hadn't actually announced an official date for her great adventure yet, but the scuttlebutt was that she'd be making a try beginning in early summer. Kate wished she were doing something extraordinary like that.

A glance at the cars parked in front of the building told her everyone had made it in. *Must be hoping for a break in the weather.*

Blustering wind and snow accompanied Kate indoors. She shut out the tempest and then pushed back her hood. The usual smells of woodsmoke and overcooked coffee met her as she stepped into the room.

"It's miserable out," she said, moving toward an ancient woodstove belching heat. "You think there's any hope it will let up?" No one answered. She looked around the room at brooding faces. Something was up.

His feet propped on the desk and a cigarette resting between his fingers, Sidney stared out the window. Kenny and Alan sat across from each other. Kenny shuffled a deck of cards. Mike glanced at her, and then he grabbed a piece of wood and chucked it into the stove. Jack was the only one who seemed content. Wearing a smug grin, he leaned against the far wall.

Alarm made the hair on Kate's arms prickle. "What's up?"

All eyes went to Sidney. He blinked, slow and resolute, then looked at Kate, as if seeing her for the first time. Furrows creased his brow, and he looked like he'd aged ten years. He took a drag off the half-burned cigarette. Ashes spilled onto his flannel shirt, but he didn't seem to notice.

"Sidney, what's wrong?"

Tears swamped his eyes. "My dad had a stroke."

"Oh!" Kate pressed fingertips to her lips. "I'm so sorry. Is he all right?"

"Doctor says he'll live." Sidney's tone was somber. "But he's not himself anymore."

"What do you mean?"

Sidney studied the cigarette, drew smoke into his lungs and then slowly blew it out. "Can't talk—can't walk—can't do much of anything."

"He'll get better though, won't he?"

"Not likely." He shrugged. "But you never know. The doctor might be wrong." He smashed the cigarette butt into an ashtray. "My mom's not doing so good."

"I'm truly sorry."

Sidney dropped his feet to the floor and walked to the window. Hands in his pockets, he gazed out at swirling white crystals. "Soon as this stinkin' weather clears, I'll be leaving. Family needs me."

Kate sat in a chair near the stove. "Do you know how long you'll be gone?"

He turned and settled a troubled gaze on Kate. "Could be a long while." He let out a breath that sounded like a wheeze.

Kate wondered just what that meant, but she didn't ask. She pressed her elbows on her thighs and rested her chin in her hands, allowing her eyes to graze over the men in the room. What would happen to the business?

"He offered me the airfield," Jack said, wearing a syrupy smile.

"That's not true. I didn't offer it to *you*."

At that moment, Kate thought she actually hated Jack. He was so full of himself. And he'd given her nothing but trouble from her first day at the airfield. He'd harassed her and made life miserable for just about everyone else on the team. And now, when Sidney was facing a family tragedy, all he could think about was himself.

Sidney looked at Kate. "It is for sale . . . to *anyone* with the money. You want to make an offer?" He tried to smile. "I need the money. It'll take awhile to find a job—not a lot of work in Kenai."

Kate's mind reeled. Jack had spoken the truth. He was the only one with any money, so for all intents and purposes the business *had* been offered to him. "Maybe one of us could manage the airfield until you come back."

"Wish I could do that, but my dad's going to need extra care and that takes cash. Mom doesn't have any. Everyone in the family's strapped right now."

Kate mentally calculated her own finances. She had barely had enough funds to see her through the winter, let alone buy the airfield. Every cent she'd set aside had gone to purchasing her new plane. She looked at Mike.

He shrugged. "I don't have it."

"There must be someone."

"Me." Jack smirked.

Sidney pulled on his coat. "Figure I'll be here 'til tomorrow. Kate . . . Mike." His eyes scanned the room. "If any of you come up with the dough, call me. Or maybe you know someone else who might want the business." His eyes moved reluctantly to Jack. "Otherwise . . . it's his."

"I'll take good care of the place." Jack puffed out his chest. "Make a first-rate airfield out of it."

Kate's stomach tumbled. Working for Jack would be torture. Of course, she probably wouldn't have to worry about it—he'd fire her the first chance he got. Her eyes locked with his. She couldn't just let it go to him. "I'll see what I can come up with," she said.

Kenny and Alan weren't concerned about who took over the airport, so it was up to Kate and Mike. They spent the rest of the day trying to find someone who would either loan them the money or buy the airport outright. They talked to everyone they knew and some they didn't. There was no one willing to buy it. Some didn't want to take a risk. Others reasoned one airfield in Anchorage was more than enough. And people like Albert and Helen were willing to help but didn't have the money.

Mike and Kate seemed to be the only ones motivated enough to work at finding a buyer, so they had decided to combine their efforts. After a day of brainstorming and seeking out anyone who might be interested, Mike invited Kate back to his place for something to eat.

It was late when Kate dropped onto Mike's sofa and watched him mix up a batch of waffle dough. She knew she ought to help but couldn't drag herself up off the couch.

"Got some of Helen's strawberry jam," Mike said, wearing a smile that didn't touch his eyes.

Kate nodded, her mind still searching for a way to keep the airfield out of Jack's greedy hands. "There must be someone out there who wants the airport."

Mike opened a hot waffle iron, slathered the griddle with lard, and poured in dough. Closing the lid, he asked, "You want some eggs?"

"No thanks." Kate planted her feet on a coffee table and folded her arms over her chest. "Who haven't we thought of?"

"What about Paul?"

Kate sucked in a breath. "I know he has enough to take care of himself, but he's obviously not a wealthy man. And he makes almost nothing as a doctor."

"Wish we had more time." Mike poured coffee into a mug. "You want some?"

"Sure."

He handed the cup to her and poured another for himself. He took jam and syrup out of the cupboard and grabbed a plate of butter off the table. "I haven't talked to my brothers in a while. They might—"

"Your brothers? You've never mentioned them before."

"They live in Chicago. They're partners in a pub. When prohibition was lifted, they stepped right into the business. From what I heard, they've done pretty well. But I doubt they'd loan me a penny. We've never been close."

"Call them. It won't hurt to ask."

"It's late." Mike studied the waffle iron. Steam rose from around the edges. "And they're four hours ahead of us."

"If they work in a bar, it's still early for them."

"I don't know. It's a long shot." Mike lifted the griddle and peeked at undercooked waffles. He closed the lid.

"It's worth a try. I'll do everything I can to help." Kate pushed off the sofa. "You've been working up here a long time. You know everything there is to know. You could do it."

"I don't know. There's a lot to owning an airport, and it wouldn't leave me much time for flying."

"We can't let Jack buy it," Kate pressed. "Life will be unbearable. And not just for me, but for all of us. You know how he is. He'll run roughshod over every one of us. And first chance he gets, he'll cut our pay." She strode into the kitchen. "I'll take care of these." She peeked at the waffles. "You make the call."

"Okay. Okay." Mike moved to the phone on the wall and flipped through a tablet that hung beside it. When he got hold of the operator, he gave her the pub's phone number, and then waited.

Kate closed her eyes and said a quick prayer. *Please, God, make this work.*

"Hello. This is Mike Conlin. Can I talk to Jerry or Robert?" He waited.

"Are they there?" Kate asked.

"They're getting Jerry."

Her stomach quivering, Kate checked the waffles again. They were done. Using a fork, she lifted them out and onto a plate. After adding lard to the griddle, she poured in more dough and closed the lid.

"Hi. Jerry? This is Mike." He waited while Jerry responded. "Yeah. I'm good." He nodded. "I know. It has been a long time. Sounds like you have a full house tonight.

"I have a proposition for you. It's a good deal." He was silent, but Kate could hear a voice on the other end. "No. It is . . . really. Hear me out. This fella I fly for is selling his airport—" Mike stopped and listened. "I know money's tight." He nodded. "Yeah, it is here too."

Kate could hear the booming sound of a voice coming from the other end of the phone.

"Sure. No problem. I understand." Mike's head bobbed. "Okay. Stay in touch. I'll see you too. Good-bye."

He hung up and looked at Kate. "He said no. I knew it was a long shot."

"At least you tried."

Mike sat at the table. "If we weren't just coming off the winter months, I'd have some money, maybe enough to hold Sidney over for a while."

Kate dropped into a chair across the table from him. "Me too." She took a sip of coffee. "So, how are your brothers?"

"Okay . . . I guess. Jerry said they're barely keeping up, like everyone else." Mike stared into his cup. "Can't imagine working for Jack. He'll run the place into the ground."

"Maybe not. He's been in the business a long time. He might do okay. But he'll probably fire me right off."

"Nah. He needs you." Mike took a big drink of coffee.

The idea of working for Jack made Kate's stomach hurt. Her gaze wandered to the waffle iron. Smoke rolled out and over the top. "The waffles are burning!" She ran into the kitchen and threw open the griddle, then poked the blackened waffles with a fork and speared them out. "Can't even make a decent waffle."

"Guess you ought to stick to flying." Mike chuckled.

Kate laughed. "You don't think I ought to take on a second job . . . say as a cook?"

"Can't think of anyone who'd hire you." He laughed and soon the two were doubled over, laughter releasing the day's worries.

When they quieted down, Mike took the fork. "I'll make some more."

"I'm not hungry." Kate shook her head. She knew how things would be—Jack belittling her, giving her the worst runs and as little work as possible. "I don't see how I can stay on." Unbidden tears pooled in Kate's eyes.

"It'll be all right. We'll work out something. And the fellas and I will stand up for you. You don't have to worry about Jack."

"He's not going to be easy on you either. And I doubt he'll get along with the customers. They'll be falling off like flies." Kate wiped away her tears, hating that she'd let someone like Jack get to her. "Thanks, but I can stand up for myself." She sniffed and grabbed a handkerchief out of her pants pocket and blew her nose, then moved to the closet and grabbed her coat. She wished Paul lived in town. She really needed him right now. "Well, I better go. Sorry we didn't come up with anyone, but thanks for your help."

"No problem. Just wish we could have figured out something." Mike opened the door for Kate. "See you tomorrow."

The following morning, Kate felt crummy. She'd lain awake most of the night, trying to come up with an answer. She even considered asking her father for the money. She was sure he had some put aside. But an airfield was a risk, and she couldn't ask him to jeopardize his savings.

While Kate washed her face, dressed, and combed her hair, melancholy wallowed inside her. She didn't bother with makeup. When she stepped outside, she glanced at the sky. It was clear. Sidney would be leaving.

She climbed into her car and prayed that something had happened overnight. Maybe Sidney's father had made a miraculous recovery, or Mike's brother had changed his mind. *God, you can do anything. Please provide the money we need.*

When Kate pulled up at the field, three cars were parked out front—Sidney's, Jack's, and Mike's. She didn't see Kenny's or Alan's. *They don't care enough to even say good-bye to Sidney*, she thought with disdain.

When Kate stepped into the shop, Mike was bent over the stove. He used a poker to stir the embers. He glanced at Kate, his expression glum. After adding kindling to the coals, he closed the door, leaving it open a couple of inches to help it draft.

She tossed Mike a nod, then turned to Sidney. Even though she already knew the answer, she asked, "Any news on your father?"

"Nothing. Figure he's the same." He settled blue eyes on Kate.

She remembered the first time she'd met him. He'd been dressed in blue jeans and cowboy boots, and he'd had on his overlarge cowboy hat. He'd looked more boy than man.

"You ready to buy the place?" He forced a smile.

"Wish I could." Kate's mind reworked the figures—if only there was a way. "Maybe if we had a little more time."

"I'm out of time." Sidney turned reluctantly to Jack. "I guess we have a deal. The place is yours."

Jack held out a bank draft. "Exactly what you asked for."

Sidney took the note, glanced at it, and then folded it and slipped it into his shirt pocket. He looked around the room. "That's it, then."

No one said a word. Wood crackled and popped in the stove.

Sidney took a deep breath. "I'm packed. Guess I better be on my way." He plopped his cowboy hat on his head, then shook Mike's hand. "It's been good working with you."

"You too."

He turned to Jack. "Take good care of the place."

"You can count on it." Jack looked like he was quaking with excitement.

Sidney took Kate's hand. He smiled. "I remember when you first walked in here, figuring you were going to be a bush pilot.

68

I thought you were full of malarkey. Didn't think you had it in you." He grinned. "I was wrong." He tipped up the brim of his hat. "Figure on seeing you in Kenai now and again."

"I'll be out that way." Kate choked back tears.

Sidney headed for the door.

Sorrow and gratitude swelled inside Kate. "Sidney. Thanks for giving me a chance." She crossed the room and threw her arms around him. "Thanks for believing in me."

He hugged her back, his eyes brimming. "It's a heck of a thing—a woman bush pilot." He opened the door and stepped outside.

— 6 —

Trepidation building, Kate stood in the doorway and watched Sidney's plane leave the runway. With Jack as her boss, life at the airfield would likely be miserable. He'd made it clear how he felt about women pilots—they had no place in the business. Finally, she closed the door and stepped back inside.

Wearing a satisfied smile, Jack sat at the desk, making a show of going through files and grumbling about the mess Sidney had left for him to sort out. It didn't take long before he was reassigning flights and spouting orders.

Kate had a mail run that day, so she disappeared into the sorting room, hoping to stay out of the line of fire. However, hiding didn't help. Jack sought her out.

He stepped into the doorway. "I expect you to keep up with that mail. No shirking your duties to go gallivanting off with that doctor friend of yours."

Kate didn't look up. "I'll get my work done."

"See that you do."

Fury trampled over prudence, and Kate straightened and looked right at Jack. "That *doctor friend* of mine is saving lives in this territory. I wouldn't call what we do gallivanting."

Jack took a cigar out of his pocket and stuck it between his lips. He lit it and puffed on the stogy. Rancid smoke drifted into the air and settled around him. He stared at her with a squint. "You're in my sights. Remember that."

Kate bristled. "I know what to do. I don't need you breathing down my neck."

"I'll breathe wherever I want." He stepped into the room. "Don't think that just because Sidney's gone you can treat me like the hired help."

"You *are* the hired help." He strode toward her and, with his lip lifted on one side, glowered at her. "I can remedy that."

She could smell the stink of cigar on his breath. Barely managing to keep her temper in check, she said evenly, "All I ask is to be treated like the rest of the crew, no better, no worse."

"I'll treat you any way I like."

Mike stepped into the room. "That's enough, Jack! Lay off her!"

Jack whirled around and glared at Mike. "Just because you're sweet on her don't mean she gets special privileges."

Mike relaxed his stance and smiled. "You sure you're not the one sweet on her?"

Kate could have melted into the floor. Where had Mike come up with that?

Jack's face turned red and he balled his hands into fists. "You're the one who's caterwauling over her." He reeled around to Kate. "You do as I say, when I say it!"

Kate followed Mike's lead and forced herself to smile, and then she saluted Jack.

His complexion went from red to purple. "That's it! You're fired!"

Kate stared at him. "You're firing me for saluting you?"

"That's right. Get out!" His voice rumbled in his chest.

"Come on, Jack. You can't fire her." Mike's tone was light, as if he were teasing. "She's the best pilot you've got."

Jack pointed at Mike. "You—dry up."

He stormed back into the main office. Kate followed.

Jack threw a venomous look at her. "And you—out! Get out!"

Kate ran a dustcloth over a goblet and wondered if the airfields in Juneau or Fairbanks needed a pilot. She'd made local inquiries, but there were no openings. With a sigh, she set the glass back on the shelf, then picked up another one. She didn't want to leave Anchorage. Her friends were here.

And what about Paul? She'd almost never see him. The thought lay heavy in her chest. He was worth more than any job. She couldn't walk away, but she couldn't imagine life without flying either.

The feel of a hand on her back startled Kate. She turned to see Helen smiling at her in that maternal way of hers. "Oh. Hi. I didn't hear you."

"I just want you to know that Albert and I are praying for you, dear. And we're confident things will work out just as they should. God has everything under control."

"I want to believe that . . . but I'm afraid I'll have to move away. I don't want to leave. I'd miss everyone so much . . . especially Paul." Kate blinked back tears. "I don't want to live far away from him."

Helen smiled. "Now how many times have I heard you say no place is that far away if you can fly there." Her blue eyes warmed as she gently grasped Kate's upper arms. "The Lord has a place for you, exactly the right place."

Kate nodded, wishing her faith were stronger.

The bell hanging on the front door jangled. "Sounds like I'm needed. I'd better get back to work." Helen moved toward the front of the store.

Kate heard Mike's voice and shrank inside. She didn't want to see him and the pity in his eyes. He'd try to make her feel better—crack a few jokes and grouse about Jack. She didn't want to pretend everything was all right.

"Hey, Kate." Wearing a broad smile, Mike peered around the end of the aisle.

"Hi." She glanced at him and ran the dustcloth over the

drinking glass. Maybe if he saw she was working, he'd just say hello and leave. She set the goblet on the shelf.

Mike's blue eyes seemed brighter than usual. "I've got good news." Wearing a teasing grin, he leaned against a shelf.

Kate wasn't up for his shenanigans. She ignored him and moved to a set of dishes.

"Don't you want to know?"

"Mike, I'm busy." She wiped dust off a plate.

He ambled down the aisle toward her.

Kate blew out a huff. "Mike, I've got work to do."

Still wearing his know-it-all expression, he stopped and folded his arms over his chest.

Kate turned and faced him. "What?"

His smile softened. "You've got your job back."

"I've what?"

"Me, Alan, and Kenny told Jack we'd quit if he didn't hire you back."

"You did?"

Mike's smile tipped sideways and he nodded. "Jack's already in a bind, now that he's stuck at the airfield most of the time."

Kate covered her mouth, but couldn't hold back her laughter. "You wouldn't really quit, would you?"

"I would." Mike shrugged. "'Course he'd have to hire me back. Can't run the place with only two pilots."

Kate thought back to the scene between her and Jack and the way he'd treated her from the very first. "I appreciate what you fellas did, but I can't go back. I won't work for Jack."

"Come on, Kate. I know he can be ornery and unfair, especially to you, but it won't be the same without you. And what are you going to do without a flying job?"

Kate knew she ought to accept the offer. She needed the job, and it would solve the problem of having to move. Besides, the men at the field had put their own jobs on the line for her. The whole thing just wasn't fair.

She shrugged, and then shook her head. "No. I can't. But thanks. And tell the fellas thank you, but Jack doesn't want me there. He'll make life miserable, especially because he was forced to take me back."

Mike's mouth lifted in a slight grin. "You've got too much pride, Kate. If you want to fly, you'll have to get over it."

He was right, but Kate couldn't stand the idea of groveling to Jack. "Maybe something else will come up."

"Oh yeah, like there are all kinds of jobs out there just waiting for you." He leaned a hip against a shelf. "Be reasonable. The depression's getting worse, not better."

Recent headlines of higher unemployment and children going hungry flitted through Kate's mind. She really didn't have a choice.

"Just swallow that pride of yours and come back to work."

"What did Jack say?"

"He was pretty mad, but he agreed that you could return and that he'd lighten up on you, at least a little."

Kate chewed her lip. Maybe it wouldn't be so bad. With a nod, she said, "Okay. But I'm not putting up with any more of his bullying. I've had it."

"It'll be all right. You'll see."

"Thanks, Mike. I appreciate what you and the guys did."

"Couldn't imagine the place without you."

The tenderness in his eyes reminded Kate of how Mike really felt about her. Instantly uncomfortable, she tucked a loose strand of hair behind her ear and glanced at the floor. "So, can I go back to work right away?"

"You bet. In fact, he has a run for you—Unalaska."

"Really? He usually takes that one himself."

"He's got too much work to do in the office." Mike grinned. "He's not going to like that part of the job. Being the boss will keep him grounded a lot of the time."

"I've never been to Unalaska." Adrenaline shot through Kate.

Mike frowned slightly. "It's a long way out to the Aleutians—harsh conditions, unpredictable weather."

"That's most of Alaska."

"Yeah. But be careful."

"Okay. Okay."

Helen joined them. "I suppose you'll be deserting me." She feigned distress.

"Do you need me to stay?"

"No. You go to work. We'll be fine. Muriel said she'd help anytime we need." She gave Kate a quick hug. "I told you everything would work out."

"You did." Kate smiled. "I guess I ought to learn to listen to you." She untied her apron and lifted it over her head. "I'd better get moving. I've got a trip to the Aleutians."

"Maybe I should go with you," Mike said. "I don't have anything going for a couple of days."

"Thanks, but I'll be fine." Kate didn't want Mike along. She'd already decided to stop at Paul's. The villages out on the chain could use a doctor, and she could use more time with him.

When Kate set down on the sandbar, Paul was on his way out in the boat. She had a shipment of medical supplies for him, which gave her a good reason to stop.

Leaving the engine running, she grabbed the package and climbed out of the plane. Angel had already greeted Paul. "Thought you might need this." She held out the parcel.

Paul took the box. "I've been waiting on this and on you." His eyes found hers and he circled an arm around Kate and kissed her.

She lingered against him, wishing work could wait. She stepped back. "I've got a run to make."

"Figured." Paul tucked the parcel under his arm. "Where you headed?"

"Unalaska, and a few villages between here and there."

"I haven't been out on the Aleutians. How they set for medical care?"

"I think Unalaska's got a doctor, but I'm sure the villages would be glad to have a doctor stop in." She raised her eyebrows. "I'm wondering if we know of one who could go."

"I can be ready in fifteen minutes."

"I was hoping you'd say that."

He kissed her. "I'll have to get some things from the cabin."

"Let me shut down the plane and I'll go with you. We'll be gone a few days, so make sure to bring some clothes and things."

"No problem. Just need to let Patrick know so the boys can take care of the dogs. Then I'll pack and get my medical bag."

"I'll talk to Patrick and Sassa for you."

"Sounds good."

Kate shut down the engine and then climbed into the boat. Paul pushed off and headed for the dock. He tied up, gave Kate a hand out, and then walked up the trail toward his cabin, Angel at his heels. Kate followed the track along the creek. When she broke into the clearing at Patrick and Sassa's place, their dogs charged toward her.

"Hey, boys. It's just me," Kate said calmly.

The dogs' bristles laid down and their tails wagged. The youngest, a pup the Warrens had adopted from the same litter as Angel's, was the first to reach her. Although larger, he looked just like Angel—a heavy-coated black and silver malamute. He nuzzled Kate's hand. The two older dogs demanded attention, and Kate gave each a pat, then headed for the two-story cabin.

Sassa stood in the doorway, wiping her hands on an apron. "Good morning. You have something for us?"

"Just a message from Paul. He's making a run out to the Aleutians with me. We'll be gone three or four days. He wants to know if the boys can look after his dogs."

"Oh, sure. No problem. Those boys, they like the dogs." Sassa smiled, her brown skin crinkling at the corners of her eyes.

"Tell them thanks for me." Kate wanted to hurry back to the plane—she had a lot of air time ahead of her. But not wanting to seem impolite, she asked, "Where's Patrick?"

"In the garden. He's getting some of the peas in the ground."

"We had snow a couple of days ago," Kate said.

"Yeah, it does that, but this time of year it doesn't stay."

"Have you heard from Lily? How is she?"

Sadness touched Sassa's brown eyes. "Not so good. She's missing home."

"I'm sorry to hear that. I thought things were going well for her in Seattle."

Sassa folded her arms over her plump middle and shook her head. "She's not happy."

"Will she be coming back?"

"Maybe. I don't know. I would like it if she did, but I want her to be happy, to have a good life." Sassa's lips tightened into a firm line. "I think maybe she doesn't feel like she fits in, and she doesn't have any native friends. Most of the people in Seattle are white. I think she's lonely, and I'm wondering if some people are mean to her because she's not like them."

"I hope not. Maybe things will get better." She glanced up the creek. "I need to get moving."

"Okay. We'll see you next week?"

"Next week."

Kate hurried back down the trail. Paul was waiting at the dock, tossing a stick for Angel.

"You all set?" Kate asked.

"You bet."

"Okay. Let's go." Kate climbed into the boat and they headed toward the plane.

With the boat secured out of the water, Paul followed Kate and Angel into the plane. He stowed his things in back.

"Ready?" Kate asked.

"Yep." He pulled the door shut and bolted it, then took his seat beside Kate. He looked at her and smiled. "I was hoping I'd see you today." He leaned between the seats and kissed her, then nuzzled her neck. "I don't see you enough."

Kate warmed inside. "Yeah, me too." She throttled up and they were on their way.

Once in the air, she said, "I have deliveries at Chignik, Perryville, and King Cove. And then we'll head out to Unalaska."

The weather held as Kate and Paul flew southwest. They stopped in Chignik and Perryville the first day and then stayed over in Perryville, where there were several cases of the flu.

Paul doled out aspirin and gave instructions on how to cope with fevers and stomach upsets. When they left the following day, Kate hoped they hadn't picked up the bug. A lot of those they'd seen had been really miserable.

The second day, they made a delivery to King Cove, a small community that depended almost entirely on local fish canneries for its existence. The village was hemmed in by the ocean, mountains, and treeless hills. There were only a few who needed or had time to see the doctor. Most were native mothers who showed up with little ones with runny noses and sore throats. One man had an infection in his hand from a fish hook that had buried itself in his flesh. Paul cleaned and dressed the wound, and he told the man not to work for a few days, but as he walked away, Paul said to Kate under his breath, "He'll go straight back to his boat."

Kate shrugged. "He's got to make a living."

They left King Cove under gray skies. Rain spattered the windshield and winds buffeted the Bellanca. "Hope the weather doesn't get worse," Kate said just as the plane dropped into a downdraft. She pulled back on the control wheel and rode a current upward.

"Kind of like bronc riding," Paul said, his voice tight. "I thought Jack usually took this run."

"He does, but he's the boss now, so he's stuck at the airfield taking care of paperwork, shuffling schedules, and rousting up business. Being the boss has its drawbacks." Kate grinned.

"What happened to Sidney?"

She reached into her pocket and pulled out a pack of spearmint gum. "Oh my gosh. I forgot to tell you." She took a piece of gum, then held it out to Paul.

"No thanks. Tell me what?"

"Sidney sold the airport."

"He sold it? Why?"

Kate unwrapped her gum and stuck it in her mouth, crumpled the wrapper, and tossed it on the floor. "His father had a stroke." She chewed.

"Is he going to be all right?"

"Doesn't sound good. Sidney had to go home to help out, and his mother needed financial aid, so he sold out."

Paul picked up the gum wrapper. "To whom?"

"Jack." Kate shook her head. "It's going to be awful. He was full of himself before and now it's worse. He fired me the first day."

"What? Why?"

"We got in an argument."

"Then who are you flying for?"

"Jack. The whole crew threatened to quit if he didn't hire me back."

Paul smirked, then laughed. "I'll bet Jack hated that. Good for the guys."

Kate grinned. "Yeah. Working for Jack's like wrestling with a bear, but it's better than being without a job. And I can stay in Anchorage. It won't be easy, though. He thinks he's the big cheese now, and he's not keen on me. I could get canned anytime."

"He'll keep you. He may be a bully, but he's not stupid."

They flew into a bank of clouds. Kate kept a close eye on her instruments, relying on them to keep her on course and level. The winds picked up and buffeted the plane, which shuddered as it flew through swirling gray.

Paul gazed out the window. "Maybe we should have stayed on the ground."

"I can't always wait for clear weather, especially out here. There are almost no cloudless days." Kate kept her voice light, but she watched the controls and prayed the clouds and turbulence would clear.

As they ventured farther out on the chain, the clouds thinned and sun splintered the sky. Below, green hills and mountains stood between the blue of the Pacific Ocean and the dark waters of the Bering Sea. Kate gazed at the splendor laid out below them. "You'd think I'd get used to the scenery, but it continues to take me by surprise. There's always something new and more beautiful than the day before. It's one of the things I love about this job."

Paul gazed at the shimmering ocean stretching to the horizon. "I wish I owned a plane. It would be easier on everyone if I could do my own flying."

"It'd take a lot of training and time, but you could do it. Of course, I've been flying most of my life and this wilderness challenges me all the time. It would take awhile before you'd be ready to go out on your own." Kate glanced at him. "And one drawback would be that you wouldn't need me."

"Oh, I'd need you, just not as a pilot." Paul's tone teased.

"Maybe I can give you a lesson one of these days."

"Just say when and where."

A crosswind bumped the plane in the side. "Well, today's not the day."

They flew over the small community of Unalaska, which sat on a large arching bay hemmed in by treeless, green hills. The earliest spring flowers splashed color across the meadows outside of town, even though the highest knolls were still buried with snow.

Kate put down with no difficulty. When she stepped out of the plane, she breathed in the smell of spring air and the sea. She turned and gazed out over the broad bay. "This is an amazing place. I'm glad Jack was too busy to make it."

A stocky man with red hair and a beard walked toward them. "Howdy." He nodded at Kate, then turned to Paul. "I'm Sam Drummond." He extended his hand and shook Paul's. "Jack told me you'd be coming. Glad to see you. Store's running short on staples and the ferry's not due for another three days."

"I'm Paul Anderson. But I think you want to speak to Kate." He nodded at her. "She's the pilot."

Kate extended a hand. "Kate Evans."

Surprise showed on Sam's face, then he relaxed and smiled. "Never met a woman pilot before, but I heard of you."

Kate turned to Paul. "Paul's a doctor, in case anyone in town has need of one."

"We got a doctor, at least part time. Not that he's in the office much. Like most folks, he fishes." Sam rubbed his right shoulder. "I've been having a pain right here." He pointed at a spot at the front of his shoulder. "Maybe you could have a look at it."

"I'll be happy to," Paul said.

After Paul checked out Sam's shoulder and diagnosed it as an overuse injury, he and Kate had a meal of fish chowder and bread at a local café.

Paul leaned back in his chair and rested a hand on his stomach. "I ate too much. You want to take a walk?"

"That sounds good to me."

Paul paid the bill while Kate strolled outside to wait. Together they headed for the docks.

Paul rested his arm over Kate's shoulders and pulled her to his side. "You don't suppose people will get any wild ideas about the pilot and the doctor, do you?"

"Maybe." Kate smiled. "I really don't care what they think." She leaned in closer.

"Well, if you don't care, then neither do I." He smiled down at her and gently kissed her forehead.

They walked along the pier and watched the fishing boats come in. The wind had stilled. The air was alive with gulls and their screeching calls as they searched for tidbits floating in the quay. Fishermen sorted their catch, then cleaned and stowed fishing gear. One man whistled a tune while he worked. He nodded at them as they passed by. Paul felt content and wished every day could be like today.

A sudden sharp breeze splashed whitecaps across the top of the swells. Kate stopped and breathed deeply through her nose. "I love the smell of the ocean."

Her large amber eyes were alive with pleasure. Paul gathered her into his arms. "I like it too. Always have. But it's even better sharing it with you. It's the one thing I really miss, living out on the creek. I've got to travel a ways to see the ocean."

"I never spent much time at the beach. My family only made the trip over the mountains a few times. But I love it."

Memories bombarded Paul. "Growing up in San Francisco,

I was at the beach every chance I got. My brothers and I did a lot of fishing with my dad and my uncles." He struggled to keep his voice steady.

Kate rested a hand on his arm. "I've never been ocean fishing. What kind of fish you figure they pull out of the Bering Sea?"

"All kinds—rockfish, salmon, probably halibut. Wish we had time to go out."

"We have time. Nothing to do until we take off tomorrow, and there's plenty of daylight. We just need a boat." Kate smiled and her eyes filled with mischief, then she hurried toward the man who had been whistling.

He had moved off the pier and was standing in a bobbing dory. Paul trailed behind Kate, and as they approached, the man looked up. His almond-shaped eyes crinkled in greeting, his teeth flashing white against his native skin. "Hello. What can I do for you?"

"We were wondering if you know anyone who'd be willing to take us fishing—just for a little while."

"Better to go in the morning."

"We'll be leaving in the morning." Kate pouted slightly, then said, "I'm Kate Evans and this is Paul Anderson."

"Billy Konig." Billy glanced toward town. "What you doing all the way out here? Too early in the year for tourists and the ferry doesn't come for another couple of days."

"I fly for an outfit in Anchorage and had a delivery to make here."

"I thought Jack Rydell made the run out of Anchorage."

"He does, but he was busy, so he asked me to fill in."

Billy grinned. "An improvement, I'd say."

Kate's grin revealed how she felt about the statement.

"So, you like to fish?" Billy shoved his fingers up under a knit hat and scratched his head.

"Yes. But I've never fished in the ocean."

He gazed out at the broad bay, then looked back at Kate. "I guess I can take you. But not for too long. My Sophie will be unhappy with me if I miss dinner."

"I can pay you," Paul said.

"No. Not necessary. Climb in." He stashed a bucket in the back of the boat. "Didn't have much luck this morning. Got plenty of bait." He sat on the short wooden bench in the back of the boat beside the engine.

Kate and Paul stepped in and settled on the other two benches. Billy pulled the starter and the engine puttered to life while Paul unhooked the rope securing the boat to the dock. Billy headed out into the bay. "I have two poles. Don't figure you want to use nets, not as much fun."

"I've never net fished," Paul said.

"We use nets to catch more fish so we can sell to the cannery, but pole fishing means a fight." Billy smiled. It was hard to tell how old he was. He looked young.

The dory bounced through choppy waters. Paul looked at Kate to see how she felt about going out in such a small boat. She was smiling, seemingly unaware of anything but the pleasure of the elements. Wind whipped her short hair away from her face, and ocean spray left droplets on her skin. She was stunning. The love he felt made his chest feel tight. He reveled in it and feared it all at the same time.

He loved her with a passion, which made the thought of losing her all the more excruciating. He wished she didn't love flying so intensely. He wasn't sure he could survive her cracking up and being killed or disappearing somewhere in the immense wilderness she flew. Refusing to allow morose thoughts to spoil their good time, Paul willed them from his mind. "We need to do this more often," he said with a smile.

"It's almost as good as flying." Kate grinned and bundled deeper into her coat.

"You know how to set up the jig?" Billy asked.

"Sure." Paul reached for a pole.

"There's the bait." Billy nodded at a bucket.

Paul lifted out a fish the size of a minnow, secured it to a large hook, and got the pole set for Kate.

"We'll troll," Billy said. "Maybe have better luck that way."

He slowed the engine. "Drop your line in and we'll see if you get a bite."

Kate lofted the line into the water and then settled back to wait.

Before Paul could get his hook baited, Kate squealed, "I've got one!" Her pole bent. She stood and hauled on it as it bowed from the weight of whatever was on the end of the line. The boat rocked and Kate nearly lost her balance.

"Careful." Paul caught hold of her arm. "Don't want you going overboard."

Kate stared at her line. "What do I do? It feels like a huge fish."

"Probably a King. Play him out," Billy said. "Let him run a little, then haul him back. Get him tired. But be careful so he doesn't break your line." His ruddy face was alight with pleasure.

"Here, I'll show you." Paul stepped behind Kate and reached around her, getting ahold of the pole. "You want to pull up like this and then let out a little of the line so he can run, but you don't want him to run too hard or too fast, so keep the line taut."

"I'm afraid he's going to get away." Kate hauled up on the pole.

Paul rested his hands over hers. "You don't want him to break free." He lowered the rod slightly, strongly aware of Kate's warmth and the slight fragrance of Evening in Paris.

Kate glanced at him. She looked so happy. Paul nearly staggered backward at the force of what he felt for her.

"Like this?" she asked.

"Yeah. You got it." Panic seized Paul and he put space between himself and Kate. He loved her, but the intensity of what he felt was more than he'd bargained for. What had he gotten himself into?

Paul pulled a weed out of the damp garden soil, then straightened and gazed down a row of poles. He envisioned green vines loaded with plump peas winding their way up and around the posts. He could almost taste the sweet vegetables and wished summer's arrival would hurry.

The pop of a branch caught his attention, and he turned to see Sassa running up the trail that led from her house to his. Sassa never ran. He shoved his spade in the ground, prepared for whatever emergency he might face. When he saw glee in the native woman's eyes, he relaxed. Curiosity replaced anxiety.

Puffing for breath, Sassa stopped in front of Paul. "I had to tell you." She pressed plump hands against her ample chest and took in a lungful of air. "Lily's coming home! Isn't it wonderful? I can hardly believe it."

Paul smiled, happy for Sassa and Patrick, but wondering what had happened to bring Lily back to the creek. "That's great news. Is she visiting?"

"No, she's coming to stay." A shadow of concern cooled the warmth in Sassa's brown eyes. She wet her lips. "I've missed her. I was afraid she'd live in that city forever." She closed her eyes for a moment. "Thank you, Lord, for bringing my little girl home."

Although Paul longed to know what had driven Lily from Seattle, he managed to keep his curiosity under control and asked, "When will she be here?"

"Her ship docks in Seward two weeks from today. She'll take the train to Anchorage. Mike's going to fly her home." A chortle escaped her lips, rising into the air like birdsong. "Patrick just talked to him on the radio." Still barely able to catch her breath, Sassa continued, "We're going to have a celebration. And we want you to come."

"I wouldn't miss it." Paul hadn't forgotten how Sassa had been unrelenting in her attempts to match up him and Lily. He hoped she didn't return to her efforts. He gave her a firm look. "You understand about me and Kate, right?"

"Of course." With a wave of her hand, she set off for home, but she wore a knowing smile that made Paul nervous.

Before leaving for the Warrens' place, Paul lingered on the porch, hoping to catch a glimpse of Jasper. He missed his companion. He peered into the trees and whistled. The raven cawed from within a thicket of birch, then swooped down and landed on his perch beside the back door. Paul rewarded him with a chunk of bread. "Good to see you, friend."

For a long while, after Paul had rescued the bird from one of his traps and cared for his broken leg, he'd stayed close, but recently he'd become more independent, his visits rare. The forest had once again become his home. Still, Jasper never seemed far away.

Paul stroked ebony feathers on the bird's head and shoulders. "Figure one day you'll find a mate and fly off for good." Paul knew that's how it ought to be, but he couldn't squelch a feeling of melancholy. He'd miss his feathered companion. "Better get moving. I've got a party to go to." He headed for the steps.

He ambled along the trail that led to the Warrens', his mind on Lily. She'd been back two days, but he hadn't seen her. He wondered if she'd changed much. Probably not—she'd been away less than a year. Sassa had kept her daughter's reason for returning a secret. Remembering Lily's enthusiasm for travel and adventure, Paul pondered over what had driven her back to the homestead. He figured he'd find out soon enough.

As he approached his neighbors' log home, their dogs set to barking. When they recognized Paul, their bristled ruffs lay down and tails wagged. He gave them each a pat as he waded through wet noses and thigh-high fur.

Eleven-year-old Douglas opened the door. A broad smile brightened his round face. "Hi." Although the oldest of the three boys, Douglas was the smallest but was built stout like his mother. He leaned inside the doorway and called, "Paul's here." Stepping back, he opened the door all the way. "Come on in."

Paul rested his hand on the boy's shiny black hair. "How you doing?"

"Good. Went fishing this morning. But I got skunked. You do any fishing lately?"

"Only a little. Been busy."

"Me and Ethan pulled out two nice ones yesterday."

Ethan and Robert crowded around the doorway, trying to get Paul's attention. They were both tall and thin like their father.

"Hi," Robert said. He tugged on Paul's hand, dragging him inside. "Mama's made the best dinner ever. And there's cake."

"Is that you, Paul?" Her hands in the sink, Sassa looked over her shoulder at him. She wiped her hands on her apron and moved to the children, flagging them away. "Go on. Get. Stop pestering him."

"Oh, they're all right." Paul breathed in the succulent aroma of fish and baked bread. "Smells good in here."

Sassa smiled. She reveled in her reputation as a good cook. "We're having baked salmon, rolls, and sweet potatoes—Lily's favorites."

"Sweet potatoes with marshmallows and brown sugar?" Paul asked.

Sassa closed the door. "That's the tastiest way to make it." She smiled.

"I have it on good authority that there's also cake?" Paul winked.

"Those boys—I've had a time trying to keep them out of it." She shook her head.

Paul looked around. "Where's Lily?"

"Upstairs." Sassa lowered her voice. "She's embarrassed. Things didn't turn out well in Seattle. She doesn't want a party." Sassa glanced up the stairs. "But she's back where she belongs and that's reason enough to celebrate." Tears filled her eyes and she mopped at them with the corner of her apron. "I'm so thankful to have her back."

Paul rested a hand on Sassa's shoulder. "I won't say a word about Seattle," he said, but wasn't sure how to avoid the topic. She'd been set on an adventure and a new life. Whatever drove her home must have been pretty bad. "Maybe a party will cheer her up," he told Sassa with a smile.

"Oh I hope so."

The old German bachelor Klaus Braun, who lived farther up the creek, stood at the front window. Like so many who lived in the bush, he'd left a past in Germany that no one knew about, and they understood not to ask. He nodded at Paul. "*Gutten Abend.*" Leaning heavily on a cane, he hobbled to an overstuffed chair and slowly lowered his aging body into it.

"Hello, Klaus, good to see you," Paul said.

The door opened and Patrick walked in. "I found a piece— oh hi, Paul. How are you?"

"Good. You?"

"Couldn't be better." He held up a chunk of driftwood. "Found this on the beach and figured Klaus might use it for one of his carvings." He closed the door and moved across the room toward the elderly man. "What do you think? Will it work?"

The old German took the wood. He furrowed heavy gray brows as he studied it. "Ja. Gut." He looked up at Patrick. "How much you vant for it?"

"Nothing. Figure God set it on that stretch of sand. It belongs to him, not me."

Paul sat across from Klaus. "You ought to be able to make something special out of that."

"Ja." He nodded, turning the wood over in his hands and running his thumb down one side. "This is a fine piece for carving."

"How you feeling these days?"

"Not so gut—old bones." He leaned back in his chair. "Glad for a celebration, though," he added with a smile.

"Sassa's put together a fine meal," Patrick said, glancing at the kitchen. "I don't know how much longer I can wait. My stomach's so empty, it's about to turn on itself."

"Heard you already have your garden in, Klaus," Paul said.

"I do." He nodded, his whole upper body moving instead of just his head. "But a bear come t' my place so I got more work t' do. He knocked over de outhouse—dragged paper all over de place." He smoothed his beard. "*Danke* to Patrick for putting things back in order or I vouldn't have a pot to . . ." He glanced at Sassa who was working in the kitchen. "Vell, you know."

Patrick and Paul chuckled, then in a more serious tone, Patrick said, "It was probably a young male—they're full of vinegar, especially this time of year. Gotta watch 'em."

Sassa stepped into the room. "Come and eat." She moved to the bottom of the stairs and called, "Lily, dinner is ready."

The men moved into the kitchen and sat at a large rough-hewn table. Sassa carried a wooden bowl with a towel draped over lumps that Paul guessed were rolls. She set it on the table.

Lily walked into the room.

"Hi, Lily. It's nice to see you," Paul said.

"Goot dat you're home." Klaus gave her a nod. "Ve'll have to go fishing soon."

Lily offered a quiet smile. "I'd like that."

"Lily, you're the guest of honor," Sassa said. "You sit. I'll take care of everything." She gave Lily an enthusiastic hug as if realizing anew that her daughter was home.

A blush darkened Lily's brown skin and she dropped into a chair. She glanced at the others around the table and placed her hands in her lap. She didn't look happy.

Poor Lily. Sassa meant well, but a party is probably the last thing she needs. Paul smiled at her. "Nice to have you back."

"Thank you." She glanced out the dining room window. "I like it here," she said, but her tone was halfhearted.

"We're real happy to have our girl home." Patrick moved to Lily and draped an arm around her shoulders, giving her a squeeze. "Not good to be rootless."

After everyone had found a place at the table and the food was set out, Patrick prayed, thanking God for Sassa's cooking and his daughter's return. He looked up, his eyes teary. He cleared his throat. "Let's eat."

Paul couldn't keep from wondering why Lily had moved back. When she'd told him about her aspirations of finding a better life on the outside, she'd been confident and determined. He had to work at keeping his questions to himself.

Conversation at the table was lighthearted, focusing mostly on hunting and fishing. And Paul's new occupation as a traveling doctor. He enjoyed sharing some of the adventures.

The meal was delicious, and although Paul's stomach told him he'd had enough, he scooped up the last of the sweet potatoes onto his plate. "Sassa, you've outdone yourself."

"Best cook in the territory," Patrick said.

She smiled. "Thank you, but it's just plain food."

Paul scooted his chair back slightly and stuck his legs out beneath the table. He patted his stomach. "I won't have to eat for a week."

"We have dessert," Sassa said as she cleared the table.

"Mom made cake." Robert leaned his chest against the edge of the table.

"How about we rest a bit before we dive into dessert." Patrick glanced at Sassa. "That all right with you?"

"Sure," Sassa said. "I'll do the dishes. By then maybe you'll have your appetites back." She stared at Paul. "A walk might help you digest all that food you ate." She slid her eyes toward Lily.

Paul suppressed a groan. She knew about Kate. What was she up to?

"A walk is good after a heavy meal," she said.

What's the harm? He looked at Lily. "Would you like to go for a walk, Lily? I could use the company."

Her face flashed with embarrassment. Her lips pursed, she cast a glance of frustration at her mother. "Sure. I guess that would be all right." She pushed back her chair and stood.

Paul moved to the door and opened it. Lily stepped onto the porch. Paul had barely closed the door behind them when Lily said, "You don't have to go anywhere with me. Mama's just being her usual busybody self."

"She cares about you. And what's wrong with taking a stroll with a neighbor?"

"I know about you and Kate. I'm happy for you. She's very nice."

"She is. And I'm crazy about her." Paul grinned and then turned his attention toward the stream. "You up for a walk? You look a little pale."

"I'm fine."

Paul followed Lily down the steps and toward the creek. "Maybe we can talk about something other than hunting and fishing. Even I get tired of it."

She smiled at him.

"It's nice to have you home. Really."

Lily looked out over the creek. "It is beautiful here. I missed it when I was in Seattle." Something in her voice said she missed Seattle more.

"Do you plan on going back, or is there some place else you'd like to explore?"

Lily shook her head. "No. One trip to the outside was enough. This is where I belong."

"You're awfully young to decide something like that. You don't know what life holds for you."

"I'm nearly twenty." Lily bent and picked a tiny magenta-colored flower. She smelled it, then twirled the stem between her fingers. "Seattle wasn't what I thought. At first it seemed exciting and fun. I got a job in a cannery and I had my own apartment. I liked that.

"But . . . it's a big city. The people are different—not like here. Even with the big population I felt alone. I never met another native the entire time I was there. And some people didn't like me just because I am native. It wasn't what I expected."

"I'm sorry."

She brushed the flower petals over her lips. "It's all right. I figure I belong here anyway."

All of a sudden, Paul saw a changed, more mature Lily. She'd grown up while she'd been away. Sometimes disappointment will do that to a person.

Lily turned dark brown eyes on Paul and acted as if she were about to say something, then walked on. She plucked another flower. Without looking at Paul, she said softly, "I met a man while I was there. He seemed nice."

Paul waited for her to continue.

Lily took a deep breath that sounded like a sigh. "He said he loved me." Her full lips tensed into a hard line. "I believed him." She tossed aside the flowers. "But the truth is, I was just a novelty to him—the Indian girl from Alaska."

The spite in Lily's voice surprised Paul. He was instantly angry at the man who'd hurt her. "You're a lot more than that."

She glanced at him, then without saying anything, she sidestepped down the bank.

"Don't let someone like him decide who you are," Paul said, following her down the embankment.

Lily sat on a log and stared at the creek. "I am just what he said—an Indian girl. I'm nothing special." She looked up at Paul. "I'm not going to pretend to be something I'm not."

"Good." Paul sat on the downed tree, making sure to leave a couple of feet between the two of them. "Trying to be someone you're not only causes more trouble."

"Yeah, I figured that out. God created me. And I've decided not to argue with him about who I am."

"Yeah, but I thought you wanted to see the world. Don't

give up on your dream. Sometimes it's not easy to fit in, and maybe we're not supposed to. But don't abandon something just because it's hard to do. When I came here, I didn't know anything about living in the bush. I was completely out of place—a real cheechako."

"You were." Lily laughed. "We all wondered what in the world you were doing here." Her eyes widened as if she realized she'd stepped into a forbidden subject. She quickly added, "I'm glad you stayed."

Paul couldn't tell her he had no choice. "I'm glad too."

"I think that some people aren't meant to leave home. God plants us where we belong. I'm not leaving again." Lily braided her long black hair, then loosened the braid and combed her fingers through it. "I don't mind living here. In fact, it feels good knowing where I'll spend my life."

"You plan to stay right here on the creek?"

"I doubt I'll stay with Mom and Dad, but nearby. I'd like to marry someone who loves this area, have a family, and maybe even live up the creek further." Her voice held no implication that she really thought it would happen.

Paul wondered why, then his thoughts wandered back to his home in California. Was he like Lily? Did he belong there instead of here? No. He was needed here, and he was doing something important. "I'm where I belong."

"And you have Kate. She'll never leave Alaska."

"Yeah, can't imagine anything chasing her out." Apprehension pitched through Paul. Kate didn't do anything in half measures. She'd give her all to Alaska. Maybe even her life.

— 8 —

Mike matched Kate's strides as she crossed the airfield. "You're working too hard," he said. "You just got back last night and now you're off for another three days?" He shook his head. "You need some downtime."

"I'm fine. I got plenty of sleep."

"What, four hours?"

Kate didn't answer. She'd barely managed that, but she wasn't about to pass up the work.

"Let me take this one for you."

"Thanks, but Paul's counting on me." And Kate needed to see him. The last time they'd been together everything had been fine. They'd had a good time together and fishing had been fun, and then all of a sudden he seemed to withdraw. Something was wrong. She knew it.

"I can take him."

"True, but I've got supplies to drop off, and I need the money." She glanced at him, not slowing her pace. "Everyone works hard this time of year—you know that."

Mike grabbed her arm. "Wait a minute."

Kate stopped, and stared at his hand. "What do you think you're doing? Let go." She planted her hands on her hips and fixed her eyes on him. "You're acting like you own me."

Mike's eyes slid away. "Sorry. I didn't mean to do that."

He shoved his hands into his jacket pocket and kicked at a stone with the toe of his boot. "I can drop a flight and go with you."

"Mike, why are you pushing this?"

"I'm taking care of my . . . best friend." His blue eyes pleaded with her.

Kate's heart softened. She wished he'd find someone else to love. "Thanks . . . really, but I'll be fine."

"What's wrong with spending a little time together? Just friends, flying buddies." He looked at her straight on. "I miss you. And not like that, but I miss our friendship. Since you've been going around with Paul, we barely see each other."

Kate knew she hadn't made time for Mike. She felt badly, but her time was limited and her heart was with Paul. She didn't know what to say. She pushed her fingers through her short hair to lift it off her face.

"So, a date just between friends?"

"A date?" Kate shook her head. "No. How can you even ask? How would you feel if your girl was out with another guy?"

Mike's expression darkened. "She is."

"Stop it! That's not fair. True friends want what's best for each other. And all you're thinking about is yourself." Kate stared at the ground.

Silence wedged itself between the two until Mike spoke up. "You're right. I'm sorry. Really, I am. It's just so hard. I can't just stop loving you. And I do care about you, and I even like Paul, but I can't help how I feel."

"You're going to have to . . . or we can't be friends. Sorry, but I've got mail to deliver." Kate walked to her plane. She knew Mike was watching her, but she didn't dare glance back.

Once in the air, Kate replayed the scene with Mike. What was she going to do about him? He'd helped her get started up here. But he couldn't keep acting this way.

Her mind turned to Paul and excitement prickled through her at the thought of seeing him. Everything between them was probably fine. Most likely he'd just been tired or moody.

But the two of them had gotten serious about each other awfully fast. Maybe too fast for him.

There was a time when she'd believed Richard was the man of her dreams and then Mike. Could she trust her feelings? Even as she wondered about her emotions, her mind returned to Paul. Just the thought of him made her feel flushed. She loved him. She was certain of it.

Kate allowed her imagination to consider what life would be like as his wife. It wouldn't all be bliss. She knew better than that. They were very different from one another. There'd be skirmishes and her being a pilot would cut into wifely responsibilities. Plus his being a doctor would keep him away a lot of the time. She wasn't sure how they'd manage a family. Would he want her to stop flying? And was she willing to do that? Kate couldn't imagine life without it.

When she set down on the sandbar, Paul was already on his way in the boat. Patrick dropped him off, waved, and then headed back up Bear Creek. Paul climbed in and pulled the door shut.

"Where we headed?" he asked, dropping a quick, almost impersonal kiss on her cheek before sliding into his seat. He smiled and briefly touched her hand.

Kate had expected more. "Ninilchik," she said, unable to keep the hurt out of her voice. "Someone radioed in that there've been some cases of measles."

"How many?"

"At least three. One's a child in the village and he's recovered. The other two are in the same family—the Gladwells. They're nice people. They actually live outside town. They have an airstrip, so getting in and out will be easy." She wished he'd reach over and give her a real kiss or at least clasp her hand.

Paul nodded, but he didn't say anything. Instead, he kept his eyes focused outside. Silence wedged itself between them. Something *was* wrong.

When she approached the village nestled on the shore of Cook Inlet, Mount Redoubt and Mount Iliamna stood on the opposite shore, making for a stunning skyline. She flew over a dark sandy beach. "One of these days we'll have to go clamming again. I heard there are lots of them to be had here."

"Sounds like fun," Paul said, keeping his eyes on the town of Ninilchik.

Most of the trip, he'd been quiet. What had happened to their usual friendly banter? Kate wanted to ask him if he was upset about something, but didn't dare, afraid of what he'd say.

***

Dropping above the treetops, Kate searched for the Gladwells' place. When she spotted their cabin perched on the edge of a clearing, she circled the runway to make sure it was clear of debris, then landed on the grassy airstrip and shut down the engine.

She let Angel out for a short run, then closed the dog inside the plane. She and Paul headed toward the cabin. On the west side of the house stood a good-sized barn. A mare grazed in a pasture while her foal trotted around her, its tail in the air. Beyond the barn a large garden sprawled toward the forest.

"Nice place," Paul said.

A tall, lanky man with a heavy beard and wearing a red flannel shirt stepped out of the barn. "Hello," he called.

"Hi, Carl," Kate said. "Good to see you."

Taking long strides, he approached Kate and Paul.

"Carl, this is Paul Anderson, the doctor. Paul, this is Carl Gladwell."

The two shook hands. "Thanks for coming," Carl said, then turned toward the house and headed across the field. "My oldest boy Nate's not too bad. He's miserable, but nothing like Gordon." His brow creased. "Gordon's been real sick."

"Everyone else all right?"

"Yeah. Me and my wife and little girl are fine so far. I'm worried about Annie, though. She's just two."

"I'll check on her while I'm here." Paul glanced at two dogs woofing and pulling on their leads. "You hear of any other cases in town aside from the one?"

"No. But since the boys got sick, we've been keeping to ourselves, so there might be some I haven't heard about." When they reached the house, Carl opened the door and stood aside while Paul and Kate stepped indoors. "You sure you wouldn't rather wait outside?" Carl asked Kate. "Hate to see you get sick."

"I had the measles when I was six. Worried my mother silly."

Carl looked at Paul. "How about you? You have them?"

"I did, right along with my brothers and sisters."

A woman with her hair twisted into a bun at the base of her neck closed an oven door, then straightened and faced her guests. "Hello," she said, her voice hushed. Her face looked drawn and the skin beneath her eyes appeared bruised, revealing her lack of sleep.

"Hi, Emily," Kate said. "Sorry to hear your boys are sick."

She tucked a loose hair into place. "I'm so thankful you've come. I'm sure now that the doctor's here everything will be fine."

Carl introduced Emily to Paul. "I've been so afraid, Gordon's been really sick," she said and headed toward a doorway off the main room. "He's back here."

Paul and Kate followed her into a small bedroom. It was sparsely furnished with two single beds and one chest of drawers. A small window allowed in the morning sunlight. The boys were bundled beneath heavy quilts. The room felt stifling.

"This is Gordon," Emily said, hovering over her son.

Paul moved to the boy's bedside. "How you doing, Gordon?"

"Not so good," the youngster mumbled.

Kate almost gasped at the sight of him. His face was swollen and blanketed with a red rash. He peered up at Paul through puffy eyes.

Paul sat on the edge of the bed and took a thermometer out of his bag and placed it under the boy's tongue. "Keep your mouth closed." Looking as miserable as any human being could, Gordon did as he was told. Paul took his pulse. His brow furrowed. "Let me have a look at you," he said, his tone cheerful. He studied the youngster's face more closely, then asked, "Can you sit up?"

Gordon pushed himself upright and rested against the wall. The effort seemed almost too much for him.

"That's a good boy." Paul lifted his pajama top, exposing more of the fiery rash. "You've got a good case, all right." He gently lowered the boy's pajama top, took the thermometer out of his mouth, and studied it briefly. "Running a pretty good temp there, champ."

"What is it?" Emily asked.

"A hundred and five."

Emily pressed a hand to her mouth. "I knew it was bad."

Concern showed in his eyes, but using a casual tone, he said, "It's not unusual for children to run high fevers, especially with the measles. We'll get his temperature down and he'll be fine." He placed a stethoscope to Gordon's chest and listened. "Can you take a deep breath for me?"

Gordon tried to breathe deeply, but a cough rumbled inside his chest. Paul left the stethoscope where it was and said, "Can you try again?" Gordon complied and this time managed without coughing. Paul moved the stethoscope. "Again." He listened closely, then straightened. "I don't hear any sounds of pneumonia."

"Thank the Lord," Emily said.

"Can you get a bowl of tepid water and a washcloth for me?" Paul removed the bedclothes.

"I'm cold," Gordon whimpered.

"I know," Paul said kindly. "It's the fever." He moved to the other bed and gave Nate the same exam as his brother. "You're doing well." He looked at Carl. "He the first to get sick?"

"Yeah. He'd been sick about four days when Gordon came down with it."

"I'm feeling a lot better," Nate said.

"I can see that." Paul stood. "But I want you to stay in bed a few more days, all right?"

"A few more days?" Nate groaned.

"Sorry." Paul grinned.

Emily returned with the water and washcloth. While explaining that bundling up the children when they are running a fever only increases their temperatures, Paul showed her how to give Gordon a sponge bath. "The water will cool his skin and bring down his fever."

Gordon shivered, his skin prickling with gooseflesh.

"Once that temp's down, you'll feel a whole lot better," Paul said. "Do you have aspirin?" he asked Emily.

"No."

Paul took a small bottle out of his bag and gave it to her. "Give him one or two every four to six hours. It will help with his discomfort and to control the fever. Make sure he rests, even when he's feeling better. If that cough gets worse, radio the airfield and I'll come out and have another look." Paul glanced at the window. "It's best to keep the room dark. Too much light is hard on the eyes."

Emily nodded. "I'll cover it right away."

"He ought to start feeling better in a few days."

"Thank you, Doctor." Emily smiled shyly at Paul.

He closed his bag and headed to the front room.

"What do we do if Annie gets sick?" Carl asked. "She's just two."

Paul set the little girl on the kitchen table and gave her a quick exam. She smiled at him and tried to grab ahold of the stethoscope. "She seems fine." Paul set her on the floor.

"And if she gets sick?" Carl watched her toddle out the door and onto the porch.

"The treatment's the same, only decrease the aspirin to half a tablet. You can crush it in some jam to get her to take it. And watch the fever. If it spikes too high, it could cause a seizure."

"A seizure?" Emily's voice sounded panicked.

"It's rare. I wouldn't worry too much about it."

100

Carl walked to a cupboard and took down a tin can. He removed the lid and fished out a couple of dollar bills. He handed them to Paul. "It's not much—"

Paul pushed the money back at him. "I'm glad to come— no charge."

Carl stuffed the money into Paul's shirt pocket. "I pay my way." He walked back into the kitchen. "Can I get you something to eat or drink before you head out?"

Paul rested his hand over his pocket. "I could use a glass of water."

"Sure." Carl looked at Kate. "You like some?"

"I'm fine. Thank you."

Carl filled a glass from a hand pump in the sink. "How about we go out on the porch and sit?"

Kate lowered herself onto a chair made of hewn lumber and gratefully breathed in fresh air. She was glad to be free of the stuffy house.

Paul took a drink. "Measles are highly contagious. Likely there'll be others in town who'll get sick. I'd like to know if there are any more cases. Hate to have a measles epidemic out here." Paul took another drink of water.

"Folks are keeping to themselves," Carl said, watching his daughter totter down the path in front of the house.

"Good." Paul eased onto a chair and looked around. "It's real pretty out here."

"We like it. Moved onto this place five years ago."

Kate let her gaze roam over the farm. "I'd love to have a place like this one day."

"Might want to look into homesteading," Carl said.

"I'm not ready for that yet. Right now a small house in town would be nice, though. And one day maybe a home-stead." Kate glanced at Paul. She couldn't keep up a farm on her own, but if she were married . . .

Carl looked out over the property. "Figure in another couple of years I'll have everything fenced off and then I'll get us a few cows. I'm building a pen for pigs right now. I'll need it soon too. Made a deal with a man in town who has a pregnant sow."

Paul drained his glass. "Good luck to you. Heard pigs are hard to keep in an enclosure."

"That's true." He chuckled. "I'll be making my pen good and strong. Don't figure on chasing pigs over hill and dale."

Paul handed him the empty glass. "Thanks for the water." He looked at Kate. "We better get moving."

Carl walked with them to the plane. He clapped Paul on the shoulder. "Thanks again, Doc. We really appreciate your coming out."

"My pleasure."

Paul cranked the plane while Kate settled behind the control wheel. She was checking the gauges when Paul dropped into his seat. "Ready?" She turned over the engine and glanced up, catching a flash of red just before hearing a sickening ka-thunk. She shut down the plane and sprang out of her seat.

"What happened?" Paul asked.

"The prop hit something!" Kate pushed open the door and leaped out, afraid at what she would find. Carl lay on the ground in front of the plane. His little girl sat beside him. She was crying.

"No!" The word exploded from Kate.

Paul sprinted past her and knelt beside Carl. He leaned over the injured man.

"Annie . . . I was trying to get Annie."

"Don't talk," Paul said, then he yelled at Kate, "Get my bag!"

She ran back to the plane, snatched up Paul's medical bag, and hurried back to him. Blood was everywhere, all over Carl, on Paul, and on the ground. She picked up the crying little girl and watched helplessly while Paul yanked open his bag and pulled out wads of gauze.

Kate couldn't stand to watch, but she couldn't wrench her eyes away either. "I didn't see him." A sob escaped Kate. "I didn't see him." Tears coursed down her cheeks.

Emily ran toward the plane, terror written on her face. When she saw Carl, she smothered a scream behind her hands and sank to her knees beside her husband. "Is he all right? Will he be all right?"

Paul glanced at her, his eyes somber. He didn't answer. Instead, he glanced at Kate. "I need your help."

"Carl. Carl." Emily rested a shaking hand on his forehead. "Please, don't leave me."

Paul had stripped off the man's shirt. His right arm was nearly severed and a ghastly wound ran from his shoulder up his neck and disappeared into his scalp. Blood gushed. Carl's face had turned pasty white. His eyes were closed and it didn't look like he was breathing.

Paul grabbed more cloth from his bag. "Kate!"

As if being awakened from a trance, she handed Annie to her mother and knelt beside Paul. He took her hand and pressed it on a spot in Carl's neck. "The artery isn't completely severed, but it's gashed, and if we don't stop the bleeding . . ." He let the sentence hang. "I need you to keep it pinched together."

Kate could feel warm blood and a weak pulse. At least he was still alive. *This is my fault. I should have been watching. If he dies* . . . She couldn't even allow her thoughts to go there.

"Don't let off the pressure." Paul dug in his bag.

No matter how tightly Kate squeezed, Carl's artery pumped blood. The pulse grew weaker. *He's dying. He's going to die right here in my hands.*

Paul threaded a needle, his hands miraculously steady. "Okay. I'm ready." He swabbed blood. "I've got to get it clear so I can see well enough to stitch the laceration." His voice revealed neither hesitancy nor fear. He handed Kate gauze. "Mop up the blood so I can see." He looked at her for a moment, his eyes gentle. "You can do it."

Paul took the tattered artery and squeezed it closed and began suturing. Blood seeped out—not so much now though.

Kate did her best to keep the area clear. The blood didn't seem to be pumping any longer, but there was still so much of it. She looked at Carl's face. His skin was ashen. Did he have any blood left? *Oh Carl, please live.*

"Is he still breathing?" Emily asked, her voice quaking. "I don't think he's breathing." Her voice strident, she bent over her husband. "Carl? Carl!"

Kate knew it was too late. He'd lost too much blood. Paul kept working on him.

"Paul. He's gone," Kate said quietly.

Paul acted as if he hadn't heard her.

She rested a bloodied hand on his arm. "He's dead. Paul, he's gone." Kate couldn't believe she was even saying the words.

He looked at her as if seeing her for the first time, then he sat back, his hands and forearms covered with blood, his expression morose.

Kate wiped her hands on her pants. They were sticky.

Emily threw herself over her husband's body. "Noooo." She sobbed. "Noooo. Lord, not my Carl. Please, not Carl."

Kate stood on shaky legs. She felt sick. She looked away, tasting salty tears.

"I'm sorry," Paul said. "I tried. I really tried. The injuries were too severe." He stood and gazed down at Carl. It had only been minutes earlier that they'd been chatting.

Kate took his hand and leaned against him. "You did everything you could. This is my fault."

"It wasn't your fault." Paul turned tormented eyes on her. "Tell me why. Why would God do something like this? He could have stopped it. Why didn't he?"

Kate didn't have an answer. Life was filled with sorrows she had no explanation for. The verse "There is a time to be born and a time to die" rolled through her mind. "It was his time," she said softly. Alison's face flashed into her mind. Sweet Alison had died too young. Had it been her time or was it Kate's carelessness? If only she hadn't taken the plane out that day. Alison would still be alive. Even in her own state of confusion and guilt, Kate heard herself say, "God is here. He sees—"

"Yeah, well, does he see Emily?" He swung around and pointed at the house. "Does he see those children?" His eyes brimming with tears, Paul looked at little Annie, stained with her father's blood, and he said bitterly, "Does he see her?"

9

Paul punched down a mound of rising bread dough. The image of Carl Gladwell remained imprinted in his mind, as did the expressions of shock and horror on Carl's widow's face and those of his children. He'd never forget.

He worked the dough. Life was tenuous. Incidents like what had happened at the Gladwell place could be counted on, especially in this territory. Every day people were snatched from loved ones. And the risk takers, like Kate, walked a more unstable road than most. Something would happen to her. She'd been lucky so far, but that would change. Paul pressed the heel of his hand into the bread and rolled it out, and then slapped it down.

Finally, he divided the dough into two sections. Almost brutally, he shaped them, then placed the yeasty loaves in baking pans and set them in the warmer.

He walked to the window and stared at the trail leading from the back of the house. Kate was a risk taker. He didn't want to love her. It meant one day he'd lose her. And with her drive to prove herself, that meant probably sooner than later. He imagined life without her—how it would feel if she were to die. An ache swelled inside his chest. It was impossible. He was stuck. What was he going to do?

I'll break it off. The sooner, the better.

But how would he fall out of love? Maybe if he didn't see her anymore, the passion he felt would ease and finally fade? Even as Paul reasoned it out, he knew there was no easy fix. He'd allowed himself to fall in love. He'd promised himself never again, but here he was—trapped by love. He rubbed his temples where a throbbing had set in.

It had been six years since he'd lost Susan. And he still thought about her every day. The longing for her remained. *But we were married. I haven't known Kate very long—less than two years. Maybe it will be different with her. Maybe I can forget her.*

He had to end it.

The dogs started barking. Paul figured it must be Patrick and stepped onto the porch. He was surprised to see Lily heading toward the cabin. He didn't want company right now, especially not Lily. When Sassa found out that he'd split up with Kate, she'd be back trying to match up him and Lily.

"Hi." Lily stopped at the bottom of the steps and lifted a pie to chin level.

"Afternoon."

"Mama and I made some pies and thought you might like one. It's still warm."

"Thanks." Paul walked down the steps and Lily handed him the dessert. "What kind is it?"

"Rhubarb."

"One of my favorites." He breathed in the aroma of sugar, spices, and fruit. "Mmm. Can't wait to try it." Sugar glistened on the golden crust and red juice oozed out of slashes cut into the shell. "It's too early in the year for fresh rhubarb."

"We still have some that we put up last year. Mama figured we'd better use it."

"Tell her thank you."

"I will."

The two stood silent and awkward. Paul didn't know what to say. It would be rude not to invite Lily in. "I was just about to make myself some lunch. You hungry? We could have pie for dessert." He hoped she would say no.

106

Lily's brown eyes brightened. "It's been a long while since breakfast. Lunch sounds good. You sure you don't mind?"

"'Course not. I can always use a little company."

"You know . . . Mama—she's likely to get her hopes up even if you and Kate are . . . well, together."

"Don't worry about that." Paul barely hung on to his cheerful expression as he stepped back and allowed Lily to walk up the steps ahead of him.

"I'm sorry about Mama." Lily stopped on the porch and looked back at Paul. "She thinks a lot of you."

"I'll have to remember to thank her." He reached around Lily and opened the door, then followed her inside and set the pie on the table. "I have soup simmering."

"Smells awfully good." Lily stared at Paul. "It's embarrassing the way Mama acts, as if I'm desperate. I'm not, you know."

"I didn't think you were." Paul took two bowls out of the cupboard. "The right man will come along."

Sadness seemed to dim the light in Lily's eyes. "I suppose so."

"Your friendship matters to me. You and your family have been good neighbors. And recently your mother hasn't said a word about us." *'Course that will change if I break things off with Kate.*

Lily lifted her lips in a half smile and raised her eyebrows. "She did send me over with pie."

Paul chuckled. "That she did." He took the lid off a pot of soup. "You like split pea?"

"Love it. But the peas aren't ready yet."

"I have a few left over from last year." He grinned. "Like the rhubarb, figured I'd better use it up. I'll need the jars soon."

"Hope the weather stays nice. That way we won't have long to wait for fresh vegetables." Lily sat at the table and clasped her hands in front of her.

Thankful to have something to do, Paul sliced bread from his last loaf and set the pieces on a plate. He placed it on the table, along with butter and a knife, then set out salt and pepper. After ladling soup into the bowls he placed one in front of Lily, the other across from her. Retrieving two spoons from a drawer, he handed one to her before sitting down.

"It looks good." Lily stirred her soup. "Smells good too." She took a slice of bread and buttered it and took a bite. She chewed slowly. "I love fresh butter."

"I have it only because your mom's generous enough to share the cream from your cow."

"We have so much we don't know what to do with it."

The two ate quietly. Paul wasn't sure how he felt about having Lily here. He forced himself to relax. It was just Lily. He'd known her since she was a girl.

An amiable mood settled over the two. "Will your mother worry?" Paul asked.

Lily smirked. "Don't be silly. I'm with you. The longer I'm away, the better she'll feel."

Paul laughed. "Suppose you're right."

"This is nice, though. I usually have my brothers talking over each other or arguing about who caught the biggest fish or hauled the most firewood . . ." She shook her head. "It's always something."

"They're just boys. It was the same in my family." Paul felt a pang of homesickness. He'd enjoyed the wrangling between himself and his brothers.

He'd imagined having a family with Kate. He'd even thought about what their children might look like with her height and auburn hair and amber-colored eyes. Without warning, the son he'd lost flashed through his mind . . . and Susan. She hadn't looked anything like Kate. He wondered what their son would have looked like. He'd had dark fuzz on his head. He might have had dark hair like Paul's.

No one could ever replace them. He spooned in a mouthful of soup but could barely swallow it past the lump in his throat. What would he say to Kate?

Eager to see Paul, Kate dropped down above the mirror-smooth surface of Bear Creek and landed on the sandbar.

She took in the lush beauty around her and doubted there was any place in the world as stunning as Alaska in June. It was her favorite time of year—long days that stretched into midnight, trees and plants clad in vibrant greens, and wildflowers carpeting the earth.

She tried not to think about what had happened to Carl Gladwell. It was too awful. It had been her plane, her prop . . . her fault. She should have been more careful, looked to make sure all was clear.

She knew better than to go down that trail of thought and turned her mind to Paul and her life in Alaska. She had the job and the man of her dreams. And she'd be spending the next two days with Paul. She couldn't wait to look into his dark brown eyes and feel embraced by his gentle smile. But after what had happened at the Gladwells', she wondered what she would see in his eyes. They'd held a haunted expression when she and Paul had parted. It unsettled Kate. She'd seen it in his eyes before, as if he possessed a dreadful secret.

Again the horrible scene intruded on her thoughts. She fought to hold it back, but it flared to life anyway. Had it been her fault? Had she been careless? She thought through the moments before the terrible sound of the prop hitting Carl. She'd done as she always had. There was no reason to worry, no reason for Carl to be where he'd been—anyway, none that she knew about. How could she have known his little girl had wandered out in front of the plane?

Things like this happened, where no one was at fault. Kate knew that if she wanted to live and work in the bush, she'd have to accept the brutality it could bring. It was part of life here and there was nothing that could be done about it.

She had done the best she could to calm her guilt, but it remained. She heard the motor of a boat and looked out the window and saw Paul standing in Patrick's dory as it moved across the creek toward her. He stood with his shoulders back, legs slightly apart, hands clasped in front, holding onto his pack and medical bag.

Kate waved. He tossed her a stiff nod. When Patrick reached the sandbar, Kate stuck her head out of the plane door and waved.

"You got any mail?" Patrick hollered.

"Not today."

"Okay."

He directed the boat up to the rocks, where Paul leaped out of the boat. Paul waved at his friend and strode toward the plane. He climbed in and tossed his pack on a seat, set his bag beside it, and then pulled the door shut and bolted it.

"Good morning," Kate said, making sure to sound cheerful.

"Hi." Barely giving Angel a pat, Paul moved up front and sat. "Where we headed?" He scarcely glanced at her.

"We've got a stop in Valdez and Cordova, then we'll swing around and head to Seward tomorrow." Kate waited for some kind of touch or hug from Paul, but he didn't even look at her. She'd expected him to be in a bad mood, but this was more than a mood. Fear tightened in her gut. "All set?"

"I'm ready." Paul watched the bank.

Kate throttled up. "Sorry I'm late. I slept in."

Paul didn't respond.

He just stared out the window. Kate had the sick feeling that something was terribly wrong. Fear jittered through her. "What happened at the Gladwells' place was a freak accident. I know that you're upset about it. But you did everything you could. We have to trust God."

"I'm sorry for blowing up like I did." Paul looked at her. "I know God has a reason for things like what happened up there. I know it," he repeated as if trying to convince himself. "But sometimes I don't understand. Sometimes it's too much. I'm not strong like you think."

Kate let off the power and allowed the plane to idle. "Is that what's bothering you?"

Paul shook his head. "No. It's more than that."

Kate caught something in his look that terrified her. "Then what is it?" The silence in the cockpit felt suffocating. "If anyone is to blame, it's me."

Paul studied his hands. "It's nobody's fault, but you don't forget something like that."

"True. But we've got to go on. I've been fighting my own demons—why didn't I see him?"

"It's just like you said—a freak accident."

He was saying the right things, but his tone seemed stilted. "Just one of those things," Kate said.

Paul nodded, slowly and thoughtfully. "Yeah. Sometimes it seems like the world's doing its best to kill off decent people."

He's thinking about his wife. He'd never told her what happened, just that she was dead. "I figure that when something like this happens, it makes you think of your . . . wife."

Paul stared at her, his expression startled and hurting. "It never goes away. Never." Again he turned his gaze out the window. "Poor Mrs. Gladwell. Can't stop thinking about her kneeling beside her husband, his blood spilled all over the ground."

He sucked in a deep breath and turned in the seat so that he faced Kate. "I didn't want to talk about this now, but there's no good time." He looked squarely at her.

"No good time for what?" Kate's insides trembled. Was Paul about to tell her the secret he'd been carrying inside?

"Death—it's everywhere." He shook his head. "We can't escape it."

"True. Everyone's going to die someday." Kate tried to keep her tone light.

"Yes, but you tempt it, Kate. Every time you get in this plane, you're asking for trouble."

"I—"

"Don't. You know you do. All the pilots do." He stared at his interlocked fingers in his lap. "I thought I could do this . . ."

"Do what?" Kate's pulse thumped. She kept her eyes on him, wishing she could stop the unbearable words she feared most.

"I thought I could love you."

"You don't love me?" Anguish shot through Kate and she gripped the control wheel.

"I do." Paul rubbed the back of his neck, then turned his serious dark eyes on Kate. "But I can't. I just can't."

"What do you mean?" Kate tried to quiet rising panic.

Paul's expression pleaded for her understanding. "Pilots go down all the time, Kate. Next time it might be you. You've already had two crack-ups and several close calls. One day your luck will run out."

"I've been flying most of my life. I'm twenty-seven years old and I'm still here. I'm not going to die in a plane crash."

"You don't know that."

"I'm careful and skilled."

"So was Frank. And so were most of the other pilots who died following their obsession."

What could Kate say? Being a pilot was dangerous. Finally she sputtered, "What do you want from me? I can't guarantee that nothing terrible will happen. No one can. And you're just as bad. You're in the air nearly as much as I am."

"You're right. I could die any day . . . just like you." He stared out the window. "But as selfish as this sounds . . . if I'm dead, I don't care." He looked at her. "If you're dead, I have to live . . . without you."

"So, what are you saying?" Kate knew, but she had to ask.

He folded his arms across his chest. "It would be better . . . if we didn't see each other anymore."

Kate's stomach dropped. "But you said you love me."

"It's because I love you that I can't see you."

"You're not making any sense."

"I can't love you. Don't you see? If I do, I'll lose you."

Kate couldn't believe what she was hearing. "If we break up, you're losing me. And whether we're together or not, if something happens to me, you lose me."

Paul's expression turned more miserable. "I know it sounds crazy, but the longer we're together, the more I'll love you, and when the inevitable happens . . ."

"You can shut off your emotions just like that?" She fought tears.

Paul worked his jaw. He didn't answer.

"Fine. It's better that I know now. What a fool I'd be to love a man who can stop caring anytime he wants." She spat the words at him.

"You don't understand. It's not like that. I can't shut it off. I love you—more every day. Every moment we spend together my love grows stronger." He shook his head. "When I lost Susan, I swore I'd never love anyone again." He sat back and looked away. "I'm sorry, Kate. It's over."

10

Kate had been dreading this delivery. She hadn't seen
Paul since they'd ended their relationship. What
should she say? Should she act like nothing happened,
treat him like any other customer?

When she circled above his cabin, her throat tightened.
There was no sign of him. Maybe he was at Susitna Station.
She hoped so. Or maybe he wouldn't recognize the plane.
She'd had to bring Jack's pontoon plane today.

And although she knew eventually they'd work together,
she couldn't bring herself to fly with him yet. Sorrow felt as
if it would squeeze the oxygen out of her lungs.

She'd imagined spending their days here, fishing the rivers
and streams, working in the garden, adding on to the cabin
for the children they'd have. She felt the familiar ache in her
chest and the frequent tears that kept her eyes red-rimmed.
She wiped them away, determined to show Paul that she was
fine.

I am fine, she told herself. *It's over, and dwelling on what
happened won't change anything.*

The plane splashed down on the quiet stream and she
headed toward his dock. When she saw Paul step out of the
shed, her stomach turned over.

Angel recognized the stop and ran for the door, her tail wagging hard.

"No. Not today, girl. You stay." Kate grabbed a box of supplies, and keeping an eye on Angel to make sure she stayed put, she opened the door and stepped out, package under her arm.

She closed the plane door and waited on the dock, watching Paul walk down the path. She loved how he carried his body, broad shoulders back and long strides. When he approached, she couldn't manage a smile and simply nodded. "This is for you."

Paul took the box and glanced at the return address. "Good. I've been waiting for these—nearly out of gauze and bandages." He tucked the box under his arm and set his dark eyes on her. "How you been?"

"Good. Busy. You know how it is this time of year."

"Yeah." Paul glanced at the creek.

"You been doing much fishing?" Kate asked.

"In my spare time. I have quite a few in the smokehouse." He glanced at the small wood structure at the edge of the clearing behind his house, then looked at the plane. "So, you're flying Jack's plane today."

"Yeah. I need pontoons." Kate looked back at the Stinson. "It doesn't fly as nice as mine."

"Well, you've got the best, right?" He gave her a stiff smile.

Kate nodded, then said, "I better get moving. I've got a lot of stops to make."

"Sure. Take care of yourself. I'll see you." He took a few steps up the trail, then stopped and looked back at Kate.

She forced a smile and waved, then climbed into the plane. She moved away from the dock. Tears blurred her vision as she lifted off the water and headed north. She felt no joy in her job—what good was it to continue to fly if it meant living without the man she loved? But as the thought pounded her mind, another niggled at her. What kind of man would insist that she choose between her love of flying and him? Anger swelled, replacing sorrow, and she swiped away the tears. Maybe Paul wasn't the man she thought he was.

Paul reached beneath a pea vine, grabbed hold of a clump of fescue, and tugged it free. He shook off excess dirt and dropped the weed into a bucket. It felt good to work with the earth.

Sitting back on his heels, he looked down the row. Small green pods, just beginning to sprout, promised a late July feast of creamed peas and baby potatoes.

"Hey Paul," Patrick called, stepping into the garden and trudging down the row.

Paul stood and wiped the dirt from his hands onto his blue jeans. "Thought you and the boys went fishing."

"Wish I had. But Sassa won't wait on that broken window frame another day."

Paul grinned. "Well, it doesn't look like you're working on a window anyway."

"I need some help. Could you lend me a hand?"

"Sure. No problem."

The two headed toward Patrick's. They hadn't gone far when Patrick said, "Heard you and Kate split up."

"Yeah." Paul didn't want to talk about it.

"Sorry to hear it. She's a fine lady."

"She is."

"Don't mean to pry, but you never said anything all these weeks. What happened between the two of you?"

Paul knew he needed to talk to someone about what was going on inside his heart, but he couldn't bring himself to reveal his fears. "Just wouldn't have worked out."

Patrick cocked an eyebrow, but didn't probe. "Can't say Sassa's unhappy about it. She likes Kate, but you know . . ." He stopped. "I thought you and Kate were well suited to each other."

Paul could see he wasn't going to get away without an explanation. "We are . . . kind of. But it comes down to her job. It's risky, too risky. I don't want to live every day wondering if this is the one when she dies."

Patrick nodded slightly. "I can see how that would be hard on you, but any one of us can die today, maybe tonight, anytime. When we fall in love and commit to someone, there's no guarantee our lives will be long. Seems to me that while you're still living, you ought to love all you can. No one's going to get out of this world still breathing."

"I know all that's true, but Kate pushes it. Her job's going to take her sooner, not later."

Patrick shrugged and pushed his hands into his pockets. "Makes no sense to me, but it's your life."

Paul knew he was being a coward and that he'd broken Kate's heart. But she'd get over him, and given time, he'd get over her . . . in time. He just hoped that when her final day came, he'd be over her.

Paul held the window frame in place while Patrick hammered in a nail. Taking another from between his teeth, Patrick pounded it in, then climbed down from a ladder and stepped back to look at his work. "Is it straight?"

Paul studied the frame. "It's slightly higher on the right than the left."

Patrick grimaced. "Yeah. I thought so too. But I figure if Sassa's not happy with it, she'll let me know."

"Let you know what?" Sassa asked as she stepped around the corner of the house. She looked at the window. "It's crooked."

Patrick half grinned. "Yep."

Sassa stared at the window. "Ah, it's good enough. You can barely tell." She turned to Paul. "How you set for canned carrots?"

"Running low. But I'll make do until the new crop is ready."

"I don't know if we ate less or if I canned more, but I've got a bunch of extra jars. Could you use some?"

"Sure. I'll take a few off your hands."

"Come on out to the shed, then. I'll put some in a box for you." She ambled around the house and down the short trail leading to the storage room.

"See you later," Patrick said. "I've got some cabinets to paint. Better get to it."

117

"Don't wear yourself out." Paul followed Sassa.

Lily nearly collided with him as he rounded the house. She had a clothes basket piled with wet towels propped against one hip.

"Sorry." Paul reached out to steady her.

"It's my fault. I was in a hurry."

Sassa opened the shed door. "Lily, can you give us a hand?"

"Sure." Lily set the basket on the ground beneath the clothesline, then headed for the storage room.

Sassa grabbed two wooden boxes and set them on a workbench before she started clearing shelves of carrots. Dust mingled with the musty smell hanging in the air. "I've got a bunch of peas too," she said, handing a jar to Lily.

"Thanks." Paul didn't need more peas but didn't want to offend Sassa, so he accepted the gift without argument.

When the two boxes were full, Sassa stood back and looked over the half-empty shelves. "I guess that's it." She turned to Lily. "Can you carry one of them over?"

Lily glanced at Paul. He could see humor in her eyes. They both knew Sassa was back to her matchmaking now that Kate was out of the picture. It would have been funny if he didn't feel so miserable about Kate.

He picked up the box of carrots. "Thanks, Sassa. This will help get me through. But Lily doesn't have to haul that over for me. I can come back for it."

"She doesn't mind, do you, Lily." Sassa smiled at her daughter.

"No. Glad to help. But I left a basket of wet laundry sitting out."

"I'll hang the clothes."

Lily picked up the jars of peas and led the way out, then headed toward the trail. She and Paul walked side by side. Neither spoke.

When they reached Paul's place he strode into the shed and set his box on a workbench. "Just put yours here beside these."

Lily placed the box on the worktable. "Do you actually need all of these?"

"Some of it." He smiled. "Your mother's a generous woman."

"She is, but I think she wanted to make sure you had enough to carry so you'd need help."

Paul chuckled. "You're probably right."

Silence sifted between them, and then Lily said, "Me and the boys are going fishing tomorrow. Would you like to come? They'd get a kick out of showing you up." She grinned.

"I haven't had much time for fishing. Sounds like fun."

"Good. I'll bring lunch," Lily said.

"And I'll bring the gear and bait."

"Seven o'clock sound okay?"

"I'll be ready." Paul felt almost lighthearted. "We can take my boat up the creek. I know just the place."

Lily's brothers loaded bait and untied the line tethering the dory to the dock while Paul started his Johnson outboard. Lily settled in the bow and the boys found seats on the benches. Paul steered toward the center of the creek, the small engine making a puttering sound.

"This ought to be fun," Douglas said. "I know just the place."

"No. Today Paul chooses where we fish," Lily said.

"I know a good fishing hole," Paul said with a smile.

Lily sat quietly, gazing at the surroundings. She looked older than she had before moving to Seattle. She'd put on a little weight. Maybe that was it. But she acted more grown up too. Odd, how a few months could make such a difference. Paul thought he detected melancholy in the young woman and wondered if something was bothering her.

"It's strange how different everything looks from the middle of the creek." Lily leaned over and dipped her hand in the water.

The boys did the same, making the boat teeter.

"All right. Settle down," Paul said. "The last thing we need is to get dunked. It may be June, but that water is ice cold."

119

The boys sat down and stared ahead. Lily lifted her face to the sun and closed her eyes.

Paul couldn't keep from staring. Her tanned skin was flawless and her black hair shimmered in the sunlight. When she turned to look at him, he quickly averted his eyes.

Acting as if she hadn't noticed, she said, "So, are you giving away the location of your favorite fishing hole?"

Paul smiled. "I've got more than one."

"I've got at least six," Ethan bragged. "And I'm not telling no one where they are." He grinned.

"Well, there are plenty of good places on this creek," Paul said.

They motored past Klaus's cabin and spotted him in the garden.

"Hi, Klaus," the boys hollered.

He waved. "Gut day for fishing."

"Hope you're right," Paul called back.

Klaus folded his arms over his rounded stomach and watched them move past.

"We'll bring you back a big one," Lily said.

"Danke." He returned to work.

"Sometimes I wonder if he's lonely," Lily said.

Robert dipped a hand in the water. "I go and see him all the time. He's really good at whittling and always likes to teach me."

Paul smiled, but figured Klaus must be lonely some of the time.

"I worry about him living out here all by himself," Lily said. "His health isn't so good."

"Has he ever mentioned moving into town?" Paul steered the boat into the deep water in the middle of the creek.

"No. He'd never do that." She stared at the old man's cabin until it melded into the lush greenery at the river's edge. Her voice thick, she asked, "Do you think he'll live much longer?"

"Hard to say. He won't let me check him over." When he noticed that all three boys were staring at him, waiting for his answer, Paul added, "He's a tough old guy. If I were a betting man, I'd say he'll be around a good while."

"I sure hope so," Douglas said. "He's grouchy some of the time, but I like him and I think he likes all of us." He turned his gaze upriver, seeming content.

The stream split into two channels and Paul followed the branch leading to the right. Lily remained in the bow, her back straight as she stared ahead. She was small and slender, but Paul could see the strength in her. She brushed her hair off her face and smiled back at him. Paul's throat tightened. He couldn't keep from comparing her sultry beauty with Kate's healthy good looks. *She's stunning*, he thought, surprised that he'd even noticed. He'd never paid much attention to Lily's appearance.

Dragging his mind back to the task at hand, he steered toward a sandbar. "Let's give this spot a try."

The boys jumped out and splashed through the water, dragging the dory onto the pebbled beach. Lily climbed out while Paul shut down the engine. He leaped over the side and helped the boys haul the boat onto shore, where he tied it to the base of a tree.

Lily lifted out the bait bucket and tackle box and Paul grabbed the poles and a canteen. The boys quickly picked out their poles and set to work baiting them. Paul handed a fishing rod to Lily. She set up the jig, and Paul did the same. By the time Lily finished, the boys were already heading up the creek.

"Stay within eyesight," Paul cautioned.

Lily made her way over the rocky beach until she found a spot alongside the creek, where she sat on a large rock and cast out her line.

Using a new, brightly colored lure Paul had seen advertised in the Sears catalog, he waded into the water. The current was stronger than he'd expected and he had to fight to keep his balance. The boys had found their spots in the stream and already had their lines in the water.

"I don't know why men have to stand in the water. The line is just as happy if you're sitting. And the fish don't care," Lily said.

"I like to stand. That way I'm ready if I get a big one on."

Lily reeled in her line and cast out again. With a glance over her shoulder at the trees, she said, "Hope we don't meet up with the bear that tore up Klaus's place."

Paul rested his hand on the pistol he had holstered at his waist. "No need to worry."

"A bear can be on you before you can even fire that thing." Lily's pole bent and she yanked it up. "I've got one!" She scrambled off her rock, keeping tension on the line. Pointing the tip of the pole toward the water, she hauled it up and toward her. "It's a big one." She let the fish run, then worked it toward the shallows. "Get the net! Get the net!"

Paul grabbed it and hurried to the water's edge. He searched the stream, trying to catch a glimpse of the fish. Lily continued to fight and finally a flash of silver glistened in the clear water.

"Looks like a nice one." Paul stepped deeper into the water, net ready. "Get him a little closer."

Lily reeled hard, maneuvering the fish toward Paul. All of a sudden, the line went slack and the rod straightened. "Crumbum!" She stared dismally at the lifeless pole. "I nearly had it." She looked at Paul. "What pound test did you use?" Her tone was accusatory.

"Twenty. Plenty strong for salmon." Irritated, he tossed the net up on the bank and headed back to his spot. He didn't need a native girl telling him what pound test to use.

Lily sat and went to work repairing her line. She glanced at Paul. "Sorry. I didn't mean to get snippy. You know what you're doing . . . even if you did grow up in San Francisco."

He looked at her, and when he caught sight of her smirk and teasing eyes, he couldn't stay mad. "I grew up in San Francisco, but I've been fishing lakes and rivers since before you were born."

"I know." Lily tied off her line. "What's San Francisco like? Is it as big as Seattle?"

"Bigger. There's not as much rain, but there's a lot of fog. Both cities are built into hillsides, but the ones in San Francisco are steeper."

"Really? I wouldn't like that much." She rested her arms on her thighs. "When I was in Seattle, I got sick of walking up and down hills every time I wanted to go somewhere."

"You get used to them." Paul reeled in.

"I didn't mind the rain, though." Lily let out a sigh. "When the sun came out, the city and mountains looked bright, like they'd been scrubbed clean. And Mount Rainier reminded me of a grand dame, standing regally above all the other mountains. It was beautiful, all white and glistening in the sun."

She straightened. "I could see it from my apartment. And Puget Sound too. I liked watching the ships come and go." Her tone was melancholy.

"I thought you didn't like Seattle."

"Some things I liked." She dug into the bait bucket, pulled out a fingerling, and snagged it on the hook.

"You glad to be back?"

She shrugged and then cast out her line. Her jaw looked tight, like she'd clamped her teeth tightly together.

"Well, I'm glad you're here. It's fun to have fishing partners." He glanced at the boys, who looked like they were expecting to have a fish on at any moment. They took fishing seriously.

Paul was alone most of the time, except when he worked with patients. He'd enjoyed flying with Kate, but that was different now . . . Since ending their relationship he'd flown with other pilots—it wasn't the same.

Melancholy grazed the edge of his heart. He didn't want to spend his life alone, growing old like Klaus with no one to share his days. His gaze moved to Lily. She'd make a good companion. But he didn't love her and wasn't about to marry someone just for companionship. He might as well get used to the idea of facing life on his own.

"Hey, when's lunch?" Ethan hollered. "We're hungry."

"If you're hungry, come and get it. I made plenty. It's in the picnic basket." Lily reeled in, rinsed her hands in the stream, and then took the basket out of the boat. She leaned her pole against a downed tree and picked up the canteen. Taking a long drink, she watched Paul as he strolled toward her. She offered him the canteen.

"Thanks." He chugged down several mouthfuls, then wiped his mouth with his shirtsleeve.

The boys scrambled over the rocks, laid their poles on the rocky beach, and grabbed sandwiches out of the basket.

"I brought along some cookies." Paul took a container out of the boat and opened it. "Oatmeal. You want one?"

"Sure." The boys each snatched two, then settled in the shade to eat.

Lily took a cookie and bit into it, chewing thoughtfully. "Good. But they could use a little more cinnamon."

Paul chose one. "Think so?" He took a bite. She was right, but he wasn't about to let her know. "More cinnamon would be too much."

Lily leaned against a willow tree. "Suit yourself, but I think—"

"I know what you think, and yes, I know your mother's the best cook in the territory."

Lily laughed, her eyes narrowing into crescents. All of a sudden, she turned pale and grabbed hold of the willow. She sank to her knees.

"Lily? You all right?"

She closed her eyes and nodded slowly.

Paul hurried to her side. "What is it?"

"I feel kind of faint and sick."

"Put your head down and breathe slowly."

Lily did as he said.

"You feeling better?"

"A little."

"Has this happened before?"

124

"Just lately." She sat on a log. Her color was slowly returning.

"Have you seen a doctor?"

Sorrow and resignation touched Lily's eyes. "Yeah. I've seen one." She took in a deep breath and looked at him. "I'm perfectly healthy . . . for someone who's going to have a baby."

— 11 —

Paul held an axe blade against a whetstone and rotated it in a circular motion, his thoughts on Lily. Ever since their fishing trip the week before, he'd pondered her situation. He knew it wasn't any of his business, but he couldn't help but care. What was she going to do? She might be a tough gal, but life was hard on single mothers. Why had she let something like this happen? As much as he hated to admit it, he was disappointed in her.

He spit on the stone to moisten it and then continued the task of sharpening. He'd like to get his hands on the man who'd taken advantage of Lily. She thought he loved her. *She's probably better off without him.*

A dull pain had settled in his fingers. He stopped for a moment and shook his hand. He'd been away from home so much he hadn't kept up with the chore of keeping the axe and hatchet sharp, which now meant more time on the whetstone. He'd rather be swinging the axe than sharpening it.

His thoughts drifted to Kate. He wondered how she was handling the disappearance of Amelia Earhart, who had gone missing several days ago. He knew it would hit her hard if her heroine was found dead or not at all. *That's what happens—people push too hard, lose all reason.* The thought made him angry. Miss Earhart had people who loved and cared about her. Hadn't she considered them when she took off on her adventure? *She's just like Kate.*

Sweat dripped into his eyes and he wiped his forehead with the back of his hand. It was hot for July. He stopped to rest the aching muscles in his forearms, mopped his face with a handkerchief, and then gulped water from a canteen.

Paul held up the axe to the light, hoping it was sharp enough. It wasn't. He could still see the reflection of light in the blade. Spitting on it, he resumed the tedious job.

He heard what sounded like a whine from outside and stopped working to listen. The whimper came again. The dogs were back. They'd headed out for a romp more than an hour ago. He set down the axe and went to the shed door and looked out. Nita stood head down in the middle of the yard. She ambled toward him, her tail barely flagging. There was no sign of the other two dogs.

"What's wrong, girl?" He knelt in front of her and ran his hand over the top of her head. "Where are the boys?"

Just as he spoke, Jackpot appeared on the trail. He limped into the clearing. Alarm clanged through Paul. He hurried to the dog. "What happened to you, boy?" He stroked Jackpot's black coat. It felt sticky and wet. Paul looked at his palm—it was coated with blood.

Dread flared. He probed and found a gash along Jackpot's left shoulder. It was still bleeding. "What did you tangle with, boy?"

Paul glanced up the trail, hoping to see Buck. There was no sign of him. He returned to his examination of Jackpot and found several lacerations. By the size and depth of the gashes, he guessed they'd been inflicted by a bear. "Looks like he got the better of you."

Paul gazed into the forest, wondering what had become of Buck and hoping an enraged bear hadn't followed his dogs home. He cupped his hands around his mouth and hollered for Buck, then waited. There was no sign of the big malamute. He called again and again. Still nothing.

His stomach roiled. Even a dog Buck's size couldn't stand

up to an angry grizzly. He should have returned with the other two dogs. Either he was too badly injured . . . or dead. Sickening possibilities tumbled through Paul's mind. And then memories pressed in. He'd spotted Buck in a litter of pups when he'd first arrived in Anchorage. They'd been comrades ever since. Dead or alive, he had to find him.

Paul looked at Jackpot, who lay in the dirt licking his wounds. He'd have to tend to him before he could search for Buck. Gently, he combed through Jackpot's hair, looking for injuries. He cleaned and sutured each one. Jackpot whimpered from time to time, but he remained still, seeming to know Paul was helping.

With Buck on his mind, Paul fought the impulse to hurry. After he'd tended to Jackpot's wounds, he gave both of the dogs food and water, then closed them inside the shed. He sprinted to the house to get his rifle, then headed to Patrick's. It would be wise to let him know where he'd gone.

He knocked on the door and waited impatiently. He didn't want to waste a moment.

"Hi, Paul," Sassa said, as she came around the corner of the house. She wore a broad smile. "Good to see you." Her smile faded.

"Is Patrick here?" Paul walked down the steps.

"He went to Susitna Station. Anything I can do?"

"No." Paul shifted the rifle he'd slung over his shoulder. "The dogs went for a run this morning. Only Nita and Jackpot came back. Jackpot's pretty chewed up—looks like a bear got to him."

"Oh, Paul. I'm so sorry. Is he going to be all right?"

"Yeah. He'll be fine." Paul's eyes wandered back toward his place. "But Buck's out there somewhere. I have to find him."

"Maybe you should wait for Patrick and go together. It'd be better if there are two of you, especially if the bear's the same one who made a mess of things at Klaus's."

"Maybe, but dogs and bears are never a good mix." He glanced at his place again. "I can't wait. Buck could be badly injured. And the bear's probably long gone by now."

"Be careful."

"Yeah. I will. You might want to keep the boys close to home. There's been bear scat around my place. If it's the same bear . . . well . . ." He shrugged.

"I'd say that bear will make a good rug." Sassa grinned, then her expression and voice turned somber. "I hope you find Buck."

"Thanks."

"Where are Nita and Jackpot?"

"I closed them in the shed. Nita's fine, but I had a lot of sewing to do on Jackpot."

"I'll check on them."

"I appreciate that."

Paul headed up the trail, his mind filled with thoughts of Buck. He'd been the largest in his litter, with great big feet and a happy disposition. He'd grown into a powerful dog, but had trained easily in spite of his determined nature. Buck wasn't the type to back down from a challenge even if it came from a grizzly. He'd fight to the death.

Sick to his stomach, Paul knew Buck was probably never coming home. Heartache swelled and he tasted the saltiness of tears. Wiping at them, he forced his mind back to tracking. He had no time to be maudlin.

It wasn't difficult to follow the dogs' trail. They'd frolicked their way through the forest, leaving a profusion of broken limbs and crushed brush.

Paul had only traveled about a mile when he came across a downed tree torn apart by a bear. It had been turned over and shredded, providing the animal with an insect feast. Had the dogs come upon him here? Paul knelt and studied prints left in the soil. It was a grizzly—a big one. Its tracks had been disturbed and partially covered by those of the dogs. They'd gone after him, all right.

Paul slowed his pace and stopped, listening for any sound of Buck or the bear. He waited and studied the foliage. Was the bear out there, watching him?

When he was reasonably certain the grizzly wasn't nearby,

he called softly, "Buck." The wilderness with its birdsong and buzz of insects swallowed his voice. There was no response from his dog.

He followed a swath of broken limbs and flattened grasses. It looked like the brush had been crushed by the pursuit of excited dogs. Paul figured the chase had started here. Watchful, he moved cautiously, not wanting to surprise the grizzly and set up a confrontation.

Continuing to follow the trail, he called Buck's name again. There was no answering bark or whimper. He came upon a heavily trampled area. The brush and grasses were bloodied. This had to be where the battle had taken place. His rifle ready, Paul stood in one spot and slowly turned, his gaze probing the trees and bushes. Had the bear fled?

"Buck," he called. Then he whistled. "Come on, boy." He searched the area, finding nothing. And then he saw it, a mound of black and silver fur. His heart thumped into his throat. "Buck!"

Fearing the worst, Paul ran to his friend and knelt beside him. He rested a hand on the animal's side. He looked like he was dead. And then beneath his fingers Paul felt the dog's chest rise ever so slightly. He was breathing! "Oh, Buck." Paul cradled the dog's big head in his lap. "Come on, boy, wake up."

Buck didn't react.

Paul quickly examined the malamute. The dog was badly injured. Along with numerous lacerations, he had a broken leg and puncture wounds in his neck and head. But that wasn't the worst of it. Paul rolled him onto his other side and his gaze fell upon what should certainly be a fatal wound. What felt like a hammer slamming against his chest knocked the wind out of Paul. The bear had laid open the dog's side.

He hefted Buck into his arms, and cradling him against his chest, he set off for home. Paul counted a hundred paces, then stopped and rested, then counted off another hundred. His arms and back screamed for him to stop. He kept going, telling Buck everything would be fine, that he'd fix him up good as new and that they'd run the trapline again.

Exhausted, Paul's legs crumpled beneath him. Sucking in oxygen, he rested a moment, then stumbled back to his feet and kept moving. Paul knew that even if they made it home, Buck probably wouldn't live. He could feel the heat and moisture of Buck's blood soaking into his coat. Still, he kept moving, checking again and again to see if the dog was still breathing.

With the trail in sight, Paul heard the crackle of branches. Was it the bear? Had it returned to finish off Buck and him too? Paul set down the dog and grabbed his rifle. His finger on the trigger, he stared into the brush. A spruce hen flushed out of the bushes. Paul's pulse raced and he let out a breath. He'd nearly wasted several rounds on a bird.

By the time the cabin was in sight, the muscles in Paul's back felt as if they were on fire. His legs would barely hold him. But the sight of the house breathed strength into him and he kept moving.

When he approached the cabin, Lily stepped out of the shed. "Paul. Thank God you found him! I was so worried." Her gaze went to Buck. "Is he . . . alive?"

"Barely. The bear got him good. How's Jackpot?"

"I think he'll be all right. He's sleeping."

Nita trotted out of the workshop and nudged Paul's leg, then she sniffed Buck. "You're looking good, girl," Paul said and headed for the house. "Lily, can you get the door for me?"

She hurried up the steps and swung the door wide. "What else can I do?"

Paul stumbled onto the porch and into the kitchen where he set Buck on the table. "I'll need more light. Bring in a couple of lanterns." He stripped off his bloodied coat while he rushed into his room to grab his medical bag. He dropped the coat over the back of a chair.

By the time he returned, Lily had two lanterns on the table. She struck a match and lit them.

"Thanks. Can you heat some water?"

"Sure." Lily filled a pot with water and set it on the stove, then she put paper and kindling in the stove and lit a fire.

Paul turned his attention to Buck, examining his injuries.

The damage was extensive. The most humane thing to do would be to put him down. Paul stroked the dog's head, considering what he ought to do. He remembered all the promises he'd made to Buck while carrying him home. He had to at least try to save his life.

"Okay. Here we go. I'll do my best." Buck made no sound, no twitch of an ear or an eye. It seemed as if he were already dead. Paul wondered if any of the head injuries had stolen the dog's mind.

He worked on the gaping wound in Buck's side first. After clipping away the hair, he washed out the gash with warm water and soap. He examined internal organs and didn't find any evidence of tears or severe bruising. Infection could still set in. He did a final cleanse with Listerine, then sewed him up.

All the while, Lily stood at his side, making sure he had everything he needed. With the warmth of the stove adding to the heat of the day, the room was sweltering. Using a washcloth, Lily mopped perspiration from Paul's forehead to keep sweat out of his eyes.

Patrick showed up just as Paul finished working on Buck's abdomen. He stepped inside and quietly closed the door. "Sassa told me what happened. Sorry to hear about Jackpot. It looks like Buck's in a bad way too."

"He got the worst of it," Paul said, his hands continuing to probe the dog for further injuries. "He's never done anything halfway."

Paul found a deep puncture. There was little to do except to swab it out. He clipped away hair from a slash on the dog's neck. If the bear had hit an artery, Buck would have bled out on the spot.

Patrick stood across the table from Paul. "Anything I can do?"

"Maybe you can keep the rags cleaned. And I'll need more. Can you find a few?"

"Sure. I'll be right back. Sassa probably has a pile of them."

Paul heard the door open and close. A few minutes later, Patrick returned with a bundle of clean cloths. Paul continued to work, clipping, cleaning, and suturing. With all the lacerations tended to, he turned his attention to Buck's hind leg. It wasn't broken but was dislocated.

"Looks like the bear got ahold of that leg and pulled," Patrick said.

"Yep." Paul manipulated the limb back into place. He listened to Buck's heart and breathing. Both were weak. There wasn't anything more Paul could do.

He looked up at Lily. "Thanks for your help."

"Glad I was here." She cleared away bloody swabs. "I'll wash these for you," she said, heading for the door.

Paul picked up his instruments and set them in the sink. Using a wet rag, he wiped up the blood on the table, then listened to Buck's heart again—it was steady.

"Thank God you found him," Patrick said.

"Yeah." Paul gazed at his dog. "It's amazing he's still alive." He draped a blanket over him. "He lost a lot of blood, and there could be massive infection. He was torn open pretty badly."

Paul made sure he sounded matter of fact, but his insides were raw and he was terrified that he'd lose his best friend. What would he do without Buck?

He felt the pressure of Patrick's hand on his shoulder. "That dog's got heart. He'll pull through."

Paul nodded, unable to speak.

He'd done everything he could. But the truth was that even if Buck made it this time, one day he would die. Everything died eventually.

With Buck at his side, Paul stepped out of the cabin and held the door open for his canine friend. Buck limped out. Paul had kept the dog indoors while his wounds mended. Most days, Buck seemed content to remain at his side, and Paul was grateful for his company. There had been days of waiting and praying when he'd feared he'd lose him. But the big malamute had struggled back, unwilling to give up his life.

Paul walked more slowly than usual so Buck could keep up. The dog was the determined sort and might hurt himself if Paul got in too big a hurry. Glancing at his owner now and then, he managed to match Paul's pace.

"Good boy," Paul said, resting a hand on the dog's head.

Buck answered with a wag of his tail.

Nita and Jackpot strained on their leads and barked at them. "I know, you want to run."

Paul put Buck in the shed, then returned to the dogs and let them off their leads. While they bounded around him, he picked up a stick and tossed it. They chased after it, Nita coming up with the prize and trotting back to Paul with the treasure.

They needed time off their leads, but Paul couldn't keep himself from worrying that they'd have another encounter with the bear or some other animal, like a wolverine or ill-tempered moose. The wilderness was alive with danger.

Jackpot had healed nicely and didn't seem the least bit encumbered by his injuries. Paul took the stick from Nita and tossed it again. This time Jackpot was the first one to grab the stick, and then took off with Nita chasing him. When they dashed down the trail, Paul forced himself not to call them back. They needed freedom to run. It wouldn't be fair to restrain them because of his fears. He watched them go.

"Make sure to come back," he said under his breath.

He sauntered toward the shed, where Buck greeted him at the door and tried to push past. "I know you want to go, but you're not ready yet." He knelt and pulled the dog into his arms, pushing his fingers through his thick coat, careful not to press too hard. "You'll have to stay close to home for a while." He stood and stroked the dog's head, then moved inside the shed and closed the door.

Paul took several leghold traps down from the wall and set them on the workbench. He examined and wire brushed each one. They were in good shape with only a few needing minor repairs. He set those aside.

As always, his thoughts turned to Kate. It had been several weeks since he'd seen her. Ever since their breakup, Jack had lined up flights for him with other pilots. But Paul knew eventually he and Kate would have to fly together again. He wasn't sure how he'd manage to work with her and keep a casual relationship. No matter what, it would be awkward. But worse than that would be sharing their lives again, only it would be impersonal. How would he pull that off?

Each day without her felt as if it were filled with barbs. Her face, her laughter and spirit haunted him. He'd hoped as the days passed that life without her would become more manageable, but her absence only taunted him. He'd begun to think that this wasn't any better than if she had died. Maybe he'd been a fool to end the relationship.

When he'd finished scrubbing the traps, he dipped them in a bucket of creek water to remove any remnants of his scent.

Using a stick, he fished them out of the pail and set them in a box, then turned to the ones needing repair.

A low growl emanated from deep within Buck's chest. Paul glanced at him, then went back to work. The dog pushed to his feet and, staring at the door, he growled again, his hair bristling.

"What is it, boy?" Paul figured one of the Warrens had come by for a visit. "Is that the way we greet guests?" He walked to the door and opened it. Buck pushed up alongside him, but Paul blocked him from getting out. He didn't want the dog's enthusiasm for visitors to override the restraints of his injuries. No running yet.

"Stay back," he said. Buck's hackles were raised as he stared past Paul's legs. Paul went to step outside and then he spotted a grizzly with a shimmering deep brown coat nosing around the porch. Alarm pulsated through him. It was likely the same bear that had nearly killed the dogs and torn up Klaus's place.

Keeping a hand on Buck, Paul watched while the bear investigated the house. He seemed unaware of Paul's presence. Then, unable to hold back any longer, Buck let out a deep-throated woof, followed by all-out barking.

The bear swung its enormous head around and looked straight at Paul and Buck. With his mouth lax enough to show off savage teeth, he blew air from his nostrils. Small black eyes bore into Paul. The grizzly moved down the steps, his hulking weight bowing a weak board. He ought to run off. Instead he lumbered toward the shed.

Paul closed the door and latched it. He didn't have his rifle. He'd left it in the house. When would he learn? In this territory a man dared not be careless. His rifle should go everywhere he went.

Buck continued to bark. "Buck. No. Quiet." The dog stopped, but he stared at the door, agitation making him quiver. Paul wondered if he was remembering his encounter with the bear.

The shop was sturdy, so Paul had little fear that the bear

would break in. But he didn't like being trapped inside defenseless and unable to get to the house. He sat on a stool beside the workbench and listened. Most likely the grizzly would explore and then move along. Paul always made sure not to leave any kind of food out, so there wouldn't be anything to hold the animal's attention.

He could hear him snuffling at the door and then clawing at what he guessed were the legs of the cache. The bear had smelled the food inside. He hoped he'd built the smokehouse sturdy enough—otherwise he'd lose his fish.

All of a sudden Paul remembered Nita and Jackpot. They could be back anytime. He needed his rifle.

Buck lay at his feet, his eyes riveted in the direction of the bear's noises. Again there was snuffling outside the door. *Please go. Just go. There's nothing here for you.*

The sound of a plane filled Paul with dread. Today was mail day. The Warrens had gone into Anchorage. They wouldn't meet the plane and he had an order due. He hoped Kate wasn't flying Jack's pontoon plane. If she landed on the creek, she could walk straight into an unpredictable grizzly.

Kate circled the creek. She didn't see Paul anywhere or the Warrens. She reached out to pet Angel, then remembered the dog wasn't with her. She'd been sick during the night, so Kate had left her at home. She missed her companion, especially today. Life seemed dismal. She'd been certain Amelia Earhart would succeed at her attempt to circle the earth. When she'd disappeared, Kate had high hopes of her being found.

Now there were rumors that the search for the pilot would be called off. It hadn't even been two weeks since her disappearance. How could searchers give up so quickly? Amelia had seemed invincible. *I guess none of us are.* Her own vulnerability engulfed her and she forced her thoughts back to work—a delivery for Paul. These days every time she stopped at Bear Creek it felt as if salt were being rubbed into an open wound. It had been her favorite stop, but now she dreaded it,

137

fearing she'd see Paul and then feeling his rebuff anew every time he refused to meet the plane.

As she passed over his place, a familiar ache tightened in her chest. She knew he wouldn't be at the dock. What little news she got about him came from one of the other pilots. Surprisingly, the fellas had seemed to understand that she needed time to adjust to the breakup. If only she would.

Mike had been his usual friendly self and hadn't pushed her for a renewal of their relationship. She was grateful for that. She never wanted to care about anyone that way again. She doubted she'd ever get married. Her line of work made it too complicated. Being a wife and a pilot just couldn't be done.

She made her approach but didn't like the feel of the plane. The float plane just didn't handle as well as her Bellanca. Still, she set down on the creek without mishap. She didn't see anyone around. Usually Sassa or Patrick met her. And some days Lily or the boys would come to the dock. Today their place looked deserted. Apprehension pricked her, but she dismissed the feeling. Today was as good a day as any to get over her jitters at delivering mail to Paul. She couldn't avoid him forever, and she didn't have anything for the Warrens anyway, but she did have a letter for Paul.

Kate glanced at the letter. The return address was San Francisco, California. Whoever sent it shared Paul's last name. It was probably one of his brothers. She wondered why Paul never saw any of his family, then shut off the thought. His business wasn't her business any longer.

She motored to Paul's dock and shut down the engine. After tying off the plane, she headed up the trail toward the house. It wasn't more than a couple hundred yards, but today it felt like a journey as she thought over what she'd say when she saw him.

She brushed aside hairy stems of straggly plants, and then she looked up the path. Her eyes landed on a grizzly, and fear vibrated through her. He was at the top of the trail and lumbering toward her. He didn't seem in a hurry. Maybe he wasn't even aware of her. Gulping down panic, Kate grappled at what she'd been taught about bear encounters, and although her first inclination was to run, she commanded herself to remain still.

His eyes found her and he stood on his hind legs as if to get a better look.

He's probably just curious. Kate stood her ground, but he moved toward her. She waved her hands above her head and shouted, "Go away, bear! Go away!"

The grizzly stopped and sniffed the air. Again, he stood and stared at her.

Kate's heart throttled inside her chest. What should she do? "Go away, bear!" she shouted.

The animal didn't move.

Was this the one that had hurt the dogs and raided Klaus's place? If he was, he could be trouble. She took a step back and glanced over her shoulder, gauging the distance to the plane. It wasn't far, maybe twenty feet. Still, could she make it back if the bear came at her? She took another step backward. He dropped to his feet, still acting more curious than aggressive.

She took two more steps and the bear moved toward her. Her mouth dry, Kate wondered if she ought to call for Paul. Where was he? She needed him. Her heart seemed to ricochet between her ribs, and her hands trembled. What did it feel like to be killed by a bear?

The air splintered with the blast from a rifle and the shock of it reverberated through Kate. Instead of scaring the grizzly off, it only seemed to enrage him. He charged toward Kate. She knew she couldn't outrun him, but she sprinted for the plane anyway. He'd be on her at any moment. She didn't dare look back.

Another shot fractured the air, but Kate didn't slow down. She pumped her arms and legs as hard and fast as she could. When she reached the dock, she sprinted across it and scrambled inside the plane. Yanking the door closed, she moved to a window and looked to see where the bear was. He was storming into the forest.

Barely able to catch her breath, her heart beating hard against her ribs, Kate leaned against the rim of the window and gazed up the trail. Paul cautiously walked toward the place she'd last seen the grizzly and disappeared into a grove of aspen only a few yards up from the creek. Kate climbed out of the plane, straining to see him. "Please, Paul, be careful."

He reappeared a few moments later and walked toward her. "He hightailed it, but he's wounded."

Kate's legs suddenly felt weak. She started to shake and wasn't sure she could stand. She sat down on the dock, the shock of what had happened breaking over her like a rogue wave.

Paul knelt in front of her. "Take slow, deep breaths."

She did the best she could, but with each lungful she shuddered. Then tears came and she couldn't stop them.

Paul pulled her into his arms and held her against him. "It's all right. He's gone. He won't hurt you."

Kate clung to him. "I've never been so scared. If you hadn't been here . . ." She couldn't finish the sentence.

"But I *was* here." He caressed her back. "Can you stand?"

"Yeah. I'm okay now." Her voice quaked.

Paul kept his arms on hers and helped her to her feet. Kate wished he was still holding her. For a moment the energy between them felt the way it once had. She looked into his brown eyes and longed for those days.

"He had me scared there for a minute." Paul glanced at the forest. "I thought I was going to lose you."

You already have. "Where were you?"

"In the shed. He came prowling around, but I didn't have my rifle. If I had, I would have downed him before he ever got close to you."

"Well, he's gone now."

"I've got to go after him. He's wounded. Either he'll lie down somewhere and suffer until he dies or he'll take his rage out on someone else."

"What if he's waiting for you? Or comes after you?"

"I doubt he'll do anything like that. I'll be fine. And I don't have a choice. Someone has to kill him. And I'm the one who wounded him, so it's up to me."

Kate knew he was right, but she wished he weren't. "Please. Be careful."

— 13 —

*P*aul knows what he's doing, Kate told herself as she lifted into the air. She glanced down at his cabin. It looked cozy and safe tucked in among the trees—a deceiving picture. The world held no true sanctuaries.

Fresh terror flashed through her as images of the bear charging at her pitched through her mind. She'd nearly been killed.

She circled the area once more, hoping to catch a glimpse of Paul. There was no sign of him. She felt uneasy about him going after that grizzly by himself. She wished he'd waited for Patrick. What if something went wrong? Clearly it was a dangerous bear and now that it was wounded . . . Kate dragged in her worry and prayed, *Lord, protect Paul. Help him find that bear and kill it. And then bring him home safely.*

With Paul in her thoughts, she headed up the river. Although they weren't a couple any longer, Kate couldn't imagine the world without him in it.

At Susitna Station, Charlie Agnak, the store proprietor, was in his usual spot. The back of his chair rested against the front of the mercantile and his feet were propped on a stump. Kate hauled a mailbag out of the plane and walked up steps cut into the side of the riverbank.

Charlie smiled at her and waved. She noticed he was

missing another tooth. Most people in the bush rarely fixed teeth—they pulled them.

"How you doing?" he asked.

"I'm good. You?"

"Can't complain." He nodded for emphasis.

Kate swatted at a mosquito. "I could live without these hungry bugs."

He grinned. "Out here you take the good with the bad." Charlie dropped his feet to the ground and stood. "By mid-August they quiet down some."

"That's another month," Kate said, unable to keep the whine out of her voice.

"Yep." Charlie grinned. He didn't straighten his spine but remained slightly hunched over. "What you got for me?"

Kate handed him the mailbag. His store was the drop-off spot for the local residents. "I've got a couple of packages too." She headed back to the plane. Reaching inside, she hefted a large parcel and lugged it up the steps, then went back for another one. "You order supplies?"

"Sure did. The women around here like to bake. Ran me out of flour, sugar, and spices." He grinned. "Can't say I mind. They usually share with me."

"Do you have a sweet tooth, Charlie?"

"I do," he said with a nod. "A'course pretty soon I won't have no teeth." He broadened his smile to show off his new gap in front and laughed.

Kate shook her head. "I hope you don't lose them all."

"Ah, who cares."

Kate grinned, remembering the one she'd had pulled. She intended to keep the rest of her teeth. "Sorry to be late."

"I don't watch no clock." Charlie set the mailbag down by the door and took the package. "So, why you late?"

"I had a run-in with a bear when I stopped at Paul Anderson's."

Charlie's dark eyes glinted with interest. "Grizzly?"

Kate nodded.

"What happened?"

"From what Paul said, he'd been sniffing around his place when I landed. My plane should have scared him off, but when I headed up the trail to Paul's cabin the bear came at me. For a minute I thought I was going to be bear food."

Charlie chuckled. "You're here, so figure Paul got him?"

"Yes and no. He wounded him, but the bear ran off."

"That's not good. Wounded bear's a mean bear."

"Paul went after him."

Charlie pushed black hair out of his eyes. "He better be careful of that critter. Grizzlies can be real smart. Sometimes they come back around on a man."

Fear shot through Kate. "Do you think he's in real danger?"

Charlie grinned. "When a man's hunting a grizzly, they're always in danger, but I figure Paul will do just fine. And he'll have a new bear rug." He chuckled.

Kate didn't want to talk about it anymore. "Well, I gotta go. I still have a couple of stops to make."

"Okay. See ya." Charlie headed inside with the packages.

Once back in the air, Kate couldn't keep her mind off Charlie's words. What if the bear circled around on Paul and came after him? *He'll be careful. He knows what a bear can do.* Kate's reassuring thoughts did nothing to comfort her. Even some of the best hunters had been killed by grizzlies. She wondered how long Paul would be out. Maybe he'd already killed the bear. She agonized over not knowing.

By the time Kate made her final delivery, she'd decided to stop at Paul's to see if he'd made it back safely. They may not be a couple any longer, but she still cared about him and wouldn't rest until she was assured he was all right. She reasoned that the bear probably hadn't gone far, and Paul would be back at the cabin. She had to check.

She turned the plane south and headed for Bear Creek, then put in a call to Jack at the airstrip in Anchorage. She prepared herself for an onslaught of taunting. He wouldn't be happy.

The radio crackled to life. "Anchorage airport, this is Pacemaker 221. Over."

"Pacemaker 221, this is Anchorage. Go ahead. Over."

"Jack, I'm going to be delayed. Putting down at Bear Creek. Over."

"Unable to copy. Say again. Over."

"Pacemaker 221 is delayed. Over."

"Where the heck are you? Over."

"Bear Creek. Over."

"Copy that, 221." A snicker carried over the airwaves. "When will you return? Over."

"Late tonight or tomorrow morning. Over." Kate knew she'd get teased when she got back.

"Copy. Over."

"Pacemaker 221, over and out."

When Kate motored to Paul's dock, she hoped to see him appear on the trail with a wave and a big smile, but there was no sign of him.

She tied off the plane, and with memories of her close call taunting her, she headed toward the cabin. No matter how hard she tried to hold them back, images of her last visit assailed her. Fear clenched her insides, and she kept looking at the bushes along the trail, half expecting to see the bear emerge. She managed not to run, but did hurry her steps.

A breeze kicked up and swept through the underbrush. Kate stopped and stared into the forest. Was the bear out there? If he was, then where was Paul? Deciding she was being foolish, Kate walked toward the cabin.

"Paul," she called, and waited for a response. The wind and creaking of tree limbs were the only answer.

If only Angel were with her. Paul's dogs started barking and Kate called to them. When she stepped into the clearing, Nita and Jackpot were on their leads, Buck woofed from inside the house. The dogs' hackles lay down and their tails beat the air.

Feeling less alone, Kate gave each dog a pat, then called Paul's name again. Still nothing. She checked in the shed, then the garden and the smokehouse. He wasn't anywhere. Maybe he was in the house. Kate walked up the steps and knocked on the door. No answer, except Buck's whining.

She opened the door and was heartily greeted by the big dog. "Hi, boy." She patted him gently and called out, "Paul, you here?" She hoped he'd appear from the bedroom, but he didn't. She looked down at Buck. "Where is he, boy?" She knelt in front of the dog and pulled him into her arms, stroking him. He was thin and his coat uneven with one large patch on his side still mostly bare. Still, considering what he'd been through, he looked pretty good.

Kate stepped inside and closed the door. Maybe she'd fix a meal so it would be waiting when Paul returned. She looked through a shelf with canned goods to see what he had to work with.

A knock sounded at the door, startling Kate. When she opened it she found Patrick looking at her with surprise in his eyes. "What in the world? We heard a plane and when you didn't take off, we figured we ought to see if everything was all right." He looked past her into the house. "Paul around?"

"No. I wish he were. He's off hunting a bear."

Lily pushed in beside her father. "He went after a bear? Today?"

"Yes. About an hour ago. That's why I'm here. I was worried. After I finished my deliveries, I came back to check on him. But he's not here." She opened the door farther. "Come in."

"Why in tarnation did he chase off after a bear?" Patrick stepped inside.

"Today while he was working in the shed a grizzly wandered in from the woods and was rummaging around. Paul figured he'd wait him out, but then I showed up and the bear met me on the trail and came at me. Paul shot him but didn't kill him."

"It must be the same one who worked over the dogs and tore up Klaus's place."

"All I know is he's big and has a foul temper."

"I wish Paul would have waited for me."

Patrick's concern only fed Kate's anxiety.

He must have noticed her increasing apprehension because

he added, "I'm sure he's fine. He's a smart man and he knows his way around the bush." Patrick rested a hand on Kate's shoulder. "But it's wise to have another man with you when you're hunting bear."

He moved to the window. "Figure I'll track him, along with that bear." Kate could see excitement in Patrick's eyes as he headed for the door. "I'll see if I can catch up to him. Better get a move on."

"You think Mama will mind if I stay here with Kate?" Lily asked.

"I doubt it. I'll let her know you're here." Patrick stepped onto the porch and headed down the steps.

Kate stood in the doorway. "What is it about men? They're always chasing after some sort of adventure or other."

Lily raised her brows. "Sounds kind of like you." She grinned.

Kate chuckled. "I guess you're right." She stared after Patrick. "So, what should we do while we wait?"

"The garden needs weeding. Paul's been gone so much he hasn't been able to keep up with it."

"Sounds good to me. I like outdoor work. And I was thinking about making some soup—we could add fresh vegetables to it."

When Kate took a close look at the garden, she was surprised at how badly it had been neglected. It wasn't like Paul. Maybe he'd been away too much. "Looks like there are more weeds than vegetables."

"He doesn't have time." Lily's tone was defensive. "The garden's important. It will feed him this winter." She sounded protective. "My family helps when we can, but we've got our own place to look after. Mama's putting up some canned goods for him."

When Kate had convinced Paul to work as a doctor in the bush, she hadn't considered what that meant for him in practical ways. She felt the swell of guilt at her thoughtlessness. How could he possibly keep up his place while flying all over the territory to care for people's medical needs? "I'm sorry about all the extra work."

"No. I'm just grousing. What he does is important. And I don't mind helping him. He's a fine man and a good neighbor."

Kate felt a twinge of jealousy. Was there something between Lily and Paul? She'd never have thought they'd make a match, but Lily was pretty and working with him would bring them closer.

Disguising her envy, Kate said, "I'm sure he appreciates everything you do."

"We're neighbors. And neighbors help each other."

"Do you see him often?"

"He comes to dinner sometimes. And we go fishing once in a while."

Lily's tone sounded artificially casual. There *was* something between the two of them. Kate was certain of it.

"Good. It's always important to have friends you can count on out here," she said, wishing Lily still lived in Seattle.

Ignoring the sting of bristly spruce needles, Paul pushed a low-hanging branch aside. The grizzly was still moving fast for a wounded animal. Rage might be driving him. He'd left a trail of blood and broken brush. If he kept bleeding, he'd weaken and would be forced to slow his pace.

The bear had followed the creek inland and then crossed to the opposite shore. Paul waded through the shallows, icy water seeping into his boots. His gaze swept across the thick brush on the far side of the stream, but he kept moving, every nerve alert. The grizzly could be anywhere.

When he reached the bank, he stopped to examine deep-set prints left in the damp earth. The hairs on his arms lifted. Studying the shadows, he listened but heard only the chirp of birds and the hum of flying insects.

With the sun dropping low in the sky, he pushed on, fatigue weighing heavily on him. He'd been tracking the bear for hours and needed to stop so he could fix himself something to eat and rest. He wished he'd brought Nita. She'd have kept watch while he slept.

He pushed on, following the bear's trail, while searching for a safe place to rest. He'd have to spend the night. The long summer days had never bothered Paul, and now he was especially thankful for them. He didn't like the idea of darkness concealing his prey, especially if the grizzly had reversed roles and Paul had unknowingly become the prey. He tried to push the thought out of his mind. He knew the dangers, and dwelling on them would not accomplish anything other than get him twitchy.

The bear had stayed close to the creek. Paul kept moving, occasionally glancing over his shoulder, feeling as if something were following him. "You've spooked yourself," he said aloud, as if the sound of his voice would drive away trepidation. The muscles in his legs complained and his feet hurt. He needed to rest.

When he came upon an open area where two trees had fallen across each other, he stopped. The trees created a natural barrier and provided a place where he could take a breather and not be surprised from behind.

He built a fire, filled a tin percolator with water from the creek, and set it in the coals. He opened a can of baked beans and placed them alongside the coffeepot. With the sound of the creek tumbling past, he opened a wool sleeping bag and stretched out on it, leaning against one of the downed trees. He'd been so intent on tracking he'd forgotten to eat. Emptiness gnawed at his middle. He took moose jerky and bread out of his pack. Stripping off a bite of the jerky, he chewed, but remained alert, wondering how much further he'd have to travel to catch up to the grizzly. Of course, the bear could double back, attracted by the smell of food.

His eyes heavy, Paul rested against the downed tree. Mosquitoes buzzed his head and bit his arms through his wool shirt. He swatted at them, but they refused to yield. "Stinkin' bugs."

The coffee boiled over, and using his gloves, he lifted it out of the hot embers and filled a tin cup with the dark brew. He took a sip and then another bite of jerky. The beans would taste good. He scooted them out of the coals and let them cool for a few minutes, then ate them straight from the can.

After finishing off the beans, he downed a slice of bread and another cup of coffee. His hunger satiated, his eyelids drooped. He forced himself awake and added wood to the fire, then moved back to his spot against the tree. The upper branches of alder and birch stirred in the breeze. The limbs of a cottonwood creaked. Soon Paul dropped off to sleep, rifle in hand.

A branch popped and Paul startled awake. How long had he been asleep? It was still light so probably not more than a few minutes. Breathing noiselessly, he listened, certain there was something in the forest shadows. He raised his rifle.

Patrick emerged from the greenery, then dodged to one side with his hands raised in the air. "Hey, it's just me. Put that thing down." He grinned.

"Patrick." Paul lowered the rifle. "What are you doing here?"

"I figured a man shouldn't hunt an angry bear all by himself." He sat across from Paul. "I was beginning to think I'd never catch you. Then I caught a whiff of coffee and knew I was close."

"How'd you know about the bear?"

"Kate told me what happened." He hunkered down next to the fire and leaned over the coffeepot, breathing in the aroma. "You mind if I have some of that coffee?"

"Help yourself. The last time I saw Kate she was headed for Susitna Station."

"She came back. Said she needed to know you were all right. She's waiting for you."

"She is?"

"Yep." Patrick dug out a cup from his pack. He filled it and stood to drink, gazing around. "That bear sure came a long ways."

"Yeah. He did." Paul's mind was still on Kate. He wasn't sure how he felt about her waiting for him at the cabin. He knew she still had feelings for him. She needed to stop caring so much. And so did he.

Patrick stood and pulled off his rucksack. "Sassa packed me some food. You hungry?"

"No. I'm good. Thanks."

"You sure? There's three sandwiches and some cookies."

Paul laughed. "Guess I could make room for a cookie."

All of a sudden an explosion of brown fur, teeth, and saliva barreled at Paul. His heart thrummed into his throat as he reached for his rifle.

Before he could fire, the air thundered. The bear dropped and the earth shuddered. The grizzly lay less than a yard from Paul.

Standing on weak legs, he stared at the animal. Quaking, he took a step back, never taking his eyes off the bear. His mind replayed his race from the shed to the house, terrified he'd be too late. What if he didn't make it in time? What if the bear got Kate? He could still smell the terror he'd felt as he aimed the rifle, took a breath, and fought to hold his shaking body still. He couldn't miss. Kate's life depended on him getting it right, just as Susan's had. This time he succeeded, but he'd failed Susan and their son. The question why resurfaced once more, just as it had a hundred times before.

"Good thing I had my gun in hand," Patrick said with a chuckle. "He nearly got ya."

Paul let his gaze move to Patrick. "If you hadn't been here . . ."

Patrick moved to Paul and slapped him on the back. "Yeah, well, I was. Figure God had it all worked out."

"Thanks for saving my life."

"Anytime." Patrick grinned.

Still shaken, Paul moved back to the fire and sat down. He looked up at his friend. "That's the closest I've ever come to dying."

"Nearly dying is good for a man—puts things into perspective." Patrick studied the bear. "Looks like a young male, in good condition. It's those youngsters you've got to watch out for." He pulled a knife out of his belt. "Better get to skinning. There's a lot of good meat here and you'll have a fine rug."

"It's yours. You're the one who shot him."

"Nah. Don't really like bear meat, and I've got a few rugs already, don't need any more." Patrick raised an eyebrow. "Figure we better get to it. There's someone waiting for you at the cabin."

"Oh yeah . . . Kate. She shouldn't have done that."

"She loves you, what did you expect her to do?"

"We're not together anymore."

"Love isn't something you can just turn off and on whenever you like."

"I know that, but it still doesn't change things." Paul pushed to his feet.

Patrick shook his head. "You're wrong about this. Not allowing yourself to love Kate won't bring your wife and child back."

Paul knew. "I'm not taking a chance on losing anyone else."

"You think living alone is better than loving and taking a risk?" His eyes bore into Paul's. "You're not dead inside, Paul. You were meant to share life with someone."

Paul stared at the hulk of brown fur. Patrick was wrong. He was dead inside, as dead as that bear. He didn't have anything to give, especially not to someone like Kate.

— 14 —

It was midmorning and Paul and Patrick still hadn't shown up. Kate sat on the top step of his porch, elbows propped on her thighs. She rested her face in her hands and watched the trail. *They should be back by now.*

Jasper squawked at her from a nearby tree. She'd tried to persuade him to fly to his perch, but couldn't convince him to trust her even when she offered him bits of bread. He'd kept his distance—like Paul had.

"Come on, Jasper. I won't hurt you." She whistled, but he held to his resolve. With a resigned sigh, she looked about and wondered what else she could do to pass the time. She'd finished most of the weeding, tidied up the house, and baked bread. She couldn't think of anything else to do.

Believing that a wounded bear couldn't travel far, she'd expected Paul back the previous evening. Buck limped from inside the house and plunked down beside her. She stroked his head. "How you doing, boy?"

He whined and leaned against her leg. He was worried too.

What if something terrible had happened? What if Paul and Patrick didn't come back? What if . . . ? She shut off the thoughts. Worrying accomplished nothing. But no matter how sensible she tried to be, she still had to fight the impulse to search for them. It was a foolish idea. She'd be of no help and would probably get herself lost. If they didn't show up by early evening, she'd call in a search team. She wondered if Sassa and Lily were worried. They hadn't been by since the previous night.

Kate could feel Lily's presence here. From what she'd said, it sounded like she had become part of Paul's life. Was she? She didn't seem like the kind of woman he'd be interested in. Jealousy ate at her.

Staring at Nita and Jackpot, Kate took in a sorrowful breath, and then slowly let it out. If only things were the way they used to be.

Nita and Jackpot both stood and stared down the trail. Nita whined. Buck pushed to his feet, his tail wagging. Anticipation buzzed through Kate. It must be them. She moved to the bottom step, her eyes on the trail.

A few moments later she spotted Paul. He pulled a litter with a brown pelt laid over a mound that Kate guessed must be bear meat. Patrick walked beside him. Relief swept over her like a cool breeze on a hot summer day.

"Paul," she said, her voice barely more than a whisper. Clearing her throat and putting on what she hoped was a casual smile, she said more loudly, "Hi. It's about time you showed up."

Paul gave her a nod. "Patrick told me you were here. Surprised you waited so long."

Kate's enthusiasm wilted. He didn't want her here.

When he reached the shed, he set down the litter.

Patrick sat on a stump and swept off his hat. Using his shirtsleeve, he wiped sweat off his forehead. "Getting too old for this kind of thing."

Kate walked to the litter, wondering what a bear fur felt like. "It's good to have you back. I was beginning to worry." She longed to embrace Paul, but he gave no inclination that he'd welcome such a greeting.

His arms at his sides, he turned and faced her. "We're fine. But it's a good thing Patrick came after me." He glanced at his friend.

154

Patrick slapped his hat back on his head. "That bear gave us a time of it." He grinned. "But we had the final word."

Paul lifted the hide, and the rank smell of warm meat and blood assaulted Kate's nose. Looking worn out, he hauled the hide off. "I've got my first bear rug to hang on the wall."

Patrick stood. "I better get home. Sassa'll have my hide if I lollygag. I'll give you a hand with that tomorrow."

"Thanks. See you."

Patrick headed toward home, his long stride slower than usual.

"You hungry?" Kate asked.

"Starved."

"I made some soup and bread."

"Sounds good. But I've got to get this hide stretched, and then I'll be in." Paul disappeared inside the shed.

"Can I help?"

"Nah. It won't take me long."

Kate returned to her post on the porch step. He didn't want to spend time with her. She knew she should head back to Anchorage. Yet she stayed.

When Paul finally appeared his eyes went to the dogs. "Better get this meat put away too."

"I'll give you a hand." Kate moved toward the litter, the idea of handling the bloody flesh repulsive.

"I've got it." Paul sounded weary.

"Okay. I'll go in and check on the soup and get some fresh coffee percolating."

It seemed like a long time before Paul opened the door. He held it opened just enough to peer inside. "Can you turn around? I had to wash up outside and left most of my clothes out here."

Her cheeks burning, Kate turned her back to him. She heard the door close followed by the sound of him hurrying across the room. Buck had been lying beside Kate. He stood and hobbled into the bedroom.

A few minutes later, Paul emerged. Without even looking

at Kate, he gave Buck a rubdown. "We don't have to worry about that old bear anymore."

He glanced up at Kate. "The soup smells good. Hope it's ready. I'm starving."

Heavyhearted, Kate set down on Lake Spenard. She was thankful Paul was safe, but the loving reunion she'd hoped for hadn't materialized. They'd shared a meal and meager conversation. Paul told her about the hunt and Patrick's quick reactions that saved him. Other than that, they didn't seem to have much to talk about. Conversation was stilted and they parried around sensitive issues.

Kate needed a long chat over coffee with Muriel, but wondered if she'd mind her just dropping in. The baby was due any day, and the last time Kate had seen her she'd been exhausted and uncomfortable. She decided Muriel might enjoy the company.

As Kate headed for the shop, she noticed Alan had his engine hood up. He looked at her, but didn't wave. He seemed like a nice enough man but only knew how to communicate with his plane, not people.

Kate smiled and waved. "How's it going, Alan?"

"Fine," he said and went back to work—a one-word answer as usual.

It pained Kate to watch him struggle with relationships. He said very little and kept to himself mostly. The only one who seemed able to break through his protective shield was Mike. But then, Mike had a way about him. Most everyone liked him.

When she stepped into the shop, Jack was the only one there. He sat at his desk, working on forms. He glanced up. "About time."

"I got here as soon as I could."

"Right." He returned to his work.

Since taking over the business he'd become surlier than ever. He didn't like being earthbound. His responsibilities meant he had time only for a few short runs.

"Everyone out . . . except for Alan?"

"Yeah. His plane's giving him trouble." He stopped and looked at her. "I could have used you today. Had a run to Kenai. You cost me good money."

Kate clenched her teeth, holding back a retort. Fighting with Jack only made her life miserable. As calmly as she could manage, she said, "I waited to make sure Paul was all right. He didn't make it back until today. If he'd needed—"

"Yeah. Yeah. Yeah." Jack shook his head. "Say what you want. We both know you're still mooning over him. Don't you get it? He's not interested."

Kate clamped down her fury. "He went out after a bad bear. Which, I might add, nearly killed me yesterday. I waited until I knew there was no need to fly him or his neighbor Patrick out."

Jack's brows furrowed. "What happened with you and the bear?"

"When I tried to deliver mail, it came at me. Paul shot him, but only wounded him. He had to go after him and finish him off."

"How honorable." He snickered.

Kate decided to ignore the comment. She walked to the chart on the wall and recorded her return time and date. "Do you have any runs coming up?"

"Nope. Lost the one and nothing since."

"Guess I'll head home. I'm available if anything comes in."

"If Alan gets his plane running, he's the next one up."

"Sure. I understand." The phone rang as Kate headed for the door.

Jack picked up. "Hello." He listened, then dropped the receiver back in place. "That was Mrs. Towns. She said her daughter's at the hospital."

"The hospital? She's having the baby?"

"That would be my guess."

"I gotta go." Kate headed out the door and hurried to her car. She slid in behind the wheel, revved the engine, and headed for Third Avenue. She'd promised Helen and Muriel she'd be there when the baby was born. She wanted to be there.

Splashing through puddles, Kate approached the four-story Railroad Hospital. She pulled into a parking area and stepped carefully through a muddy drive. Hurrying up a wooden walkway that cut a path through the middle of a flower-strewn lawn, she tried to quiet her worries. Things could go wrong when having a baby.

Kate took the front steps two at a time, swung open the front door, and walked into a small lobby. She stopped at the front desk to ask directions, and then headed for the waiting room.

Helen sat, appearing calm, her knitting needles clicking. She looked up. "Oh, Kate. I'm so glad you're here."

Albert and Terrence stopped pacing momentarily.

"Hi," Albert said.

Terrence nodded and tried to smile. He resumed pacing.

"Is Muriel all right?" Kate asked.

"The doctor says she's fine." Helen rested her hand on the chair next to her. "Come. Sit. It's going to be awhile."

"How long do you think before the baby gets here?"

"Too long," Albert said with a chuckle. "Babies always take too long."

A smile lifted Helen's lips. "Babies arrive exactly on time." She settled calm blue eyes on Kate. "And don't worry about Angel. Our neighbor offered to check on her."

Kate nodded and sat down. She hadn't even given Angel a thought.

Terrence pushed fingers through his light brown hair and adjusted his wire-rimmed glasses. "I wish we'd hear something." He glanced at a door leading from the room. "Something."

The tension in the room made Kate feel edgy. She folded her arms over her chest, sucked in a breath, and let it out slowly. She stretched her arms over her head and then rolled her shoulders back. Helen seemed completely relaxed. Kate wished she knew how to knit. Maybe it would help.

It was an interminable five hours before Muriel presented Terrence with a son.

When a nurse finally allowed family into Muriel's room, Kate hung back while Terrence met his child. Helen and Albert went in next. He glanced at Kate. "You coming?"

"I'll wait. This is for family."

She leaned against the corridor wall, studying pallid green walls. So, Muriel was a mother. It was a wonderful thing. Really. So why did she feel so melancholy? She *was* happy for Muriel and Terrence, but thoughts about life without Paul—and the family they could have had together—made the contrast all the more painful. She wanted it to be her. What if it never was?

With effort, she tried to shake off the dark thoughts. Staying on that path would do her no good.

The door opened and Helen peeked into the hallway. Her face radiated joy. "He's beautiful!" She motioned for Kate to join her. "Muriel wants to see you."

Putting on what she thought was an appropriate smile, Kate walked into a room with several beds. Cotton curtains provided privacy for other new mothers. Propped up on pillows, Muriel rested in a bed near a window. Terrence hovered beside her, gazing down at his little boy. Muriel held a swaddled bundle in her arms.

She looked up at Kate. "I can hardly believe he's here."

Muriel's blonde hair was plastered to her head and her face was splotchy red, but the joy in her eyes made her look beautiful. Hunger for a child of her own engulfed Kate.

"How are you?" she managed to ask without revealing her inner feelings.

"Tired. But I've never felt better or happier. The doctor says he's perfect." She looked down at the infant. "I'd like you to meet Gerald Kenneth Stevens."

Kate stared at the baby. His eyes were closed and he had a pudgy fist pressed against his lips. "He's so cute." Happiness for Muriel flowed in like a tide, covering Kate's emptiness.

"Would you like to hold him?"

"May I?" Kate allowed Muriel to lay Gerald in her arms. Gently she cuddled him, feeling slightly clumsy. She pressed her cheek against his and breathed in the fragrant scent of newness. Her heart constricted. Looking at Muriel, she said, "How amazing—you're a mother."

"I can hardly believe it." Muriel looked up at Terrence and took his hand. "We're a mom and dad now."

"Was it terrible, the birth I mean?"

"At first, but then they gave me something and I barely remember his being born."

"Can I hold my grandson?" Helen asked, moving in beside Kate.

Kate placed the baby in Helen's arms.

Helen kissed his forehead. "Oh, you're so handsome," she said and moved to a chair, cradling Gerald against her.

Kate turned to Muriel. "He is perfect."

With love lighting her face, Muriel gazed at her son.

All of a sudden, Kate knew that being a pilot wasn't enough. She wanted more. She felt submerged by loneliness and longing. "I better go. I've got a flight." She needed to get outdoors and away from the happy family scene before she exposed her heartache.

"Congratulations, Terrence and Grandma and Grandpa." She leaned down and kissed Muriel's forehead. "I'm so happy for you." Kate meant it. She just wished that being a wife and mother was something she could share with Muriel.

Fighting tears, she headed to the airport. It was late, but maybe Jack had a run for her. She'd feel better if she could work. Getting up in the air always cleared her head.

Kate stepped into the shop. Jack hadn't moved. "Hi. Any flights come in?"

"What are you doing here?"

"Muriel had her baby and she's fine, so I figured I'd check to see if you had a run for me. There's plenty of daylight."

"You missed one while you were gone. Alan took it." Jack sounded almost gleeful.

Kate wondered if she ought to stay. She didn't like Jack's

company but going home to an empty room seemed worse. "I think I'll stick around for a while and see if anything comes in. My plane needs cleaning anyway."

"Suit yourself."

Carrying a bucket, Kate wandered out to the Bellanca. Opening the door, she climbed inside and went to work, picking up bits of trash left over from mailbags and items that travelers had left behind. After that, she swept it out with a hand broom.

The sounds of a plane caught her attention and she looked up to see Mike's Fairchild gliding toward the runway. The wheels touched down and the plane took one small hop before Mike taxied into the grass and stopped.

She swept out the last of the dirt and moved onto the steps. Mike climbed out of his plane and waved to her. In his usual relaxed style, he ambled toward her. Just seeing him made Kate feel better.

"How you doing?" he asked, playfully punching her arm. He looked more closely. "Something wrong?"

"No. I'm fine. Muriel had her baby." She tried to sound cheerful.

"She did?" He pushed his fingers through unruly brown hair. "What she have?"

"A boy. They named him Gerald. He's really cute."

"Well, how about that." Mike grinned. "Muriel's a mama."

Jack stepped out of the shop and hollered, "Hey. Mike. Got a run for you."

Mike lifted a hand to Jack, then turned to Kate. "You been waiting?"

"Uh-huh." Kate clenched her teeth. This trip ought to be hers.

She and Mike walked toward the shop. Jack waited outside the door.

"What's up?" Mike asked him.

"A call just came in for a rescue. A couple of climbers got themselves in trouble and need a lift out."

"No problem," Mike said. "But Kate's here and she's been waiting."

"I need a man on this one."

"Why? One of the climbers badly injured?"

"Yeah."

"How bad?"

"I don't know. Pretty bad, I guess."

"Did he make it to a pickup point?"

"I guess." Jack's eyes slid away, but only for a moment.

"Well, if he can make the pickup point, I figure he's doing good enough for a woman pilot to get him home. Doesn't sound like she'd have to carry him." Mike crossed his arms over his chest. "I'm beat. I'd rather not go out again."

"I'm ready," Kate said.

"Fine." Jack thrust a map at Kate. "The coordinates are there. You ought to be able to get close enough to give them a lift."

Kate swallowed her anger and managed to say, "I'm on my way."

Mike walked alongside Kate. "Hey, you mind if I tag along?"

"I thought you were done in."

"Yeah, but this sounds like fun, and I wouldn't mind hanging out with you for a while." He grinned and looked over his shoulder at the shop.

"Okay. I could use the company."

Kate headed her Pacemaker toward Mount McKinley while Mike studied the map. "The hikers are on the south side, low elevation. Shouldn't be too thorny a pickup."

Mike and Kate fell into their usual amiable banter. It was like old times. Kate felt more lighthearted. She didn't know what had come over her at the hospital. Maybe she was worn out. There was more to life than being a mother. Children weren't everything.

On McKinley there were no easy landings, but these hikers were waiting at one of the more accessible locations. Kate had no difficulty getting the plane down. One of the climbers had an arm trussed up, but didn't have any trouble getting around and refused help climbing into the plane.

With the two onboard, Kate took off and headed for the

airfield. A few miles out, the engine sputtered and the plane dipped as it lost power. Mike tinkered with the mix and it evened out for a while, then sputtered again. Kate checked the magnetos and the carburetor.

"We better get this bird down," Mike said.

"We're nearly home. Maybe if I switch the tanks."

"I'll do that. And the choke might need adjusting."

"What's wrong?" one of the men in the back hollered, his voice near hysteria.

"Nothing to worry about. We're fine," Kate called. She focused on the airport in the distance. She could see the wind sock flapping lazily. *Nearly there. Come on. Come on.* She fought her natural response to grip the control wheel too tightly. If she did, she'd lose the feel of the plane.

"You concentrate on getting us on the ground and I'll take care of the mixture," Mike said as the plane backfired.

"What was that?" one of the passengers demanded.

"Just priming the engine," Mike called. He glanced at Kate, then turned his attention back to the controls.

Thankful Mike had decided to join her on this trip, Kate dropped down just above the trees as they approached the field. Barely clearing them, she brought down the plane a little fast. It hopped a couple of times, but she held it steady, and finally they rolled to a stop.

"I thought we were going to die," one of the climbers said.

Kate barely noticed him, her mind on what had just happened. As the men unloaded, she managed to smile and stood at the door.

Mike helped haul the supplies to the office, then they returned to the airfield. "We better have a look at the plane," he said. "Check the gasoline mixture. Maybe we got a bad batch. Don't want any of the other pilots having trouble." In a friendly gesture, he slapped Kate on the back. "By the way, you did a good job getting us down."

"Thanks." She stopped at the plane. "I'm glad you were with me to help."

"We're a good team." Mike's expression turned gentle.

Kate felt an unexpected rush of pleasure. "Yeah. We are."

"How about having dinner—my place." Mike glanced at his watch. "Uh, I mean a late-night snack." He grinned. "Dinner was hours ago."

"I'm starved. What do you have?"

"Some sardines and crackers, a few eggs . . ." He shrugged. "I'll have to look. It's been awhile since I went to the store."

"I don't know. I want to have a look at the plane."

Mike glanced at the darkening sky. "It's late and I'm beat. We can have a look in the morning."

Weariness weighed on Kate. "Okay. I'm tired too." Kate liked the idea of spending time with Mike. He was fun. And she could use some casual time. Life had been too stressful. Mike was the perfect guy to help her loosen up.

— 15 —

Kate drained off a small amount of gasoline into a clear glass and held it up to the light. She studied the liquid. Water. And a lot more than would accumulate from condensation.

"Hey Kate, you find anything?" Mike asked as he approached.

She extended the glass to him. "There's water in the gasoline. It's a wonder we stayed in the air at all."

Mike examined the plane's fuel tank. "Looks sound. You figure you got some bad gas?"

"Most likely." Kate fixed her eyes on Mike. "You don't think Jack would do something—"

"No. Never. He's surly and pompous, and he doesn't like you much." Mike flashed a grin, then quickly sobered. "But he wouldn't purposely hurt someone, especially not a pilot. And even though he's cantankerous as a cornered coon, he admires good pilots, even you."

"Me? Every day I leave here, he'd just as soon I didn't come back."

Mike chuckled. "He just wants you to think that." He rubbed a day's worth of whiskers. "If it was done intentionally, it was probably some kids goofing around. We'd better check all the gasoline in stock and keep it under lock and key. I'll talk to Jack about it."

"No. I'll tell him. It's my plane, my flight." Kate wished they'd found an explanation. She wouldn't relax until they did. "I'll check the fuel supplies. But first I've got to empty and clean my tanks. I need to get back in the air."

"Okay. I'll have a look at my own gasoline and tell the fellas to do the same. See you later." Mike took a step toward the shop, then stopped and looked at Kate. "By the way, I had a good time last night."

"Me too."

"Maybe we can get together again?"

Kate hesitated. Her heart was still tied to Paul, and she wasn't ready to give that up. But being friends with Mike, hanging out together, was something she really wanted. Hopefully he could handle just that. "Sure," she said. "Only next time let me do the cooking. I'm not a great cook, but I can do better than sardines and crackers." She laughed.

"You got it." He strode toward the office.

Kate watched him go, thinking back over the previous evening. Mike had been full of stories and jokes that she'd never remember. And he'd managed to beat her at several hands of rummy. They did have fun, but she wished she'd been with Paul instead. *I've got to stop thinking about him. He's not in my life anymore*, she thought, frustrated with herself.

Kate knew that if she wanted to enjoy what she had, she needed to accept things as they were. And Mike was no slouch. He was good-looking, fun, and crazy about her.

Over the next several weeks, Kate and Mike spent more time together. Although Paul was often in the back of her mind, Kate enjoyed Mike's company and found herself thinking about him more and more.

Kate was scheduled for a flight to Fairbanks, along with Mike, who was picking up a plane and flying it back. She was giving the plane a final inspection when he showed up.

"Hi there," he said. "Kind of late getting started."

"Yeah, guess the farmer had trouble transporting his

stock—car trouble or something. So we'll be chasing the sun all the way north."

The cargo was unusual, but in Alaska pilots hauled all sorts of freight. Today Kate's delivery was a trough, with piglets in it. When she saw what was being shipped, she laughed. A pilot's life was never boring. She hoped the little critters traveled well.

Mike helped Kate load the trough while piglets scurried back and forth, squealing at the top of their little lungs. "Figure by the time we make Fairbanks, the plane will stink to high heavens." He lifted his hat and resettled it on his head. "They're cute."

"And noisy."

While Mike cranked the plane, Kate dropped into her seat and went through a checkoff list.

"All set," Mike called from outside.

Kate lit off the engine and the piglets squealed their fright. She glanced back at them, hoping they'd quiet down. Just the idea of listening to that noise the entire flight gave Kate a headache.

"Hope they simmer down," Mike said, taking the seat beside Kate.

"Me too." She looked back at the cargo. Angel hovered over the trough, her tongue lolling and tail wagging. "Angel, you leave them alone," Kate ordered. "I can't have her eating the shipment." She laughed, but watched until Angel curled up on the floor next to the trough.

When the plane headed down the airstrip and lifted off, the piglets raised a horrible racket.

"This is going to be a long trip," Mike said, sinking deeper into his seat.

Once in the air and on course, the piglets seemed to adjust and settled down. But a stink soon replaced the noise, and Kate thought she might prefer the racket.

"I heard you found a couple of cans with fouled gasoline in them."

"I did." Kate shook her head. ""Finally got through all

the inventory of fuel. I'm going to talk to the supplier the minute we get back. Jack said he'd talk to him, but I figure it couldn't hurt to give him an extra chewing out."

"Yeah, you'd think they'd be more careful. This is the last straw. We'll be finding a new supplier. Jack isn't about to put up with that kind of carelessness." Mike folded his arms over his chest and leaned back in his seat. "A lot better ride today."

The words were barely out of his mouth when the plane hiccupped.

Kate tossed a meaningful glance at him.

"It's nothing."

Kate looked at the forest below and wondered if there was a place to put down if they had to. *You worry too much*, she told herself, and then the Pacemaker cut out again, then sputtered. Power seemed to drain from the engine.

Mike was no longer casually sitting back. "This isn't good." He adjusted the mixture, but the plane continued to run rough. "Brother! What is it this time?" He glanced at her. "You check the fuel before you filled it up?"

"Yes. It was fine."

Mike gazed down at the forest below. "We need to find a place to land."

Kate dropped down over the Susitna, hoping for a sandbar big enough to put down.

"There!" Mike pointed upriver. "That looks good."

Kate headed for the spot. "Radio Jack. Let him know where we are."

Mike grabbed the handset. "Anchorage airport, this is Pacemaker 221. Over."

The radio crackled to life. "Pacemaker 221, this is Anchorage airport. Go ahead. Over."

"Anchorage, we're in trouble. Over."

"Unable to copy. Say again. Over."

"We're having engine trouble. Over." Mike shouted into the radio.

"What's your location? Over."

"We're putting down on the Susitna River. Over."

"I need more than that. Over."

Even with radio buzz, Kate could hear the strain in Jack's voice. He was worried. For a moment she almost liked him.

While the plane bucked, Mike grabbed the map and searched for their location. "Where are we?"

"We just passed Gold Creek."

Mike looked out the window. "Anchorage, Pacemaker 221 is north of Gold Creek. Over."

"Say again. Over."

"North of Gold Creek. On the Susitna. Over."

"Copy that, 221. We'll get someone out to you. Over."

"We'll be here. Over." Mike looked at the horizon. "Not much daylight left."

Kate couldn't worry about the daylight. She had all she could handle just to keep the plane in the air. The trees were close, nearly tickling the plane's underbelly. "I need a few hundred more yards."

Mike primed the engine, and instead of getting any lift, it backfired.

"It's going to be close. Hang on." As the water and trees came at her, Kate's mind flashed to Rimrock Lake. She fought to keep the nose up and feathered the pedals to maintain level. The sandbar seemed out of reach. As she came in, she checked for debris. A log had washed up and lay to the left, she turned the plane right, hoping there'd be enough room to stay clear of the log and the water on the other side. The wheels hit hard and the plane bounced. Pigs squealed as Kate managed to bring the plane in. It slowed and then came to a stop.

"You did it!" Mike whooped and grinned.

"You like this kind of thing, don't you."

"Sometimes." He shrugged. "Makes life interesting."

"I could do with a lot less interesting." She looked around. "It would have been easier if I'd had Jack's pontoon plane."

The engine sputtered and died as Mike headed for the door. "I'll take a look at the engine." He grabbed a toolbox and climbed out.

169

Kate followed with Angel behind her. The dog took off across the small island and sloshed into the shallows.

"See anything?" Kate asked.

"It's almost too dark to see." He rummaged through the toolbox and came up with a flashlight and took another look. "Huh. You've got a loose wire running to the carburetor. Must have shaken loose." He looked more closely. "It actually looks kind of ragged, like it's worn out."

"I should have caught that," Kate said.

"Can't find everything. We'll need to replace the wires before we can take off."

"I've got some extra supplies."

Mike jumped down. "It'll have to wait until morning. We don't have enough daylight to fix it and get off the ground and still make Fairbanks." He sloshed through the shallows. "Better find a place to make camp for the night." Angel appeared from the brush and leaped on Mike. "Hey, girl. You been on an adventure?" He patted her.

"Mike, sometimes you drive me crazy. You act like *this* is an adventure. We nearly crashed and now we're stuck out here."

Mike leaned against a tree and watched Kate splash to shore. "Might as well make the best of it." His easy smile lit up his face.

None of it seemed humorous to Kate. The last time she'd been forced down she'd been stranded with Nena and wondered if they'd survive. It had been October and the nighttime temperatures had been below freezing.

"Won't be too bad," Mike said. "As long as the bugs don't eat us alive."

Kate gazed at the darkening sky, where lacy clouds sifted over a pink background. Mike was right. She needed to lighten up.

He walked down the shoreline. "We'll need a fire. Once the sun sets, it's going to get cold."

While Angel sniffed her way along the edge of the forest, Mike and Kate gathered wood. Mike soon had a fire going. With darkness pressing in, he and Kate hunkered down close to its warmth. Kate was thankful she wasn't alone. She prided herself on being independent, but company was always welcome when stranded in the Alaskan wilderness. "You hungry?"

"Starved. What you got?"

"Not much. I wasn't planning on spending the night out here." She picked up the flashlight, pushed to her feet, and headed for the plane. "I suppose we could have roast pig," she teased.

"Sounds good to me."

Kate climbed inside the plane. She checked the piglets. They seemed content, sleeping in a pile. She dipped water out of the river into a container and set it in their enclosure, then scattered grain for them. They immediately came awake and snuffled up the meal. Kate grabbed a couple of blankets and her pack and headed toward the fire.

Mike met her. "What, no little pig for the spit?" He chuckled. "Here, let me give you a hand."

Kate handed him the blankets. "They're too cute to eat. I'd hate to be stuck here long enough to actually have to do that."

"Don't worry. We'll be on our way in the morning."

The two sat down close to the fire, and Kate took crackers and a can of sardines out of her pack. "Sorry. I promised not to serve you sardines, but it's the best I can do tonight."

"I like sardines." Mike fished a tool knife out of his pocket and cut open the lid. He took out a small salty fish and handed the can back to Kate. She held out another can. "And this one?"

He looked at the label. "What, dog food in a can?" He shook his head and opened Angel's dinner. "You're one spoiled dog," he said, shaking the contents onto the ground in front of Angel.

Kate took crackers out of a tin and placed a sardine between two of them. She took a bite and handed the tin to Mike. "Not bad." She heard something splash in the river and looked into the darkness to see what it was.

"Probably just a fish." Mike leaned back and ate another

sardine along with a cracker. He munched on the small meal. "Got anything else?"

"I made some ginger cookies." She grabbed a stack of them wrapped in waxed paper, opened them, and handed a couple to Mike.

He stuffed one into his mouth, then smiled with his cheeks bulging. "Delicious. Don't ever tell me you can't cook," he said around the mouthful.

"I try." Kate felt a flush warm her face. She didn't feel like a good cook and taking a compliment felt awkward. She had no difficulty accepting praise about her flying. But that was different; she knew she was a good pilot. Cooking was domestic. And right now she felt anything but that.

Kate sat with her knees pulled up to her chest and her arms circled around her legs. She watched orange, yellow, and blue flames lick at wood and hot coals. "This almost feels like a campout."

"Yeah. Not bad." Mike gazed at her in a way that made Kate's cheeks heat up. "Can't say I mind being stranded with you." The light of the fire flickered in his eyes.

Kate didn't know what to say and mumbled, "You're good company." Was it possible that he could be more? She felt self-conscious, realizing he was still watching her. He'd never replace Paul, but he was a good man. She tried to imagine what it would be like to spend her life with him. *It might be nice*, she thought, then told herself, *it's just the romantic setting here. Keep your head on straight.*

Quiet settled over them. The hoot of an owl cut into the hush of the night. A rustling came from inside the plane as the piglets established their sleeping places. "I'll be taking another load of baby pigs out to Patrick and Sassa next week."

"What, have you become a barnyard pilot?" Mike chuckled.

"Guess so. Lily radioed in an order to a local farmer. Sassa said they lost several of theirs to a hungry fox."

Mike nodded, and then a long silence dragged out between them. Finally, he cleared his throat and said, "That's really something about Lily, isn't it?"

172

"What about Lily?"

"You know . . ."

"Know what?" Kate felt her interest pique.

"Well . . . that she's in a family way."

"Lily's pregnant?"

"Yeah. I thought you knew."

Kate shook her head. "I haven't heard anything."

"Maybe I wasn't supposed to tell anyone. Just figured everyone knew—the way word travels through the bush."

"How do you know?"

"I made a delivery out at Susitna Station the other day and Charlie told me."

"You think it could just be one of those gossipy things and not actually true?"

"Charlie doesn't lie. He likes a good story, but he's not the kind to say anything malicious."

"That's true." Kate wondered who the father was. Lily'd only been back a few months and she didn't have a local beau. Only man she was even friends with was Paul. Kate remembered how Lily had talked about helping him out with his garden and how they'd gone fishing together.

A thud went off in Kate's head. Paul? No. It couldn't be him. Even if he did have feelings for her, he wouldn't do something like that.

"Did Charlie say who the father is?"

"Nope. No one's talking, but the scuttlebutt is that it has to be someone she met in Seattle. If the rumors are accurate, she's due in the fall."

Mike pushed a piece of wood into the fire with the toe of his boot. "Have to say it shocked me. I thought Lily was a nice girl."

"She is," Kate snapped. "Why is it that whenever something like this happens, it's the woman who gets blamed? How do we know what happened?"

Mike stared at Kate a moment, then said, "You're right. Sorry. But no matter what, Lily will be fine. She's a strong gal. And Patrick and Sassa will see to it that the father does right by her."

Kate nodded, her mind on Paul. How did he feel about it? Would he come to Lily's aid, maybe even deliver the baby? It made sense. He was a doctor and they were neighbors, after all.

Mike studied her. "You okay? You look a little green around the gills."

"I'm fine. Just don't think that fish agreed with me." She pressed a hand to her stomach. What was wrong with her? Paul had called it quits two months ago. He could care about anyone he wanted to. He'd find someone and so would she.

Mike picked up one of the blankets and moved close to Kate. "Here, lay down. Try to get some sleep."

Kate obeyed. He draped the blanket over her, and then tucked it around her shoulders. He was so close she could feel his breath on her cheek. "You know, I still love you," he said.

"I know." She looked up at him. He made her feel cared for, protected. She wanted to love him.

"I know you don't feel that way about me, but maybe with time. I want to share my life with you, Kate." He sat beside her, leaving a hand on her shoulder.

Kate wanted to lean against him, to feel the warmth of his tenderness and love. She needed to be loved. Taking a deep breath, she said, "There's no one like you, Mike. You're my best friend."

"Friendship's only a place to begin. I want more than that. I know couples who started out just as friends." He gazed down at her. "I'd make you happy."

Kate looked into his charming blue eyes. "I believe you just might." A smile touched her lips. "There's no one I trust more than you." She willed the words "I love you" from her mouth, but she couldn't say them.

Mike leaned closer, his breath caressing her face. His lips barely grazed hers. She felt an unexpected heat in her belly. He kissed her again. This time their lips embraced. Warmth became a flame.

His face only inches from hers, Mike ran a hand over Kate's

forehead and eased back a loose strand of hair. Kate studied his handsome features. Even now he seemed at ease.

"I remember the first day we met. You sidled into the shop with that trouble-free smile of yours." Kate didn't love him the way he needed . . . but maybe in time it would come. "You've always been special to me."

If it were possible, Mike's expression warmed even more. He gently pressed his lips to hers, then deepened the kiss. Passion building, Kate's arms circled his neck and pulled him closer. They held each other for a long while.

Mike loosened his hold and looked down at her. "Will you marry me, Kate?"

She could see hope and passion in his eyes. How could she turn him down? Maybe it was time for her to be practical. She wanted to say yes.

Instead, she said, "Can you give me a little time to think about it?"

— 16 —

The most delicious moose roast I've ever eaten," Kate said.

"You'll have to get the recipe." Mike rested a hand on his stomach.

"We're thankful you're here. The two of you could have been killed when your plane went down." Albert wiped his mouth with a napkin. "What happened anyway?"

"A wire came loose. I must have missed it when I did my inspection," Kate said. "I'll be more careful from here on out."

"Thank goodness you're safe and sound." Helen started to clear the table.

Kate picked up a plate.

"Oh no you don't. It's Albert's turn to help." Helen took the plate from Kate.

"The guys probably want to talk. I'm more than happy to help."

"Why don't you and Mike take a walk? It's a beautiful evening."

Mike stood. "Sounds a heck of a lot better than doing dishes." He winked at Kate.

"Okay." Kate gave in. She'd been avoiding being alone with Mike. She knew he was waiting for an answer to his marriage proposal. Although she cared for him deeply, she wasn't sure whether she should marry him. What if the kisses they'd shared and what they'd felt when they were stranded that night had more to do with a clear summer evening, a crackling fire, and the thrill of survival than it did with love?

"Let me get my sweater." Kate headed toward the front door and took the sweater out of the closet. "It's chilly out." She pulled it on quickly before Mike could help her.

He opened the front door and held it for Kate, then followed her out. They walked down the front path to the road. He stopped at the edge of the yard. "Which way?"

"Doesn't matter to me."

"How about toward the creek." He looped his arm through hers. "I like it there. It's kind of romantic." He lifted his brows and smiled.

Kate gave him a teasing look. "Sure." He expected an answer. He'd waited patiently for three weeks.

They strolled down the road.

"So, you have any more trouble with your bird?" Mike asked.

"Nope. Since the repairs were made it's been running perfectly. I had to make a couple of trips using Jack's pontoon plane. I don't know why he brags it up. It doesn't carry close to the load mine does, and it's not nearly as stable in rough conditions."

"You know Jack. He's always got to have the best."

"You would have thought I'd never flown the plane before the way he gives me detailed instructions about how to fly the dang thing." Kate shook her head. "I hate having to use it."

"Don't let him get to you." Mike took her hand and gave it a squeeze and kept hold of it. "He does the same thing to me and everyone else."

Kate liked the feel of her hand in his. "I wish I could get one of those amphibian planes."

"They're not making them for our kind of flying, but they will. Just be patient."

Kate nodded. "The sooner, the better."

When they reached the bridge, Mike released Kate's hand

and leaned on the rail, gazing down at a tumbling stream. Neither of them spoke. The air smelled of wildflowers and pollen. The breeze blew leaves into the air.

"Fall's coming."

"Seems like summer gets shorter and shorter." Kate knew she was stalling.

Mike straightened and faced her. "Okay, Kate. I don't know if I can wait anymore. If deciding is so difficult, maybe that's your answer."

"I just want to make sure that I don't make a mistake. I've thought I was in love before and then things went bad."

He circled his arms around her waist and pulled her close. "So, you think you're in love?"

"Maybe," she answered with a teasing lilt to her voice. She looked into eyes the color of a fall sky, and then her gaze moved to Mike's lips. They always seemed to hold a bit of mischief. He was a good man, a perfect match for her. Why was she hesitating?

"Do you want me to do this properly?" He took something out of his pocket and dropped to one knee.

"Mike. Get up." Kate looked up and down the road, embarrassed and hoping no one could see them. The street was empty.

"I want to do this right." He held out a small box. "Kate, I love you. I want to spend my life with you. Will you marry me?" He opened the box and Kate could see a ring resting inside.

She had to answer. She closed her eyes and thought back over their friendship and the experiences they'd shared. They *were* right for each other. They belonged together. She smiled. "Yes. I'll marry you."

Mike let out a little whoop, lifted out a gold band with a small diamond in it, and slid it on her finger. "It's nothing fancy, but I'll get you something better later."

"No. It's fine. It's perfect. You know me—I'm not a fancy sort of gal."

He pulled her into his arms. "I'll make you happy. I promise." He kissed her tenderly.

Happiness swept over Kate. This was right, she was sure of it. And then Paul's face flickered through her mind, and with it came doubt.

Mike's breath against her lips, he said, "Everything will be perfect." He kissed her again. "Mrs. Mike Conlin. I like the sound of that."

"How about Kate Conlin? The pilot Mike Conlin is married to?" She chuckled.

"It's fine with me, either way."

Kate's heart battered in her chest. She did love him, didn't she? And even if she didn't, romantic love was overrated. It usually left you with a broken heart. She could live without it. A steady, respectful love was long-lasting and more dependable.

She planted a sweet kiss on Mike's lips. "I'll be the best wife I know how. 'Course I'll have to take cooking lessons from Helen and Muriel."

"Don't worry about that." He smiled broadly. "So, when?"

"When what?"

"When should we get married?"

Kate laughed. "I don't know. It'll take some planning. I want my parents to be here."

"Okay. When you have it figured out, you tell me and I promise to be there." Taking her hand he said, "Come on. Let's tell Albert and Helen."

Her mind full of wedding plans, Kate headed for the airfield. She hoped Mike hadn't left yet. She needed to ask him about the date for the wedding. She'd considered the first week in October. It was a busy season for her parents, but if she waited until November they might not be able to make it up.

Her thoughts jumped unexpectedly to Paul, and her jovial mood slid downhill. Would she always love him? Maybe when he got married, she'd be able to let him go completely. But she doubted he'd ever marry. He'd never allow himself to get close enough to anyone to make that kind of commitment again.

She rested a hand on Angel, who sat on the seat beside her. "So, you think you'll like living at Mike's house?" Angel pressed her head under Kate's palm and moved closer to her.

Kate's thoughts lingered on Paul and Mike. She couldn't keep from comparing how she felt about the two. She didn't feel the same passion for Mike that she'd had for Paul, but that didn't mean she loved Mike less, just differently.

She slowed and turned toward Lake Spenard. Mike should be at the airfield. He and Kate both had runs scheduled. When she pulled into the airport, she was disappointed that his plane wasn't there. She'd missed him.

Kate parked her car in front of the shop. She stepped out and stood for a moment to collect herself. She was on edge, but didn't know why. Taking in a breath of cool September air, her gaze settled on the Chugach mountain range. She never tired of looking at them. The power of the steep, jagged peaks bolstered her.

She headed for the shop and stepped inside. Jack was the only one there. "Good morning."

"Figured you'd be here earlier. Mike said you were supposed to meet him here this morning."

"I was. Where is he?"

"Set out at the crack of dawn." Jack tapped the end of a pencil on the desk.

"Really? I didn't know he wanted to leave so early."

"Said something about company for dinner?" Jack cocked an eyebrow.

"Yeah. We're getting together with friends."

"You better get a move on if you want to get back in time. There's a lot of mail." Jack narrowed his eyes. "What's so important about tonight anyway?"

"Nothing."

"Didn't seem like nothing to me. Mike was wearing a big fat grin the whole time he was here." Jack studied her, squinting. "Something's going on . . . I can feel it."

Kate shrugged. "Can't guess what." She hoped she sounded innocent.

"Yeah. Well, he said he wanted to get back early so he could make dinner."

"Really?" Kate smiled furtively and walked into the back room. Muriel and Terrence would be at Mike's by seven o'clock. Mike planned to announce their engagement. They'd sworn Helen and Albert to secrecy, and Kate wasn't about to let Jack know about her and Mike before her best friend heard.

She wondered what life with Mike would be like. *Exciting and unpredictable*, she guessed. They wouldn't be bored. And Mike already owned a house, which meant she could use her savings for something else.

It would be fun to do some traveling. As pilots, they could fly most any place they wanted. She imagined trips across the United States and Canada. There were so many places she wanted to see. And traveling with Mike would be fun. He knew how to have a good time.

Wearing a smile, she placed sorted mail into a bag. When it was filled, she set it to the side and picked up another canvas sack. Jack had been right when he said there was a lot of mail.

Her mind flitted back to wedding plans. Maybe October wasn't such a good idea. It would be hard for her parents to get away. It was a busy season on the farm. A summer wedding would be nice, but that meant waiting months. She knew Mike wouldn't like that.

The squawk of the airport radio disrupted the quiet. Kate didn't pay attention, not at first. Then she heard Mike's voice. "This is Fairchild 323. Come in Anchorage. Over." His voice sounded tight. Something was wrong. Angel whined.

Kate moved to the doorway.

"Fairchild 323, this is Anchorage. Go ahead. Over."

"Engine's out. I'm going down. Over."

"Fairchild 323, give me your location." Jack's voice was anxious, but steady. He repeated. "Fairchild 323, I need your location. Over."

Static was the only response. "Fairchild 323. Report your location." Nothing. "Mike." He waited. No word came back. "This is Anchorage airport to Fairchild 323. Come in. Over."

Panic swelled inside Kate. Her stomach tightened and her heart hammered inside her chest. She strode into the office. "Call him again."

"Mike. This is Anchorage airport. Are you there? Over."

Static sizzled through the room.

"Fairchild 323, this is Anchorage. Come in." Jack stared at Kate, unable to disguise his alarm.

Kate stood immobile, then years of experience kicked in. "Where was he heading?" She tossed aside the mailbag.

"North of Palmer. He was dropping David Clarkson off at his homestead."

"Okay. I'm going. I'll have a look."

Jack nodded, his expression morose.

Kate ran for the door. She opened it, then turned and looked back at Jack. "I'm sure he's fine. You know Mike. He can get out of any tight spot." She gripped the doorknob. "But you'd better get some pilots up to search for him."

Kate sprinted across the airfield, Angel beside her. When she reached the plane, she threw open the door and Angel jumped in. Kate cranked the flywheel, climbed in, and turned over the engine. With only a quick glance at her gauges, she headed toward the airstrip and, quickly picking up speed, lifted into the air. *He's got to be okay. Please be okay.*

With the engine roaring in her ears, she skimmed the top of the trees bordering the airport. Her mind worked through all options and visualized the countryside between Anchorage and Palmer. If he'd gone down in farmland, it wouldn't be hard to spot him. And he could probably set down without serious damage. But if he'd crashed north of Palmer, the terrain was forested and mountainous. A plane would be hard to see.

She scanned the open fields dappled with patches of forest. If he knew he was in trouble, where would he set down? *Show me, Lord,* Kate prayed as she flew, trying to believe that she and Mike still had a future.

When there was no sign of him, fear knifed through Kate. What could have gone wrong? Where was he?

She flew in a pattern over the Matanuska Valley. Finally she radioed back to the airfield. "Anchorage, this is Pacemaker 221. Over."

"Anchorage airport. Go ahead. Over."

"Any word on Mike? Over."

"Nothing. You see anything? Over."

"No sign of him here in the valley. Over."

"Pacemaker 221. I have two more planes in the air. Another on the way. Over."

"I'm heading to the Clarkson place. Over."

After that, all Kate heard was static so she shut down communication. The minutes seemed to tick by in slow motion. There was no sign of Mike or his plane. Kate's thoughts returned to the time she'd spent stranded after crashing into the lake near Mount Susitna. While friends and family had feared the worst, she'd been alive and waiting for rescue. Aside from being cold and hungry she was fine. Nena had suffered a terrible injury, but she'd pulled through. Kate told herself Mike was safe and waiting for someone to find him.

Her mind reeling with questions and fears, she flew over the Clarksons' airfield. Mike's plane wasn't there. She set down, and leaving the engine running, Kate ran toward a small cabin.

Julie Clarkson stepped onto a porch with a wooden railing, her two-year-old son in her arms. She wiped her free hand on an apron draped over a rounded stomach. She was due to have another baby in a few weeks.

"Kate?" She squinted against the sun. "I thought David was flying out today with Mike."

"He's not here?"

"No. Should he be?" The tenor of Julie's voice rose.

Kate combed her fingers through the thick hair on Angel's neck. The dog had stayed with her instead of heading off to investigate, as if knowing Kate needed her. "Mike and David left early this morning. Mike sent in a call for help, saying he was putting the plane down. I was hoping he'd made it here."

Although her insides quivered with anxiety, Kate managed

to maintain a facade of composure. "I'm sure they're fine. Probably just had a little trouble with the engine and Mike found a safe place to set down. He's one of the best pilots you'll ever find, and he can land just about anywhere. We've just got to find him." She forced a smile.

Julie pulled the toddler closer. Her eyes brimmed with tears. "Where do you think they are?"

"Don't know just yet. But we've got several planes out searching. I'd better get back in the air. We'll have David home soon." The color had drained from Julie's face, and Kate feared she might faint. Resting a hand on her arm, she asked, "Are you all right?"

"I'm fine." Julie brushed at her tears. "Just find David for me."

"We will. Maybe you should lie down. Try not to worry."

Wishing she were able to follow her own advice, Kate loped back to the plane. When she climbed aboard she heard the crackle of the radio. "Pacemaker 221, this is Anchorage airport. Over."

Kate scrambled into the front seat and picked up the radio. "This is Pacemaker 221. Go ahead. Over."

There was a pause, then the radio came to life again. "We found Mike. Over."

Kate's heart pummeled against her ribs. "Is he all right? Over."

No answer, then Jack said quietly, "Sorry, Kate. Mike . . . ," the radio crackled, ". . . make it. Neither did David Clarkson. Over."

Kate couldn't believe what she'd heard. "You're breaking up. Say again. Over."

"Mike and David didn't make it. Over."

Kate dropped the handset. The world tipped. Didn't make it? No. It wasn't possible. Mike was the best. She stared at a lone spruce. He couldn't be dead. Terrence and Muriel were coming for dinner and he was going to announce their engagement.

Kate broke into sobs. "No . . . No . . . Not Mike."

Her eyes trailed to the cabin. She'd have to tell Julie.

Sidney, Kenny, and Paul joined three other friends of Mike's and carried his casket out of the church, down the front steps, and to a waiting hearse. Kate followed. Her heart ached and felt as if it were made of lead. Helen stood at her side and circled an arm around Kate's shoulders. Kate leaned against her, then looked back at the church. This was the place they'd planned to begin their life together. Instead Kate was saying good-bye.

She rested a hand over the tiny gold airplane that hung around her neck—the one Mike had given to her at Christmas. She remembered her surprise at the special gift. He'd had it made just for her. Anger mingled with her sorrow. Why had he died? He didn't deserve it. Where had God been?

She gazed out over the parking lot packed with cars. Everyone loved Mike. She loved Mike. Why had she waited so long to let him know? So many days wasted. Tears blurred her vision.

Albert moved down the steps and reached out to help her take the last one. He kept a gentle hold on her arm as she walked along the pathway. Again, her fingers found the necklace. Had she known all those months ago that she loved him? Even when she'd been seeing Paul? Maybe what she felt for Paul had been infatuation. From the first day she and Mike had met, she'd cared about him and knew she always would. Mike was supposed to always be there. Now he was gone. Alison's death had been hard enough, but this was unbearable.

Mike's casket was lifted into the hearse and slid inside. Kate had a horrible sensation that the hearse was swallowing him. Her legs went weak and she feared she might faint.

She leaned against Albert as he steered her toward his car and then opened the door. Kate sat on the backseat. Helen moved in beside her. She took a handkerchief out of her handbag and gave it to Kate.

"Thank you." Kate dabbed at her unending tears. Albert

turned onto the street and followed the hearse on its journey to the cemetery.

When the men placed the casket beside an open grave, Kate couldn't look at it. Mike didn't belong in the ground. His place was in the sky. And then Kate remembered—he was flying, with the Lord. The clarity of that knowledge warmed her heart.

Stiffly, she made her way to the graveside where friends had gathered. Helen and Albert remained at her side. Muriel caught her eye and nodded reassurance.

As the reverend spoke, Kate twisted the engagement ring around her finger. She wondered if she should have placed it in the casket with Mike. She looked up to find Muriel staring at the ring. Their tear-filled eyes met and Muriel smiled gently.

Kate tucked her hands behind her back and allowed her gaze to roam across the small cemetery. The close-cropped grass was adorned with small pink, yellow, and blue wild-flowers, the last of the season. Radiant fireweed trembled in the breeze, seeming to whisper condolences. The arms of an oak protectively sheltered the grave site. Mike would have liked this spot.

The minister ended with a prayer and then a woman from the church, whom Kate barely knew, sang "Jesus Is Passing This Way." When she finished, the crowd slowly dispersed. Kate remained. She didn't want to leave Mike. He'd be alone.

She rested a hand on the casket. *Why did you have to go? We were just beginning.* The weight in her chest grew heavier and she choked back sobs. She looked up and caught sight of Paul. He stood several yards away and seemed to be waiting for her. Brushing at her tears, she blew into the handkerchief, then turned back to the casket. "You were my best friend. I'll never forget you. Never."

Her legs barely held her as she walked toward the car where Muriel, Helen, and Albert waited. Paul moved toward her and she felt rising panic. She couldn't talk to him. Not today. This day belonged to Mike.

Having no alternative, she threw back her shoulders and waited.

Paul stopped, leaving only a couple of feet between them. When he acted as if he might reach out for her hands, she hugged herself about the waist. "Kate, I just want you to know how sorry I am. Mike was an upstanding person. I admired him."

"He liked you too."

Paul glanced at Albert and Helen. "If there's anything you need, please let me know."

"Sure." Kate squeezed back tears.

With a slight bob of his head, Paul turned and walked away. He held his shoulders high and his spine straight. He didn't look back.

— 17 —

It was mid-September, and the chill wind of fall swept up small whitecaps on the lake, sifting a fine spray across the tops of the waves. Kate's hair blew into her eyes. She didn't mind. She liked the wind. It made her feel alive.

The days since Mike's funeral had dragged and the nights were interminable. His absence had left an emptiness in her—a constant ache that she felt even in the dead of sleep. Since their first meeting he'd been her friend, someone she could count on. What would she do without him? Work. She needed to work.

Coughing into her sleeve, she headed for the shop, Angel at her side. The dog had stayed close since Mike's death, seeming to sense Kate's loneliness and the need for companionship.

Feeling a sneeze coming on, Kate pulled a handkerchief out of her pocket and blew her nose. She'd picked up a cold somewhere, but was determined to fly anyway. Jack had kept her grounded and fear had niggled its way into her thinking. She had to get back in the air before it took hold.

When she reached the shop door, she stopped. Facing the guys would be hard. She hadn't seen them since the funeral. She didn't know how to act. Did she behave as if nothing had happened? Or should she talk about Mike? No. She couldn't do that yet.

She opened the door and stepped inside, her hand resting on Angel's head.

Jack, Kenny, and Alan looked at her. No one spoke. Kenny gave her a nod and then shoved a piece of wood into the stove. Keeping his face turned away from her, he reached for another piece and thrust it into the fire. Alan turned back to working on a piece of equipment at the bench.

Jack puffed on a cigar. "Didn't figure you'd be back so soon. We're not busy right now. Maybe a little more time . . ." His tone was uncharacteristically cordial.

"Thanks, but I'd rather work." Kate moved to the back room door. For a moment, she expected to find Mike sorting mail for her. She stood in the doorway. He wasn't there. He'd never be there again.

"It's only been a few days," Alan said in his quiet voice. He offered a sympathetic smile.

"I've had enough time."

"You're sure?" Jack stubbed out his cigar.

Tears demanded release, but Kate held them back. "I'm ready to work."

"Okay then." Jack looked at the schedule. "Paul has some calls to make. You want to take him?"

Paul? Kate had hoped for something less personal—a scouting crew or a homesteader needing a ride back to his family. "Sure," she said. "No problem. I'll need a flight plan and I'll be on my way." She coughed.

"You sick?"

"Just a slight cold. I'm fine." The room swirled momentarily and Kate held on to the doorframe, hoping Jack hadn't noticed her unsteadiness. She probably didn't even have a cold—this was probably caused from all the crying she'd done. If she could stay busy, she'd feel better. After all, stuffing down her feelings for Paul had gotten easier each time she'd had to work with him over the summer. So being with someone like Paul would help her hold back her tears.

Kate took the list of stops from Jack and scanned it. There were several between Anchorage and Kotzebue and then she'd hopscotch from Kotzebue to Fairbanks and then back down to Nenana, Talkeetna, and Palmer. It would take several days, which Kate normally wouldn't mind, but she didn't want to spend too much time with Paul.

Get used to it. It's part of your job. A stab of misery hit her. There'd been a time when she'd longed for more trips with Paul. Now it was Mike she missed. There'd be no more runs with him, no teasing or burned meals, or sardine dinners.

Kate headed for the door. "I'll stay in touch and see you in a week or so." As she said the words, the reality that she might not make it back hit her in the gut. Every good-bye for a pilot could be their last.

With the engine roaring in her ears, Kate checked her instruments. In her mind she could see Mike following the same procedures. He'd always been methodical, checking everything to make sure all was in order. What good had it done him? Fear swirled through her. She closed her eyes and took a deep breath, which made her lungs hurt.

"You ready, girl?" she asked Angel, giving her a pat. The dog put a paw on Kate's arm as if to say yes. "All right, then. Time to get back at it." Shaking off a sense of dread, Kate taxied onto the runway and turned the plane into the wind.

It would be a bumpy ride, but she'd had her share of those. She barreled down the length of the airstrip, feeling every jolt and thump. When the wheels left the ground, the plane felt heavier than usual, not quite right. Was something wrong? Her pulse picked up.

Stop it, she told herself, refusing to let what had happened to Mike victimize her. The nights were worse. She dreamed about him and his accident and she'd wake up, wondering if he'd suffered. She knew that, just like Mike, one day her luck could run out.

Helen and Muriel had been a comfort. Helen brought food and good wishes with her every day when she came into the store. One day, Kate had broken down and Helen just held her. The words of comfort she shared came back to Kate now like a balm. "God knows when it's our time to go home. And his hand is upon you, Kate. Trust in him, not in circumstances."

"Trust him," she said, forcing her mind back to flying. She thought over the route. She'd pick up Paul and they'd head north. It would be good to see Nena and Joe and the kids. Nena was sweet and full of love. And the children made her laugh.

Against her will, her mind trailed back to Mike and the life they could have shared. They'd have had beautiful children. He would have been a terrific father, full of fun and surprises. Tears trailed down her cheeks and she didn't bother to wipe them away.

A crosswind hit the plane, thumping it hard. Fear thudded through Kate. It wasn't unusual to be hit by crosswinds, and her Bellanca was barely bothered by them. She knew that. Still, she seemed to have no power to stop the alarm that bristled through her.

She was relieved to spot the Susitna River. Bear Creek was close.

When she reached the creek, she buzzed it, making sure her landing site was clear. The trees and brush reached out over the sandbar. It didn't look like there was enough space. She shook her head. She'd put down here a hundred times. There was plenty of room. At the last moment, Kate pulled up and climbed above the trees, trying to control the quaking in her hands.

Stop it! You're being foolish.

She came around again, staring at Patrick and Sassa's rooftop and the smoke drifting from their chimney. Everything was as it should be. Kate relaxed her grip and dropped her shoulders. "Get ahold of yourself," she said. "Nothing's changed. You're the same pilot you were before Mike died, a good one. And you've got a dependable plane." Angel whined. Kate reached over and buried her fingers in the dog's ruff. "It's all right, girl. We're fine."

With fresh determination, she circled back and set up her approach. This time she stayed on her heading and gently set the plane down on the sandbar. Paul was already waiting there for her, medical bag in hand and pack slung over one shoulder.

Kate had barely stopped when he climbed in. He tossed in his pack and closed the door, then set his bag on a seat and made his way to the front. "Hi. What happened? You having some kind of trouble with the plane?"

"No. Just wasn't lined up right. Better safe than sorry." Kate did her best to keep her voice relaxed. "So, Patrick drop you off?"

"Yeah." He looked at her kindly. "You all right?"

"I'm fine." Her voice sounded nasally.

"Didn't expect you. Figured one of the other pilots would pick me up."

"We're short on pilots," Kate said dryly, then blew her nose into a handkerchief.

"Maybe you should have taken more time off. It's only been a few days since the funeral."

"I needed to get back in the air. That's what Mike would have done."

"Yeah, I suppose." Paul reached over and gave Kate's arm a squeeze. "You feeling all right? You don't sound too good, kind of hoarse."

"I've got a cold . . . or something. Nothing to worry about." She sniffled into her handkerchief before heading to the end of the sandbar and setting up for takeoff. Again, fear crept into her mind. She ignored it and kicked up her speed, lifting off without difficulty.

Hoping to keep things businesslike, Kate immediately started going through the schedule. "We have stops at a couple of homesteads. One has an elderly parent who's not doing well and the other family has a child with tonsillitis. After that, we'll stop at the mine. There's always a ration of troubles there."

Paul chuckled. "Those miners would have a whole lot fewer problems if they'd stay out of the hooch and learn some basic hygiene."

Any other time, Kate would have laughed and bounced back a snappy reply. Today she didn't have it in her. There was no laughter inside. She ignored Paul's teasing and continued to read off the list of stops.

"It'll be nice to see Nena and Joe. How've they been?" Paul's tone was cheerier than usual.

"Fine, last I heard."

Conversation fell off. Finally, Paul said, "Kate, you don't have to talk about what happened. But sometimes it helps."

"It doesn't. I . . . I can't talk about it, not yet."

"I know it's painful, but maybe you should try."

Kate wasn't ready. Anger and frustration flamed. "How would you know? You've never talked to me about what happened in California. As far as I know, you've never talked to anyone about it."

Paul started to say something, then set his jaw, folded his arms over his chest, and stared straight ahead. Finally, he said, "It's not always so easy. When you lose someone you love, it leaves a hole inside. And it feels like nothing and no one will ever fill it."

Immediately guilt swept over Kate. Paul hadn't deserved harsh words. He was only trying to help. "I'm sorry. I shouldn't have snapped at you. I know you've had a hard time. I'm not myself." Kate coughed. Her chest felt tight.

"That's a cold. Doesn't sound like you should be working." Paul eyed her paternally.

"It's nothing," she said, but Kate knew she was getting worse. Her head felt stuffed up and she could feel a wheeze in her chest when she breathed. "I'll be fine." She didn't want Paul to check on her, to be that close. And she didn't want him to care, not now.

They stopped at two homesteads. At the first one, Paul gave an elderly man a thorough checkup and left instructions with his daughter on how to care for him. He advised the parents at the second stop to schedule their son for surgery to remove his tonsils. The next place was the mine. By the time they'd finished doctoring several men, it was late in the day and they were forced to stay over. Kate's accommodation was a tent and a cot. The tightness in her chest had developed into a cough. That and a plugged nose made sleep nearly impossible. Paul checked on her once during the night and gave her something to quiet the cough. After that, she managed a few hours' sleep.

Morning arrived with gray clouds and drizzle. While Paul had a look at a couple of miners he hadn't gotten to the previous day, Kate readied the plane. She did her best to ignore the pain in her throat and chest, and her throbbing head. With the engine warming, she huddled in the cockpit, unable to get warm.

By the time Paul showed up, she was losing patience. They had a lot of miles to cover before they reached McGrath. She was already thinking about a warm bed and a good night's sleep.

Paul finally climbed into the plane. "Sorry," he said, dropping into his seat. "But one of the men sliced up his hand pretty badly with a hatchet while cutting kindling this morning."

"Oh," Kate croaked, feeling guilty at her irritability.

"You don't sound good. Maybe we ought to stay put for a couple of days so you can rest."

"No thanks. A tent and a cot isn't what I have in mind for tonight." She headed the plane down a rough, grassy airstrip. Rain splattered the windshield and the window fogged up. Kate could barely see. It was too late to abort the takeoff, so trusting her instincts, she increased speed and guided the plane into the air. Her confidence grew.

The next two days passed in a haze of coughing and pain. Kate's head and face throbbed in spite of the aspirin Paul dispensed. She pushed on, unwilling to give up. Besides, working helped keep her mind off of Mike.

When they landed in Kotzebue, it felt like winter had already arrived. The ground was covered with frost and a chill wind blew in from Kotzebue Sound.

Joe and Paul secured the plane while Kate drained the oil. She couldn't risk it freezing. With that done, the three of them covered the fuselage with a tarp and then headed toward town. Angel trotted ahead of them. She knew where they were headed.

Nena greeted Kate and Paul with a smile. "Good to see you." She pulled Kate into her arms. "I'm so sorry about Mike. We weep for you and know you must be missing him terrible. He was a good man."

Kate didn't know how to answer. Everyone was sorry, but their words didn't help. "Mike lived the way he wanted" was all she could think of to say.

The Turchik children sprinted toward Kate and embraced her around the legs. She gave them each a hug, fighting back tears. It felt good to be loved, but somehow the affection only made her feelings of loss more intense. Angel pushed between Kate and the children, demanding attention. Laughing, the children buried her with hugs and kisses.

Nena enfolded Kate in her arms, and then held her away from her. "You have a fever." She studied Kate. "You're sick?"

"Just a cold."

"I can hear it and see it. You have more than a cold." Nena looked at Paul.

"She won't let me help." He shrugged. "Stubborn."

Nena led Kate to a chair. "You sit and let the doctor fix you."

Kate was too tired to argue, so she sat down. Nena took her coat.

Paul set his medical bag on the table. He palpated Kate's neck. "You've got some very unhappy glands." He took a tongue depressor out of his bag. "Open your mouth and stick out your tongue." He grinned.

Kate almost smiled.

He examined her throat, then using his stethoscope he listened to her heart. "Take a deep breath." Kate did as instructed, which set off a bout of coughing. When she quieted, he moved the stethoscope from place to place, each time asking her to breathe. "I don't hear any pneumonia. That's good."

He took a thermometer out. "Under your tongue."

Kate did as he asked, but she felt uncomfortable. His touch seemed too familiar.

Using his thumbs, he gently pressed on her face, first above her eyes. "Does that hurt?"

She nodded.

He put pressure on her cheeks. "Here?"

"Uh-huh," she mumbled around the thermometer.

Paul removed it and after a quick glance said, "A hundred and one. I'd say you're good and sick. Probably a sinus infection to go along with your bronchial infection." He looked straight at her. "You need rest. And I want you to breathe in some hot steam."

"Okay. I'll rest."

"I have soup," Nena said. "And a cup of hot tea will be soothing."

"Tea sounds good," Kate said. "Thanks, Nena."

"I'll heat up some water and you can eat and then go to bed," the native woman said with a maternal smile.

Two days later, when Paul and Kate left Kotzebue, Kate was still sick, but her fever had abated and her cough was better. Her head still felt congested and she'd had an occasional dizzy spell. The best thing for her was to get home.

They had fewer stops to make on their way back to Anchorage, so she figured she'd be in her own bed in two or three days. The atmosphere between her and Paul had warmed since they'd first set out. His kindness and concern made her feel cared for. They felt like friends again.

On their second day out, Kate woke up to pressure in her head and ears. She said nothing to Paul about it. All she wanted was to get home. The sooner they got started, the sooner she'd get there.

As they approached Palmer, the world suddenly dipped sideways, then began to whirl. Kate waited for the sensation to pass. Instead it got worse. The earth and sky merged and spun out of control. Kate couldn't read the instruments. She couldn't get her bearings and wasn't even certain whether the plane was upright or not. Nausea swept over her. She'd heard of vertigo but had never experienced it.

She pushed the palm of her hand against her left ear, the one that had the most pressure. It didn't help. She tipped her head to the side, but the movement only made the vertigo worse. She did her best to focus on the instruments, but no matter how hard she tried, she couldn't read them. Kate's nightmare was coming true. She was about to die and kill another person she loved. She should have stayed on the ground.

"Paul, I'm in trouble. I'm dizzy."

"Dizzy? How bad is it?"

"Bad. Everything is spinning. I . . . I can't fly. I can't tell up from down." Kate gripped the control wheel, fighting panic. She needed to stay calm. She closed her eyes and tried to separate the motion of the plane from what the inside of her head was telling her. She loosened her hold on the wheel and listened to the engine to make sure she was maintaining speed.

"Hold your head absolutely still and keep your eyes closed."

Kate did as he said, but the world continued to spin behind her eyelids. "It's no better. I . . . think I'm going to be sick."

"That's normal with this kind of thing."

That didn't make Kate feel any better. Alarm rising, Kate fought for composure. Her life and Paul's depended on it. "Look at the inclinometer and tell me if we're flying level."

"The ball's floating to the left."

Kate adjusted with a touch to the pedals. "Better?"

"No. Too far. We're banking right." Paul's voice remained calm.

Kate tapped the pedal.

"Okay. Good."

"You're going to have to fly and land the plane. But I'll help you."

"You sure you can't do it?"

"No. I can't even tell up from down."

"Okay."

If Paul was frightened, Kate didn't hear it in his voice. Her stomach rolled and she willed away the nausea. "Do you have a coin or something flat you can use to free the control wheel?"

"Yeah. I've got a quarter."

"Okay. Turn the screw at the base of the wheel shaft. That will release it."

Kate felt pressure against her leg as Paul reached across her. "Okay. Got it."

"It pivots, so swing it around to your side."

"Done."

"The plane is yours now."

"What should I do?"

"You need to get a feel for the controls. We're going to use gentle changes. I want you to move the nose back and forth with the rudder pedals at your feet. Push the right pedal and the nose should move right."

"Okay."

"Now, push the left pedal and the nose will turn left." Kate could feel the change, but couldn't distinguish how far they'd moved. Everything was distorted by the spinning.

"Watch the nose on the horizon and see how it moves. How do the wings look? Are they level?"

"Mostly level."

"Which one is down?"

"The right wing is lower."

"Move the control wheel to the left a bit. See if you can find level."

Kate waited. She opened her eyes and the spinning intensified, so she closed them again. "You got it?"

"Yeah. I think we're fine." There was a trace of tension in Paul's voice.

"Paul, I can hear the engine slowing down. Push the control wheel forward . . . gently. Okay, that sounds better." She licked dry lips. "We've got to find a place to put down. I'm pretty sure there's an open field coming up that should work."

"There's lots of farmland, but there are fences."

"No. Look farther out. I'm sure there's a big enough field."

"Yeah. I can see it—looks like four or five miles ahead."

198

"Okay. Good." Kate held her emotions in check, barely hanging on to calm. "Now, use the rudder in gentle increments to point us toward the field."

"Gotcha."

"You've flown in this bird a lot. You probably know more than you think. You're going to do fine."

"Darn right."

Kate was calmed by the humor in his voice. "How's it feel to you?"

"Not bad. I'm starting to get the hang of this. Actually, Mike let me fly his bird a couple of times."

Bless you, Mike. "Have a look at the altimeter. What's our altitude?"

"Two thousand feet."

"We've climbed a smidge, but that's all right. Keep bringing us down. Remember small increments. And pull the power back another notch."

She listened to the sound of the engine. Paul was doing well. Kate managed a smile and dared to look at him. "You having fun?"

"Yeah. I can do this."

"I know you're up to it, but stay focused. And remember, this bird wants to fly."

"Got it."

"Keep making those rudder corrections to keep turning us toward the field. Reduce the power a bit so we can start a gentle descent. We want the nose a bit lower. But don't shove it down. Remember, gentle. Wings level?" She felt the correction, but he was a little heavy on the controls. "I'm going to use a bit of trim. If you're ready, glance at the airspeed and now back to the nose."

"Looks good," Paul said.

"All right. Let me know when you have the field lined up. I want to be at eight hundred feet when we're about four miles out."

"We're there, but my altitude is too high."

"What is it?"

"A thousand feet."

"That's okay. Keep bringing us down. Remember, small increments."

The spinning suddenly intensified, and Kate grabbed hold of the side of her seat for stability. She tasted the bitterness of bile and tried to swallow it away. "We don't want to go too slow or this bird will decide to quit flying. Keep the nose slightly down."

Kate opened her eyes to see if the spinning might have slowed. It hadn't. "Okay, here's the toughy. Once we get close to the ground, say fifteen feet, you'll gradually pull back on the control wheel, but not too fast. Things will seem to be happening faster as we get close to the ground. I need you to talk to me. We'll work as a team."

A few minutes passed in silence. She heard Angel whine. "What's happening? Where are we?" Kate asked.

"The ground's coming up fast," Paul said, his voice tense. "The left wing is down."

"Move the control wheel to the right gently and throttle back." Kate's grip on the seat tightened. "And pull back on the wheel."

"The ground's right below us. We're almost down." Paul's voice had taken on a strident tone.

The bird bounced up and back down hard, careening when they made contact and wobbling back and forth.

"We're veering right!"

Kate tried to see and then she felt the plane slow down, its weight on all three wheels. It lost speed too rapidly. She could feel the tail coming up and leaning to the right. The prop dug into the ground and the Pacemaker hesitated and wavered, then came to a stop balanced on the prop and the right wing.

"Out! Out!" Kate cried. "There could be a fire." Trying to hurry in her spinning world, she felt Paul's hand on her arm. "Where's Angel?"

"She's right here," Paul said as he helped Kate climb out of the seat and guided her toward the back of the plane. Barely able to see, and certain that at any moment she'd lose her breakfast, Kate managed to scramble out.

Paul kept an arm around her waist and steered her clear of the plane. When he stopped, he shouted, "We did it!"

Kate sat on the ground, pressing her hands on the grass, searching for something solid and still, but the world continued to spin. She closed her eyes and felt Angel nuzzle her. She grabbed the dog around the neck. "We did it, girl." Releasing the dog, she tried to look around but could barely make out anything in the whirling world. "Now, we've got to find our way out of here." Normally that wouldn't be too difficult in this part of the country, but Kate still couldn't distinguish up from down, and any movement made the spinning worse. She couldn't remember ever being so ill.

Paul sat beside her. "How are you feeling?"

"Terrible. But glad to be alive." She smiled and leaned against him. "Thanks."

"Thank you. Can you call Jack and have him fly someone out to get us?"

"Sure."

Kate looked up at the sky. Blue and white swirled. "I nearly killed us."

"It's not your fault. You didn't have any control over what happened."

"I did. I had some dizziness before we left today and pressure in my ears. I knew better. When my cold got bad, I never should have flown. It was stupid of me." And then she knew an awful truth. She was done with flying.

"I'm never flying again. Not ever. I'm through."

— 18 —

Kate had said her good-byes. She didn't want to say them again, but Muriel and her parents had insisted on seeing her off at the train station.

Albert pulled the car into a parking spot, and Kate's gaze traveled to a passenger train sitting in front of the depot. Was that the one she'd take to Seward?

The reality that she was leaving Alaska suddenly hit her. She'd been sick in bed for a week, but had stuck to the decision she'd made the day Paul landed her plane. It was time for her to go home.

Muriel had been struggling to hold in her tears. She stroked her son's downy hair and sniffled into a handkerchief.

Running her hand over Angel's neck, Kate pulled the dog close and fought to control her own emotions. She was tired of tears. She stepped out of the car, leading Angel out on a leash. People milled about, and Kate wondered where they were going and why.

Albert opened the trunk and lifted out Kate's bag. "You travel light."

She shrugged. "I don't have a lot, never needed much." She glanced at her watch. "I'd better see about getting Angel and my bag checked in." She reached for the suitcase.

"I've got it." Albert headed toward the terminal. Kate followed.

It took only a few minutes to purchase a ticket and check in. When Kate led Angel into the crate that would carry her all the way to Seattle, she wondered if she'd made the right decision in bringing her. The trip would be long and the weather in Yakima might be hard on a heavy-coated dog. She'd considered leaving her, but couldn't bring herself to do it. She knelt and stroked her friend through wood slats. "I'm sorry, girl. But we'll be home before you know it." She forced herself to stand and walk away.

The train in front of the station wasn't Kate's. It was headed north. Steam billowed around the engine as it moved away from the terminal. Kate placed her ticket in her purse and stepped out of the depot and into the cool autumn air. She stood on the wooden platform and gazed down the tracks.

"So you're all set, then?" Helen asked, her eyes glistening.

"I am."

"Are you sure that overnight case is all you're going to need until you get on the ship?"

"It's adequate." Kate held up the case. "Angel and I ought to be settled on the ship by this evening."

Helen handed Kate a basket. "I made you a little something to eat along the way. You'll likely be hungry before you get to Seward."

"Thank you." Kate couldn't imagine being hungry. Her stomach churned and ached. Fresh tears threatened at the thought of Helen's kindness.

Muriel and Helen sat on a bench with Kate between them. Muriel bounced her little boy on her lap. Albert stood, leaning against a railing.

"I don't know what I'm going to do without you," Muriel said. "You're certain I can't persuade you to stay?"

Kate stared at her hands clasped in her lap. "It's time for me to go home, where I belong. Nothing in life is meant to last forever." She took Muriel's hand and squeezed it. "I'll write. And who says we can't visit on the telephone now and then?

Maybe you can come for a visit. I'd love to show you the Ya-kima Valley. It's a beautiful place, but very different from here."

Muriel hugged Kate, tears spilling onto her cheeks.

The whistle of a train reverberated from the hills above the station. "That must be your train," Albert said, leaning over the railing and looking up the line.

The train hissed and rumbled its way into the station, then chugged to a stop, steam swirling around the platform. Kate stood, holding the basket of food against her abdomen. This was it. The moment she'd dreaded—the final good-bye. "I guess it's time."

She looked back at the terminal and then at the bay that stretched toward the horizon. She'd miss Alaska. Did she belong here?

Passengers disembarked and then a man walked alongside the train and called, "Board! All aboard!"

"Oh, it's time." Helen's hands played with a large button on her coat. "I'll keep praying for you, dear." She pulled Kate into her arms. "The Lord knows the path for you. He'll show you the way."

"He already has." Kate smiled while trying to keep her tears in check. She held on to Helen. "Thank you for being such a dear friend. You've been like a mother to me. I don't know how I would have managed without you." She stepped back. "I'll miss you terribly." Trying to lighten the mood, she added, "And your cookies."

"I included some of the recipes. They're in the basket." She smiled. "Now with an adequate kitchen you'll have a chance to try baking some of them."

"My mom and I can do it together." She turned to Albert and hugged him. "Thanks for everything." She kissed his cheek. "I hope you and Helen will come and visit."

His eyes shimmering, Albert said, "We'll do our best."

A blast resounded from the train. Kate watched a cart go by piled with luggage and Angel's crate. The sight of her caged up was disturbing. Kate wished there were some other way to get Angel to Yakima. Even as she considered the idea, she knew there was—they could have flown. But just the idea made her stomach churn.

Muriel was crying openly now. She wiped at her tears with one hand while cuddling her son with the other. "Oh, I'm going to miss you."

Kate dropped a kiss on the baby's head and rested her cheek there for a moment. "You're a lucky little boy. You have the best mama in the world." She smiled at Muriel. "Thanks for being such a good friend."

Muriel's eyes filled with new tears and her chin trembled. She nodded, then hugged Kate with her free arm. "What am I going to do without you?"

"You'll be so busy you won't even know I'm gone."

"That's not true. You come back, okay?"

Kate hugged her more tightly. "We'll see. Maybe." She had no intention of ever returning. Alaska was behind her now. She had a new path to walk.

"You won't be able to stay away. You're an Alaskan."

"No. I'm not."

"You are. I know it."

"I know what . . ." Her sentence dragged off. Paul walked toward her, his hands tucked into his coat pockets. She'd never expected him to show up.

Muriel turned to see what Kate was staring at. "Oh, my goodness. What's he doing here?" She sounded annoyed. "Mike's funeral was only weeks ago."

Helen took Muriel's arm and led her away. Kate watched Paul, wondering why he was here. His expression seemed pained.

"I heard you were leaving. I couldn't let you go without saying good-bye."

"I planned a trip out to the creek, but it just never happened. I don't fly anymore, so getting out there . . . well, it's not so easy without a plane."

Paul glanced at the train. Passengers were boarding. "I wanted to tell you good luck and that . . . well, that I'll miss you."

"Will you still work as a doctor?"

"Yeah. I'm needed, and I'm sure I'll be able to find flights. But without you it'll be more difficult . . . and not nearly as much fun." He took his hands out of his pockets and acted as if he were going to touch her, then he pushed them back into hiding. "I hope you'll return someday. It would be good to fly with you again."

Kate focused on the basket instead of him. "Like I said, I don't fly anymore." She was afraid, terrified in fact. She managed to look at him and, with as much conviction as she could muster, said, "It's time for me to return to a reasonable life. Settle down." She tossed her hair off her forehead. "That'll make my mom happy."

"How 'bout you?"

"Me too." Even Kate could hear the forgery in her statement.

He nodded. "If you change your mind, I'll be here and I'll always be happy to fly with you." He gently grasped her arm. "Kate, maybe it's too soon . . . maybe you should wait awhile before making this big a decision."

Kate looked at his hand. "No. I've made up my mind. It's the right thing for me to do." She glanced at the train. She needed to board. "Jack's going to sell my plane."

Paul nodded, watching the boarding passengers.

"Make sure to say good-bye to Sassa and Patrick and the boys. And Lily too. I suppose she'll be staying close to home . . . what with the baby and all."

"Yeah. I'll be close by though, if she needs me."

Kate's heart winced. *Did he mean as a doctor or something more?* "I'm sure she's counting on you."

A blast from the train alerted passengers of its imminent departure.

"I have to go." She gave Paul what she meant to be a quick hug, but he held on to her. Finally, she stepped back. "I'll write."

"I'll watch for your letters." He smiled, but there was no light in his eyes. "Take care of yourself."

"I will." Kate moved toward the train.

Muriel ran to her and gave her one more hug. Albert waved and Helen blew a kiss. "Bye, dear. I'll be praying," she called.

Kate climbed the steps, stopping at the top. Paul was still watching her. The ache she felt was so intense it was as if someone had buried a knife in her heart. With all that had happened, she still cared for him. Shame engulfed her. Mike had been gone less than a month.

She turned and stepped inside, making her way down the aisle of the car. She found a seat near the back and had barely managed to sit down when the train jerked forward and headed out of the station.

The terminal was on the opposite side of the train, so she looked out at Cook Inlet. Tears washed into her eyes and she dabbed them away. New ones replaced them. Through a blur, she stared at the bay, not really seeing it. She rested her cheek against the window. It was cold.

She was cold.

Paul watched until the train disappeared, a heavy sadness enveloping him. He'd chosen to live without her, but she'd always seemed close because he'd see her often. Now, she was truly gone, and life wouldn't be the same. He should have tried to stop her.

Albert and Helen approached him. "Paul, we didn't know you were in town," Helen said kindly.

"I had some things to take care of and decided I'd come down and say good-bye . . . since I was here." He didn't want them to know the truth, that his entire reason for coming into town was to see Kate. His throat tightened. "Didn't think she'd actually leave. She loves Alaska."

"Maybe she'll move back one day," Helen said. "I hope so."

"So, how's Sassa and Patrick?" Albert asked.

"Fine. Busy, though. You know how it can be this time of year, getting in the last of the produce and preparing for winter."

Albert nodded. "I suppose they're especially concerned, what with Lily . . . well, with Lily being in the family way."

Helen shot him a "shut your mouth" look. "What he means is they'd be extra worried with winter coming on and them being so far from a hospital."

"Well, they've got a doctor right next door," Paul said, irritated that Lily and her condition had come up. It wasn't something people ought to be talking about. With Lily not being married, it felt like gossip.

"Well, of course," Helen stuttered. "That must be reassuring."

Silence wedged itself between Paul and the Towns.

In an obvious attempt to change the subject, Helen said, "Fall is a beautiful time of year."

"It is." He tipped his hat. "Well, I better get a move on if I want to get home before dark."

"It was nice to see you," Albert said. "We'll watch for you, sometime next month?"

"I'll be in before winter."

Helen laid a hand on his arm. "And please tell Sassa we'll be praying for her . . . and the family."

"I'll tell her."

Paul had barely docked the boat when Douglas, Patrick's oldest boy, scampered down the trail to meet him. "Hi. You have a good trip?"

"Yeah." Paul tossed him the rope and the boy tied off the boat.

"Mama wants to know if you'd like to have dinner with us. It's caribou and she made berry pie." He licked his lips to emphasize how much he loved pie.

"I'd like that. It'd be nice not to have to cook for myself." Paul climbed out of the boat and headed up the trail after the boy. "Give me a few minutes to clean up and I'll be over."

"Okay." Douglas dashed off toward home, leaping to grab a tree branch as he went. He stopped and turned. "Oh yeah, I already fed the dogs."

"Thank you. I appreciate you taking such good care of them for me."

The boy grinned and ran up the trail.

Paul hauled his canned goods into the shed, and then went to greet his dogs. He gave them each a rubdown before heading indoors.

Once inside, he filled a bowl with cold water, then removed his shirt. He leaned over the bureau in front of the mirror and using a straight razor shaved off two days of whiskers. The house seemed extra quiet. He imagined Kate riding the train south. He'd made the trip before. It was beautiful country and part of the time you could see the ocean. He wished he were sharing the excursion with her.

He'd lived alone for six years, but today he felt extra lonely. He couldn't stop memories of Kate from bombarding him— medical runs with her, the chats and arguments they'd had, her laughter. And how she'd waited for him when he'd gone after that bear, even after he'd broken off their relationship. She'd been strong and steady when she'd been sick and had to help him land the plane. Her decision to stop flying had shocked him.

He scraped off stubble from his neck, then cleaned the blade on the edge of the bowl. For so long he'd hoped she'd give up flying, but now that she'd walked away from it, he could see what a mistake it was. Being a pilot was part of who she was. Quitting was like cutting off an arm or a leg. What would happen to her if she didn't fly, if she wasn't living in Alaska? She belonged here.

He rinsed off the blade, wiped the excess soap from his face, then splashed it with water. He bathed with a washcloth, then dressed. He needed a fire, but there wasn't time. It was already late and Sassa was probably waiting dinner for him. He'd build a fire when he got back.

Patrick opened the door to Paul's knock. "Howdy, neighbor. Good to have you back. How'd everything go in Anchorage?"

Paul knew Patrick cared about him, but he also wanted to know all the news and whether or not Kate actually got on the train. "Fine. I picked up a few supplies and said good-bye to Kate."

Patrick closed the door and moved toward the front room. "It's a shame she took off like that. Wonder if she'll be happy."

"Dinner's almost ready," Sassa said. She smiled at Paul, her round cheeks dimpling. "Nice to have you here."

"Thanks for inviting me. If not for you, I'd be eating cheese and bread tonight."

Patrick lowered himself into his favorite chair. "How'd Kate seem to you?"

Paul shrugged. "Resigned, I guess."

"How do you mean?"

"She's decided to go, but she's not happy. I could see that."

"'Course she's not happy. She's leaving her home."

"I don't think she's coming back. I hate to think of her spending her life doing something other than what she was meant to do and then wishing she'd done something else." Paul moved to the front window and gazed out at the creek. "I know how that feels."

His mind wandered back to the life he'd left. What would it be like to return to San Francisco with its crowded housing, the busy streets, and his work at the hospital? He'd grown used to quiet isolation and a slow pace. If he did return, could he adjust? Did he want to?

"Dinner's ready," Sassa said.

Paul turned just as Lily walked into the room. She flashed him a friendly smile. Her hand rested protectively on her rounded stomach.

"Hi, Lily. How you feeling?"

"Good. Except the baby's keeping me awake. He spends half the night kicking me."

"Just means he's healthy and strong," Sassa said. Like any mother with a daughter in Lily's condition, Sassa had grieved, but she'd accepted what life had offered and now seemed to embrace the idea. She placed a pot on the table.

"How do you know it's a boy?" Ethan asked.

"I can tell by the way she's carrying him," Sassa said with confidence.

The conversation over dinner was casual and fun, just what Paul needed. There were no more questions about Kate. When they were done eating, Sassa, true to form, suggested Lily and Paul go for a walk.

Paul had come to expect it, and he didn't mind spending time with Lily. She was an interesting person, full of stories about life in the bush.

As soon as they were out of earshot of the house, Lily said, "I'm sorry about Mama, she just won't give up."

Paul smiled. "I don't mind. I enjoy your company and I understand, your mother wants you settled with someone, especially now that you'll have a baby to raise." He hesitated, uncertain whether he ought to ask what was on his mind. He decided to leap in. "Does the father know? A child should have a father."

Lily let out a long sigh, sat on a stump, and pressed her hands against the small of her back. "He knows." She squared her jaw. "He doesn't care." She rested her hands on her stomach as if caressing her unborn child. "We'll be just fine on our own."

— 19 —

Mists swirled about the ship as it maneuvered through the waters of Puget Sound. Kate stood on deck, huddled in a coat and peering through the fog, hoping for a glimpse of Seattle. After six long days at sea, she was anxious to get off the ship and step back into the life she'd once known.

Her parents were meeting her in Seattle, and she could barely wait for the comfort of their arms. Although she'd offered to take the train from Seattle to Yakima, saving her mom and dad a trip over the mountains, they'd insisted on being at the dock to greet her. Now, she was glad they had. She wasn't sure she could stand to wait any longer. And she knew Angel was anxious to be free of her crate. Every day during the journey, she'd taken her out for a walk at least twice a day, but that wasn't nearly enough.

In some ways the trip had been good for Kate. She'd had time to think and to pray. Her thoughts had bounced between wishing she'd stayed in Anchorage and believing she'd done the right thing by leaving. Mike felt close. She tried to imagine what he would say to her. Every time it was the same. He'd have told her to do what she loved—only now she didn't know what that was. And she couldn't help but consider that he'd done what he loved and it had killed him. She wished he was with her, helping her to be strong and making her laugh.

Chilled, she pulled her coat closer and lifted the collar around her neck. He was probably disappointed in her. She'd given up, chickened out. He never would have done that. *I'm not him. I'm sorry, Mike, but I can't do it anymore.* Tears burned her eyes and she swiped them away. She'd shed enough of them.

Staring into the mist, she wondered what she would do now. Go back to working for her parents? It didn't feel like enough, but it would do temporarily.

This was the busy season—apple picking and processing, cider making, and canning the last of the vegetables from the garden. Working for her parents would fill her time while she figured out what she wanted to do with her life. And they could use the help.

Kate loved this time of year in Yakima—warm days, morning frosts, the smell of ripening apples, and family and friends working together. There'd be harvest celebrations and pumpkin carving, then Thanksgiving. It was a good time to return.

Beyond the fall season lay a void. Kate didn't know what she'd do then. She'd always counted on being a pilot. Now she didn't know what she wanted. Perhaps, while she figured it out, she could work at the local grain store or the mercantile. And there was always the possibility of being a wife and mother. She just needed someone to love who loved her back.

Sunlight pierced the haze and slowly the fog thinned, revealing the city. It was startlingly large, unlike the towns and villages of Alaska.

Squat buildings huddled along the bay and beyond, skyscrapers towered over them on stacked hillsides. Her eyes moved east past the business district. Quiet neighborhoods nestled on the hillsides where broad-limbed trees and tall evergreens shaded the homes. White-capped mountains stood in the distance, shimmering beneath a blue sky. Her home lay in the valley beyond. Kate could hardly wait to see it.

She hurried to her stateroom, grabbed her overnight bag

and her suitcase, and then made her way back to the deck. She'd be home soon.

Guided by tugboats, the ship approached a pier where a throng of people waited. Kate searched the crowd, hoping to see her parents. She felt a moment of panic when she couldn't find them. Maybe they hadn't made it.

"Katie," she heard someone shout.

She looked for the source of the voice. And then she spotted her father, wearing a broad smile and waving at her. Kate waved back, picked up her suitcase, and moved toward the walkway. She watched men throw out huge braided ropes and then tie off the ship. While she waited, her suitcase seemed to grow heavier. She tapped her foot. It was taking forever.

Finally passengers were allowed to disembark. Kate wanted to hurry, to push past the throng, but she forced herself to move with the crowd. She'd barely set her feet on the dock when her father captured her in his arms.

Kate dropped her bags and hugged him. "Oh, Daddy! It's so good to see you." A flood of tears took Kate by surprise.

"Katie," he said, smoothing her hair, seeming to know instinctively that she needed more than just a hug.

She hung on to him, all the fear and sorrow surfacing. Kate remained in her father's embrace until she caught sight of her mother standing patiently at his side.

"Mom."

Her mother pulled Kate into her arms. "How good to have you home." She held Kate close and swayed back and forth as if she were soothing a small child.

Reluctantly, Kate stepped back. "I'm glad to be here." Even as she said it, Kate knew that at this moment she was thankful for them and for a home, but she was unnerved by the feeling of instability that hovered over her. She really didn't know what she was going to do with her life. She'd always known, and now it felt like she'd been set adrift on an ocean of uncertainty.

"You only have the two bags?" her father asked.

"That's it," Kate said, "plus this basket from Helen. She

had it packed with food. I managed to eat everything she sent."

"Well, you could do with a little weight," her mother said. "I declare you're skin and bones."

"I'm fine, really."

Bill took the bag. "I thought you brought your dog?"

"I did, but we have to wait until the cargo is unloaded and then check her through into the state."

While Bill put her bags in the trunk of his Chrysler sedan, Joan tucked an arm into her daughter's. "How was the trip? Did you have good weather? Are you tired?"

Kate smiled. "The trip was fine. So was the weather. And no, I'm not tired."

The three of them headed toward the shipping office.

"We can stay over at a hotel if you like," Joan said.

"If you don't mind, I'd really like to get home. And I can't wait to introduce Angel to the farm. She'll love it. Do you mind making the trip over the mountains today, Dad?"

"Not a bit. We got in yesterday. And you know how things are this time of year—even a couple of days away means there will be catching up to do."

"Now you have me to help."

Kate spotted Angel and her crate. The dog whined and wagged her tail. After signing a release form, Kate opened the crate and caught the dog in her arms. "We're almost home, girl. Not far now." She hooked on a leash while her parents both greeted the dog.

"It'll be nice to have her around the place. Just hope the weather's not too hot for her," Kate's mother said, giving the dog a pat.

"We'll just have to make sure she doesn't get overheated," Kate said and headed toward the car.

Bill opened the back door for Kate and Angel, then hurried around and opened the front for Joan. He climbed in behind the wheel and looked over his shoulder. "So Katie, you ready to go home?"

"Yes. I can't wait." And she meant it. The sooner she got

there, the sooner she'd find her new life. She draped an arm over Angel and eased back into the seat, suddenly weary.

Her father merged into a line of traffic exiting the terminal and made his way onto First Avenue. Seattle seemed huge to Kate. It was so much larger than Anchorage, and louder.

Making their way out of Seattle meant climbing one hill after another. Bill steered through heavy traffic. Buildings rose skyward on both sides of the street. Sidewalks were congested with pedestrians. Kate was glad they weren't staying in the city. It was noisy and smelled of exhaust. When they reached the outskirts of town and headed toward the mountains, the tension eased out of Kate.

"The pass was clear when we came over yesterday," Joan said, "but we had some rain last night, so there might be snow today."

Kate gazed out the window at huge evergreens pressed up alongside the paved roadway. "I'd forgotten how big the trees are here. Most areas I fly . . . used to fly . . ." A twinge of sadness shot through Kate. "Most areas up north have small trees and fewer evergreens. And there are vast areas that don't have any trees at all."

"Why is that?" Joan asked.

"I'm not sure. My guess would be the weather and the permafrost."

"I remember when we were up there it was a stunning and daunting place." Joan looked back at Kate. "We can be thankful we don't have to worry about frigid temperatures here. The winters are cold, but nothing like what you've had to endure."

"I didn't *endure* it," Kate said, unable to conceal the irritation she felt. She wasn't sure why she was annoyed. She'd decided to leave the territory. "It's just that you get used to it."

Joan nodded and turned her attention to the road ahead of them.

Kate slid her legs out in front of her and leaned against Angel, who had made herself comfortable on the seat. She stroked the dog and thought about home. Had it changed since she left? How would it feel to live in the same old farmhouse where she'd grown up? Maybe she could find a place of her own after she got settled and found a job. The car dropped into a pothole, knocking Kate's head against the door handle. She plumped up a pillow her mother had brought, rested her head against it, and dozed off.

Kate awakened as they descended the mountains. Excitement built and memories bombarded her. This is what she'd always known. It was so different from Alaska. The pine trees were heavy bodied and red pine needles carpeted the bare ground beneath them. Leaving the mountains behind, they drove through hillsides that rolled gently downward. Yellow grasses looked soft and seemed to shimmer in the fall sunlight.

As the road wound through the hills, the broad green Yakima Valley sprawled out toward the prairie. Kate had forgotten how beautiful it was.

When they turned onto Canyon Drive, her nerves popped. They drove up the hill and Kate gazed at rows upon rows of apple trees. When they turned into their driveway, she could barely believe she was home. Her father waved at a man carrying a ladder. The man gave him a wave back.

When Bill stopped in front of the two-story farmhouse, Kate didn't get out immediately. She stared at the home she'd known all her life. A large covered porch sprawled across the front. It looked like it always had—hanging baskets overflowing with flowers, woven furniture, and a book on a table where her mother always read. Everything was the same, but she was different.

Had the time she'd spent in Alaska meant anything? Had she made a difference? She thought back to the people and remembered the injured and sick that she and Paul had helped. She recalled the woman who'd had a baby on one of her flights. Mike had helped then. She hadn't been a failure, so why did she feel like one?

Her father opened the door for her and she stepped out. Kate looked around. The yard was green and clipped short. Her mother made sure to keep it watered. The dahlias were still vivid, but many of the flowers were done for the summer. She walked to a rosebush with a display of pale pink flowers and bent to smell one. The fragrance was sweet, but faint.

"These are beautiful, Mom. You should enter them in the fair."

Joan smiled and tipped her head to the side. "Maybe I will one of these days. Perhaps you can help me with them next year."

Next year. The words reverberated through Kate. This is where she would be next year and the year after. It's where she'd spent most of her life. Her Alaskan adventure was over. Now what did she have to look forward to?

"Come on in. I'm sure you must be hungry. I've got some leftover pot roast I can warm up."

"That sounds good."

Kate let Angel out and the dog busily investigated her new home. When Kate went indoors, Angel followed, seeming comfortable and happy. "You're going to be just fine here, girl," Kate said, stroking the dog.

While her mother rustled around in the kitchen, Kate walked up the stairs to her room, Angel at her side. Her father had already brought up her bags and left them on the bed. She sat on the mattress and rested a hand on its walnut headboard. The same white dimity bedspread she'd had for years still dressed the bed. The room was spacious and had been painted a frosty green. She remembered how she and her mother had tusseled over the color. Her mother had wanted a soft yellow. Kate had refused. She smiled at the memory, still liking the green.

Green cotton curtains with yellow daisies had been freshly washed and now fluttered in the breeze at the window. Kate looked down on the front yard. She liked being able to see who was coming and going. She turned and gazed at the room. It felt familiar, but it didn't feel like home. She missed her little room in Anchorage.

With a sigh, she set her overnight case on her bureau and then undid the straps on her suitcase. She took out her clothes and placed them in the chest of drawers. She hung her leather flight jacket in the closet and pushed it to the back. She didn't want to look at it. With her clothes put away, she stashed the suitcase on a shelf in the closet. She put her personal things in the upstairs bathroom and then stashed the overnight bag in the closet beside her suitcase.

Angel lay on the floor beside the bed, her head resting on her feet. She seemed content.

Kate sat on the edge of the bed and opened the drawer to her nightstand. A book on aviation history sat inside. She'd forgotten it was there. As she flipped through the pages, an ache tightened in her chest. It was over—the adventure she'd always dreamed of was behind her. She set the book back in the bureau and closed the drawer.

A knock sounded at her door. "Come in."

Her mother opened the door. "I left things just as they were." Tears sprang into her eyes. "I never thought you'd come home." She sniffed and smiled. "And as much as I love you and want you here, I'm truly sorry. I know this isn't where you intended to be. And Mike . . . I know you cared deeply for him. Everything must seem awful to you right now, but it will get better. I promise you that."

It took all Kate had not to break down. She pushed off the bed and moved to her mother. "I'm fine. I like it here." She swallowed hard. "And Mike died doing what he loved." She squeezed her mother's hands. "Everything will work out just as it should."

Joan smiled and draped an arm over Kate's shoulders, giving her a gentle hug. "And how is Paul? Is he still working as a doctor?"

"Yes. He loves it."

"And you? How are you feeling . . . about him?"

Kate didn't know how to talk about Paul. Her feelings were all mixed up. "I . . . I miss him. But just thinking about him makes me feel like I'm being unfaithful to Mike."

"You loved them both. And love can't just be shut off the way you do a spigot." She smoothed Kate's hair. "Your heart will heal. Give it time."

Kate leaned against her mother, thankful to be home. This is what she needed.

"So, you hungry?" Joan asked in a cheerful tone. "Dinner's ready."

The following morning, Kate headed into town with her mother to help her with some shopping. It seemed to be a day when everyone was out. She met old friends and neighbors. Everyone greeted her warmly, making her feel welcomed. It almost felt like being home. Until she remembered Anchorage and wondered what Muriel and Albert and Helen might be doing. Her thoughts wandered to Paul. He was probably out on a run, doctoring people in the bush. She'd miss that.

She placed a bag of flour in the shopping cart. When she looked up, she saw Alison's mother, Lauraine Gibson, staring at her. Kate felt as if the wind had been knocked out of her.

Mrs. Gibson looked old. Her dark brown hair had gone gray, her skin was sallow, and her cheeks hollow.

Joan approached her. "Lauraine, how nice to see you."

"It's been awhile." Mrs. Gibson's eyes darted to Kate. "I heard you were back in town."

Kate couldn't think of a thing to say.

"I'm sure you must have hated to leave Alaska."

"It's nice to be home."

"Welcome back." She took a step away and turned to Joan. "You must be ecstatic to have your daughter home. It would be wonderful." Her voice trailed off.

Kate wanted to say something that would make her feel better, but knew that nothing she had to say would be welcome.

Mrs. Gibson tried, unsuccessfully, to blink away tears. "Well, I better be moving along. William's waiting for me in the car." With a stiff nod toward Kate and her mother, she walked away, her steps short and rigid.

Kate stared after her. "Nothing's changed. She still hates me."

Joan rested a hand on Kate's arm. "She doesn't hate you.

She's still grieving. She's never been able to get over losing Alison. Poor dear."

The rest of the shopping trip was ruined. Kate couldn't get Mrs. Gibson out of her mind. She was thankful when her mother suggested they head home.

Once in the car, Kate said, "Seeing Mrs. Gibson is one of the reasons I left. I can't believe I ran into her on my first trip to town."

"Maybe you should talk to the Gibsons. A lot of time has passed. I'm sure she'd welcome a visit from you."

Kate shook her head. She'd tried once to speak to them. They'd blamed her and told her to never set foot in their house again. "I can't. They don't want me there, ever."

At home, Kate helped unload the groceries, then headed for her room. She needed to be alone.

Her father stopped her at the foot of the stairs. "I ran into Richard today."

"Oh?"

"He asked if he could stop by and say hello."

"No. Not yet. I can't talk to him right now. Not after what I did."

"You went after a dream," her mother said.

"Yeah, on the day I was supposed to marry him," Kate said dryly.

"Oh Katie, I'm sorry. I thought you wouldn't mind." Her father pushed his fingers through his salt and pepper hair. "I told him it would be all right to come by anytime."

"You didn't."

"I did. I'm really sorry. He said he'd be by after supper."

20

K ate dried the last dish and set it in the cupboard. "I'll take care of the rest of this," she said, glancing around the kitchen.

"You don't have to do that. You've barely gotten home. Consider yourself a guest." Joan smiled. "At least for the rest of the day."

"No. I want to."

"That's fine, then, but we'll have plenty for you to do in the days to come. You know how it is this time of year. Apples are ready to be picked, and I can barely keep up with the garden."

Kate thought she heard a car and her pulse picked up. She glanced out the window, but there was no sign of Richard. She didn't know what she'd say to him.

Her mother spread a tablecloth on the table and set a vase of dahlias in the center. "You don't have to see him. A phone call is all it takes."

"I know, but . . . I'm not sure what I'd say. 'Don't come over'?" She grimaced. "And if I make up an excuse, he'll know. I've never been any good at lying."

"Well, I'm glad for that." Joan smoothed the tablecloth. "Do what's best for you."

"Guess I might as well get it over with." Kate leaned on the counter. "Why does he want to see me? What I did was

222

pretty awful—leaving on the day we were supposed to get married. If I were him, I wouldn't speak to me."

Her mother shrugged. "I guess he still cares about you."

"I'm not ready to date, especially not Richard." Kate's throat tightened as she said, "Mike's only been gone a few weeks."

"Richard understands that. I'm sure he's only interested in renewing your friendship. And because he cares about you, he wants to be helpful. After all, you two have been friends most of your life." She rested a hand on Kate's cheek. "Accept the friendship. Good friends are hard to come by."

Kate nodded. "I guess I better freshen up."

After pulling on a sweater, Kate stepped onto the porch and sat on a woven patio chair. Angel sat beside her and rested her head in Kate's lap. She seemed happy here. "How you doing, girl? You like your new home?" Angel nuzzled Kate's hand, then lay down on the slatted wooden porch.

Kate looked out over the orchards. The sun rested on the tops of the hills and slanted rays washed the farm in gold. A cool breeze rustled the long slender limbs of a weeping willow in the front yard.

She clasped her hands tightly in her lap and tapped the heel of one foot. She had no notion what to say to Richard. Maybe he wouldn't show up. Her stomach rumbled and she wished she'd eaten more dinner, but she'd been too nervous to eat. The sound of a car carried up from the road and she watched the driveway. No one appeared.

Chickens moved through the yard, clucking and scratching at the ground. One hen had a new clutch of chicks. Like a shadow they moved with her, scrambling beneath her protective wings at the slightest hint of danger. *That's how I need to be—hiding in God's shadow.*

The cow mooed from inside the barn, asking to be milked. Kate's foot stopped tapping and she unclenched her hands. Everything was as it should be.

She noticed a cloud of dust at the end of the driveway. It must be Richard. A few moments later she spotted his pickup. That's what she'd seen last, the day she left Yakima—Richard's pickup speeding down the driveway, furiously kicking up dust and rocks. Tonight he moved more slowly, accompanied by a small swirl of dust.

Kate stood, wiping damp palms on her skirt. Angel moved to the top of the steps and woofed as Richard pulled up in front of the house and turned off the engine. Suddenly eager to see her old friend, Kate walked across the porch and down to the yard.

Richard climbed out of the car, his blue eyes trained on her. Lifting his hat, he ran a hand through his short-cropped blond hair, he said, "Kate. Good to see you." He glanced at Angel. "And your dog?"

"This is Angel. My best friend."

"Well, hello, Angel." Richard knelt and let the dog approach him. He ran his hand over her heavy coat. "Beautiful dog."

"She was a gift from a friend."

He stood and took a step toward Kate, wearing an uneasy smile. For a long moment, they stood at arm's length, saying nothing. Then Richard's smile broadened. "What the heck." He pulled her into a friendly hug, then stepped back and studied her. "You look good."

"Thanks. So do you." Kate felt herself relax. They were still friends.

Shaking his head slightly, he said, "You're a sight for sore eyes. Alaska must have been good to you." He shifted in embarrassment. "I mean—"

"I know. It's all right."

"I'm sorry about what happened." He shoved his hands into his jeans pockets. "Sounds like Mike was someone special."

"He was." Kate let her gaze roam around the yard and then out to the orchard.

"Figure you're missing Alaska."

"A little. I like it here, though. It's warm, at least during the day."

224

"You want to take a walk?"

"Sure."

They wandered into the orchard, Angel between them. Kate looked up into a tree and took a deep breath. "Smells good."

"I always thought the air smelled kind of vinegary this time of year." He reached into the tree and plucked a yellow apple. "Looks like these are ready to pick."

"Dad has some pickers coming this week."

"Won't have any trouble finding enough. There are still a lot of people out of work." Richard shined up the apple on the front of his shirt, then took a bite. He chewed and his eyes seemed to smile. "Good."

"The reds and goldens are ready, but the winesaps have a way to go. Hope the cold holds off."

"It'll be nice having you around for the harvest celebration this year. Your dad said he'd have it up here and combine it with cider making."

"That ought to be fun." Kate's mind wandered to the fair in Palmer. She had missed it this year.

"Heard they had quite a time down at the Johnstons' last fall. A few of the fellas from town brought out some hard cider." He grinned.

"You weren't there?"

"Nah. I was working up north." Richard took another bite of his apple. "I'll be around for it this year, though." His cheek bulging, he added, "The CCC has me working on a local project."

"It'll be nice to work closer to home."

"Oh yeah. Thanks to President Roosevelt's work program I've got a job. I don't know what to expect, though."

"I heard the economy's supposed to pick up by next year," Kate said. "I hope I can find a job."

"It'll improve. I plan on ringing in 1938 with a celebration of hope. It's got to be better, right?"

"Maybe," Kate said with a sigh. "Things seemed better for a while and then the economy took another dive."

She leaned against the trunk of a tree and gazed back at

the house. The lights were on. The sight of it made her feel warm inside. Coming home had been the right decision.

"So, you have plans?"

"Plans?"

"I mean, you going to work for your parents or do something else, maybe work at the cannery or some place in town?"

"I figure, for now, I'll help out Mom and Dad. After that, I'm thinking I'd like to work in town, maybe at the feed store or one of the shops. I've had plenty of experience. That's what I did in Alaska when I wasn't flying."

Richard nodded. "Heard they have great fishing up there. You do any?"

"Not much. I never seemed to have the time." Kate wanted to apologize to Richard for leaving him so abruptly, but she didn't know how to begin. And then the words just tumbled out. "I'm sorry for what happened."

He stared at her, but she couldn't read his expression.

"I mean about leaving the way I did and then not writing to you for so long. It was wrong of me."

Richard shrugged. "You had to do what you had to do." He stepped over the irrigation ditch that ran down the row of trees. "I got over it." He held out a hand to Kate, helping her cross, and they walked along the open ground between rows.

"You'd never have been happy if you didn't go. You had to try."

"Yeah, but I went about it all wrong. And I'm really sorry."

"It's in the past now. Forget it." He glanced down at her. "Sounds like you did real well. I'm proud of you."

"Thanks," Kate said, but all she could think was that she'd failed—run away . . . again. She felt like a coward.

"Hey, you want to go fishing tomorrow? I found a real sweet spot on the river."

Kate didn't know how she felt about spending time with Richard. She didn't want him to get the wrong idea. "I don't know. I just got in and I'm pretty tired. Plus Mom and Dad have a lot of work that needs to be done. Besides the apples, there are green beans and corn to be picked and canned. Doesn't seem right to play while Mom and Dad work."

"Sure. I understand."

Even if it hadn't been such a busy time of year, Kate would have found a way to say no. Spending time with Richard didn't seem right. "We better get back to the house. It's getting dark."

They stopped at his truck. "I gotta head home. It was good to see you." He turned his gaze toward the house. "We've been friends a long time. I'd like to get back to that, if it's all right with you."

Kate was surprised at the declaration. Did he mean they should be buddies or something more? "We'll always be friends," she said.

He smiled and Kate felt the old comfort she'd once known with him.

"Come by tomorrow. Maybe I can find time to get away . . . for a quick fishing trip."

"Okay." He climbed into the cab of the truck and swung the door closed.

Kate stepped back while he started the engine and backed out. He lifted his hat to her and then drove off. She watched until she couldn't see him anymore, then turned and walked up the yard, feeling more at ease than she had in a long while.

Kate sopped up the last of an egg yolk with her toast and took a bite. Talking around her breakfast, she asked, "So, what're we going to do today?"

"Your dad's already out. He's picking reds."

Kate watched her mother as she worked around the kitchen. She wore a soft smile. Her mom was happy. It seemed like a long time since Kate had been truly happy. Life had been so confusing, and then when she thought she had it figured out, Mike died.

She finished off her breakfast. "That was good, Mom.

Thanks." She scooted her chair away from the table and carried her plate to the sink.

"I'm glad to see you eating well. You're too skinny."

"I'm fine. It's just that in Alaska I didn't do much cooking. Here, I'd better be careful or I'll get fat."

"I doubt you have to worry about that. You're always busy and you like work."

"I do and I want to help, so where do you need me today?"

"I've got some carrots that need to come out of the ground before they get woody. And I'd like to can them right away." Joan looked at her daughter with love in her eyes. "You know, your father would enjoy it if you spent some time with him. I'll be fine on my own."

"You sure?"

"Absolutely."

"There's nothing you want me to do?"

"I just want you to be happy." Joan dropped a kiss on Kate's cheek.

Remembering why she was in Yakima, Kate felt a lump tighten in her throat. Happiness felt far away. "Well, I better get out to the orchard."

Angel trotted alongside Kate as she walked to the work shed. Kate found a canvas bag and slung it over one shoulder, then grabbed a ladder that rested against the side of the building and headed for the orchard.

It didn't take long to find her father. He was picking from the upper branches of a tree.

"Hey, Dad," she called up to him. "You need some help?"

He peered down at her through the limbs. "I sure do. I have a couple of guys working the end of the row, but the main crew can't be here until next week. The reds are ripening in a hurry. And the goldens aren't far behind."

"Okay if I pick next to you? That way we can talk."

"Sure. Let's get this tree finished and then we can move on to the next."

Panting, Angel plopped down at the base of the tree. Kate leaned the ladder against the other side and climbed up. "It feels like it's going to get hot this afternoon. Angel's already suffering. Afraid she's not made for this kind of weather."

Bill wiped sweat from his forehead. "Have to make sure she gets plenty of water." He watched Kate work for a moment. "Remember to leave the stem on. Otherwise the apple will spoil. And make sure to set them in the bag gently so they don't get bruised."

"Dad, it hasn't been that long since I've picked apples. I know what to do." She cast him a disparaging look and then smiled. "I've spent more time in an apple tree than just about anywhere else."

"It's good to have you back."

"I'm glad to be here," Kate said, and at that moment she meant it. It felt like a perfect day.

"You're not missing Alaska even a little? What about your friends?"

"I miss it and my friends, especially Mike."

Her father placed an apple in his bag. "I have to say I was kind of surprised when you said you two were getting married. I thought you and Paul were meant for each other. Didn't think you felt the same about Mike." He plucked an apple. "Did you love him, Katie?"

Kate hadn't allowed herself to think about that. She wasn't completely certain what she'd felt for Mike. "Yes, I loved him, but not in the same way I did Paul. It was more like absolute admiration and trust. I still can't believe he's gone."

"I'm sorry about what happened. I liked him."

For several minutes they worked without speaking. Kate liked the feel of the apples in her hands and soon fell into the rhythm of picking.

"I was thinking about taking my plane up this afternoon. Would you like to go? It'd be like old times."

Kate had pushed her fear of flying from her mind. She'd known her father would invite her and had dreaded his asking. "No, I can't. I'm going to help Mom with some canning."

"Ah, come on. It'll be fun."

"I said no." Kate swallowed hard before continuing. "I'm

not flying anymore. Please don't ask me again. I'm done with it."

"Done with what?" came a voice from below.

Kate looked down to find Richard standing at the base of the tree. "Oh nothing."

"Hi, Richard. Good to see you." Bill removed his hat and wiped the sweat from his brow with the back of his hand.

"I heard you might need some help."

"You got that right." Bill climbed down. "The apples are ready but the crew isn't." Hauling his ladder, Bill headed toward another tree. "Why don't you finish this up with Kate and I'll get started on the next one."

"Sure. No problem." Richard placed the ladder he'd brought along against the trunk and climbed up into the heart of the tree. He smiled at Kate. "How you doing?"

"I'm getting back into the swing of things."

"I was thinking that when we get done we might go for a swim. It's hot."

"I thought you wanted to go fishing."

"Yeah, well, it turned out hot today."

"I don't know. Maybe." Kate didn't want to rush this friendship thing between her and Richard.

The next couple of hours passed quickly. Kate and Richard talked about the old days and the pranks they'd pulled and the fun they'd had while in school. It was as if the romance they'd had never happened, and had been replaced by the camaraderie they'd shared before all of that. It felt good.

"I'm done here," she said, climbing down her ladder, her sack full. Gently tumbling apples into a box, she looked up to see her father driving the tractor and trailer toward her.

He stopped. "Let's get these boxes loaded and then have some lunch. I'm starved." He looked down the row. "We've gotten a lot done for one morning."

Kate set a box of apples on the trailer. "Well, you've been out here since dawn."

"No other way to do it." He chuckled. "If I know your mom, she's already got lunch made for us." He threw an arm over Kate's shoulders as they headed toward the house. Richard walked on the other side of her. Angel padded along beside them, panting heavily.

Kate downed a glass of lemonade and held it out to be refilled. "Mmm. That's good. Could I have a little more?"

Her mother refilled the glass. "How about you, Richard?"

"You bet." He held up his glass. "You make the best lemonade in the valley."

"Well, thank you." Joan set the pitcher on a small table and sat in a chair beside Bill.

"Knew there was a reason I married you." Bill winked at his wife, then took a bite of his ham sandwich. "I've got to work on the tractor after lunch. It's running rough. And I'll need it in good shape before the pickers arrive."

"Oh," Kate said. "Do you mind if I leave the boxed apples where they are or should I haul them to the end of the row?"

"Just leave them as they are. Maybe your mom could use some help."

"I've got carrots in a water bath now. I was going to do some weeding when they're done."

"I'll give you a hand."

"No need. It's my last batch today, and all you've done since you got home is work. Why don't you and Richard go and do something fun?"

Kate didn't know what to say. Was her mother matchmaking? It was out of character for her.

Before she could respond, Richard asked, "Maybe we could go for that swim?"

"That sounds like a good idea." Bill stuffed the last of his sandwich in his mouth and followed it with a gulp of lemonade.

Kate felt trapped. How could she get out of the invitation without sounding rude? She didn't mind working with Richard, but swimming was something else altogether. "I don't know. I'd planned to help Mom."

"I'm fine, really. You two go have a good time."

Kate looked at Richard. "Well, okay. I guess a swim would feel good." She glanced at her dog, panting in the shade of the porch. "Angel would like it. I think she's overly hot." She turned to her mother. "Do you know where my suit is?"

"Yes. I'll get it."

Kate followed her mother indoors. When she was certain they were out of earshot of her father and Richard, she said, "Mom. Wait."

Her mother stopped and looked at her. "What is it, dear?"

Kate wasn't sure how to express herself without sounding ungrateful. "I . . . Why are you pushing Richard and me together?"

Her mother's eyes widened. "Oh. I didn't mean to. I just want you to have a good time." A look of regret flickered across her face. "I'm sorry for being insensitive."

"It's okay. But after this, please let me decide. Okay?"

"Of course." Joan gave Kate a hug. "I'm sorry."

———————

With a shift covering her swimsuit and a towel rolled up under one arm, Kate headed for Richard's pickup. Angel jumped into the back while Richard hurried to the door and opened it for Kate. She slid onto the seat. Maybe this would be fun.

Richard climbed in. "All set?"

"Yep."

He backed out and headed down the driveway. Once they were on the road that followed the river, Kate leaned on the open window and gazed at the brown hillsides, covered with sunburnt grass and sagebrush. Clusters of bright yellow flowers speckled the landscape.

"Wonder if the rope swing is still intact," Richard said.

"How long's it been since you were at the swimming hole?"

"Not since you were here."

Kate stared straight ahead. It seemed that a lot of things

had come to a halt for Richard when she'd left. And now . . . what now?

She decided not to worry about it. It was a beautiful October day and she was going to enjoy herself. She leaned closer to the open window and allowed the wind to tousle her hair. Closing her eyes, she breathed in the fragrance of sage, dry grass, and hay. "It's awfully warm for October."

"Well, it just got started. And we can always do with an Indian summer. I'm not complaining."

"It feels good," Kate said as they passed an area of rangeland dotted with huge stacks of hay bales.

Richard turned onto a side road and drove toward the river. Bushes, small trees, and willows hugged the banks. "This is it." He pulled to a stop. "Looks the same."

Kate climbed out of the truck and her mind flooded with memories of picnics, laughter, and friends. She ran for the tree that hugged the bank and grabbed hold of the rope. "It's still here." She smiled and tugged on it.

"You swimming in that dress?"

Kate had nearly forgotten her shift. She suddenly felt embarrassed. Taking it off would feel like she was undressing in front of Richard. He grabbed the rope and swung out over the water. With a whoop, he let go and dropped into the river.

Kate lifted the shift over her head and tossed it to the base of the tree. "Here I come," she called, grabbing hold of the rope and pushing off. With a squeal, she swung out and let go, falling into the pool beside Richard. The water sent shocks of cold through her. "It's freezing." She laughed.

Angel didn't waste any time jumping in and following Kate out to the middle of the pool. She lapped up mouthfuls of water as she went.

Richard flattened his hand and pushed it across the water's surface, splashing Kate. She reciprocated and soon they were in the midst of an all-out water fight.

"I give. I give," Kate finally hollered and swam for shore. She stepped across the rock beach and climbed the bank.

After wrapping her towel around her, she sat on a grassy spot. It felt good to laugh.

Angel exited the stream, looking soggy but cool. She shook off the excess water and trotted away to do some exploring. Kate gazed out over the water to the reeds on the far bank and the hills beyond.

Richard dropped down beside her. "I love it here."

"Me too. I'd almost forgotten how much."

"We've had some good times here." He smiled at her, and his gaze turned tender. Kate knew he was remembering not just the fun, but also the embraces and the kisses they'd shared. She looked away and stared at the river.

Neither spoke. Kate allowed her thoughts to carry her further back to the fun-filled days of childhood. She and Richard had been buddies then. "Do you remember the day you convinced me to skip science class and come fishing?"

Richard chuckled. "Old Man Reynolds wasn't one bit happy."

"I can't believe he actually got someone to take his class and came down here to haul us back to school."

"Guess he was fed up. It's not like it was the first time." Richard grinned.

Memories cascaded over Kate. "Those were good days."

"Glad to have you back," Richard said, his tone gentle. "I've missed my fishing and swimming pal."

"I've missed you too," Kate said, realizing how much he meant to her. She needed a good friend. She'd lost too many.

Silence settled over the two. Richard leaned back on straightened arms and asked, "So, how was it up there?"

"Wonderful . . . and horrible." Kate pulled her knees up against her chest. "I loved it. Alaska's one of the most beautiful places I've ever seen. There are powerful, endless mountain ranges that seem to reach right up to heaven. And the forests aren't anything like what we have in the mountains here. Some of the spruce are huge, but most of the evergreens are small and sparse. There's endless tundra covered with greenery that looks like burnished brass in the fall. And fields of flowers and berries are everywhere. In the summer it stays light nearly all night, and during the winter there are only a few hours of daylight. I didn't like the bugs. Sometimes there were so many mosquitoes they'd look like a cloud. And the black flies were almost as bad."

"Don't figure I'd like that much. What about the winters? They as awful as I've heard?"

"Worse." Kate laughed. "Well, sometimes. They can get really bad. And the cold is like nothing we ever see around here. If you're not careful, the storms will do you in."

"You have any close calls?"

"A couple." Kate didn't want to talk about that.

Silence descended again. Richard finally said, "Heard you're not flying anymore."

"Yeah. Enough's enough."

"Back before . . . before you left, I was unfair to you. I was thinking only about me and what I wanted. But I was proud of you, Kate. I just wanted to keep you to myself."

"It doesn't matter now. I'm not flying anymore." Kate pushed to her feet. She didn't want to talk about any of that. "I'm cold. Let's go."

21

Paul peered down at the creek as Kenny Hicks set up for a landing. The forest blazed with autumn colors and smoke rose from a mound of brush behind Patrick's house. He and the boys stood around the fire. They gazed up at the plane and waved. Paul returned the gesture, glad to be back. His mind moved to the list of chores he had to do to prepare for winter. Being away had cut into his work time.

His gaze moved to Klaus's cabin and he thought it odd that there was no smoke rising from his chimney. It had been cold. He studied the German's place, hoping to see the old-timer, but there was no sign of him. He'd probably made a trip to Susitna Station.

Kenny set down on the creek and motored toward Paul's dock. He grabbed his medical bag and his pack, and then headed for the door. "Thanks for the ride. See you in about a week?"

"Sure thing." A black curl flopped onto Kenny's forehead and into his eyes. "If I'm out on a run, Jack'll make sure someone picks you up. Alan maybe. See ya."

Paul nodded and climbed out. He was glad to be free of the plane. It was more compact than the one Kate had flown, and uncomfortable. He pressed his hands against the small of his back. And Kenny's flying made him nervous. He was at best a mediocre pilot, not nearly as vigilant or as gifted as Kate and Mike had been. Given enough time, he'd probably crack up. Paul hoped he wasn't with him when it happened.

Paul waved to Kenny as the plane headed toward the middle of the creek, then he started up the trail toward his cabin. The dogs barked. He stopped to savor the homestead. The air was chilled and filled with the scent of ripening berries and cedar. He gazed at the pale blue sky, where whispers of white clouds reached from west to east.

Paul glanced up the creek toward Klaus's place. He ought to go check on him. He'd see to the dogs and then go on over.

He set his bags on the porch steps and then went to greet the dogs. They whined and lunged against their leads. "Did you miss me?" he asked, giving Nita a pat.

She rubbed against his pant leg while he scratched behind her ears. When he unclasped her lead, she bounded away, her nose investigating every new smell. Jackpot barked at him, and when Paul released him, he sprinted after Nita. Buck strained against his rope. "You're looking good, boy." The dog jumped up on Paul, planting his paws on his chest. His tail wagged enthusiastically.

Paul wrapped his arms around the big malamute. "I'm glad to see you too." Buck had recovered from his grizzly encounter. The only visible scar was on his side. The hair grew slightly out of its natural pattern and a fine bald line ran around the edges of the untidy patch of hair.

He headed toward Klaus's cabin. The dogs loped along the trail ahead of him, and when he reached Patrick's place, they tousled with the Warrens' dogs.

"Howdy, neighbor," Patrick called. "Good to have you back."

"Good to be here. Did Klaus go up to Susitna Station?"

Patrick shoveled a batch of rotting brush onto a pitchfork and tossed it on the fire. He stuck the pitchfork in the ground and leaned on it. "Not that I know of. I was at his place last night and he didn't mention anything about going. Why?"

"When I flew in, I noticed there's no smoke coming from his chimney and it's pretty chilly today."

A crease of concern appeared on Patrick's forehead. "We better have a look."

When Patrick told Sassa he and Paul were headed for Klaus's, she insisted on joining them. "He could be sick or injured," she said. "And no one would know. I've been feeling uneasy about him. He's not been looking so good lately."

When they approached the cabin, there was no sign of their neighbor, and his boat was still moored at the dock. Paul climbed the steps and knocked on the door. Patrick and Sassa stood close behind him. There was no answer. Paul knocked again. Still nothing.

Paul opened the door and walked inside. He spotted Klaus immediately. He was sprawled facedown on the kitchen floor. Paul hurried to the old man and rolled him onto his back. He felt for a pulse but knew he wouldn't find one. Klaus's skin was a deathly shade of gray and there was no visible sign of breathing.

"Oh, dear Lord," Sassa said. "Is he gone?"

"Yes." Paul let out a desolate breath. He knew this would happen one day, but the realization of it was worse than imagining it.

Sassa pressed her hands to her chest. "How long has he been lying here?"

"Quite awhile, I'd say. He's beginning to show signs of rigor mortis." Paul felt sick inside. He'd seen too much of death, too many friends gone. He rested a hand on the old man's chest. No one had been with him at the end. Is that what he would face one day?

"Anyone know if he had family?" Paul asked.

"He never talked about anyone," Sassa said, dabbing at tears with the corner of her apron.

Patrick moved to the door and stared out. "I figure he'd want to be buried here on his place."

Sassa and Lily prepared Klaus's body while Patrick built a casket. Paul and Patrick's two oldest sons dug a grave. The boys had picked a spot on a small rise. They thought it would be nice if Klaus could see the creek.

When everything was ready, Paul joined the Warrens at the gravesite. Sassa stood with her arms protectively around her three boys while Paul and Patrick lowered the casket into the grave. Lily stood several paces back, clutching a bouquet of yellow and white asters, the last of the season. Her eyes were red from crying.

Patrick removed his hat and cleared his throat. He looked at the small group. "Does anyone have anything they'd like to say?"

Douglas stepped forward. "I'm going to miss you . . . Klaus." He swallowed hard. "You're the best whittler I ever knew. Thanks for teaching me. I figure you might even teach Jesus now that you're up in heaven." He wiped away tears and stepped back.

Robert, who was barely seven, clung to his mother but said in a raspy voice, "Sometimes you were kind of cranky, but I knew it was because you were old and not feeling so good. I'm never gonna forget how we used to go fishing together."

Silence settled over the small group. Paul thought he ought to speak but didn't know what to say. All he could think about was that poor Klaus had died alone.

Patrick cleared his throat. "Well, Klaus, you were a good neighbor and friend. We're gonna miss you, but I figure you're a lot better off now. You loved God, so I know you're with him. There'll be no more sorrow and no more tears for you. Thanks for being a fine example to my children and to me and Sassa too." He looked at the others, his eyes brimming with tears.

The boys sniffled and wiped their noses, Sassa cried into a handkerchief. Lily remained stoic, but stepped forward and dropped the flowers onto the casket. She stared at it, then turned and walked away.

Patrick pushed his hat back on his head. "Well, I guess we better get to it." He gave Sassa a knowing look.

"Okay, boys. I need help cleaning out the chicken house." She ushered them away.

Patrick picked up a shovel and scooped dirt onto the casket. His heart heavy, Paul used the other shovel and helped bury the old man. After Patrick pounded a wooden cross into the ground, Paul walked home, feeling empty. Life was a puzzle. A man was born, lived, and then died. What was the meaning of it all? Paul's soul ached for an answer. Was doing good while one lived enough? He'd always believed in a God of mercy who loved his children. So great was his love that he offered his own Son. Paul had never doubted . . . and then Susan had died. Why?

That night, Paul had barely fallen asleep when a knock at his door startled him awake. Still mostly asleep, he stumbled to answer it. "Who's there?"

"Me. Patrick." He sounded agitated.

Paul opened the door. "Is everything all right? Has something happened?"

"It's Lily. The baby's coming."

"Are you sure? I thought she wasn't due for nearly a month."

Patrick shrugged. "She's acting just like Sassa did every time."

"Come on in. It'll only take me a minute to get dressed." Paul hurried to his room and pulled pants and a shirt on over his long johns. He pushed his feet into his boots and laced them. If Lily's doctor, in Seattle, had been correct, the baby was several weeks early. That could mean problems, especially for the baby. Panic tried to bully him.

He hadn't delivered many babies. Since losing his own son, he'd done his best to steer clear of laboring mothers. He'd counted on Lily having an uncomplicated birth, which meant Sassa wouldn't need him to help bring her grandchild into the world.

He grabbed his medical bag and followed Patrick into the night air. As they walked up the trail, the lantern cast shadows on the bushes. Paul's mind was busy calculating what could go wrong. Babies born this early sometimes had difficulty breathing. Or they might not breathe at all. Premature infants sometimes didn't have the suckling reflex. They were susceptible to illness and there was a whole list of other maladies they might face.

Carrying an air of confidence Paul didn't feel, he followed Patrick into the house. It felt overly hot and smelled of cooked fish.

"She's upstairs," Patrick nodded toward the stairway.

Paul hurried up the steps. He glanced in the first door. The boys were huddled on their beds, looking anxious. "Hi, boys," he said cheerfully.

"Hi," Douglas said. "Is Lily going to die?"

"No. Of course not."

"Is she going to heaven like Klaus?" Robert asked.

"No. She's just having a baby. She'll be fine, but it takes awhile and it hurts."

"She was moaning real loud and crying."

"That's normal. Try not to worry."

"Okay." Robert sat more upright. "I'm not so scared with you here."

Paul nodded. He'd do his best, but that might not be enough. He hurried down the hallway to the next door. A groan came from inside. Sassa sat on a chair beside a bed, holding Lily's hand.

Paul moved to the bed and leaned over Lily. "Hi, neighbor."

She looked at him. "I'm so glad you're here. The baby's not supposed to come yet."

"Don't worry. I'm sure it's just fine." Paul fought to keep a tone of assurance in his voice. "When did the contractions start?"

Before Lily could answer, Sassa said, "Just after we buried Klaus. But they weren't bad, so I thought they were just those early pains a mother gets. But they didn't go away. Then awhile ago she lost her water and the pains got real bad." Sassa glanced at Lily, who had rolled onto her side and was holding her abdomen. She let out a whimper. "She's so early we thought you should come."

Paul checked Lily's pulse. It was fast, understandably so. "How are you feeling?"

"How do you think?" Lily rolled onto her back and wiped damp hair off her face. "That was a bad one."

"Let me check you over," he said, placing a thermometer in Lily's mouth. He took a stethoscope out of his bag and listened to her heartbeat, then the baby's. "Sounds good and strong." He took the thermometer out of her mouth. "No fever."

He smiled down at her. "Everything seems fine."

"But I'm not due until the end of the month."

"Babies have a mind of their own, and sometimes they get here before we expect them to and they do just fine." Paul didn't see any reason to tell her about all the possible problems.

Lily closed her eyes.

"Try to relax and rest while you can."

Lily took several deep breaths.

Paul placed his hand on her abdomen. He could feel the muscles tighten.

"Another one's coming." Her voice sounded panicked. She grabbed hold of her mother's hand.

"Breathe slowly," Paul said. "Don't tighten up."

Lily blew out a breath and took in a slow, deep one and then blew it out gradually. "It's getting . . . worse," she panted.

Paul left his hand on her abdomen. "Okay, it's easing off. It'll be over soon." He looked at Sassa. "How often are they coming?"

"Every couple of minutes."

"Paul, they're getting worse. Really bad," Lily said. "I don't know if I can do this."

He smiled. "You *can* do it. Remember, you're the woman who can do anything."

"Not this."

Using a washcloth, Sassa patted the sheen off her daughter's face. "You will do well. I know it."

"Listen to your mother. You're one of the strongest women

I know." He turned to Sassa. "I'll need some hot water and washcloths. And do you have a birthing blanket?"

"Yes. I'll get it." She hurried out of the room.

Paul turned back to Lily. "Have you had any pressure on your bottom?"

"Yes, with the last two pains."

"You feel like you need to push?"

Lily shook her head no, then she took a deep breath as another contraction hit.

"Probably won't be long now."

Lily grabbed his hand. "I'm afraid."

"I know. But it's going to be all right," Paul said, his tone steady and calm.

Lily panted. "But the baby . . . it's too soon."

"All you need to think about right now is bringing this child into the world. I'll take care of the rest," he said, but couldn't keep from wondering if he could. What if the baby wasn't ready for the world? Did he know what to do if it was too premature? He hadn't been able to save his own son or his wife. What made him think he was ready for this? He wanted to walk out and not come back.

"I'd better wash up."

He passed Patrick in the doorway. His brows furrowed, he stared at his daughter. "Is she going to be all right?"

Paul pressed a hand on his friend's arm. "She'll be fine." He kept saying the words, but he was afraid.

"And the baby?"

Paul wasn't about to lie to Patrick. "I don't know. We'll have to wait and see. It's pretty early." He moved into the hallway and hurried down the stairs and to the kitchen, where he washed his hands thoroughly in the sink.

Sassa had washcloths and towels draped over her shoulder and a heavy blanket folded in her hands. "I'll come back for the water."

"I'll get it," Paul said.

Sassa headed up the stairway.

Paul toweled dry, lifted the cast iron pot off the stove, and headed up the stairs. When he walked into the room, he set the water on the bureau next to Lily's bed. Paul helped Lily off the bed and allowed her to lean on him while Sassa removed the bedding and replaced it with the birthing blanket. Paul kept a hand on Lily when she lay back down.

"I'm so glad you're here," she said and then groaned. "Oh, I have to push."

"Okay," Sassa said, stroking Lily's forehead. "Listen to your body. It will tell you what to do."

When the contraction passed, Paul said, "Lily, I'm going to have to check you to see where the baby is."

She nodded. While Paul examined her, Lily stared at the ceiling.

He couldn't see the head, so he felt to determine the infant's position. It hadn't moved very far into the birth canal. "Everything's fine, but it's going to take some extra work to get this baby down. It's in a posterior position."

"What's that mean?" asked Sassa.

"Most babies come out looking at the floor, but he's facing the ceiling. It's more difficult to birth a baby in that position and more painful. I may have to turn him."

Lily labored two more hours and finally her little boy entered the world. His cry was weak, but he was breathing on his own and his color was good. Relief filled Paul.

"Oh, thank the Lord," Sassa said, pressing her palms together.

"You have a little boy, Lily," Paul said, clamping the cord and cutting it. He listened to the baby's heart and breathing. "He sounds healthy." He handed the infant off to Sassa.

She cleaned and swaddled him and then placed the little one in Lily's arms. "He's perfect." Her eyes brimmed with tears as she looked at her daughter. "All babies are a blessing from God. This little boy is God's creation."

Lily took her mother's hand and squeezed it. "I love you." She turned her attention to her son, then smiled up at Paul. "Thank you for helping."

"Glad to." Paul gazed at the baby. "He's a fine-looking

boy." His heart stirred at the sight of mother and son, and a longing for his own son welled up inside of him. What would life have been like if he had lived?

"Do you have a name for him?" Patrick asked.

"I have been thinking on that. I think I would like to call him Theodore Patrick Warren. I had a good friend in Seattle. We worked together and he had great faith. His name was Theodore." Her eyes moved to her father. "And your name will bring honor to my son."

Patrick's eyes glistened and he leaned down and kissed Lily on the cheek. "I love you. And no matter what anyone might say, you are a daughter to be proud of." He hugged her, then quietly left the room.

After checking the baby over and making sure all was well with Lily, Paul said, "It's time for me to get home and for you to get some rest. You stay in bed unless it's absolutely necessary to get up, at least for a few days." He closed his medical bag. "I'll be back tomorrow to check on you."

Lily nodded without looking at him. She stared at her baby, a soft smile on her lips.

Paul's throat tightened at the sight. He longed for someone to love. He longed for Kate.

22

Kate walked into the kitchen and pulled off her work gloves. "Hi, Mom." The mix of sweet and tangy smells wafted through the room. "It smells good in here."

Joan lifted the lid off the canner and steam whooshed into the air. Wearing cooking mittens, she used canning tongs to lift out hot jars, then she set them on a towel on the counter.

"I love canned rhubarb." Kate pulled off a flannel shirt she'd worn over her blouse and draped it across the back of a chair. "When I went out this morning it was cold, now I'm sweating."

"I like that about October. Cool mornings and warm afternoons."

"You mean hot afternoons. Poor Angel is lying in the yard under the weeping willow, panting away. Sometimes I wonder if it was wise to bring her."

"She'll adjust. You both will. It's just that you're used to the cooler weather up north." Joan set the last jar on the counter. "And it's not going to stay hot. I heard the temperatures could drop into the twenties tonight. I'm worried we'll lose a lot of our apple crop."

"Dad's ready. He has the oil and pans all set just in case."

"A letter came for you, from Helen. I put it on the occasional table in the living room."

Eager for news from Alaska, Kate headed into the front room and picked up the envelope. Dropping onto the sofa, she settled back to read.

Helen had a lot to say. She talked about the annual fair in Palmer and the fun they'd had. And she gave details on a storm that blew in, dropping snow on Anchorage. The store had nearly sold out of kerosene and oil. Muriel's husband, Terrence, had brought down a moose his first day out, and the baby was getting fat and was already rolling over. She talked about what a happy little boy he was and how much she loved being a grandmother.

Kate smiled. Helen would be the world's best grandmother. Returning to the letter, she read about Lily and the baby. Helen was happy for a new life but was concerned for Lily and the stigma that would follow her and her son. Even though they lived out at the creek, gossip about Lily's circumstances had been bantered about the bush and even been carried into town.

Melancholy swelled inside Kate. It was true that Lily had stumbled, but she was still a fine person and she'd be a good mother. She hated how unfair people could be—as if *they'd* never sinned.

She wondered how Paul felt about it all. He'd helped deliver the baby. Did he have special feelings for the infant? And what about Lily? Had the two of them grown closer? Sadness enfolded Kate. Would there ever be anyone for her? Would she ever be a mother?

She returned to the letter.

Helen and Albert planned to expand the store. Business had picked up and they needed more space. Kate wondered if they'd utilize the back room that had been her home. The idea made her a little sad.

Kate folded the letter and slid it back inside its envelope. Just as she headed for the stairs, she heard the sound of a car out front. Wondering who had stopped by, she glanced out the window. It was Richard. What was he doing here? She opened the front screen door and stepped onto the covered porch as he climbed out of his truck. Angel greeted him, her tail wagging.

He stroked her head. "Hi, girl. How you doing?"

In answer, the dog leaned against him.

Richard looked up at Kate. "Hi. I was just going by and thought I'd drop in."

Kate pushed the envelope into her back pants pocket. "Where you heading?"

"I was on my way home from work."

"Isn't this a little out of your way?"

He grinned and placed a foot on the bottom step. "There's a double feature playing in town. You want to go?"

"I'm a mess. I just got in from working all day."

"There's plenty of time. I can run home, clean up, and then come back."

"I don't know. Daddy might need me tonight. The temperature is supposed to drop, maybe into the twenties. If it does, we'll have to set out smudge pots."

"We wouldn't be late. And I doubt that it's going to get that cold. It's still hot."

Richard was probably right. Her father had a tendency to be extra careful when it came to his trees. Kate wasn't sure she wanted to go, no matter what the weather did. Swimming on a hot afternoon was one thing, but the movies felt more like a date.

"*Captains Courageous* is playing along with the new Shirley Temple movie, *Heidi*."

"They're both s'posed to be good." Kate blew out a breath. "Okay. What time?"

"How about an hour?"

"All right."

Richard glanced at his watch. "I'll be back at five. Maybe we can get some dinner afterward?"

"Okay. See you in an hour."

Kate was putting on lipstick when she heard a car pull up. She went to the window and looked down at the yard.

Richard climbed out of his pickup. Her father met him at the end of the yard and they talked. Maybe he'd convince Richard to stay and help in case of bad weather. But while Kate watched, her dad clapped the young man on the shoulder and then headed for the barn. Richard walked up the yard toward the porch.

Kate took a last look in the mirror, ran a brush through her bobbed hair, and then headed downstairs with Angel at her side. When she made her way down the stairs, Richard was visiting with her mother in the front room.

"You're just on time," she said.

He looked at her and she could see admiration in his eyes. She wished she hadn't accepted his invitation. He might get the wrong idea.

"Kate, you look lovely." Her mother folded her arms across her waist and studied her. "Richard said you two are going to the movies."

Trying to sound nonchalant, Kate said, "There are a couple of good ones playing, so we thought why not." She smiled at Richard, hoping she wouldn't see any expectations in his eyes. Thankfully she saw only fun.

"Ready?" he asked.

"All set." Kate grabbed a sweater out of a closet near the front entry. "We won't be late," she told her mother and walked to the door. Angel followed. Kate stroked the dog. "Sorry, girl, not this time."

Richard reached around Kate and opened the door. "Night, Mrs. Evans."

All the way to town, Kate wondered if she'd made a mistake in accepting Richard's invitation. What if he expected something more than friendship?

She seemed to be the only one worrying. He was relaxed and talked about inconsequential things. By the time they reached the theater, Kate felt more comfortable. Maybe they could be just friends.

When Kate stepped into the line of people waiting in front of the theater, she spotted Mr. and Mrs. Parkins from church.

She groaned, knowing Mrs. Parkins would jump to conclusions about her and Richard.

Wearing her sweetest smile, the woman approached. "Kate. Richard. How wonderful to see you two."

"Evening, ma'am," Richard said.

"Hello." Kate had heard the excitement in the woman's voice. She would tell everyone she knew that she'd seen them together. Kate frantically searched for some way to explain why she was with Richard.

"Kate and I are crazy about Shirley Temple movies," Richard said. "So, we decided since we're friends we might as well see it together." He smiled. "Friends. We're just longtime friends." He grinned.

"Oh. Well of course." Mrs. Parkins took a step back. "Enjoy the movie." She walked toward her husband.

Kate buried a giggle beneath her hand. "Thanks, Richard. I appreciate that."

"No problem." He paid for their tickets and opened the theater door. Kate stepped inside. She loved the atmosphere. It reminded her of Saturday matinees as a child. "Do you remember when we used to come down on Saturday afternoons?"

"Oh yeah. Silent movies. I never was a fast enough reader." He leaned against her. "But I liked it when you read the captions to me."

"You liked the snacks," Kate said.

"Still like Hershey bars." He grinned. "Figure I'll get myself one before we sit down. You hungry?"

"Maybe." Kate moved to the snack bar and studied her options. "Milk Duds sound good."

Richard stepped up to the counter. "One box of Milk Duds, two Hershey bars, and a bag of popcorn." He looked at Kate. "You want something to drink?"

"How about a Coke."

"Two Cokes, please." Richard slid the change across the counter.

As they headed for the theater, Kate looked at him. "Some things never change."

"What do you mean?" he asked, stuffing the candy bars into his shirt pocket, while supporting the bag of popcorn against his chest and holding his pop with the same arm.

"You love to eat." She chuckled. "You won't want anything afterward."

"Wanna make a bet?" he chuckled.

When Kate dropped into her seat, she felt relaxed and happy. It seemed like forever since she'd done something as simple as go to a movie. Life in Alaska, with its joys and sorrows, seemed far away.

After a rousing ending to *Captains Courageous*, the screen went black and the theater lights came on. Richard and Kate headed for the lobby.

"That was a good movie," Kate said.

"They both were."

"What about the cartoon? You're not a fan of Donald Duck?"

"I absolutely am." Richard draped an arm over Kate's shoulders and gave her a teasing hug.

When they stepped out of the theater, cold night air nipped at them. It had settled over the valley in a hurry, and now frost glistened in the car lights on the street.

Kate bundled deeper into her sweater. "It's cold. Too cold." She hurried her steps. "I need to get home."

Richard ran around and opened the truck door for her, then slid in behind the wheel and started the engine. They hurried toward Kate's.

"I should have stayed home."

"Calm down," Richard said. "It's not that cold yet. I'm sure everything's fine."

"I hope Dad has help," Kate said, gazing at the rows of trees as they drove past. Lights bounced through the orchards and most of the farms had smudge pots burning already.

When they headed up the driveway, Kate saw her father and mother out among the trees. "Stop here," she said. The truck

251

was still moving when Kate opened the door and stepped out. Richard left the lights on so Kate could see as she ran across the orchard to her parents. "How bad is it?"

"We're staying on it," her father said. "The only trees we've got to worry about are the late apples. Can you grab some of those cans and set them out?"

"Sure." Kate hurried to her father's truck and grabbed a batch of buckets.

Richard picked up two cans of kerosene and followed her. "I'll pour the fuel."

"Thanks." Kate set a bucket down in the center of the row. She wished she weren't wearing her dress shoes; they made walking difficult. Richard poured fuel into the bucket and Kate lit it off. The flame illuminated his face. "Even though it wasn't the best timing, thanks for tonight."

"I shouldn't have asked, not with the possibility of a freeze."

"I wanted to go."

He smiled. "Okay. So let's save as many apples as we can."

Working frantically, Kate and Richard moved down one row and then on to the next.

Two laborers who'd been staying on at the farm set out pots several acres away. Kate's parents joined forces in the next orchard. It took more than an hour to get the pots out and lit. By the time they'd finished, Kate was exhausted. She stood with her hands on her hips and gazed out over the farm. It looked eerie with flickering flames and smoke illuminated in the light.

Her father joined her. "Good work, Kate."

She leaned against him, enjoying the feel of his arm around her. She felt safe. "Will the apples be all right?"

"I'll tell you in a minute." He picked an apple off a tree and using a pocket knife, cut it open. He studied the fruit. "This one looks good, just a little frozen around the outside edges. Didn't get into the core." He moved to another tree and picked an apple, cut it open. "Same here."

Kate sat on the tailgate of the truck. Even in the cold she

felt hot. She took in a deep breath of gratitude. She exhaled and the air fogged. "Where's Angel?"

"We thought it would be better if she stayed indoors." Kate's father leaned against the side of the truck. "Thanks for your help." Taking off his hat, he rotated it in his hands and then resettled it on his head. "I think we're going to be fine."

"I should have been here."

"You couldn't have known. You worked all day—no reason not to go out and have some fun. You've had little of it."

Richard sat on the tailgate beside Kate. "It was my fault. I asked her out. I knew it was supposed to get cold tonight."

"Well, at least you were here to help. I needed you."

Richard gave him a nod. "I'll be here anytime." He looked down at Kate and his look implied he meant that for her too.

She purposely bumped against him, thankful for his friendship. It had been right for her to go to Alaska. She needed to live her adventure, but now it was time to learn to be content with a simpler life.

23

Paul set his medical bag and a box of supplies on his kitchen table. He needed to restock for his next trip out. He went through the bag to see what items he was short on, then sorted through the box of supplies, replacing sutures, sterile gauze, a thermometer that had broken, two bottles of aspirin, and one bottle of morphine, which he needed for the worst of injuries. Morphine wouldn't have helped Carl Gladwell.

An image of the bloodied man burst into his mind. He wondered how Carl's family was managing. More than likely, his wife and children had moved back into town or were living with family.

He slid a bottle of alcohol into a pocket on the inside of the bag and then dropped in adhesive tape. He closed the satchel and set it on the bureau in his bedroom. He'd be prepared if he were called out on an emergency. He was scheduled for a trip later in the week.

The dogs started barking and Paul looked out the window. Lily was in the yard and she'd stopped to visit the dogs. She carried Theodore in a side sling. The dogs sniffed at the baby. Teddy, as Lily called him, gazed at the animals, his head bobbing. He wasn't old enough to hold his head up well.

Lily walked toward the cabin, and Paul opened the door and stepped onto the porch. "Hi. What brings you here?"

"It's sunny and almost warm, so I thought Teddy and I ought to get a little fresh air and sunshine." She caressed the baby's nearly bald head. "He likes to be outside." She looked up at Paul. "I hope you don't mind."

"No. I was just stocking up my medical bag." He moved onto the porch. "How's he doing?"

"See for yourself." She walked up the steps, hefted the chubby baby out of the sling, and handed him to Paul. "Do you mind if I get a drink of water? I'm thirsty."

"Help yourself." Holding the infant against his chest, Paul stepped aside to allow Lily into the house. He followed and closed the door. Hefting the baby, he smiled at him. "You're a big boy." He glanced at Lily. "He's strong. He's already trying to hold up his head." Theodore's chin dropped to his chest. "Well, sort of."

"He can only hold it up a few seconds," Lily said, taking a cup out of the cupboard and filling it from the hand pump.

Theodore grinned.

"And he's smiling too?" Paul bounced him. "I'd say you have a precocious young boy here."

"I don't think he knows he's smiling." Lily looked at her son with devotion. "Mama agrees with you, though. She says he's real smart, that she can tell. I just think he's lovable and sweet." She sipped from the cup. "He sleeps most of the time."

Paul cradled the baby in one arm and smiled down at him. "He looks like you."

He bounced the baby gently, his heart squeezing. He'd never been able to hold his own son. He had never taken a breath. If he'd lived, he would be six years old. Paul remembered when Susan was pregnant he'd imagined how it would be—he'd teach him to hunt and fish. Maybe he'd grow up to become a doctor one day, like his old man. And then the dreams had ended.

"When he gets older, maybe I'll take him fishing," Paul told Lily.

255

"Sure," she said and laughed. "But it'll be awhile."

Paul studied Theodore. It would almost be like having a son of his own. He could help Lily and be Theodore's Uncle Paul. The idea made him smile.

Lily stroked Theodore's cheek. "He looks more like his father than me."

Paul handed the baby back to Lily. "Did you ever hear from his father?"

"No."

"Hard to believe a man's not interested in his own son."

With a shrug, Lily took Theodore and propped him against her shoulder. "I don't care anymore." She gently patted the baby's back. "It's just me and Teddy. We don't need anyone. And there won't be a man who'd take me now."

Then acting as if the subject hadn't even been brought up, she said, "Mama asked me to come and see if you wanted to go into Anchorage tomorrow. Me and Teddy are going with Daddy to get supplies."

"I already made a trip in, but I wouldn't mind a change of scenery. You sure you won't be too crowded?"

"Daddy's already got a lot of the winter staples, so it should be fine."

"Okay. What time you leaving?"

"First light. It's a long trip there and back." She headed for the door and stepped outside. "It'll be Teddy's first trip to Anchorage. I wonder if he'll like being in the boat." She kissed the top of his head, then settled him in the sling. "I hope the weather stays clear." She glanced at the blue sky as she walked down the steps. "See you tomorrow."

Paul waited on the dock while Lily settled on the middle bench of the boat. He blew on his hands. It was cold, and he wondered if it was a good idea to have the baby out. He kept his concern to himself. It wasn't his business.

Patrick started up the engine while Paul untied the rope and then sat on the bench in the front. The slight breeze created by the boat's movement intensified the cold air's bite. "Hope it warms up."

"It will," Patrick said. "It's barely daylight. Once the sun rises, it'll heat things up." He gazed at the deep blue of the morning sky. "It's a fine day."

Lily kept the baby bundled inside her coat, cooing at him from time to time. "I hope it doesn't turn windy when we reach the inlet. The chop can get bad out there."

"We'll be fine," Patrick said, resting his hand on the tiller and keeping his eyes on the water in front of the dory.

"I'm just worried about the baby. Maybe I should have stayed home."

"He's got to be tough if he's going to live out here. Might as well start now." Patrick steered the boat into the Susitna. He glanced at his daughter. "We'll have fine weather. I promise. I'd be feeling it in my bones otherwise." He kicked up the throttle. "Actually I'm feeling kind of spry, especially for a grandpa." He grinned.

They headed up the Susitna. Ice frosted the banks and the gold, red, and yellow leaves on the trees glistened. "Looks like this will be the last trip of the year," Patrick said. "Won't be long before things freeze up."

Paul gazed ahead. "Hope we'll see some wildlife—whales, sea lions, or otters."

"Me too." Lily looked at the brightening sky. "And I'll be glad to see the sun."

Patrick chuckled. "It is nippy." His brow furrowed, he kept his eyes on the river. His skin was weathered from years spent outdoors in the Alaskan weather.

Paul liked his friend's toughened look. His life's experiences could be seen on his face. Paul trusted him more than anyone else in the territory. He had few friends, which suited him fine, but at least those he had were true-blue.

They approached the mouth of the Susitna where it flowed into Cook Inlet. The transition created rough water and the boat bounced as Patrick guided it into the huge bay. Once out in the open, the water calmed into gentle swells. The sun was up, but it was still too early to feel its heat.

Paul pulled his coat closer and kept his hands in his pockets. He searched the waves for any sign of animal life. When his gaze landed on Mount Susitna, he could see the figure of the Sleeping Lady. As always, he remembered Susan and how she'd once gazed up at the sky in the same way. The pang of loss he felt seemed less intense today. Was he beginning to miss her less? The idea brought comfort and fear. He didn't want to completely let go.

The winds remained calm. The only animal life the travelers saw were sea lions sunning themselves on harbor buoys.

Once in Anchorage, Patrick hurried through his errands. He wanted to be home before dark, so there was no time for lollygagging.

Before noon, they stopped for lunch at a downtown café. Sitting at a booth across from Patrick and Paul, Lily rocked back and forth with Theodore against her shoulder. He was fussing. "Please, let me eat, and then I'll feed you," she told him.

When a waitress came to the table, Patrick scanned his menu. "I think I'll splurge today. How about chicken and dumplings, and a piece of mince pie for dessert?"

Lily moved Theodore to her other shoulder, but his whimpers were growing louder. "I'd like an egg salad sandwich with a piece of apple pie."

The waitress wrote down the order and turned to Paul.

He was still reading the menu. "Hmm. I . . . guess I'll have a slice of ham with baked beans." He slapped the menu closed. "And, how about a piece of lemon cake for dessert?" He smiled at the waitress.

"Oh and bring us some coffee too, please. We need warming up," Patrick said.

The baby's whimpers had turned into demanding wails. Lily bounced him, but it didn't help. "He's hungry. I'll have to feed him." She looked around, searching for a place with privacy.

"How about the lavatory?" Patrick nodded toward a door in the back of the café.

"I don't want to do that."

"Don't see any other choice." Patrick rested his arms on the table in front of him. "Maybe you can feed him just enough to quiet him down."

"Okay. I'll be back." Lily stood and walked to the lavatory and disappeared inside with Theodore wailing. Some customers watched, their expressions showing irritation.

"I'll be done eating before she finishes feeding that baby. He's got a big appetite." Patrick took off his hat and set it on the bench beside him. His jovial mood faded. He glanced at the lavatory door. "That Lily, she's a good mom. I feel bad that she's got such a tough road ahead. It's not easy being a mom, especially when you got no husband. And people have kept away."

"They'll get over it."

"That little boy's special . . ." Patrick's eyes glistened. "He doesn't deserve to be treated no different from any other kid."

Paul nodded. "People who reject him wouldn't be good for him anyway." He reached across the table and rested his hand on Patrick's arm. "It'll work out fine. You and Sassa are good parents and you'll be good grandparents. He'll grow up to be a fine man."

Patrick nodded, took a handkerchief out of his back pocket, and blew his nose. "And no matter what anyone says, Lily's a good girl."

"She is, and some man will come along who loves her, who'll be a good husband and father."

The waitress returned with coffee and cups. She filled the cups and left.

"I hope you're right about her finding a husband." Patrick took a drink of his coffee. "In the meantime, Sassa's enjoying being a grandma." He managed a smile.

Patrick and Paul were nearly finished eating by the time Lily emerged. "Sorry it took so long. He was really hungry." Lily sat down with the baby cradled against her shoulder.

"I'll take him while you eat," Paul said, scooping up his last bite of lemon cake. He pushed the plate aside and reached out for Theodore.

"Thanks." Lily draped the burp cloth over Paul's shoulder and handed him the infant.

Paul settled into his chair with the sleeping child and patted his back.

Lily started on her sandwich. "Thanks, Paul. I'm starved. One day you'll make a good dad."

Paul doubted he'd ever find someone to share his life, but he didn't say anything about it. "I like taking care of him." Theodore burped and milk dribbled from his mouth. Paul wiped it up and returned to patting his back.

After Lily finished eating, Paul handed Theodore to her and they headed for the shoe store. The boys needed boots. Patrick picked out a pair for each of them.

"One more stop," he said. "I need a few things from the general store. And I hate to come to town and not see Albert and Helen. I hope they're both working."

Paul opened the door and waited while Lily and Patrick stepped outside. "You want me to carry Theodore for you?" Paul asked Lily.

"Sure."

He took the sleeping child and rested him against his shoulder. He liked the feel of him and his little baby noises. He almost felt like a father.

"Wish I had time for a game of checkers with Albert," Patrick said.

When they entered the mercantile, Paul spotted Albert right away.

Patrick headed straight for him. "Good to see you." He clapped his friend on the back. "It's been too long."

"You can say that again. You spend too much time out there on that homestead of yours."

"I like it out there."

"I've been hoping you'd come in. Been practicing my checkers game." He smiled devilishly.

"No time today. Gotta get home before dark."

"Why not stay over? Me and Helen can put you up."

"Sassa would worry."

Albert nodded. "Okay. But next trip give yourself more time." Albert turned his attention to Lily and Theodore. His expression was slightly discomfited, but he smiled at Lily. "You're looking fine. Heard you had your baby." He took a closer look. "A boy?"

"Uh-huh. His name's Theodore. I call him Teddy."

"Real cute." Albert turned to Paul. "So, how's business? You still doctoring?"

"I am. In fact I'll be heading out later this week."

"You still liking the work?"

"Love it," Paul said with a nod.

Albert turned back to Patrick and asked, "So what can I do for you?"

The two men headed toward the back of the store. Lily took the baby and walked down a row containing household goods. She looked very domestic. Paul was about to join her when Helen stepped in front of him.

"Paul, how nice to see you. I've been wondering when you'd be back in. Have you heard from Kate?"

"No. I doubt I will." He didn't want to talk about Kate. "I've been expecting a letter, but nothing yet."

She looked over her shoulder at Lily, then taking his arm, led him toward a side aisle. "I know this is none of my business, but I've been . . . concerned." She took in a breath.

"Is there something I can do to help?"

Her blue eyes softened and she said in a hush, "I've just been worried about Lily. Is she doing all right?"

Paul felt a stir of irritation. Why did people think that just because a woman wasn't married she was in some kind of trouble? "She's great. The baby's healthy and Lily's a good mother. Her parents are a great help too."

"Has the father done anything to help?"

"No. From what Lily says, he's not interested."

"Really?" Helen's eyes widened. "I'd think a man would want to care for his own flesh and blood."

"Lily's made peace with it. And I don't think it's anyone else's business." Paul's tone was sharp. He was surprised at Helen. She'd never seemed to be the type to nose in on other people's affairs.

The color drained from her face. She looked mortified. "You're right. I'm sorry. It is none of my business. But if there's anything Albert and I can do to help, please let us know."

"I will." Right now all he wanted was to get away. He detested gossip, and although he was certain Helen meant well, he was offended by her probing. And he knew the next topic would be Kate and he couldn't bear to talk about her.

From the moment she'd gotten on that train, he felt as if the oxygen had been sucked out of his lungs. He'd never be the same. Every day since she'd gone, he'd prayed for her return.

K ate pulled on a sweater as she hurried down the stairs. She breezed into the kitchen where her mother was finishing up the breakfast dishes. "I could have done those for you."

"Don't be silly. There were only a few to take care of."

"Well, I'll do them tomorrow. I promise." She glanced around. "Do you know where Angel is?"

"Oh, she went off with your father this morning. They've become pals." Joan smiled. "So, where are you off to?"

"I've got to go into town. Do you mind if I take the car?"

"You can use it any time—you know that."

"Thanks." Kate dropped a kiss on her mother's cheek. "You're the best. Do you need me to pick up anything?"

"Mayonnaise. And another dozen quart jars." She opened the icebox and peered inside. "I thought I had a full jar of mayonnaise, but my memory must be going." She held up a nearly empty jar. "I'll need more to make the potato salad for tomorrow's festivities."

"It should be fun. Do you expect a lot of people?"

"Just about everyone we know." Joan smiled. "You remember how it is at the end of the season."

"Oh yeah. My first fall in Alaska, I was so homesick. I'd think about you all here and imagine the fall activities.

263

Sometimes I could actually smell the cider." She smiled. "I was glad to be in Alaska, but I also wanted to be here with you and Dad and our friends. It'll be nice to take part this year."

"We're one of the last farms to make cider, so everyone decided to meet here." Joan let out a sigh. "It's a lot of work."

"I'll help as soon as I get back. I won't be long."

"Why the trip to town?"

"I need some stationery. I'm almost out. A friend of mine had a baby, so I'd really like to get a letter off to her." Kate didn't want to explain about Lily. She took a step toward the front room.

"Who had a baby?" Joan wiped off the counter.

"Lily. She was on my mail route."

"I remember you mentioning her. How nice. I didn't know she'd gotten married."

Kate didn't correct her mother's assumption.

She picked up the car keys from an occasional table in the dining room alcove. "I won't be long."

Kate hurried out the front door and across the yard to her parents' Chrysler sedan. It started right up. Her father was a stickler for proper maintenance of his car and truck. He was the same about his plane. Kate backed out of the driveway and headed down the hill toward the main road.

The day was clear and warm, so she rolled down the window and rested an arm on the window frame. White clouds, reminding her of cotton candy, swept across a pale blue sky. Kate looked toward the mountains and felt a tug for the wilds of Alaska. The mountains there had seemed to explode from within the earth.

Dust flew up from the dry road and in the window. Kate could taste it. In Alaska, the air would be cold and smell of fermenting berries and moist earth. Snow might still carpet the ground from the storm that had blown through. When she'd first settled there, she'd missed Yakima, especially the cool fall mornings and warm afternoons. Sadness rose inside her. Now it was as if she had two homes. If she lived in one, she missed the other. Melancholy rippled through her. Would she ever be content?

She gazed at the brown hillsides. She'd always loved their look—velvety and warm. All she needed was a little time and this would be home again.

She pulled up in front of a market with pumpkins piled in a bin outside the front door. The windows were plastered with posters advertising sales on sugar, flour, and spices. Stepping inside, she glanced about. Where would they keep the stationery?

A redheaded woman she'd never seen before stood at the cash register. She smiled and her freckles seemed to stretch across her cheeks and nose. "Can I help you?"

"I'm looking for greeting stationery. Oh, and I also need canning jars and mayonnaise."

The girl stepped into the aisle. "The writing materials are down at the end." She pointed at an aisle on the far side of the store. "The mayonnaise is in the next aisle over. And canning jars are straight down this one." She turned to the row behind them.

"Thank you." Wondering what she ought to say to a woman who'd had a baby out of wedlock, Kate set off toward the end of the store. She imagined that some people had probably judged Lily harshly, but she figured Lily would come to terms with what she'd done and enjoy being a mother. Living out on the creek with her parents would make it easier.

And then lost hopes and dreams swamped her as Paul's face filled her thoughts. She'd once envisioned them raising a family there on the homestead. The hurt ran deep. Would she ever stop loving him?

As she approached the section with paper, pencils, and pens, she spotted a man who looked vaguely familiar. His dark hair and the way he held his muscled body reminded her of someone. He turned and Kate's heart skipped. It was Charles Gibson, Alison's brother.

Blue eyes, filled with loathing, bore into her. His lips tightened into a line over his teeth. "What're you doing here? I thought you moved to Alaska."

"I did, but I'm back now." What else could she say? This kind of meeting was what Kate had feared. Alison's family hated her. Back when the accident happened, they'd refused to speak to her. In a small town like Yakima, the chances of running into them was likely.

Charles continued to glare at her and folded his arms over his chest. "Maybe you ought to consider going back."

Kate swallowed hard. There were no words. "I know how you feel—"

"You *don't* know how I feel."

"I'm sorry about Alison."

"Being sorry doesn't change anything." He held his fixed angry stare a few seconds longer, then turned and walked away.

The burden of guilt and shame pressed down on Kate. Charles was right. Saying she was sorry didn't make things better. Alison was gone. Kate understood that God had forgiven her, but clearly there were people who never would.

She turned and faced the cashier. The redhead stared at her as if she'd just figured out who Kate was and she didn't want her in the store.

Without saying a word, Kate walked out. She was hurt and angry. When would it end?

Driving home, she didn't see the blue sky or the golden hills. All she could see was the loathing in Charles's eyes. Her mind flashed to the accident, the icy water, Alison's body being pulled from the wreckage. It felt as if a great stone of shame hung from her neck. And it glared at her in the same way Charles had.

By the time she pulled into her driveway, she'd managed to rein in her tears. She headed inside the house and up the stairs. She caught a glimpse of her mother but pretended not to see her. Once secluded in her room, she threw herself across the bed and released her sorrow. Deep sobs shook her body. *God, I'm so sorry. Please free me from this. I don't know what to do.*

She heard the door open and knew it was her mother. She didn't look up. The bed gave slightly and Kate felt a hand on

266

her back. She rested her cheek against her dimity bedspread and closed her eyes.

"What happened?" Her mother's voice was warm and protective.

"I don't want to talk about it." Kate rolled onto her side and wiped away tears.

Joan handed her the handkerchief she kept tucked in her shirtsleeve.

Kate softly blew her nose. "I didn't get the mayonnaise or the jars. I'm sorry."

"I don't care about that. Your father can go. Right now I care about you."

Kate sat up. "I ran into Charles Gibson at the market." She blew her nose again. "He hates me."

Joan's eyes revealed her own grief. She pulled Kate into her arms. "I'm so sorry, Kate. But you have no control over what he feels. He's allowed bitterness to poison him."

Kate dabbed at the last of her tears. She hated to cry, especially in front of people, even her mother. "I don't know what to do. This is a small town. I'm bound to see him and his parents when I'm out. It's what I hated about living here before. What should I do?"

Joan thought for a while, then said kindly, "Maybe it's time you talked to them."

"I tried to. Remember? They wouldn't speak to me."

"That was a long time ago. A lot could have changed."

"Obviously it hasn't with Charles."

"He's young."

Kate mulled over the idea. "Maybe I could talk to Mr. and Mrs. Gibson. But I don't know what to say."

"Pray about it. God will show you."

Kate nodded. The idea of meeting with the Gibsons was terrifying, but she knew it was the right thing to do. "I'll call them."

Joan smiled gently. "I think that's a good idea." She stood. "Dinner's on the table. Come down when you're ready."

Kate sat at the table, but she couldn't eat. Her stomach

tumbled as she thought about the call she had to make. After the dishes were finished, she dialed the operator and asked to be connected to the Gibson residence. Her hands were wet with perspiration and her heart drummed. When she heard Mrs. Gibson on the other end of the line, her mind went blank. She almost hung up. Finally, with her voice quaking, she said, "Mrs. Gibson, this is Kate Evans."

"Oh." There was a long pause. "Hello, Katharine. What can I do for you?" Her voice wasn't unfriendly exactly, but it wasn't warm either.

"I was hoping I could come over and speak with you and Mr. Gibson."

Another long silence. Kate held her breath.

Finally, Mrs. Gibson said, "I suppose that would be all right. When did you want to come by?"

"Whatever time is best for you."

"I'll have to speak to William. Can I call you back?"

"Of course. I'm staying with my parents."

"Fine, then. I'll get back to you and let you know when."

"Thank you."

Mrs. Gibson said, "Good-bye," and hung up before Kate could respond.

She set the phone back in the cradle and turned to her mother. "She said okay. She's supposed to call and tell me when."

"Good. If you'd like, your father and I can go with you."

"No. This is something I have to do on my own." She smiled at her mother. "But thanks."

Lauraine Gibson called the following morning and suggested they meet that afternoon at two o'clock. Kate worked alongside her mother, preparing for the evening's party, but her mind was with the Gibsons. All she could think about was what she should say and their possible reaction. The joy of the day and the fun of the upcoming party were squeezed out by dread. She kept looking at the clock. Time dragged.

Finally at half past one, she stopped working and went to freshen up. She chose her dress with care. It was important that Mrs. Gibson approved. She didn't use any makeup or perfume, just in case the Gibsons found them offensive. Finally, she hugged her mother and headed for town.

Her heart seemed unable to find an even rhythm. Her hands were damp, her mouth dry. White and black billows of clouds sat on the mountaintops. Kate kept looking at them while trying to sort out what to say.

The Gibsons lived in a cozy neighborhood. Kate remembered it well. She pulled into their driveway and shut off the engine, then stared at the house—a small two-story with clapboard siding. It looked just as it always had—tidy flowerbeds and a large walnut tree in the front yard. Her eyes went to a window under the eaves—Alison's room. Memories of sleepovers, practicing dance steps together, and listening to their favorite songs on the radio swept through Kate.

She gripped the steering wheel and rested her head against it. *God, help me.* She straightened and threw back her shoulders. Nine years had come and gone. It was time to resolve this.

Kate opened the car door and stepped out. A cool breeze swept up the street and tossed her hair into her eyes. She brushed it aside and took a quieting breath before walking to the front door. She stared at it a moment, then knocked.

Almost immediately the door opened. Lauraine Gibson stood with a hand on the knob. "Katharine. You're right on time." Her dark hair had gone partially gray and sorrow had taken the light from her brown eyes.

"Hello. Thank you for seeing me."

She opened the door wider. "Please. Come in."

Kate stepped inside. A stairway leading to the second floor was directly in front of her. She remembered racing up those stairs to the privacy of Alison's room. On her right was a small living room. It looked just as it always did. A tan davenport with a swirl floral design rested against the far wall and two matching armchairs sat in front of a bay window.

The mantel over the fireplace had been repainted a bright white, but the same blackwood clock rested there, its pendulum softly murmuring the passage of time. Mrs. Gibson had always kept fresh flowers in the house. Today a vase with red roses brightened the room from its perch atop an occasional table.

"Please have a seat," Mrs. Gibson said. "Can I get you something to drink?"

"Yes. Thank you," Kate said, her dry mouth making her tongue trip over her words.

Mrs. Gibson disappeared into the kitchen. Kate waited, her hands pressed between her knees. She wondered if Mr. Gibson would be here.

Mrs. Gibson appeared with a tray of glasses and a plate of cookies. "If I remember correctly, you like lemonade."

"I do. Thank you." Kate took a glass and sipped.

"Cookie? They're apple raisin."

Kate's stomach tumbled. The last thing she wanted was to eat, but she didn't dare refuse, so she took one.

William Gibson walked into the room. He seemed smaller than Kate remembered. "Kate," he said.

"Mr. Gibson." She stood. "Thank you for meeting with me."

He moved to the sofa and Mrs. Gibson sat beside him. She didn't rest against the cushions, but kept her spine straight and sat on the edge of the sofa. A furrow ran across her brow.

"Now then, Kate, what is it you wanted to talk about?" Mr. Gibson's voice was sterile and polite.

Kate sat back down. "I ran into Charles at the market yesterday."

"He told us."

"He's angry, and he has a right to be. I thought it might help if we talked . . . about what happened." Kate looked at her glass and took a drink. "We never did talk."

She rubbed a damp palm on her skirt. "That day . . . it was *all* my fault. I asked Alison to go with me. And when I saw the fog, I should have stayed clear of the lake. I just thought . . ." She fought tears. It didn't help that Mrs. Gibson's eyes had filled and that she had a viselike grip on her husband's hand. "I thought we would be fine. That I was a good enough pilot. But I wasn't. I tried to set the plane down, but I got mixed up and we went in sideways."

Kate couldn't stop the tears. "I tried to save her."

Mrs. Gibson dabbed at her eyes with a handkerchief.

"I really did. I wish it had been me who died instead." Kate was crying and barely holding back sobs. "When we went out that day, I never thought anything bad would happen. Alison was my best friend. I loved her." The energy seeped out of her voice. "I miss her . . . every day."

Mrs. Gibson looked at her husband, then back at Kate. "We know you do. And we understand that what happened was an accident, a terrible accident."

Mr. Gibson stood and walked to the window. His hands in his pockets, he stared out. "When we first heard, we couldn't fathom that our Alison was gone." His voice wobbled. "We needed to blame someone." He looked at Kate. "And so we lashed out at you."

"We're sorry," Mrs. Gibson said. "It was unfair. You were barely more than a child. We should have talked to you. We just didn't know what to say. And as time passed it became more difficult, so . . . we just let it go."

She turned to Kate. "We can see now how wrong that was."

The weight Kate had carried for so long suddenly felt lighter. "Can you forgive me?"

Mrs. Gibson reached out and took Kate's hands in hers. "We forgave you a long time ago, Katie. We're just so sorry we didn't say anything. It was difficult to even speak about Alison. And when we see you, we see her." She patted Kate's hand.

Kate had never expected this much grace and love. "I don't know what to say. Thank you. I'm so grateful. I've been afraid to talk to you." She remembered her encounter with Charles. "What about Charles? He hates me."

Mrs. Gibson nodded. "He's had a harder time of it. He's young. I'm sure he'll come around, eventually."

Mr. Gibson sat beside his wife. "We heard about your pilot friend . . . we're sorry."

Kate felt a tightening in her throat. "We were supposed to get married."

"Oh, Katie," Mrs. Gibson said.

"Will you be heading back up north?" Mr. Gibson asked.

"No. I'm here to stay. I'm not flying anymore. It's not for me."

"You know, Alison loved to fly." Mrs. Gibson smiled. "She thought you were a wonderful pilot. She was so proud of you."

"Alison was the best friend a person could have."

Mrs. Gibson leveled a kind look on Kate. "She'd never want you to give up flying. She always said she thought you were part bird." Her eyes brightened and she looked younger. "Don't give up something you love out of guilt or fear."

"It's not that. I just don't think it's wise. And it's about time I settled down to a normal life, maybe have a family."

"Kate, you were never like anyone else. That's one of the things Alison loved about you. I don't think you were meant to live a normal life. That's not how God made you."

Tears choked Kate. She knew that walking away from flying meant she was leaving behind part of herself. But maybe it was time to find a new Kate.

— 25 —

Kate's mind whirled with all that had happened. She felt lighter, happier. The Gibsons didn't hate her. And Charles . . . well, she could only hope and pray that one day he'd find a way to forgive her. All things were possible with God. She knew that—why did she have to learn the lesson again and again?

Just the idea of a God who could do anything carried her thoughts back to what Mrs. Gibson had said about her and flying. Was she supposed to be that woman who had challenged the Alaskan wilderness? The one who had flown that vast territory? Is that who she was meant to be? Did that person even exist anymore?

Fear and disappointment rolled through her. If she couldn't be who she'd been, who would she be? She was too afraid to fly. Just the thought sent fear shivering through her. She tried to visualize herself in her plane, soaring over the bush and the frozen tundra. No. She couldn't do it. And what sense did it make, anyway? Who, in their right mind, lived like that?

Mike's quiet blue eyes, his laid-back demeanor, and his love of flying caught hold of Kate. She missed him. If only she could talk to him. He'd know what she should do. She remembered their first trip together and the lunch they'd shared on the beach in Homer. He'd told her then to go home, that flying in Alaska was too dangerous. Yet, he had stayed, and she knew he respected her for staying.

She visualized his easy smile, and how his eyes were always full of affection when he looked at her. An ache tightened in her throat. Why had he died? He was a good man, full of life and fun. He didn't deserve death. Anger flashed through Kate. *Why, God? You could have prevented it.*

Kate knew better than to question God about things that only he understood. It accomplished nothing. There were no answers for tragedies like Mike's.

He should have listened to his own advice and stopped flying. Kate tried to imagine him doing something else, but couldn't. He was meant to fly. But isn't that what she'd believed about herself?

She pulled into the driveway and chickens scattered. Her parents were sitting on the front porch. She knew they'd been praying and they'd want to know what had happened, but Kate wasn't ready to talk about it yet. She'd carried the burden for so long, none of this seemed real. She needed time to contemplate and relish the change.

She slid out of the car and closed the door, then walked up the path that led to the porch. Taking the steps, she wished there were a way to avoid a conversation about all that had happened.

"Hi," she said.

Her father smiled at her. "How'd it go?"

Her mother stood. "Can I get you some iced tea?"

"No thanks." Kate sat in a wooden rocker. She clasped her hands in her lap, closed her eyes, and leaned her head against the back of the chair. A breeze cooled the afternoon heat and carried the scent of fermenting apples.

Her mother settled in her chair. "Don't give up, honey, I'm sure the Gibsons—"

"Actually everything is fine. The Gibsons were kind and accepted my apology with grace. They said they forgave me a long time ago and were sorry they hadn't contacted me."

"Oh, that's wonderful."

"We had a good conversation." Kate smiled softly. "We talked a little about Alison and the way things used to be." She licked dry lips and wished she'd accepted the offer of tea.

"I'm so glad to hear that." Her mother rested a hand briefly on Kate's arm. "I just thought by the look of you . . . well . . . you look unhappy. Is something else bothering you?"

Kate blew out a breath. "I'm confused. I don't know what to do."

"About what, Katie?" Her father leaned forward and rested his arms on his thighs. "How can we help?"

Kate didn't even know how to express what she felt. She brushed hair out of her eyes and looked at her parents. They were wise and they loved her. Maybe they *could* help.

"When I went to Alaska, I was absolutely certain I was doing the right thing. I wanted the challenge, and I needed a new beginning. And then everything went bad."

"Everything?" Her dad lifted an eyebrow. "Seems to me a lot of things went right."

Kate stared at him, hoping he'd help her see what she was incapable of seeing.

"You remember the day you got the job at the airstrip? You called us, even though it was a long-distance call. You were so excited you couldn't stop talking." He took her hand and squeezed it gently. "You'd accomplished one of your dreams. And in the weeks and months that followed, you proved yourself to be a gifted pilot. You saved lives and served the people of Alaska. You faced challenges most people wouldn't even dream of attempting. And you made good, solid friends, people you could count on."

"But what about all the terrible things that happened, like Frank dying in a crack-up and then Mike—"

"Those were bad, I'll grant you. But life holds good and bad for all of us." He straightened and said quietly, "I suppose you can surrender—stay here holed up on the apple farm. Give up on your dreams."

"You don't think I should be here?"

He looked straight at her. "No, Kate. I don't." He glanced

at Joan. "It's not that we don't want you here. We love having you home. But you don't belong here any longer. Alaska's your home now."

Kate shook her head. "No. I don't even fly anymore. I can't go back."

"Why not?"

"I'd be too embarrassed if I'm not flying. And everyone who flies eventually dies. I . . . I'm afraid. I can't live like that, thinking that any day I might be the one. And I don't want to kill anyone else."

Bill's lips lifted in an understanding smile. "You don't have to fly, but I think you'll be missing out on what God intended for you if you don't." He grinned. "I've been flying a good number of years and I'm still alive." His expression turned more serious. "And Katie, you didn't kill anyone."

"How can you say that? If not for me, Alison would be alive. And her parents would be happy. They've forgiven me, but they're so sad." She pushed out of her chair and moved to the railing.

"Katie," Joan said, using Bill's pet name for her daughter. "I know you understand that God's forgiven your part in Alison's death, but I don't think you've forgiven yourself."

Trying to control her trembling chin, she said, "But it was my fault." She gazed out over the orchard, feeling trapped by guilt and confusion. She needed a way out.

"You're taking an awful lot of credit for another person's life."

Kate looked at her mother. "What do you mean?"

"God has the power over life and death, not us. You did everything you could that day to save Alison." Her gaze was steady. "Either we trust God or we don't." Joan moved to her daughter and placed an arm around her shoulders.

Kate leaned her head against her mother, wishing she were still a child and all it took to cure a wound was a hug and a kiss. She was all grown up now, but her mother's presence still calmed her. Kate felt the torment seep away.

"You didn't kill Alison up there on that lake. We don't

276

know why God allowed Alison to die, but he did." She gave Kate a gentle squeeze. "You're not God, Kate. He made the choice."

Kate felt as if light had eased into her soul and had illuminated the truth. "I love you." She hugged her mother, tears squeezing from her eyes.

"I love you too."

Kate stepped back. "I think I'll take a walk before everyone gets here. You know, clear my head a little." She looked at Angel, who lay beside her father's chair. "You want to go, girl?"

Angel lifted her head, but didn't move.

Kate crossed to the dog. "Guess it's too hot, huh?" She smoothed Angel's heavy coat. "I understand," she said, straightening and walking toward the steps. "I won't be long."

"You have plenty of time," her mother said.

Kate headed for the orchard. Most of the apples had been picked. Boxes stood stacked at the ends of the rows. Some would be stored, others shipped. The ones they'd use to make cider were already boxed up and sitting near the cider press.

Maybe a party was just what she needed. Richard would be there. She wondered what he'd say about whether or not she should go back to Alaska.

* * *

The following morning Kate came down the stairs early before anyone else was up. Her parents had gone to bed late the previous evening, after everyone had gone home. It seemed like most of the farmers in the valley had been here. Kate had a fine time. There'd been good conversation, laughter, and tasty food. Some of the local fellows brought their fiddles and harmonicas, so people danced.

Kate found her niche, making cider. She and Richard worked together to help bottle the juice. She drank so much she'd felt it sloshing around in her stomach and she'd gone to bed with a stomachache.

She headed for the kitchen to make coffee. Her parents

would want some when they got up. She rinsed out the percolator and filled it with fresh water, then scooped coffee into the bin, put the lid on, and set it on her mother's new electric range.

She heard footsteps and turned to see her father. "Hi, Dad. Good party, huh."

He smiled, the creases at the corners of his eyes deepening. "One of the best." He walked into the kitchen and glanced out the window. "It's going to be a beautiful day."

"Yeah. I hope it's not hot. All that cider needs to be canned."

Bill leaned against the kitchen counter. "You wouldn't want to go up for a morning flight with me before your mother wakes up, would you?"

Kate's heart thumped. "I don't think so. I'd better stay around so I can help Mom."

"She didn't get to bed until one o'clock. She won't be up and ready to work for another hour or so. Come on. It'd be good for you." He pulled a cap out of his back pocket and tugged it onto his head.

Kate met her father's challenging gaze. "Dad . . . I'm afraid. I . . . don't think I can fly anymore."

"Sure you can. You know me. I take good care of my plane, and I'm a first-rate pilot." He glanced out the window. "We couldn't have better weather." He was silent for a moment, then added, "If you don't go up, you'll never be happy with yourself."

Kate knew he was right but wished he weren't. She glanced out the window, took a deep breath, and said, "Okay. I'll go."

"That's my girl." He slipped an arm around Kate's shoulders and gave her a squeeze.

At the airstrip, Kate stared at her father's yellow Stinson. Her heart beat faster with each step she took toward the plane. Her palms were damp and she kept wiping them on her slacks. When they reached the plane, she stared at it, trying to convince herself she could fly again. She wanted to run the other way, but her pride wouldn't let her. Besides, she'd known this day would come. She had to face this.

278

"Climb on in," Bill said.

Kate pulled on her flight helmet and clambered in, dropping into a small seat up front. She felt cramped and her stomach gallumped so badly she wondered if all the juice she drank the night before might come up.

"You all right?" her father asked.

Kate nodded, then said, "No. Not really."

"You'll see. Once we get up there you'll feel differently."

"Just get us off the ground." She tried to sound light-hearted.

Bill taxied to the end of the runway, bumping over uneven ground. "All set?"

Kate gave a nod.

They headed down the runway, picking up speed. Kate gripped the edge of her seat. A picture of her as a child on her first flight flitted through her mind. She'd been terrified then, just like now.

She was ready to shout at her father to stop when she felt the plane lift and leave the ground. For a moment her stomach remained earthbound, and as they soared over the trees she felt almost faint.

"How's it feel?" her father asked, glancing at her.

She looked down, and joy bubbled up inside. She was airborne! The world below looked like a giant patchwork quilt. She did love flying. They lifted skyward and headed toward nearby hills.

"It's beautiful," Kate hollered over the roar of the engine. "I love it." She smiled and leaned over to squeeze her father's arm. "Thanks, Dad."

He grinned. "I knew if I could just get you up here, you'd be fine." He flew over rows of apple trees. "Where you want to go?"

Kate knew where she needed to go, but could she face it? "Rimrock Lake?"

Her father's eyes widened. "You sure?"

"No. But I need to go."

"Okay. Rimrock Lake it is."

"Is there a place to set down near the lake?"

"I think there's an open field on the south side." He banked the plane and turned toward the mountains.

Kate gazed out at the scenery and wondered how she could have imagined giving up flying. She knew that if Mike could see her, he'd be smiling.

As they approached the lake, the accident looped through Kate's mind. This time, instead of pushing it aside, she allowed the memories their freedom. She needed to remember.

It had been a day like this one, only colder. She and Alison had been laughing and talking about Alison's new boyfriend. Life was full of adventure and promise.

Kate looked down at the brilliant blue water. In autumn the lake was partially drained, so there were areas of lake-bottom visible. Since the accident, the lake had seemed dark and cold. But today, it felt like Kate was seeing it anew—the waters were blue, with sunlight reflecting off the surface. A pine forest grew right up to the edge, creating a dark green frame for the pristine waters.

Bill dropped down over the trees, and when he spotted an open area, he flew over it. Kate knew he was checking to make sure it was clear of debris or ruts that might cause trouble. "Looks good. You want to land?"

Kate nodded, the lump in her throat preventing her from speaking.

The landing was a little bumpy, and Kate grabbed the edge of her seat. Then she let loose. Everything was fine.

Once the engine was shut down, she climbed out and walked to the bank, drawn by the high mountain waters. She stood there for a long while, staring at the lake and listening to birdsong and the chirps of squirrels. She heard the screech of a hawk and caught a glimpse of it as it glided beyond the trees. This place didn't seem fearsome at all. The water glistened in the sunlight like thousands of sparkling crystals. She felt her father's presence beside her.

"The last time I was here was the day of the accident," she said.

"That was a terrible day." He gazed at the blue sky. "But today's not."

Kate smiled at him. "No. It's not." She breathed in the scent of pine. Alison felt close. Kate knew if she were here, she'd pull Kate into a tight hug and ask her what was wrong. Why wasn't she flying? She'd laugh and goad Kate on. A smile played at Kate's lips. Alison had been so much fun. The weight of guilt that had begun to lift the previous day now drifted off her shoulders.

The crash had been an accident. It wasn't her fault. And once in the water, she had done everything she could to save her dear friend.

Kate closed her eyes and envisioned Alison's warm smile, knowing that if she could see her now, she'd be laughing and congratulating Kate on finally getting back her good sense.

All of a sudden, Kate knew what she had to do. It was clear now. God had a plan for her and it wasn't living in fear or hiding on a Yakima farm.

She hoped Jack hadn't sold her plane.

— 26 —

While flying back to the farm, Kate kept up a lively conversation with her father even though her mind swirled with possibilities and questions. She didn't share her feelings about what she ought to do with her life. She wanted to speak to him, but it was important that her mother was there too. She needed both of their opinions.

She wondered how difficult it would be to reestablish herself in Alaska. She'd have to rebuild trust. Jack might not even take her back.

"You seem distracted," her father said. "You all right?"

"Yeah. Just thinking."

Bill raised his brows and the furrows across his forehead deepened. "Mind letting me in on those thoughts?"

"I haven't got things figured out yet, but I do want to talk to you . . . and Mom."

"Really?"

Kate gave him a nod and smiled. "I feel good, better than I have in a long time." With a smile on her face, she gazed at the farmland below and to the rolling hills that reached toward flat golden plains. She imagined what the tundra in Alaska looked like. If it was free of snow, it would be burnished gold fused with warm oranges and reds. She wanted to be there.

Her mind carried her back to the anxiety over whether

Jack had sold her plane or not. What would she do if he had? *Settle down. Nothing's been decided yet*, she reminded herself. She still needed to talk with her parents, but she was pretty sure what their response would be.

The plane approached the airfield. "Didn't expect to take so long," her father said. "Your mother's probably fit to be tied." He grinned. "She hates it when I take side trips and don't tell her until after I get back."

"She's used to it." Kate chuckled. "You've always been like that. I doubt she's upset at all."

When they set down, Kate was the first one out of the plane. Dark clouds rolled toward them from the north, and wind swept up dirt and debris.

"We better tie her down and get a tarp over her," Bill said. "Looks like we're in for a real storm."

By the time they'd finished putting the plane to bed, clouds covered the sun, the temperatures had dropped, and the winds were stronger than ever.

"I'll milk the cow now. Won't want to go out later." Her father headed toward the barn.

"I'll take care of the chickens." Kate strode alongside her dad.

While he milked, she watered and fed the chickens and checked for eggs. Chickens generally laid eggs in the morning, but there were always some stragglers. Today there were four eggs left. With two in each hand, Kate walked alongside her father toward the house. Clouds swirled and tree limbs danced.

Bill studied the sky. "Looks like a doozy of a storm."

When they reached the house, he hurried up the steps and opened the front door, holding it for Kate.

She stopped at the top of the steps. "I think I'll stay out here on the porch for a while. I love strong winds and maybe we'll get some lightning and thunder."

"Okay. I'm going to take a shower. That sassy cow got me with her tail twice." He stared at Kate. "You sure you're all right?"

"I'm fine." She held out the eggs, smiling back at her father.

"Okay." He took the eggs, stepped inside, and closed the door.

Kate leaned on the railing and looked across the yard to the rows of apple trees, breathing in the delicious scent of rain. She would miss this place, but she missed Alaska more.

The first drops fell and Kate leaned out, catching them in her palm. Dry earth soaked up the moisture and plants seemed to reach toward the wetness. Kate wanted to step out into the shower. Instead, she turned and faced the house. It was time to speak to her parents.

The first thing Kate noticed in the kitchen was the deep boiler on the stove. She could see shimmering silver lids beneath bubbling water.

Her mother picked up a canning jar filled with golden liquid from the counter and wiped it with a damp cloth. "Hi, Kate. I heard you and your father had a nice time."

"We did. Rimrock Lake's a beautiful spot." A fresh sense of freedom welled up inside Kate. Ever since the accident, she'd been unable to think about the lake without sorrow and shame piling on her. "I haven't been there since the accident, and I needed to go back." She closed her eyes for a moment and visualized the mountain lake. "I think God led me there. I'm at peace about what happened. I feel like I've been set free."

Joan set down the jar. Her eyes shimmered. "Oh Kate, I'm so happy to hear that. I've been praying for such a long time." She pulled her into her arms. Holding her close, she smoothed Kate's hair.

Content, Kate snuggled against her mother. "I'm happy, Mom. Really happy." She finally stepped back. "I'd forgotten what it felt like. I didn't even know how tied up in knots I've been until they were untied." She folded her arms over her chest. "I do need to talk to you and Dad, though."

"He'll be down in a few minutes. He's cleaning up." Her mother retrieved another jar from the kettle. "I'm just finishing up this batch and then we can sit in the living room and chat."

Feeling calm, Kate seated herself on an easy chair across from her parents, who sat side by side on the sofa. She settled a gaze on her father. "First, thanks, Dad, for convincing me to go flying with you today. I needed someone to give me a push."

"I didn't think it would take much." He winked at her.

"When I was at the lake, I think God spoke to me." She gave a wave of her hand. "I know that sounds kind of strange, but I had a strong sense of his presence, and I think I know what he wants for me."

She pressed the palms of her hands together. "I've been thinking about what you said about God being in control of our lives, and I agree. I can trust him more than anyone or anything. Whether I live or die, he's the one directing my life.

"And when I talked to the Gibsons, Mrs. Gibson told me she didn't think Alison would want me to give up my dream of being a bush pilot. And that my love of flying was given to me by God and it would be wrong for me to walk away from that."

Her father nodded, wearing a knowing smile.

Wind whipped against the front window as if in jubilation.

"I'm not afraid anymore." She studied her hands resting in her lap. "I think I'm supposed to go back to Alaska." She looked at her parents. "What do you think? I know what you said about my going back, but do you still feel the same?"

They both smiled, but Kate could see a touch of sorrow in her mother's eyes. Even though it was the right thing to do, saying farewell would be difficult.

Her parents looked at each other. Bill took Joan's hand in his. "We've talked about this. And we agree with you. Alaska's where you belong."

Joan blinked back tears. "It's been wonderful having you here and it won't be easy to say good-bye, but I want you to be happy. And if that means you need to live in Alaska, then that's where you should be."

Kate felt her parents' love wash over her. "You guys are

the best." She got up and hugged them both. "I love you." Taking a step back, she said, "You can come to visit, and I'll fly down to see you." She headed for the kitchen. "I have to call Jack. I'll pay the long-distance charges."

"Jack?" Bill asked.

"He has my plane. I've got to make sure he doesn't sell it. And make arrangements to get it repaired."

Knowing her plane was still waiting for her, Kate had one more task to take care of. She needed to speak to Richard. They'd arranged to meet at the soda fountain. She arrived first and sat at a table in the back, farthest from the door. She'd already ordered a Coke and was sipping on it when Richard walked in.

With a wave, he headed for the table. He pulled out a chair and sat. "Is everything all right? You sounded kind of tense on the phone."

"Everything's fine." Kate knew that the news she had to share wasn't something he wanted to hear, and she wished she didn't have to hurt him again, but there was no way to avoid it. "Do you want something to eat and—"

Before she could finish her question, a pretty young waitress with dark hair and deep blue eyes walked up to their table, a pad and pencil in hand. "Can I get you something, sir?" She smiled softly at Richard.

Richard glanced over his shoulder at her. "Sure. How about a chocolate malt?"

"Anything else?" Her blue eyes seemed to hold a special interest in Richard.

Kate hoped so. Richard deserved someone special in his life. And the waitress seemed like a nice girl.

He thought a moment. "Yeah. I'd like a burger too."

"How would you like it?"

"Rare. No onions."

"Coming right up." She smiled and walked away, tossing a glance over her shoulder as she moved toward the counter.

Kate smiled to herself. From the looks of it, the waitress was definitely interested in Richard.

He leaned on the table. "Now, what is it that couldn't wait?"

Kate could see concern in his eyes. She took a deep breath and blew it out.

"Uh-oh. That sounds like a worry breath."

"It's not . . . exactly. I just need you to know that . . . I'm moving back to Alaska."

Richard closed his eyes for a moment, then looked straight at her. "I figured you'd go back." He clasped his hands on the table in front of him. "It was just a matter of time." He tried to smile. "Will you be working as a pilot?"

"Uh-huh."

"So, you're over your fear?"

"Yeah, mostly. I'm still a little nervous. But you always are." Kate felt like she ought to say more, but she didn't know what.

He gave one nod. "Well, you're a good pilot." The waitress brought his malt and flashed him a smile. "Thanks," he said, and used his straw to stir the ice cream mixture. "As much as I hate to see you go, I think that's where you belong."

Kate could have kissed him, only she didn't want to make saying good-bye more complicated. "I appreciate your saying that. You're a good friend, Richard."

He half grinned. "I am. And if you ever need anything . . . anything, you call me. Okay?"

"Okay." Kate reached across the table and took his hand. There was nothing more to be said, so she simply squeezed it.

"And hey, don't forget I'm here."

"I won't."

November was upon them and the weather was already a threat to travel, so Kate dared not wait any longer. Within the week, she, her father, and Angel were headed north. Kate hadn't been specific with Jack about her intentions, but he knew she was coming and that she wanted to keep her plane. Kate hoped he'd also want a pilot.

Time dragged as the miles passed. Kate wanted to get back to what she knew—Alaska, her friends, and flying. Albert and Helen had offered her the use of the apartment, so she'd be able to settle in easily, as if she'd never left. But Kate knew it wouldn't be easy. She'd have to prove herself all over again, especially to Jack. She knew he saw her as a quitter. He wouldn't make life easy. He'd test her. That is, if he'd even give her a job. It depended on whether or not he needed a pilot.

"So, what's your plan?" her father asked.

"First I've got to talk to Jack. See if he needs a pilot."

"Oh, he will. He knows a good one when he sees one and you're good."

"I hope you're right."

"And after that?"

"I'll settle back into my apartment, hopefully get my mail run back, and go out to see Patrick and Sassa and the kids. And Paul of course. I've got to take the box of apples to him. He'll love that. He always used to talk about how much he missed fresh apples."

The idea of seeing Paul made her tremble. How would she react when she saw him? She knew better than to expect anything more than friendship. If she were lucky, she could be as good a friend to Paul as Richard had been to her.

"I can hardly wait for a trip to Kotzebue. I've really missed Joe and Nena and the kids. I hope I can get a run up that way soon."

Her father nodded. "They'll be glad to see you." He looked down at Seward as they flew over. "Won't be long now. Glad we pushed hard. Looks like bad weather's moving in."

Kate turned her gaze to the northwest. The clouds were dark and deeply stacked. She gazed down at the jagged peaks rising up beyond the small town of Seward, which huddled between mountain peaks and the ocean.

They'd be in Anchorage soon. Her heart kicked up, and she realized she was clasping her hands tightly. She was afraid. What if she couldn't step back into her old life? What if she was gutless and too nervous to fly into the bush? She closed her eyes and prayed for peace and for God's help.

She turned to her father. "Am I doing the right thing?"

He glanced at her. "It's a little late to second-guess your-self."

Kate shrugged. "It's been awhile, and I won't have Mike to help me. I depended on him. Things won't be the same."

"Of course they won't. But you have a lot of friends here who care about you. They'll stand with you. You'll be fine."

Kate wanted to believe him, but he was her father. He loved her and that might distort his perspective. "I hope you're right."

"And what about Paul? I thought you loved him once."

"I did." She didn't want to talk about her feelings for Paul. "But we're just friends now. Things change. I hope we'll travel together again," Kate said casually, but she felt anything but casual about spending time with him.

When Anchorage came into sight, Kate's stomach tumbled from a mix of excitement and trepidation. Now her new life would begin. If Jack was working, she'd have to face him right off.

Wind bounced the plane and swirled snow against the windows. "Looks like we made it just in time," her father said.

When they touched down, Kate stayed in her seat. Her dad smiled at her, then reached out and squeezed her arm. "You're going to be great. Stop worrying."

Kate nodded. "I guess I better talk to Jack—get it out of the way." She climbed out of the Stinson and spotted her plane right off. It looked like it was in good shape. She headed across the field, her eyes fixed on the Bellanca. Putting off the meeting with Jack for a few more minutes, she walked around it, her hand trailing over the fuselage and wings. Excitement pumped through Kate. It looked just as it had. Jack had done a good job of repairing it. She climbed inside and went through her things. Everything was still there—her gear and supplies. It seemed as if it had been waiting for her.

Memories of Mike and the adventures they'd shared bombarded her. They'd been a good team. Tears burned from behind her eyes, but she blinked them away. "Well, Mike, I'm back."

She saw Jack through a window. He trudged across the field toward her. He looked just as he always had, except he was carrying a few extra pounds, which emphasized his stocky build. He walked like he had a head of steam up. As always, he had a cigar clamped between his teeth.

Kate climbed out of the plane and stood, ready to face him.

He nodded at Bill, then turned to Kate. He didn't offer a handshake or a greeting. "So, you're back."

"Yep." Kate reached for courage. She glanced at her father, whose eyes held a hint of mischief. She couldn't imagine what was funny.

"So you think you'll stay this time?" He took the cigar out of his mouth and blew smoke in her face.

"I'm here to stay." She figured she might as well ask right up front. "I need a job. Do you need a pilot?"

Jack narrowed his eyes. "Can I count on you to stay?"

"I told you I'm staying."

He glanced back at the shop. "I've got a fella who's willing to move up from Ketchikan who has a lot of experience."

"So, that means you've got Kenny, Alan, and this other pilot and that's all?"

He didn't say anything for a moment. "I fly when I can."

"You and I both know that to run this outfit you have to stay put most of the time. So you don't count." Kate looked at her father and he gave her a nod of encouragement. "I'm a good pilot. And you need me."

Jack puffed on the cigar. He watched the smoke rise, then his gaze settled on Kate. "Okay. But it's not a fifty-fifty split anymore. You get thirty percent, that's it."

Kate folded her arms over her chest. "No deal. Either I get fifty percent or I go and find another outfit."

"Forty."

Kate shook her head, no. She wasn't about to let him have the upper hand. It would only make him feel more powerful.

Jack glared at her. "All right. Fifty percent. But you'll fly where I want and when I want. And you owe me for the repairs." He didn't wait for a response, but turned and stormed back to the shop.

Kate barely managed to contain a whoop of joy. She hugged her father. "Well, I guess I'm back in business." Although she sounded confident, fear that she might mess up niggled at her. What if something went wrong right off the bat?

Paul swung his axe and brought it down on a round of spruce. The wood popped and split into two pieces. He tossed them into a pile and set up another chunk. A chill November wind caught the smoke from his chimney and carried it toward the ground where it swirled around him. He liked the aroma of burning wood. And the assurance that an abundant supply would keep him warm through the winter, which was fast approaching. It was only a few weeks until Thanksgiving.

The holiday season always hit him with a bout of loneliness. He'd be glad when the New Year arrived and the celebrations were behind him.

His family would gather for merrymaking. They'd discuss him and wonder why he remained so distant. He wasn't really. His mind and heart would be there with them. When he'd first come to Alaska, he was thankful to put space between him and the memories, the accusations. If only he'd insisted Susan be admitted to the hospital.

It was so long ago. And now the idea of time with family seemed to invite him. He should go and see his mother. There was no telling how long before she left this earth. She wasn't young. It would be nice to see his family. *Next year*, he promised himself.

His mind wandered to Kate. Maybe he should write to her.

He hoped she was happy. Normally, she would be caught up in preparations for the upcoming holiday, but it had only been a couple of months since Mike's death. He doubted she was yet able to relinquish the grief, which would undoubtedly intrude on the holiday cheer. He wondered if she'd managed to get back in the air.

He hoped so. He wanted Kate safe, but the idea of her not flying didn't seem right. She'd never be fully content. To cut that out of her life seemed tragic.

He wanted her back. The idea of going after her flickered through his mind. No. It wasn't right. He knew better. She was grieving. And even if she weren't, she wouldn't want him, not after what he'd done to her.

He set up another chunk of wood and glanced at the gray sky, wondering if snow would be on the ground before the day was out. In spite of the cold air, he was overheated, so he stripped off his coat and laid it over a stack of wood.

After wiping his brow, he swung his axe up and brought it down on the large piece of spruce, splitting it into two sections. He tossed the smaller piece in the pile, cut the other in two, and chucked them onto the pile.

"Looks like you're working hard," Lily said.

He looked over his shoulder at her. She stood with the baby in her arms.

"Hi. I didn't see you." Paul put the axe head on the ground and leaned on the handle. "How are you and Theodore doing?"

"We're fine."

Paul moved toward them. "Glad you came by. I can use a distraction." He patted the little boy on the belly. "How you doing, champ?"

In answer, the infant offered him a toothless smile.

Lily held out the baby. "You want to hold him?"

"Sure." Paul took the youngster and held him up in front of him. "Hey there." Theodore gazed at him, his brown eyes crossing. Paul chuckled. "I'll bet he'll be glad when he stops seeing two of everything." The baby chortled and his plump red cheeks rounded. "So, you think I'm funny looking, huh?" Paul hefted him up and then down. "Feels like you're eating good."

Lily laughed. "He's always hungry. He's getting fat, but Mama says that's good." Her eyes glowed with love as she gazed at her little boy. "I never get tired of looking at him."

A blast of wind from the north blew through. Paul cuddled Theodore against his shoulder. "It's cold." He glanced at the sky. "And it looks like snow."

"It's coming. I can feel it."

"You want to go inside and warm up? I've got coffee."

"That sounds good." Lily bundled deeper inside her coat. "I'm cold, but he seems fine."

"Babies are sturdier than we think." He rested his cheek against Theodore's. "He is cold." Glancing at Lily, he said, "I made some cranberry muffins this morning. They're not bad, even if I do say so myself."

"I love muffins. And I'm always hungry—can't seem to get enough to eat these days. I'm going to get fat right along with Teddy."

"You're feeding two people. You're supposed to eat more." He headed for the porch.

"In that case, I'll have two muffins."

Paul felt lighthearted as he walked up the steps. He opened the cabin door and stood aside while Lily entered.

He handed Theodore off to his mother. "Coffee's still hot from this morning." Paul filled two cups with the dark beverage.

Lily sat on one of the chairs at the table and set the baby on her lap. His big brown eyes gazed around the room. Paul wondered what it was like to see the world for the first time— to not know fear or sorrow. He longed for such innocence.

He set a cup in front of Lily along with a can of milk, then took a plate of muffins out of the warming oven above the stove and placed it on the table.

"Those look good." Lily bounced Teddy on her lap and played pat-a-cake with him. Each time she brought his pudgy hands together, he chortled in delight.

"Strong for his age," Paul said. "I'd say he's developing early—even lifting up his head and laughing. He's bright." Paul grinned. "It won't be that long before he wants to go fishing."

Lily tilted one side of her mouth in a sideways grin. "You men, can't you think about anything else?"

"Time goes by fast and he'll want to go. You wait and see. He's got a lot of people who can teach him. Plus your dad can teach him to hunt and drive the dogsled."

"And so can I." Lily lifted her chin and set defiant eyes on Paul. "Just because I'm a mother now doesn't mean everything has to change. I'm still going to fish, hunt, and drive the dogs."

"Well, sure. I never meant—"

"I get tired of people assuming that I'll settle into the role of a little homemaker. I've got to do it all—be a father and a mother. He'll need that."

"You won't be on your own all your life, Lily."

"What man will have me now?" Tears glinted in her eyes. She set the baby in her lap and folded her arms around him. "We'll be fine . . . just me and Teddy."

Paul sat across the table from her, coffee cup in hand. He wasn't sure what to say so settled on, "You're right. Sorry. I forget sometimes how self-sufficient you are. He looks like he'll be a strapping young man one day. Probably be able to handle a team of dogs with no trouble." Paul took a sip of coffee and then made a face. "Been on the stove awhile—kind of bitter."

"It's fine." Lily bit into a muffin. "Mmm. Good."

"I got the recipe from your mom. And everyone knows she's the best cook around," he added with a grin.

Paul took another drink of coffee, his mind on Lily's determination to be self-sufficient and to live on her own. He knew what that was like and he didn't like it. Neither would she. He understood that most people would judge her harshly. The majority of men wouldn't give her a thought because of her circumstances. But surely an honorable man would come along who could see what a prize he'd have in the two of them.

"Someone will come along. Don't worry."

"I'm not worried." She kissed the top of Teddy's head. "I'm just thankful to have him." He grasped one of her fingers and tried to stick it in his mouth.

Lily looked at Paul. "I've been thinking about his father. He might feel different now that Teddy's here. I was wondering if I should write to him."

Paul took in a deep breath and let it out slowly. "Well . . . if it were me, I'd want to know."

"His father's nothing like you. I don't think he'll care a whit, but it seems right to tell him he has a son. I'm going to send a letter with the next mail plane."

"Good. I think it's the right thing to do. Maybe he'll surprise you."

"I'm not going to hold my breath. You don't know him. He thinks only about himself. And he'd probably see a baby as nothing but a bother."

"I know this is none of my business, but how did you get involved with a man like that?"

Lily gazed out the window. "In the beginning he seemed nice and acted like he really cared for me. I was alone and lonely. And just a foolish girl. He saw me as an easy mark, a naïve country girl he could fool."

Paul nodded. He'd known men like him. He wished there were something he could do to help. "Well, I'm here, if you need anything."

"There's nothing anyone can do now. I wish you'd convinced me to stay here on the creek instead of gallivanting off to Seattle. This is where me and Teddy belong. Our roots are here."

She rested a penetrating gaze on Paul. "Don't misunderstand. You're a good neighbor and friend, but you're kind of like me. One day you just appeared here, all the way from California, no explanations. I know you left something or someone there. Maybe it's time you dealt with whatever you ran from."

Paul pushed to his feet and walked to the window and gazed out at drifting snowflakes. "I'll know when it's time to go home. And it's not now."

— 28 —

Kate took long strides, swinging her arms at her sides as she headed toward the mercantile. The cold bite of the wind and the light snow falling invigorated her. It was wonderful to be back in Anchorage.

"Hey, slow down," her father called.

Kate looked back at him and forced herself to a more leisurely pace. "Sorry. Since we left Yakima, I've been imagining this reunion. I can barely wait to see Albert and Helen. I hope Muriel's there."

Her father smiled and looped an arm through hers. "I'm excited too."

When they reached the general store, Kate allowed her father to open the door for her. Angel leaped in ahead of them both. She seemed just as excited to be home as Kate. The sound of the ringing bell carried a flood of memories.

"I'll be right there," Helen called from the back of the store.

Kate waited, anticipation building. A few moments later, Helen stepped out from between two rows stocked with canned goods. Her eyes fell upon Kate.

"Oh, good Lord!" She pressed her hands to her cheeks. "We didn't expect you until tomorrow." She rushed to Kate and pulled her into her arms. "Blessed day!" When she stepped back, she noticed Bill. "How good to see you." She gave him a friendly hug.

"It's a real pleasure to be here," he said. "Sorry about our early arrival, but the weather was turning bad, so we slept less and flew more, hoping to get here ahead of the storm."

"I'm so glad you're early. I've been having a terrible time waiting." She bent over and stroked Angel's heavy coat. "And you look absolutely beautiful." She wrapped her arms around the dog's neck and gave her a hug.

"Where's Albert?" Kate asked.

"He went home to put wood in the fire. With the temperature dropping, we figured the stove would need some extra to keep the house warm. He should be back anytime."

Helen stood, hands on her hips, and studied Kate. "You look wonderful, dear—tanned and robust."

Kate glanced at her father. "Mom and Dad spoiled me, plus I spent a lot of time working out in the sun."

"She was a big help to us."

"I can imagine." Helen's gaze moved to the door. "Oh, here's Albert."

The bell rang and Kate turned just in time to see him walk in.

"Why, Kate, what a surprise." He headed straight to her. "Wish I'd known, I'd have picked up Muriel and the baby on the way."

Kate wrapped her arms around her dear friend. "It's so good to see you and to be back. I can't wait to see Muriel and the baby."

"A quick call will fix that. She'll be here in a jiffy." Albert shook Bill's hand. "Welcome. And thank you for bringing Kate back to us."

"This is where she belongs," Bill said.

"I'll call Muriel." Helen headed for the telephone.

Albert gave Angel a pat. "Nice to see you again." He glanced at Kate. "She looks happy to be home."

"She is. I'm sure she knew exactly where we were when we landed. She hurried to the door, her tail in high gear." Kate smiled, her joy feeling as if it would spill over.

"So, you're going back to work for Jack?" Albert asked.

"It looks that way. He gave me my old job. I wasn't sure he would, but he needs another pilot, so I'll be going in tomorrow."

"Not even a day to rest and to catch up?" Helen asked.

"I'd love to do that, but I don't want to give Jack any reason not to keep me. Besides, I don't have much to do to settle in—just a couple of bags to unpack."

"And I've got to head south," Bill said. "Need to get back to Washington before the winter weather hits." He glanced out the front window. "I'm hoping this one blows through in a hurry."

"I don't think it's going to be much. But we've had some good snows the last couple of weeks." Albert ruffed up Angel's fur. "I figure you'll be happy to see the snow again."

"She loves it. Yakima gets snow, but not like here."

Helen's blue eyes glowed with some sort of secret pleasure. "Your living arrangements probably aren't going to be what you expected." She looked as if she were bursting with a surprise.

"Oh. I thought I was going to stay here, at least for a while. Did you decide to go ahead and renovate right away?"

"We're not ready yet, and of course you can stay, if you like, but I think you'll probably want to make a change."

"This'll be fine, as long as you don't need the room."

Helen's smile brightened as she walked to the register. Opening a drawer, she took out a bulging envelope. "This came for you a couple of days ago. We would have told you about it, but you'd already left Yakima." She handed the envelope to Kate.

Opening it, she slid out a document. It was Mike's will. Tears immediately surfaced. Kate scanned the paper, but couldn't read it through her tears.

"What is it?" She looked at Albert and Helen.

"Mike's will and the deed to his house. He left it to you."

Astonishment welled up inside Kate. Wiping her eyes, she looked back at the papers. "He gave me his house?"

"Uh-huh." Albert swung an arm over Kate's shoulders and hugged her from the side. "The attorney handling his affairs was a little slow getting the paperwork done. And I guess there was an argument from Mike's brothers about the whole thing, but as it turns out, the house is yours." He took a set of keys from the cabinet drawer and handed them to Kate. "You own it free and clear."

Kate pressed the papers against her chest. "I can barely believe it." She closed her eyes and tears leaked onto her cheeks. The house was supposed to be theirs, not hers.

Bill stayed two extra days to help Kate with her move, then it was time for him to fly south. Kate hated good-byes, and this one felt more permanent than any other. She clung to her father. "I'll try to get back in the spring to visit. Tell Mom I love her."

"I will." He climbed into his plane, and settled into the front.

Kate stepped back and watched him take off. He maneuvered beneath a heavy layer of clouds and Kate prayed for good weather.

Jack gave Kate a week off to settle into her new home. It wasn't like him. Kate wondered if he was getting soft. She hoped so.

The house had been sitting empty for a couple months and needed some sprucing up. Kate also added a few personal touches—some fresh paint, a carpet in the center of the front room, a lace doily on each end table and the coffee table, and a few pictures here and there.

The previous evening, she'd had the Townses, plus Muriel and her husband and their little boy, over for dinner. It was the first time she'd ever entertained on her own and prepared a meal for company. Everyone seemed to have a good time, and the food wasn't bad.

Now the house felt empty. It would take time to adjust. She expected to see Mike at any moment. Everywhere she turned, it seemed that he should be there.

She dusted a photo of her parents and set it on a shelf beside a picture of Mike. She picked up the photograph of him standing beside his plane. Her heart ached. Maybe she hadn't loved him with a romantic love, but he was one of the finest people she'd ever known, and her dearest friend. She'd never stop missing him.

She set the photograph back on the shelf and turned to look about the room. She remembered her first visit here. Mike had made spaghetti and they'd played cards.

The phone jangled, startling her. It was Mike's phone. No, it was hers now. She picked it up. Jack was on the other end.

"Hey, that you, Kate? I've got a job for you. How soon can you be ready?"

"Right now. I'll come in right away."

Jack didn't respond and the phone went dead.

Kate stared at the receiver. "Everything's back to normal." She smiled at Angel as she hung up. "You ready to go flying?"

Angel stood, her tail wagging.

Kate's mind went to the flight. Where was she headed? Her stomach tightened with trepidation, but she told herself everything would be fine. She'd be fine.

When she stepped into the shop, Jack was hunkered over a map. He looked up and leaned back in his chair. His eyes went to Angel. "Still got that dog, huh?"

"We're partners."

Jack fired off the assignment. "I've got two hunters coming in. They need a ride to Kotzebue. Think you can pull that off?"

"Sure. No problem. It'll give me a chance to see friends of mine who live up there."

"You won't have time to lollygag with friends. The fellas you're flying up are hunting polar bears. And while they're out on the ice, I've got some other runs for you."

Kate felt the lump in her stomach tighten. "Am I taking them out on the ice?"

"No. Just to Kotzebue. They'll catch a ride on a sled from there. While they're out, I need you to make a pickup in Fairbanks and then drop it off in Talkeetna."

"That sounds fine," Kate said glibly, but her nerves were jumpy. This was her first trip and it was no easy run. Plus she'd miss Thanksgiving with the Townses. That was what piloting in Alaska was all about, though. She couldn't worry about holidays. She glanced out the window. "At least the weather's clear."

"For now." Jack chewed on the end of a cigar. Looking out from beneath heavy brows, he leveled a serious expression on her. "Make sure you've got your survival gear. Never know what to expect up there."

Kate thought she'd heard concern in Jack's voice. That was something new. "Sure. I always do. When are my riders supposed to be here?"

He glanced at a clock on the wall. "In about thirty minutes."

By the time Stanley Greenwood and his buddy Ralph Donaldson arrived at the airfield, Kate and Angel were ready to go. The plane was packed and warmed up.

Both men seemed friendly. Stanley was tall and slender with shockingly blond hair. He was more reserved than his heavyset friend Ralph, who was talkative and outgoing.

While Ralph and Stanley helped Kate load their gear, they teased one another and bet on which one of them would bring down a bear. Angel sat up front, ready to go.

Once they were in the air, Ralph asked, "How long you been flying?"

"Since I was a girl," Kate hollered over the roar of the engine.

"You that woman pilot everyone's been talking about?" Ralph asked.

Kate shrugged. "Hard to know. I've been out of town for a couple of months—visiting family in Yakima, Washington." She looked at him. "What are people saying?"

Ralph acted like he was sorry he'd brought up the subject. He glanced away, then said, "Just that you've had a hard time of it, losing a plane and then your fiancé this last year."

"Yeah, I'm that pilot." Kate clenched her jaws, determined not to show any emotion.

"But I also heard you're a darned good flyer." He smiled. "Glad you're back in the air."

"Me too." She stroked Angel's head and shoulders. "Isn't it kind of early in the season to be hunting polar bears?"

"Yeah, but our friend Seth said the ice is in, and I've been itching to bring down one of those big white bears." He grinned. "Done every kind of hunting except that."

Kate nodded. As many times as she'd flown hunters in and out of the territory, she'd never really understood what drove them. Hunting for food was one thing, but a lot of hunters were after trophies or bragging rights about their remarkable hunting experiences.

The weather held all the way to Kotzebue. Even so, mountain currents made the plane buck, and frigid temperatures created a lot of extra work for Kate. The days were short, so getting the plane on the ground before dark was a challenge all its own. By the time Kate spotted Kotzebue, she was weary, but the trip had helped to rebuild her confidence. When they approached the landing field, the sun lay low on the western horizon, turning the sky the color of an overripe peach.

Joe had set out the firepots, making it easy for Kate to see the landing site. She brought the plane down smoothly and turned onto a cleared area. Nena stepped out of the cabin at the edge of the runway, her smiling face peering out from within a parka hood.

As soon as Kate opened the door, Angel leaped out. Ralph and Stanley grabbed their bags and rifles and climbed down the ladder. Kate followed.

Nena greeted her with a big smile and open arms. "I have missed you. I'm glad you come back."

Kate hugged her friend. "I'm glad to be here. It's so good to see you."

Nena studied Kate. "You're almost brown." She grinned. "Like me."

"It was warm in Yakima."

"I might like to see such warm days."

Kate turned her attention to her passengers. "I'll be back in a week to pick you up. Meet me here before daybreak. If you need to get ahold of me, I'll be at the general store, the Turchiks' place."

"Okay," Ralph said. "Thanks for the ride."

Stanley gave her a wave and the two men walked toward town.

Kate drained the oil, then Nena helped her tie down the plane and cover it with a tarp. The two friends looped arms and headed for the village.

"Joe is cooking," Nena said. "Hope it's edible."

"Is there some doubt?"

"Yes." Nena giggled.

When Kate stepped into the Turchik home, their three children swamped her and Angel with hugs. They exclaimed their happiness over her visit and wanted to know where she'd been. When she told them, they were full of questions about the place called Yakima. Peter and Nick ran to get carvings they'd made from pieces of driftwood so they could show them off.

Kate watched them sprint toward the back of the house. "They've grown since I last saw them."

Nena nodded. "Yes. Too fast. I cannot keep up with the sewing."

Joe stepped into the front room from the kitchen. "Kate. It's very good to see you." He hugged her briefly. "How long will you be here?"

"I'm heading to Fairbanks in the morning, then I've got a trip down to Talkeetna."

"I wish you could stay longer," Nena said, disappointment in her voice.

"I'll be back in a week to pick up my passengers."

"You are busy, already."

"It's my job." Kate smiled. "And I'm glad to be back at work."

After a meal of overcooked caribou and homemade bread,

Joe sat on the floor in the front room with the children. He told an ancient Inuit tale. Kate loved to listen to his stories. He always made it fun, using animated gestures and expressive voices.

After the tale had been told, Kate and the children played a game of tag. There was a lot of squealing and giggling. Kate got a sideache from laughing. And then it was time for bed. Each child got a hug and then off they went.

Her energy spent, Kate was thankful to climb between her blankets on the sleeping pad and close her eyes. She stayed awake just long enough to consider how grateful she was to be back in Alaska.

Nena woke her the following morning, and after a hurried breakfast, Kate set out for Fairbanks. It was just her and Angel as they flew across the frozen tundra. Kate's nerves had quieted.

Everything was going to be okay.

Six days later, Kate approached Kotzebue. This time, the weather fought her. Gray clouds churned east from the sea and wind whipped up billows of ice and snow. The temps were below zero. Kate knew she'd made it back just in time. The storm blowing in was a tempest. She hoped Ralph and Stanley were safely tucked away at their friend's house and ready to leave in the morning. If not, they could be in terrible trouble.

Joe met the plane. He tied it down while Kate drained the oil. They worked together to cover the fuselage with a tarp.

The wind blew what felt like slivers of ice into her face. "Joe, did the men I brought in last week stop by your place?" she hollered over the storm's wail.

"No. Seth took them out, and I know he's not back yet. His father was here this morning." Shielding his eyes, he looked out toward the frozen bay. "They better come soon. This is a bad storm."

Kate gazed out over the sea of ice. A feeling of impending

doom pressed down on her. If the men were stuck out there in this kind of gale, they might not survive.

As the storm intensified, Kate was thankful to be tucked safely inside the Turchiks' home, but she couldn't quiet her mind. It remained on Seth, Ralph, and Stanley. There'd still been no word from them.

After sharing a meal with the family, Kate helped Nena clear away and wash the dishes. The unrelenting howling wind grated on her. How could anyone caught out in such a blizzard survive? They'd taken a heavy canvas tent and had firepots for heat, but Kate couldn't imagine any tent standing up to these kinds of winds.

With the dishes done, she tried to sit, but couldn't. She paced.

Finally, Joe said, "Kate. Sit down. Worrying will not help."

"I can't stop thinking about those men. They'll surely die."

"Seth knows how to survive up here. When he saw things were getting bad, he probably built an ice house for protection. They have food and heat. They will be all right." Joe lifted Mary onto his lap. "It is all in God's hands. There is nothing we can do."

Kate nodded. He was right.

That night the wind howled and Kate slept little. Several times during the night she climbed out of bed and stared out of a tiny window facing the street. Snow piled against the homes and businesses. Her thoughts on the men, she begged God for mercy.

The following day the blizzard continued to pummel the village. No one went out. No one came in. The streets were empty.

The third day the wind quieted. While Kate paced, Joe went to Seth's home to see if he and his friends had made it back, but the news was not good. There'd been no sign of them.

"Where do you think they are?" Kate asked.

Joe stared at the icy bay. "Out there somewhere, probably north."

"Do you think they survived?"

He shrugged. "Maybe. Seth is a smart, determined man."

Kate stepped outside. The wind still gusted, but the worst of the storm had passed. Light snow drifted from the sky. Bursts of wind swept smoke from chimneys and swirled it toward the ground. A loose piece of tarpaulin hanging from a window flapped. Kate stepped back inside.

Nena toasted sourdough bread in the oven. "You want coffee?"

"Sure. Thanks." Kate wanted to search for the men. She looked at Joe. "Do you think the storm is over?"

He shook his head no. "It is only resting. There is more to come."

"How can you know?"

"I've seen this before. I know."

Kate stood at the window. Someone had to find the hunters. They could be dying. "How long before the storm picks up again?"

He shrugged. "Maybe five minutes, maybe a couple hours."

She was the only one who could help. They'd die if she didn't go after them. And if she did . . . she could be the one dying. Did it make sense to sacrifice her life for men she barely knew?

This is what Kate had feared—not having the courage to do what she should. Helping people in jeopardy was part of her job. When she'd signed on as a pilot, she'd made a pact with herself and her passengers—they counted on her.

She looked at Joe and Nena. "I'm going after them." She pulled on her parka.

"No. You stay. It's too dangerous." Nena stepped in front of Kate. "When the storm is done, then you will go."

"I have to go now. If I wait, they could die."

Joe shook his head. "They might already be dead. Adding your life to theirs will not help."

Kate pulled on gloves. "I'm going." She opened the door and Angel stepped outside. "Sorry, girl, not this time." Kate led her inside. "I'll be back. I promise."

Remembering her mother's words that God was in charge

of life and death, Kate pulled the door closed. She hurried toward the airstrip, keeping her head down to shield her face from the cold. Soon, Joe trudged along beside her. "Kate, you are crazy."

She ignored him but figured he was probably right.

While Kate unleashed the tarp, Joe got a fire going in the cabin. Kate scooped hot coals into a bucket, added wood, and set it beneath the engine to warm it while Joe heated the oil.

Kate went over the plane, scraping away ice and frost. As soon as the oil was added, she climbed behind the control wheel. In spite of her heavy winter clothing, she shivered. Joe cranked the flywheel while she prayed the engine would turn over. It refused the first effort. She tried again. It whined. Finally on her third try the engine lit off.

Kate waved to Joe. She needed to hurry before the storm kicked up again. She moved onto the airstrip, blasts of wind buffeting the plane. Was she being a fool? Maybe, but men like Ralph and Stanley were why she was here, why she'd come back to Alaska. She wasn't going to let them down.

She headed northwest, over the ice pack, searching the white world below, hoping and praying for some sign of the men. They'd be hard to spot, especially if they'd built an ice house. The winds increased, bucking the plane. Kate knew she should turn back, but she couldn't make herself do it. The hunters might be waiting and praying for rescue. She wasn't going to let them down.

"God, I need your help. Show me where they are."

Snow blasted the window, and visibility was poor. It was hard to distinguish the ice pack from blowing snow—it blurred together into one sheet of white. Kate knew if conditions got much worse, she'd have no references and could easily fly the plane into the ground.

Please help me find them, she prayed. She was running out of time. If something didn't happen soon, she'd be forced to turn back.

Kate headed farther north, though she doubted they'd come this far. *Just a few more minutes*, she told herself. Finally, knowing the storm had won, Kate turned back toward Kotzebue. Sick inside, she fought to keep the plane aloft in the violent winds. Now, she had to think about saving her own life.

Still, she continued to search as she flew. And then she saw something in the swirl of white—a flash of brown and black. Probably nothing more than a seal or sea lion. Kate dropped to a lower altitude and flew directly over the splotch of color.

A dog huddled in the snow. Then Kate saw another one. Her eyes searched the white landscape. Were the men here? Were they alive?

She thought she saw some kind of movement. Someone was waving something blue. It had to be them. They were alive!

Kate circled back, searching for a place to put down. The ice was rutted and in the white maelstrom it was nearly impossible to know what she was setting down on. *God, you know. Make it right.*

She made two more passes and spotted what looked like a long patch of smooth ice. She wouldn't be able to back-taxi—the runway needed to be long enough to land and take off without turning around. If she tried to turn around, the crosswind would lift the wing and tip her over. There wasn't anyplace else, so this would have to be it.

Fighting to keep the plane stable, she dropped down until she was just above the ice. Downdrafts pounded her and would make takeoff difficult. The wind speed would mean she'd need less space to take off, but the downdrafts could slow her speed. *I'll deal with that when the time comes*, she told herself. Right now she needed to concentrate on getting down. She'd have to nail the landing. The nose couldn't come up too high and the tail couldn't drag and she'd have to watch for berms. With the wind behind her, she dropped down just above the ice. She waited . . . then felt the skis touch the surface. And she was down. The ice was uneven and rough. The plane bounced and rattled across the strip of ice. The plane slowed and she prayed it would stop soon enough to allow room for takeoff.

By the time Kate got to the door, Stanley, Ralph, and Seth

were making their way toward the plane with their gear. She scrambled out and met them.

Ralph smiled at her. "Well, if you're not a sight for sore eyes. You've got moxie, lady."

Kate didn't have time to think about thank-yous. She needed to get the men in the plane and get back to Kotzebue. "Is everyone all right?"

"Yeah," Stanley said. He looked back at the dogs. "We lost all but two of the dogs—no room in our tiny snow cave for them and us. Can we bring them along?"

"Okay. Get 'em. But hurry. We've got to get out of here." As if to emphasize her words, a powerful wind gust pounded them. "Hurry!" Kate shouted.

With passengers and dogs on board, Kate lined up on the runway. There wasn't a lot of room for a takeoff. She'd need all the speed she could grab to get up and to fight the downdrafts. If the gusts were too strong, they'd hold down her speed and she wouldn't have enough power to get off the ground. She revved the engine and waited for a lull in the gale. "Hang on. It's going to be rough."

Everything seemed quiet. This was it. Kate moved down the open ice. White swirled at her. She lost sight of the ground. She had to get up. "Come on, come on." She needed more speed.

She felt the plane lighten as the skis left the ground. She pulled back on the wheel. And then the swell of ice slipped beneath the plane and they were in the air.

Shouts of jubilation went up from behind her.

Kate laughed. It would be a rough ride to Kotzebue, but she knew they'd make it. God had shown her where to find the men and he'd carry them home.

Kate relaxed. She'd done what she had to. And she hadn't let anyone down.

It was a perfect winter morning—clear weather, light breezes, and a landscape glistening white in the sunlight. It was Kate's first time out on her old mail run, and she'd had fun reconnecting with people on the route. They were happy to have her back and enjoyed telling their most recent adventures, introducing new babies, and sharing baked goods.

Bear Creek was her next stop, and as Kate headed there, she felt anxiety encroach on her good mood. She didn't know how she'd feel when she saw Paul. She hadn't seen him since she'd returned to Alaska. And try as she might to extract him from her heart, she still loved him. What would she say when she saw him? How would she hide her feelings?

The time would come soon when she'd be called to transport him on a medical run. They'd be forced to spend hours together in close quarters. She'd decided to keep the relationship casual and businesslike. It would be simpler that way.

The apples she'd brought for him from Yakima were with her, but she considered not giving them to him. She'd deliver Patrick and Sassa's mail and be on her way. It would be easier.

She wondered if Paul would ever marry or if he'd spend his life alone. The thought made her sad. He deserved more, to be loved. Why couldn't he accept her as she was? Why couldn't she be the one for him? Flying was the barrier. He'd made it clear—no flying. Could she give it up? Should she? Kate swallowed past an ache in her throat. She'd given up everything for flight, and to walk away from something she loved to please a man would only make her bitter. How could a couple begin a marriage on that kind of foundation?

He'd have to take her as she was or not at all. And she knew he wouldn't do it. She'd have to accept life without him.

Kate clicked her thinking in another direction. She was single, strong, and independent. She didn't need a man in her life. She could manage on her own and still find happiness. She liked the freedom of answering to no one but herself and God. *I'm yours, Lord, and I accept your will, whatever it is.*

When she flew over Paul's cabin, she saw him with the dogs. He looked up and Kate's heart jumped. She wanted to see him, but what would she say? She spotted Lily sitting on the porch with a baby in her arms. In spite of the pledge she'd just made, jealousy flickered to life. Had Paul found someone else? Lily was beautiful and kind, wise in the ways of the Alaskan bush.

Taking a deep breath, Kate set up for a landing on the frozen creek. She reached out and buried her fingers in Angel's thick ruff. "It's just you and me, girl."

Angel pushed her nose up under Kate's palm.

The landing area had been cleared, and Kate brought the plane in smoothly. After what had happened on Kotzebue Sound, any landing was a cinch.

Kate shut down the engine, moved toward the back of the plane, and opened the door. Cold air washed in, reminding Kate that even though the sun was shining, this was December in Alaska. Angel jumped out and sprinted across the ice.

Kate reached into the mailbag, fished out the letter to Patrick and Sassa, and tucked it into the front of her coat. She picked up the box of apples she'd brought for Paul. *Might as well get it over with*, she thought and headed for the door.

With a heavy coat on over a long dress, Sassa hustled across the ice, her mukluks kicking up powdered snow. Wearing a broad smile, she waved, and then patted Angel on the head. The dog moved off to explore the frozen world.

As Sassa came closer, Kate set down the box of apples. The native woman bundled Kate in her arms. "I knew you would come back." She hugged Kate more tightly. "I have missed you."

"I've missed you too."

Sassa planted a kiss on her cheek, then stepped back. "So much has happened." She smiled broadly. "I'm a grandmother now," she announced, as if daring Kate or anyone to disapprove. "You should see our little Teddy. Such a sweet boy."

"I've been looking forward to meeting him." Kate glanced toward Paul's cabin. She knew Lily and the baby were there. "In fact, I have some apples to deliver to Paul, and I saw Lily and baby at his place from the air."

"Yes. She took over a batch of fresh cranberry muffins for him."

Squelching her jealousy, Kate pulled out an envelope. "I have a letter for you, from Homer." She handed it to Sassa.

"Ah, from my sister." Sassa glanced at it and then said, "Now, I will take you to meet my grandson." She smiled broadly. "And I'm sure Paul and Lily will be happy to see you."

Her stomach in a knot, Kate picked up the box of apples just as Patrick walked up.

"Hello, Kate," he said in his easy way. "Nice to have our favorite mail lady back." He leveled a friendly smile at her. "I didn't think you'd stay away. I know a true Alaskan when I see one."

"You think I'm a true Alaskan?" Kate couldn't keep from smiling.

"Yep. You sure are."

"I plan to stay and one day I'll be a sourdough." She grinned and shifted the box. "It took me awhile to figure out where I belong. I've been having a time of it since I got here though."

"We heard on the Mukluk News last week that you were back at work. How long since you returned?"

"Nearly a month. I took some time to move into my new place. Mike deeded his house over to me."

Patrick nodded thoughtfully. "That's just like him."

"I'm grateful—still getting used to it though. I'd barely gotten moved in when I took a run up to Kotzebue and Fairbanks. This is my first day back on the mail run." She glanced at Paul's cabin. "It's been good seeing old friends."

"I'll bet it has." He looked at the box tucked under Kate's arm. "Who are the apples for?"

"Paul. They're from my parents' farm. He always said he missed fresh apples so I brought him some. I'm sure he'll share with you and Klaus."

Sassa's eyes dimmed. "Oh. You don't know. Klaus died just after you left."

"No. I didn't know." Kate felt the weight of new sorrow. *Klaus.* She hadn't expected him to go, not yet. "Something about him had felt permanent, like he'd always be around. What happened?"

"Just old, I guess," Patrick said. "Paul thinks it was his heart." He turned toward Klaus's place. "We buried him up there on the knoll."

Kate's gaze wandered to the old German's property. "He was a nice man. I'll miss him." Tears pricked Kate's eyes. One more friend gone. "Does he have family, someone who will move into his cabin?"

Patrick shrugged. "Not that we know. I figure someone will take over the homestead eventually . . . we'll just have to wait to find out who that is."

"Well, let's take those apples to Paul and introduce you to our grandson," Sassa said.

"I'll carry the box for you," Patrick offered.

"No. I've got it." Kate wanted to give them to Paul herself. This was the moment she'd longed for and had dreaded. Walking alongside Sassa, Kate fixed her thoughts on the positive facets of meeting again. Paul would be a good friend and she'd enjoy working with him. They were a first-rate team—life would be interesting and exciting. But she dare not hope for more.

315

She attempted to calm her breathing and her battering heart. She tried to quiet her love for him, not wanting him to see it.

As Kate stepped into the yard, Paul tossed a stick for the dogs and they tore after it. Angel joined in the chase.

He turned and looked at Kate. For a long moment he just stared at her, not saying a word, as if she'd resurrected from the dead. Finally, he said, "Hi, Kate." His tone was tender. "I heard you were back in Alaska." He talked as if he were out of breath. A smile emerged. "You look good."

"Thanks." All thoughts of what she ought to say slipped from her mind, so she turned to Lily, who still sat on the porch, a baby in her lap. She stood.

"I heard from good authority," she glanced at Sassa, "that you have a beautiful son." She moved toward Lily.

"I do." She smiled, her brown eyes warm and friendly. "I was so glad to hear that you were back." She gave Kate a one-armed hug.

Kate gazed at the baby. Dark hair framed a round face and big brown eyes looked at her. "He is so cute." She leaned close to him. "Hello there, little man." He smiled and flailed his arms as if he were trying to reach Kate.

"Would you like to hold him?"

"Can I?" Kate set the box of apples on the porch step, then lifted the little boy out of Lily's arms. She hadn't held many babies in her life and wasn't sure exactly how to go about it. "Do I need to hold his head?"

"No. He's strong for his age," Sassa said, pride in her voice.

Paul watched, looking awkward, as if he didn't know what to do or say, yet eager to say something. Kate kept her attention on the baby. She didn't know what else to do.

Theodore gazed at Kate.

"You are a cutie, yes you are," she cooed. He offered Kate a toothless grin. Instinctively she held him close and kissed his cheek, which felt soft as a rose petal. "He's wonderful." She cradled him against her shoulder and longed for the day she would have a child of her own.

"I'm thrilled for you," Kate said, and she meant it. She handed the baby back to his mother.

"I never knew having a baby would make me so happy." Lily cuddled the child against her. "It's not all fun, though. There's a lot of work." At that moment Theodore spit up a portion of his last meal. It oozed down the front of Lily's coat. She held him away from her. "Like that." She chuckled. "Well, let's go home and get cleaned up." She turned to Kate. "Good to have you back."

"Thanks. I'll see you again soon."

Patrick headed toward the trail. "I've got wood to split. This nice weather won't hold out. We'll see you, Kate." When Sassa didn't follow right away, he stopped. "I could use some help . . . hauling that firewood."

"I'm coming." She flashed a smile at Kate. "Nice to see you." She trundled off behind her husband.

Paul moved to the porch. "So, what do you have here?" He nodded at the box.

"Apples . . . from my parents' farm. I brought them for you. They're a few weeks old, but they're almost as good as fresh." She picked up the box and handed it to him.

He took out one and held it under his nose, breathing deeply. "Smells like heaven." He smiled. "Thanks for thinking of me."

I'm always thinking about you. "No problem. I remembered how you said you missed fresh apples." She shrugged. "Since I knew I'd be coming out this way, I figured I might as well bring some."

"I'm glad you're here. You have time to sit awhile, maybe eat an apple with me?" He picked up one and offered it to her. He seemed anxious, as if he was afraid she'd run off.

Kate barely managed to keep a façade of composure. "Sure. I have a few minutes."

They sat on the porch steps, munching on apples and watching the dogs frolic. It felt right to be sitting there together. Neither of them spoke for a while. Kate didn't know what to say and guessed Paul was having difficulty finding a suitable topic.

Finally he asked, "So, you staying at the Townses' apartment?"

"No." Kate hesitated. For reasons she didn't completely understand, she didn't want Paul to know she was living in Mike's house. But Paul was waiting for an answer. "Before Mike died, he willed his home to me. That's where I'm living."

"So, you have a house. That's terrific. It was good of Mike." He gazed at her, his brown eyes tender. "It was a terrible thing, his being killed like that. I'm real sorry."

"I miss him. But it's the way he would have wanted to go."

Paul nodded, a shadow of hurt touching his eyes. Kate wondered what he was thinking. Now what could they talk about? She said, "Lily and the baby look good."

"They're doing well. She's blessed to have such a kind and loving family. She and the baby will be fine. Lily's a strong woman."

Kate didn't mean to probe, but she couldn't help herself. "And how do you feel about them?"

Paul gave her a puzzled look, then his mouth tipped sideways and his eyes lit up with humor. "You mean is there anything special between us?"

Kate shrugged, embarrassed. "You just seem like very good friends."

"We are . . . and nothing more."

He didn't love her! Kate knew that didn't open the door for them—she was still a pilot—but somehow she felt a glimmer of hope.

Kate bit into her apple. Paul wasn't bound to Lily. He was free to do whatever he wanted. But she wasn't what he wanted—he'd made that clear.

"Now that you're back, maybe we can make some trips together again. I miss flying with you." He leaned against her, just slightly.

Kate felt a shiver go through her. "I'd like that. Anything I can do to help—that's why I'm here." Being close working partners was better than nothing. And spending time with someone like Paul would make life more enjoyable.

Strong and single, Kate reminded herself. She should be thankful. She was living her dream. Why, then, couldn't she be content?

Kate finished her apple, then stood and tossed the core into the bushes. "I better get back to work. I've got a stop at Susitna Station."

"I'll walk to the plane with you."

"Come on, Angel. Time to go," Kate called, wishing she could stay.

The dog trotted up to Kate and Paul, then headed toward the creek. She hadn't forgotten her way.

They walked down the snowy path. Paul kept a hold on Kate's arm to make sure she didn't slip. She liked the feeling of being protected and the pressure of his hand on her arm.

He walked all the way to the plane. "I'll crank her."

"Thanks." Kate moved toward the door.

"Kate. Wait." Paul gently took her arm and turned her so she faced him. "I'm glad you're back, Kate." He gazed down at her.

Was it love she saw in his eyes or just affection? "I'm glad to be here." She managed a tremulous smile.

"Kate . . . I . . . well, I don't know how to say this. I know I don't have the right. I've made a mess of things." He glanced at the plane, then turned a fervent gaze on her. "I pushed you away. I tried not to love you. I was callous. Can you forgive me?"

Kate's mind was overrun by her heart. All she knew was that she wanted to be in his arms, to tell him that she loved him.

"I wished a thousand times that I'd found a way to stop you from leaving, to tell you how I really felt. I wanted to come after you, but it didn't seem right." Paul held Kate's face in his hands. "I know it hasn't been all that long since Mike died, and that I'm being very forward, but I can't wait anymore. I need you to know that I love you."

Kate placed her hands over Paul's. "I love you too. I never stopped."

The devotion in Paul's eyes turned to heat. He kissed her,

gently tasting. And then hunger and passion denied for too long claimed them. They clung to one another.

Reluctantly Kate stepped back. "I'm still a pilot. That won't change."

Paul nodded. "I know. But I've learned that it's easier to live with the risk than to live without you." He kissed her again. "I was a fool to think I could be happy without you."

"It won't be easy. My job is still dangerous and I work long hours and—"

"And so do I." Paul smiled. "But we'll work it out . . . together."

He pulled Kate into his arms and she rested her cheek against his chest, listening to the beating of his heart and breathing in the smell of flannel and hard work.

They'd find a way.

Acknowledgments

The creation of a book takes more than a single author. It requires the combined efforts of many. I am grateful for all those who joined me in this project.

Saying thank you is not adequate to express my appreciation to Gayle Ranney, one of Alaska's flying champions. You gave of your time and your experience to make the flying scenes in this book possible. You came alongside me, sharing your knowledge and know-how so I could bring the pilots and their flying adventures to life.

And to my family who are Alaskans and who love one of God's most glorious creations—thanks to my mother Elsa, my sister Myrn, brother Bruce, and cousins Billy, Kenny, and Sue. Your experiences and your love for the state of Alaska enriched and brought the scenes in this book to life.

I owe a big thank-you to Mark and Cheryl Barrett of Barrett Orchards in Yakima, Washington. They graciously sat down with me and answered my questions about what it means to be an apple farmer. They ought to know—the Barrett family has been farming in the valley since 1908.

I would be foolish to write a book without the partnership of my critique group—Ann Shorey, Judy Gann, and Sarah

Sundin. You guys are the best. When you had no time, you made time—you brainstormed when I needed your creative minds—searched out and exposed my blunders and brought out the luster in my writing. Thank you.

Kelli Standish, of PulsePoint Design, thank you for contributing your original thinking and energy to creating a stunning website where I can introduce my books and my thoughts to readers. There's no one like you. Bless you for your commitment to excellence and your dedication to serve the struggling writers of this world.

I owe a great deal to my Revell team. It's an honor to be a Revell author. Thank you, Lonnie Hull DuPont, Barb Barnes, Michele Misiak, Cheryl Van Andel, and all those working behind the scenes who helped create this book. Your hard work and guidance helped me attain my best.

And to Wendy Lawton, my agent. I can't imagine making my way through this world of writing without you. When I need your business savvy, you're there. When I'm down, you lift me up. And your faith in me helps keep me on track. I can't thank you enough.

Bonnie Leon dabbled in writing for many years but never set it in a place of priority until an accident in 1991 left her unable to work at her job. She is now the author of several historical fiction series, including the Sydney Cove series, Queensland Chronicles, the Matanuska series, the Sowers Trilogy, the Northern Lights series, and now the Alaskan Skies series. She also stays busy teaching women's Bible studies, speaking, and teaching at writing seminars and women's gatherings. Bonnie and her husband, Greg, live in southern Oregon. They have three grown children and four grandchildren.

Visit Bonnie's website at www.bonnieleon.com.

Meet Bonnie at
www.BonnieLeon.com

Sign up for her newsletter, read her blog,
and learn interesting facts!

Become a fan on
f Bonnie Leon
and
f Bonnie Leon's Fan Page

"Vivid writing. Bonnie Leon immerses the reader in the time period, in the setting, and deep into the hearts of the characters. I didn't want to leave them behind when I closed the book."

—Lena Nelson Dooley, author of
Love Finds You in Golden, New Mexico

An adventurous young female pilot with a pioneering spirit makes a new start in 1930s Alaska Territory.

Revell
a division of Baker Publishing Group
www.RevellBooks.com

Available Wherever Books Are Sold

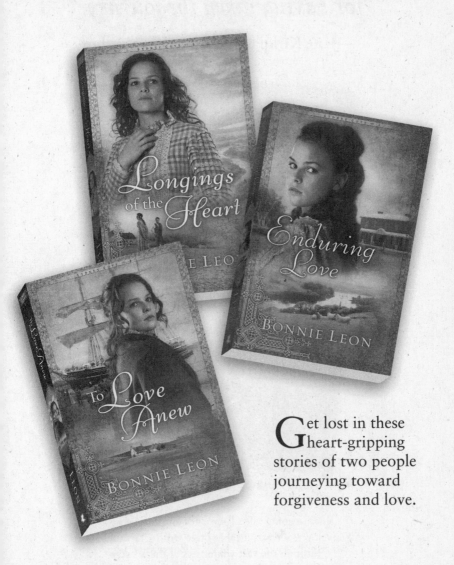

"*You'll disappear into another place and time and be both encouraged and enriched for having taken the journey.*"

—Jane Kirkpatrick, bestselling author

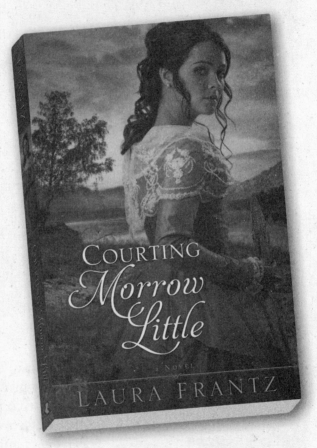

This sweeping tale of romance and forgiveness
will envelop readers as it takes them from a Kentucky fort
through the vast wilderness of the West.

Revell

a division of Baker Publishing Group
www.RevellBooks.com

Available Wherever Books Are Sold

"Laura Frantz portrays the wild beauty of frontier life."
—Ann Gabhart

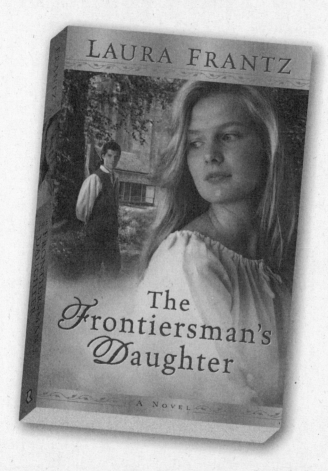

As she faces the loss of a childhood love, a dangerous family feud, and the affection of a Shawnee warrior, it is all Lael Click can do to survive in the Kentucky frontier territory. Will an outsider be her undoing?

Find yourself immersed in this powerful story of love, faith, and forgiveness.

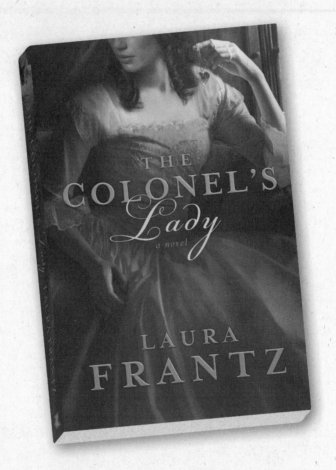

In 1779, a search for her father brings Roxanna to the Kentucky frontier—but instead she discovers a young colonel, a dark secret . . . and a compelling reason to stay.

Revell
a division of Baker Publishing Group
www.RevellBooks.com

Available Wherever Books Are Sold